# The
# Dark
# Fantastic

*by STANLEY ELLIN*

ANDRE DEUTSCH

First published in Great Britain 1983 by
André Deutsch Limited
105 Great Russell Street London WC1

The characters in this story are fictitious, and
any resemblance between them and any living person
is entirely coincidental.

Printed in Great Britain by
Hazell Watson and Viney Ltd. Aylesbury

ISBN 0 233 97596 9

# THE DARK FANTASTIC

*For Jeanne and Sue and George and Stacey*

*THE DARK FANTASTIC*

# Charles Witter Kirwan

$S$IT BACK, LIGHT UP, THE TEXT IS YET TO COME.

A professional joke. A professorial joke. Harmless. Not even worth wincing at.

The fact is that I'm not all that easy with this microphone and tape-recorder thing. Dependent on it, so it seems, but made uncomfortable by it. With pen in hand, I can instantly muster my thoughts into neat ranks and march them right along in close order. With microphone or whatever it's called in hand, I find these thoughts as disorderly as a crowd of torch-bearing villagers in a Frankenstein movie. Tumultuous, incendiary, and not quite identifiable. Hard to pick the right one out of the crowd and start it on its way. So my little professorial joke was intended to get the phlegm loosened and the words coming.

They appear to be coming now.

So.

Whoever you are—curiosity-seeker, sensation-seeker, or seeker after truth—and that's a rare bird, isn't it?—what you are now hearing.

Correction.

What you are now reading.

Because hearing will apply only to the police, who will, of course, be holding a private audition of these tapes before they're converted into print.

Of course.

And having gotten their astounding earful, they will then pass it along to our lord mayor in Gracie Mansion so that he can appear before assembled television cameras to explain and passionately denounce the grand event—oh, the horror and madness of it!—while in his palpitating, panicky, white middle-class heart of hearts he revels in it.

You doubt that? I mean the secret revelry? But hath not our mayor eyes? Hath he not hands, organs, dimensions, senses, affections, passions? And granting him these attributes, which he shares with you and me, is it possible that never in his troubled mind he happily imagined just such a grand event?

Rest assured he did.

Only wondering, no doubt, who would emerge from nowhere to finally set it off.

Well, he won't have to wonder any longer.

Nor will you.

Because by my precise instructions—signed, and in the possession of my attorney—every one of these tapes is to be transcribed uncensored and in full for the benefit of the public.

The paying public.

You.

I don't even have to ask in communications jargon, "Do you read me?" Obviously you are reading me.

Good.

Now for a troublesome aspect of this presentation. The grand

[2]

event I address myself to has not yet taken place — about three more weeks are needed to lay its entire groundwork — so I am speaking these words into this machine well before the event, and you are reading them God knows how long after it. As you read, bear in mind that you actually know more about its results than I do — or ever will — and that hindsight, despite its favorable press, has a curiously distorting effect on one's view of any great event. Why? Because it so easily confers a sense of omniscience on the otherwise well-balanced mind and thus turns one from human understanding to godlike judgment.

Don't play God in my case, friends. Just try as well as you can to play Charles Witter Kirwan.

So.

A presentation. This is what you're getting.

Not a confession. Not at all. There's a sour smell of *mea culpa* about that word "confession," and believe me there is no *mea culpa* here. Not in me, not in this marvelous package I'm handing you. A rejoicing, yes. Samson knew that rejoicing when he suddenly found the pillars of the temple yielding to his reborn strength. When, in that instant before the temple crashed down on him and his doomed tormenters, he saw the incredulity and terror in their faces. Let us, as they say, hear it for Samson.

But if you want guilt, friends, if you expect any beating of the breast, you'll have to shop elsewhere. Because what you'll find here is no more or less than a setting forth of precise facts. Yes. Adding up to a text which I imagine will be rich in history, anthropology, and tribal lore, sociology and psychology.

Oh yes, and sex. A whole colorful, perverted sexual adventure — already initiated — to be recounted in detail.

And will an account of this adventure have redeeming social value? Will it really be necessary to this presentation?

Yes. Since I am moved to set forth the unvarnished truth, it has and does.

Incidentally, it's a heterosexual adventure. Sorry to disappoint our ever-increasing faggot populace, but that's the way this twig was early inclined. To those who ask my credentials, I will confide that during my service in the Second World War, during the Anzio campaign, I shared blankets one night with an importunate captain

[3]

of the artillery, highly symbolic that, and discovered that while he did provide almost instant relief he also provided an embarrassment so intense that it curled the intestines into a deep knot for days and weeks to come, and ever afterward I clearly understood my sexual preferences.

But I digress and I must not. There isn't time for it. Or strength. I ride euphoria and must always keep an ear cocked to the sound of air starting to escape from its tires.

Better if I move directly to my pedigree and my thesis.

Well then.

I am Charles Witter Kirwan, age sixty-eight, white, male, retired associate professor of history, and a widower.

My address is 407 Witter Street in the East Flatbush section of Brooklyn. I was born in this house, have spent my entire life in it, and for the next three weeks will continue to do so. After that, by my instructions, my ashes will be added to my grandfather's already in that bronze urn — identified by his name — in this house, and thus I will continue, so to speak, in residence.

Here I hasten to clear up a possible confusion. My middle name was not taken from the street on which I was born, as one might suppose. Quite the contrary. When my forebear, Jan Uitter — that name starts with a proper Dutch *U* — carved farmland and an estate out of the Flatbush wilderness some 350 years ago, a wilderness then known as 't Vlackbos, the lane that ran through the property was, of course, Uittersveg, and that, in time, became Witter Street. And because the name Kirwan is an adoptive name, my natural father having been Henry Witter, lineal descendant of Jan, I am, in fact, the last surviving Witter of Witter Street.

As for this community, Flatbush Avenue is of course its main thoroughfare, and for landmarks hereabouts it offers the old Dutch Reformed Church and Erasmus Hall High School. The graveyard of the church across from the school is generally open to visitors during daylight hours, and among its most ancient gravemarkers there you will find three bearing the name Uitter with appropriate descriptions in Dutch. Church Avenue, incidentally, was so named after that church.

But, as noted, the 400 block of Witter Street, once Uitter farmland, is the setting for this presentation. I am owner and sole resident

[4]

of Number 407. I am also landlord of Number 409 next door, a four-story walk-up apartment building with twenty-four rental units. The building has a tax valuation of one hundred thousand dollars and an actual cash value of somewhat less than zero.

I trust you're put off by these dull facts and figures, but they are vital to an understanding of the grand event. There may be a way of enlivening such details, but, as I've discovered just now, old habits aren't easily changed. I lectured on history for almost thirty years, and as I sit here speaking into this machine I sometimes find myself the lecturer again — *Herr Professor* Kirwan? — rather than the Charles Witter Kirwan that I am.

I am also under considerable physical stress at this moment. The familiar recurrent pains. Considerable.

However, I'll continue this session a bit longer. No martyrdom involved. This opening up of myself — this unveiling of the soul — is as therapeutic in its way as any medication.

Well.

Not to mince words, I have a terminal cancer of the lungs, a cancer which has already metasticized wildly. For excellent reasons, I have refused surgery or any other futile treatment which might prolong my life even one excruciating day beyond the very few months allotted me by the medical profession.

In fact, I am going to reduce those few months to a very few weeks. About three weeks.

No question about that. No doubts.

Because, as I found, however one may first respond to the announcement of his impending death, it can come to him that this news makes him a totally free man.

A miraculous condition. And I am living witness to that miracle. First the shock and fear, then the bitter resentment, then, miraculously, the awareness of freedom. The savoring of it.

Therefore

Yes. Let's put it this way.

Therefore, I, Charles Witter Kirwan, being of sound and disposing mind, am going to blow up that structure — that apartment building at 409 Witter Street — three weeks from this day.

Blow it, in the fine old phrase, to hell and gone.

For the information of the police, the materials making the grand event will consist of seventy-two sticks of dynamite described as containing thirty percent nitroglycerin and fifty percent sodium nitrate, in addition to essential carbonaceous fuels and absorbents. The blasting caps are mercury fulminate, standard commercial. The detonator is electric spark, hand-held.

By my close calculations the building walls will fall inward. The one unknown concerns explosions due to the instant ripping apart of gas mains. The volatility of natural gas makes this seem likely, as does resultant widespread fire through the rubble.

Which, as I've remarked, is police business. My own concern in it, of course, ends the instant I press the detonator switch.

There is intended to be — there should be — a heavy loss of life. At least sixty people reside in the building; I am choosing a time for the explosion when most will be right there to share it with me. Destruction of the building alone would be mere entertainment. Destruction of life on any such scale will be a lesson burned deep into the public consciousness. An instantaneous, raging, fiery course of study in the social history of this time and this place.

Oh yes.

Oh yes indeed.

# John Milano

"Bᴜᴛ ᴛʜᴇɴ, ᴍʏ ꜰʀɪᴇɴᴅꜱ, ᴛʜᴀᴛ ᴍɪɢʜᴛʏ ʜᴀɴᴅ—that infinite and eternal and all-powerful hand!—shall reach down from heaven and rest on the ground before you. And with your faith in your Savior you will step right up on that hand——"

Eyes closed, Milano fumbled for the button of the radio-alarm, found it and pressed it. Silence prevailed. Next to him, Betty stirred. "What was that?"

"Sunday morning come to Jesus."

"Morning already?"

"Just about."

He hauled himself out of bed and tilted a slat of the venetian blind

[7]

to squint at the world outside. Over the East River the sky showed pink; over the Hudson it was dark with some pale stars speckling it. In Central Park far below, glowing street lamps made a spider web tracery. A party of joggers—there must have been two dozen of them—flowed across the emptiness of Columbus Circle and into the spider web.

Milano made his way to the bathroom, showered, shaved while at it under an almost scalding jet of water, and reflectively toweled himself dry. He wiped mist from the mirror over the sink and studied the face in it. As sometimes happened lately, it was not an altogether familiar face. With a little concentration—a few seconds' controlled schizophrenia—he could view it as the face of an utter stranger. He passed up that opportunity now. Instead, he held up the hand mirror to reflect by way of the sink mirror an unsteady view of his scalp. The last time he had done this a few weeks before he had detected an almost naked patch of skin there about the size of a half-dollar. There was no almost about it now.

"Sheesh," Milano said tiredly.

Betty came in, naked, tousle-haired, sleepy-eyed. Her jaws opened wide in a yawn and shut with a click. "What's all this about?"

"Business."

"Sunday morning at dawn? What business?"

"Private investigator business. Somebody's landing here from the Coast just about now. I'm meeting him in the office in half an hour."

"From Hollywood?"

"Nope."

"Don't worry, I'm not trying to pry business secrets out of you. Hey, I almost forgot. Happy birthday."

He grunted.

"Oh come on," Betty said. "It isn't really the end of the world, is it? So far you're still only one year more than thirty-nine."

"Which adds up to forty. Four-oh. Hell, I don't even remember making thirty. Fact is, I sometimes get the feeling I'm stuck around twenty and faking all the rest of it, know what I mean?"

He knew as he asked it half-seriously that she didn't. Imagination was not her strong point. Pretty was her strong point. And amiable. And competence at her job. She worked for the Intercontinental Credit Bureau, and after a couple of dates she had finally paid off by

[8]

regularly providing on request the kind of confidential information from Intercontinental's computer bank otherwise obtainable only through subpoena, if that. In her late twenties, living with her people on Staten Island, she had become for the past couple of months a constant in his life, attractive, amiable, unimaginative, and a little desperate. The desperation had been sharpened by her introduction to the Central Park South co-op; she hadn't suspected he really lived on that scale. And it manifested itself in outbreaks of domesticity, the small adjustments she began to make in the arrangement of the furniture, the small additions she made to the kitchen equipment. Pretty good in bed, too, but always holding to the Staten Island rules, so that there was never anything rightfully disorganized and wanton about those sessions.

Hell, when the time came it would be like shipping a spaniel puppy off to the pound.

Meanwhile, she was endlessly amiable and she did have a key to those Intercontinental computer banks.

Now, faced with his question which, however hypothetical, inched past her bounds of imagination, she took her usual course of steering around the question. She said, "How long'll you be with this whoever from the Coast? All day?"

"No, couple of hours at the most. But then I'm supposed to get over to Brooklyn. Bath Beach. Kind of a family thing for my birthday."

Betty looked downcast. "Oh. I thought with the weather so nice —"

"Well, if you want to join the party —" He regretted it as soon as it was out. It was certainly a stupid way of trying to loosen the ties that bind. But he was given no time to reverse course. Betty said happily, "That's even better than I planned, getting together with the family and all."

"Remember, you hardly know any of them."

"I met your mother and sister. And you saw how we got along."

In fact, they had gotten along almost too well. From his mother's angle, since her forty-five-year-old maiden daughter Angie, the bigshot lawyer, was never going to produce grandchildren, it was all up to sonny. And here was this Betty he seemed to be keeping company with, a nice Catholic girl obviously made to turn out small

[9]

Milanos. And from sister Angie's angle, it was not only time for her to have some nieces and nephews to fuss over, but definitely time for the kid brother, now forty and showing a bald spot and at least the suggestion of a thickening waistline, to get off the merry-go-round and settle down with some loving helpmeet. Angie, rabid for female rights, female dignity, female self-sufficiency, exercised the old double standard when it came to Betty. She didn't think much of Betty's brain power but rated her high in the loving helpmeet department. "That's what she's made for," Angie informed the aging kid brother in so many words, "and that's what you need."

Families.

He went into the bedroom, Betty trailing along. Getting into his clothes, he said to her, "Another thing. I'm not sure what the atmosphere there'll be like. Angie already sent up storm signals."

"About what?"

"The usual. Outside working hours she's stuck in the house with Mama — her choice — but she thinks I ought to share her misery. Do a lot more visiting and handholding."

"If that's all it comes to — "

"What it comes to is that I pay my dues in cash. For the rest of it, Mama is a miserable, troublemaking old witch. When she reforms, I'll reform. But that won't stop Angie when I get there. So if you want to stay clear of it — "

"No, it won't bother me, I'll just mind my own business. Want me to fix you some breakfast?"

He gave up. "I'll have coffee in the office. Just be ready to leave when I get back. Meanwhile you can catch up on your sleep."

"I was thinking that meanwhile I could do some straightening up around here."

"There's nothing to straighten up. And the service comes in tomorrow."

"There's plenty to straighten up."

At the front door she offered him a kiss, and it struck him that this would be a first for them, kind of an interesting first, her completely naked body against his completely clothed one. *Déjeuner sur l'Herbe.* It was no surprise though that as their lips met she arched her body away so that there was no contact. More of the Staten Island style.

The Watrous Associates office was at Madison and 60th a few

minutes walk away. Despite the hour the world here was not completely empty. A couple of horse carriages were already stationed at the entrance to Central Park opposite the Plaza Hotel, the horses' muzzles deep in feed bags. One of the coachmen was, in fact, a coach person, a buxom, freckled redhead chestily straining an *I Love New York* T-shirt to its limits. And on the curb before the fountain fronting the hotel were sprawled a pair of youthful leftovers of a bygone era, barefooted, in ragged jeans, and with sweatbands pulled down over their eyes in lieu of sleep masks. One male, one female, both, from the look of it, stoned out of their shaggy skulls.

Doin' the urban sprawl.

In the lobby of his building the weekend security man had him sign the register in which were already recorded the signatures of W. Watrous, S. Glass, H. Greenwald, and D. Hale, indicating that the client had arrived and was being properly hosted. On the thirtieth floor, looking down the carpeted length of corridor which marked Watrous Associates territory, Milano had the thought that the partnership was suffering its own form of urban sprawl, devouring more and more of the thirtieth floor with each passing year. It had started with a couple of rooms twelve years before; it was now developing hefty corporation dimensions, what with departments handling a wildly growing volume of computer fraud, electronic sweeps, and personal security for nervous tycoons, not to mention good, old-fashioned industrial espionage, missing persons, criminal investigation, and that occasional jackpot — John A. Milano's specialty — the recovery of high-priced missing merchandise for insurance companies who, however blushingly, were willing to tiptoe just outside the law to cut their losses. Jewelry and fine art most notably, the smoothly professional theft of which was now promising to become America's largest industry.

So Watrous Associates was on that jet-propelled spiral where the more it made this year, the more it was duty-bound to make next year. And where was the spiral headed for? Eventually renting the thirty-first floor, then the thirty-second, then going public?

Why?

Troublesome question.

On the other hand, why not?

Evasive answer. Convenient, but not comfortable.

[11]

Shirley Glass, office manager and matron of the works since its founding, was waiting in the reception room. A handsome Mark Cross suitcase, the client's no doubt, was conspicuous there. "You're late," Shirley said. "They're all sitting around making talk in Willie's office."

"Get them into my office. And I want coffee. Skip the cream and sugar."

"Whatever side of the bed you got out of this morning——"

"Coffee, beautiful. And bring along your pad and pencil."

Willie's office was just an office. Milano's office — walnut, leather, crystal, and Rouault low-number prints predominating — gave warning to the client that the bill was going to be steep, reduced initial resistance that much. The client in this case was Pacifica Inland Insurance of San Francisco, its representative a Douglas Hale. About forty himself, California cleancut vacuous, but, Milano took note, with some heavy worry lines creasing that tanned forehead.

Hy Greenwald, college fine arts dropout and leg man in training, arranged chairs around Milano's desk while Willie grunted introductions, dribbling cigar ash on the carpet during the process because Willie, the retired police lieutenant who had never gotten the precinct locker room out of his blood with his off-the-rack bargain suits, dingy neckties and twenty-cent cigars, seemed to take pride in being the company slob. Yes, and undeniably, for all the carbohydrates Willie stuffed into himself and for all the six-packs he washed them down with, he looked, at the graveyard age of seventy plus, as trim as a lightweight contender. Luck of the genetic draw, Milano decided resentfully. When Shirley dealt out coffee all around Willie thickened his with several heaping teaspoons of sugar.

Hale's attaché case was lizard with gold trim. He extracted a folder from the case and laid it on the desk. "Everything you asked for," he told Milano. "Copies of the inventory along with attributions and provenances for both works. Photographs. And the police reports."

"And the story?"

Well, to put it in a nutshell, Henry Grassie of Grassie Construction was the policy-holder, Pacifica Inland the insurer. Wednesday morning — that would be four days ago — it was found that two major works of art had disappeared from the Grassie Collection. Grassie's fault to some extent. The collection of twenty pictures was hung in what used to be the Grassie mansion's conservatory. That room, opening on the garden, was particularly vulnerable, its alarm system notoriously erratic.

Anyhow, the police were called in at once, Pacifica Inland immediately afterward. The top expert of the San Francisco police force took personal charge —

"Al Rauscher?" Milano cut in. "Lieutenant Rauscher?"

Hale nodded. "He's the one. Yes. And from what he put together this was plainly an outside job but a highly specialized one."

"Selective?"

Hale nodded again. "That's the word he used. He believes the pictures were ordered by someone who hired a skilled professional to get them. And that right now they're very likely on their way to a middleman working out of New York."

"Rauscher recommended Watrous Associates to you?" Willie said disbelievingly.

"No. Grassie did that after checking with various museum people he knows. His main concern is to get those pictures back. When he was told about you people he advised me that if Pacifica — underwriting all expenses of course — could get you to take the case, he'd delay entering an insurance claim for the time being. Highly irregular, of course, but considering the amount involved — "

"What makes it so highly irregular?" Willie asked, as if he didn't know. He always relished, once they were on his hook, putting these starched-underwear insurance company shitkickers in their place.

Hale's eyebrows went up. "Well, when it comes to paying someone for merchandise he stole — and your own merchandise at that — "

"You mean," Milano said, "you've never been involved in anything like this before? Never had any of your insured art works lifted?"

"As a matter of fact, no. Pacifica doesn't insure art works. The Grassie Collection is the only one we do cover."

"Personal favor?"

"Well, we write up over ten million dollars a year for Grassie Construction. When he stuck us with it, that made insuring the collection a necessary courtesy. Leaving us with just one question: whether or not you take the case."

Milano opened the folder. The two colored photos were on top of the material it contained, the essential data inscribed on the back of each. *La Plage, Trouville. Eugéne Louis Boudin. 1879. Panel, 14" × 7".* And *La Plage. Eugéne Louis Boudin. 1880. Panel, 14" × 7".* Beach scenes, both of them, and they had to be among Boudin's inspired best. A sweep of sand, a few figures walking, it fully realized though barely suggested a vast horizontal expanse of windy, cloudy sky. All in fourteen by seven inches. Two scenes not frozen in time but kept alive through time. Milano felt the familiar twisting in the gut as he took them in, the visceral knot Moses must have known when he faced the burning bush.

Hy Greenwald, who in full beard and granny glasses looked like a college senior disguised in full beard and granny glasses, reached for the photos and contemplated them. "Good," he acknowledged. But it was plain that Hy, the fine arts major brainwashed by Abstract Expressionism and Pop and Op and Minimalist, was still not one to get any visceral jolt from burning bushes.

Milano flipped through the rest of the folder's contents. "Three hundred thousand coverage on each?" he said to Hale. "The last Christies' auction brought in four-eighty for its Boudin."

"I know. But these policies were written up several years ago."

"And never revised. So even if you're stuck for the full insurance you're getting a bargain."

"A pretty painful bargain," said Hale.

"And that's a fact," said Milano. "All right, we'll take the case." He motioned with his head at Willie. "Mr. Watrous tends the cash register."

Willie leaned forward to crush out his cigar stub in the Steuben ashtray, grinding the slimy end of it down hard. He wiped his wet thumb along his trousered thigh. "It's the way I told you on the phone," he said to Hale. "Fifteen thousand up front. Not refundable. That covers one month, expenses included. After that, it's five hundred per diem. And you can cancel out any time you want, no hard feeling."

"Understood. But you mentioned a commission if you recovered the pictures. How much of a commission?"

[14]

"I didn't mention any commission. I said percentage. That includes the payoff money for the pictures if we nail them down. The ransom, you might say. Whatever's left over, well, that's our cut."

"All right, but what's the percentage?"

"Forty," said Willie. "Forty percent of the total insured value."

Hale blinked. "Two hundred forty thousand dollars?"

"If we get your pictures back. That still saves your company about three hundred and fifty grand."

Hale considered this, then turned to Milano. "If I agree to this — and it's not giving away trade secrets — how would you even know where to start?"

"Through connections. Get the word out through certain connections that Watrous Associates is in the market for those works. Make a competitive situation of it. If nothing else, that'll freeze the action while people think things over. That's what we need to start with: the action frozen right where it is."

"And then?"

"And then," said Milano, "it's all trade secrets."

# Charles Witter Kirwan

A DAY MISSED.

I intended to record at some time every day certain reflections on the past and present which, after the grand event, would fully explain it. Yesterday — Sunday — I learned that I'll have to be flexible in this.

Because it was yesterday at eight in the morning that I was roused from sleep by an insistent ringing of the doorbell. I had put in a bad night. At four in the morning, saturated with Percodan, I had finally fallen asleep. The doorbell, for all I tried to block it from my consciousness, shrilled on and on. I made my way downstairs, and there was Vern Bailey at the front door. Vern, age eighteen, his older brother Odell, his younger sister Lorena, and their mother, the certified Mrs. Bailey, inhabit Apartment 2-C in my building next door. I add with regret that an older sister Christine, who had once shared those rooms, moved to Manhattan a few months ago. The regret is heartfelt. I used to get glimpses — sometimes more than glimpses — of Christine through her bedroom window and now that she visits next door only occasionally I find myself deprived. To put it crudely, this splendid female is the stuff of which wet dreams are made, if one is of the age for them. Or, as an army friend once confided to me in Italy about the faraway love of his life, she could make a statue horny, buddy boy.

Yes.

This is not to deprecate the charms of younger sister Lorena who, at fifteen, suggests another Christine Bailey in the making. And I am fit judge of that, because I am already in the happy process of seducing Lorena, quaint as that word may sound. Before I was miraculously transformed into this Charles Witter Kirwan I did think the word quaint. Archaic. The stuff of glossy fiction. No more. Not when Lorena, by my schedule and for my payment, moves back and forth stark naked through this very room. Three days a week, an hour or so each day, stripped to her gleaming skin, she walks, bends, reaches, lifts, providing me with even better than those x-ray eyes every employer wishes for himself, as his secretary leans over his file cabinets.

Untouched, yes. No touching, so far. But that step will be taken very soon. And other steps will follow quickly in ascending order. Or, if you prefer, descending order. Lorena doesn't know it yet, but she and I are destined to spend the brief remainder of our lives at this game.

So.

Be that as it may, the Baileys are longtime tenants of 2-C. Like the vast majority of the block's population they are of the dark-skinned persuasion — Hamitic — and while Mrs. Bailey and Lorena manage a comprehensible English, Vern and Odell seem to have reverted to the original language of their dusky tribe.

"Gobble gobble gobble," Vern said to me as soon as I opened the door. "Gobble gobble hah wah, y'know?"

I don't speak the tribe's language, but in the classrooms I once

[17]

presided over and in dealings with my tenants I became attuned to
it. Thus I understood that there was no hot water in Apartment 2-C,
which meant there was no hot water in 409 Witter, its boiler picking
this time to break down again.

Right now I am not only landlord of 409, I am also its self-elected
janitor. A month ago when my plan for the grand event took shape,
I saw that one hindrance to it was the presence of the then janitor on
the scene, occupying an apartment on the ground floor rent free and
spending much of his time in the basement. But that basement had
to be entirely mine, forbidden territory to anyone else, and so when
the janitor abruptly disappeared — his tenure had been an unusually
long one of several months — I simply didn't replace him. No matter
what effort it required, I would serve as janitor and repairman with
occasional help from Mr. Al Bunting, building superintendent —
janitor — of Number 416 across the street, who could take care of
manhandling garbage cans as required and do such sweeping and
wet-mopping of hallways as was necessary. I will note here that Mr.
Al Bunting, for his exorbitant, tax-free gratuity each week, has so
far been faithful in his duties.

But that means that the boiler is now my province, so yesterday
morning until noon I was at work disassembling and testing its
starting mechanism until it functioned again.

Then, noticing that a leakage of water from the boiler extended
under the door of the padlocked tool room, I had a bad moment.
The three cartons of dynamite, two dozen sticks in each carton, were
on the floor of the tool room, and if dampness had gotten to them it
spelled trouble. That meant my spending an hour in the tool room
while I checked through the contents of the cartons piece by piece.

Thank God, no harm done.

But when I finally got home I was exhausted and in extreme pain,
the worst so far, the pain extending from my diaphragm to my right
hip bone. Breathing was difficult, coughing uncontrollable. I took
two hundred grams of Percodan and wound up spending most of the
day in bed in a sort of twitching haze. As my head cleared somewhat
I was moved to add to my tapes but then found that the simple act of
trying to speak into this microphone was too demanding.

Instead, I settled for playing back the original tape. I thought it
went well, but was distressed to hear it so often punctuated by my

coughing. Obviously, it isn't enough to turn the head away when coughing, the sound still penetrates. I will solve that problem, as I am doing this time around, by simply switching off the machine during the spasms.

Yes.

But muddled as I was under those conditions, two concerns did make themselves plain. First, that I may not have sufficiently impressed on my listeners — my readers — that the grand event is no act of vengeance. It is not. Formalized in the vendetta by Latin peoples who have nothing to be proud of but their pride, it is the nadir of brainlessness.

So the grand event is not an act of vengeance. What is it then? It is an inevitability. A seminal historical event. A prophetic crying-out. Psychohistorians, you newest breed of scholastic quack, be especially warned. For God's sake, don't try to find meanings here. Just let me speak for myself.

Well then.

Where was I?

A second concern. Yes. A troublesome one.

The subject of these talks, whatever their digressions, is to be the dark-skinned people of Witter Street. The descendants of some African tribesmen who, having been conveyed to the North American shore in slave ships, and after the most bloody and unnecessary fratricidal war in history, wound their way northward to utopia. To New York. To Brooklyn. To Witter Street. Where money grows on trees and foodstamps may be plucked from untended hedges.

By any calculation they are now more than ninety percent of this block. Taking 409 next door as a measure, of its twenty-four apartments they occupy twenty-three. Including what had traditionally been the janitor's apartment, which I rented out last week. One white couple, the Friedmans, drowning in the dark tide, desperately hang on against it in their top floor apartment behind triple bolts. The Friedmans have been tenants there for thirty years, but it isn't sentiment — love for the dear old neighborhood — which keeps this pair of malignant, whining old Jews on the premises. Hardly. It's rent control which does that, a *noblesse oblige* imposed on me by the City of New York which, in effect, makes these ancient Hebrews my pensioners.

[19]

# THE DARK FANTASTIC

So the dark-skinned are in possission now, they are the theme of these tapes, their alpha and omega, and the question troubling me was how to designate them. By what title? What name?

Negro? Sound and proper but removed from the American language by tribal edict. I graciously defer to the tribe in this.

Black? Not really a racial designation but a threat.

Afro-American? Pretentious. As that ancient tribal hero, Marcus Garvey, was pretentious.

Well then, what about the good old-fashioned slang word derived from Negro? The white cab-driver's favorite improper noun? Or, for that matter, my grandfather's? The ultimate  gentleman scholar merchant, he never to the best of my recollection, used any but this word when referring to a member of the tribe.

I can't. In the mind, yes. Not for the public record. Why? Because — and there's something almost comical about it — much as I've come to detest the stupidity and self-destructiveness of liberalism, social and political, I have been lobotomized by liberalism. Conditioned like a Pavlovian dog to wince at the sound of a racial epithet.

And it doesn't even have to be an epithet. I still remember my astonishment when I was informed by a colleague in the history department — he'll recognize himself as soon as he reads this — that it is insulting to call someone a Jew even though he happens to be a Jew. It is correct form to call him Jewish.

And to demonstrate liberal lobotomization at its most subtle, it now requires an effort for me to say the word Jew aloud. I suppose it comes more easily to the Jewish.

So.

With every logical title for the tribe placed out of reach — a growing irritant — I didn't find a solution as much as have it thrust on me.

*The* solution.

Out of a novel I take pleasure in returning to every few years. *South Wind* by Norman Douglas. From all accounts he was an unpleasant fellow, but how much have those accounts been colored by the fact that when he sat down with pen and paper he was a remorseless truthteller?

Glimmers of a passage in the book kept rising to mind. Something addressed to an acquaintance by the story's protagonist, the Anglican Bishop of Bampopo in Africa. Something about the imaginary

[20]

African tribesmen the good Bishop once served. I have the book before me now; I will present the passage verbatim.

"And your friends, the Bulanga! To think that I once baptized three hundred of them in one day. And the very next week they ate up old Mrs. Richardson, our best lady preacher. The poor dear! We buried her riding boots, I remember. There was nothing else to bury. . . ."

Uncanny.

When I look out of any window of this study I see them up and down the block, the Bulanga of Witter Street.

Not imaginary. Real. And that is the obscene truth of it.

# John Milano

$M$ONDAY, MILANO CAME INTO THE OFFICE AT NOON just in time to meet the thundering charge of thirtieth-floor personnel heading for the elevators and lunch. Willie was having lunch at his desk, a full-sized pizza with all the trimmings and a quart of beer.

"Where've you been?" he said. "On those pictures?"

"Uh-huh. Shaking the grapevine."

"How's it look to you?"

"Not too bad. I think we might owe Rauscher one."

"Yeah? Well, don't ever let him know it. Only thing that asshole hates worse than insurance companies who pay off under the table is the agencies that do the paying off for them. That reminds me. The money part is settled. Pacifica'll have it ready on forty-eight hours notice any time it's called for. All you have to do, Johnny boy, is make sure we have to call for it. And that we wind up with a very big slice of it."

"Depends. Meanwhile we've got that fifteen thousand up front. Enjoy it."

"When you'll be blowing it on expenses inside a week?" Willie was not altogether joking about it. "Wait a second," he said as Milano headed for the door, five minutes alone with Willie amounting to an hour under a dental drill. "Suppose Rauscher's faking it? Giving that Hale a bum steer just so's any agency on the case would be up shit creek?"

No surprise. After all, this was the Willie Watrous who was reputed to be so cagey that he wouldn't enter a confessional without taking his lawyer along.

Milano found Hy Greenwald in his cubicle, hard at work according to instructions. The floor was littered with files of agency reports, decks of index cards, and shoebox-sized plastic containers heaped with newspaper clippings.

"Any of the pieces coming together?" Milano asked.

"Maybe. But I've got some questions."

This was the first real test for Hy who had been with the agency only a few weeks and so far had served as Milano's apprentice on an earn-while-you-learn basis. For all that beard and those granny glasses he was a bright boy, kept his eyes and ears open, and absorbed information like a sponge. At this rate, in a year or two he'd be ready to take himself off and hire out to another agency for twice the money Willie would be willing to pay him. It had happened before. Meanwhile questions were in order.

"Whatever," said Milano.

"All right then. This cop in San Francisco — this Rauscher — takes a look around and says it's a selective theft. What makes him so sure?"

"Did you check out the inventory of the Grassie collection?"

"Yes."

"Then let's say that when nobody's looking you sneak up to that collection some night with your shopping bag in hand, ready to hit the jackpot. You look around and along with some second-rate stuff

[23]

you see a couple of Monets from his middle period, and two Cezannes, both gems. And of course those two Boudins. Now which do you load into your bag?"

Hy weighed this. "You mean whoever it was didn't pick the superstars. But those Boudins are only fourteen by sevens. Small and handy. Maybe that was their attraction."

"They're both on panels, not canvas, and when it comes to walking out on the street with a million dollars worth of stolen art on you, panels are a stiff pain. Highly dangerous. And if you're thinking, well, it's easier to lift a panel off the wall than slice a canvas out of a frame, it's not that much easier. Take my word for it."

"All right, I will. And you see it Rauscher's way. You believe those paintings are heading in this direction right now."

"So the odds say. Now what've you got so far? Sticking to what I asked for."

Hy bent over his notes. "In the past couple of years, eighteen thefts of major works of the Boudin period—let's call them pre-Impressionist—where they nailed the dealers in Europe who were handling them. The thefts were from collectors here and in Europe. Included some prime Courbet, Jongkind, and early Manet. Two dealers took the rap, a Gerard Ost and a Nassos Fountas."

"Bespoke dealers," said Milano.

"Fences," said Hy.

"I was being polite and high-toned." Milano seated himself at the table and closed his eyes in reflection, conjuring up the images of a series of paintings—mental filing cards—which he flicked through his mind's eye. A necessary exercise and, as bonus, a highly pleasurable one.

"Well?" said Hy.

"Gerard Ost," said Milano.

"Right. He and Fountas are both in jail now. In Switzerland."

"Figures. Anyhow, the way it goes is that some billionaire who plays strictly by his own rules—it's pretty much South America and the Middle East nowadays—needs some pieces to round out his very private collection, except those pieces are not for sale. So guys like Ost and Fountas help solve that little problem. Now it looks like some fat cat out there is building himself a real nice pre-Impressionist show, and you can't leave Boudin out of that, can you?" Milano pointed at the clutter on the table. "Did the name Rammaert turn up anywhere in that stuff? Wim Rammaert?"

"No. Who's he?"

"Rammaert Gallery over on Fifty-seventh. Small, select, and, to those in the know, smelly. The interesting part is that Rammaert is Gerard Ost's cousin."

"Oh?" Then Hy gave it added thought. "But Ost is in jail."

"Leaving someone in the family to fill in for him. They've got a very hot cousins' club operating there."

"I see. Then this someone gives the order for the Boudins to Rammaert who lifts them ── "

"Has them lifted."

"Has them lifted and is supposed to make delivery to the billionaire customer. So now you get together with Rammaert for a deal before delivery can be made."

"Not that fast. If I show him my hand and he isn't the guilty party, I'm wide open for disaster. He could have himself a real fun time stringing me along about a possible deal while some total stranger is stashing those Boudins away somewhere in downtown Kuwait. Or in somebody's castle on the pampas."

Hy looked doubtful. "I don't know. If I was Rammaert ── "

"I'm talking out of painful experience. I've been taken like that by Rammaert's kind of people. Willie'll gladly tell you about it any time you ask."

"Yeah, but if Rammaert is the one, what about him getting in touch here? You told Hale that's how you'd handle it. Was that just talk?"

"Not altogether. When word gets around that we're interested in those paintings—and if Rammaert is the one—he might get in touch. Or he might not. But we don't sit and wait. Right now, for instance, you're taking a little trip to the Rammaert Gallery."

"Incognito, you mean."

"Just another bug-eyed college art major. See if he runs the place alone, or, if there's help, how the help shapes up. Friendly and chatty? Knows the inventory? That kind of thing. And bring back any brochures. There might be a branch office listed at a foreign address. Basel would be good. Ost worked out of Basel. Buenos Aires and Rio would be good. And be ready in case Rammaert asks you any questions."

[25]

"I'll be wise as the serpent," Hy said solemnly.

"Don't strain yourself," Milano told him. "When it comes to being the serpent Rammaert's got you outclassed all the way."

He was at his own desk indexing descriptions of some lost, strayed or stolen rare coins when Hy returned two hours later looking pleased with himself. Yes, the place was open and Rammaert was there but not on the scene. He and Mrs. Rammaert were in their apartment, one flight up over the gallery. Rammaert did some extensive traveling on business now and then, but he hadn't been out of town for several weeks. Nor his wife.

Best of all, there were branch offices, three of them. One in London, one in Cannes, one in Basel. All listed in the gallery's fancy brochure.

"Talk about pieces fitting together," Hy said. "London for the petrodollars, Cannes for the gaucho gold, and Basel for the numbered bank accounts."

"Very shrewd surmise," Milano said. "But somebody there had to give you this stuff. Who?"

"Kind of a triple threat. Receptionist, secretary, guide. Not that she's any art expert. She was faking it. Making echo talk."

"Belgian, by any chance? Another one of Rammaert's helpful cousins?"

"American," said Hy. "Black and very beautiful. Her name's Christine Bailey."

# Charles
# Witter
# <u>Kirwan</u>

A GOOD NIGHT LAST NIGHT, A GOOD DAY SO FAR.

Slept soundly, woke with the realization that I was suffering almost no pain. I sometimes see that pain as a venomous snake coiled in its nest under my breastbone and slithering out along wellworn paths through my body. Now the snake appears to be coiled tight in the nest biding its time.

Only biding its time, I know that. Any minute, it may stir again and I'll have a different tune to play.

Oh yes.

I've had a few such gratifying spells during the past months. Had even been fooled a couple of times into allowing thoughts of possible remission to enter my mind. No more of that gullibility. Never.

Strange thing, I didn't rejoice in those thoughts, I was terrified by them. All my strength now stems from the finality of my death sentence. Cancel it — even postpone it — and I would be nothing.

Less than nothing.

I can savor this easing of pain though. Cancer does offer its victim that one pleasure: there are actually moments when he may forget it's devouring him. My wife enjoyed a few of them before the very bad final stretch. Lymphatic cancer, that was. Such medical sadism as radium and chemotherapy didn't help in that final stretch either.

Poor miserable puking soul.

Doctors. God's witnesses on earth to the joys of brutal, greedy, unrepressed egomania.

Never mind.

I'll just say that I woke up feeling comparatively well and it showed. An objective observer remarked on it. Mrs. Bailey, my Bulanga domestic, here for the Tuesday housecleaning, Tuesday being the day reserved for me. To Mrs. Bailey — to all the world except those doctors who put me through their tests — I have a bad bronchitis. Mrs. Bailey attended to my wife before the hospital phase; now she is inclined to attend me and my cough. So I invented the bronchitis to keep her at bay, bearing as well as I can her Aunt Jemima solicitude.

In fact, she is as much an Aunt Jemima as I am a bronchitis patient. She has the face and swollen proportions, she can ooze sweetness as the sugar maple oozes sap, but, a true Bulanga, she is the born petty thief and easy liar. Or a magician. A silver creamer is found missing from its shelf. A convincing anguish is expressed about this by its owner. The next day, the creamer miraculously reappears in a sideboard where it had never been stored. In another case, eight half-dollars, the last of a trove in a kitchen canister suddenly becomes seven. No public notice is taken. The seven becomes six.

In her final year, my wife had her own bedroom, and I knew her personal possessions well. After her death it was our teary Bulanga who cleaned up that disheveled and sour-smelling room. When I got around to gathering together those possessions I saw that she had not lost on the deal.

[28]

But things even up. Yes they do. Because with an irony Norman Douglas himself would have relished, Mrs. Bailey has of her own free will given me the use of her pet, her chief concern in life, her Lorena. Planted the idea in my head by her incessant talk about Lorena this and Lorena that and the trouble bringin' up a nice girl in today's world, keepin' 'em away from drugs and such and from them turkeys, them studs, you know what I mean, Perfessor, who only look to get a girl in a mess. The kind shows her a fat wad of green and say, baby, you just point at anything in that window and it's all yours. Girl needs some money of her own, else she buys that talk, you know what I mean? And who got the money to give her, the way things are? Even with Christine willin' to chip in. When she got it to chip in.

So the litany. The old Charles Witter Kirwan would have heard it through, outwardly sympathetic, inwardly twitching with impatience. The new Charles Witter Kirwan, under death sentence, twitched himself into action.

Fearfully of course. With apprehension. But then, can anyone abruptly decide to transform his most heated fantasies into glorious reality without apprehension? I couldn't. Not even as my new self. So I made my offer hesitantly, and, an added irony, I think it was my hesitance, my evident embarrassment, that told the doting mother the offer was simon-pure.

Certainly it was plausible. There are at least a couple of thousand books in the house. I wanted them catalogued and if Lorena thought she could handle the job, well, it was all hers. Say, an hour every Monday, Wednesday, and Friday right after school. And I'd be willing to pay five dollars for each hour. It was less than I'd have to pay a professional, of course, so I'd be making a saving and Lorena would have her pocket money.

Could anything have been more plausible?

And, in fact, when this sullen Bulanga maiden first appeared for duty I did introduce her to the stack of blank index cards and pencil and pencil-sharpener and to the brimming bookcases scattered through the building, most notably to those in the second-floor tower room, my study, as it had been my grandfather's, where work was to commence.

One card for each book. Author's last name, first name, title of book, publisher, date of publication. All explained very solemnly. Any questions?

"Yeah. How many of these things supposed to get done in an hour?"

"As many as you can without making mistakes. There's no rush."

"An' I get paid off after every time? No waitin'?"

"Paid in cash. No waiting."

She worked. I sat at my desk pretending to take notes from a textbook before me and watched. If she knew I was furtively watching, she gave no sign of it. It was gratifying to observe that Lorena, only fifteen, only a second-year student at Erasmus Hall High School, had already mastered the alphabet, a rare achievement among the Bulanga youth. It was even more gratifying just to observe Lorena, all skintight jeans and revealing T-shirt, at this close range. Shoes off after awhile. Dark-skinned, pink-soled, beautifully-shaped feet.

No time for a lengthy courtship here. How well I knew that. Yet, when the moment came two days later to make my move I didn't have the courage to do it. I hit bottom afterward. I went through a shivering, sweating, self-hating emotional crisis questioning whether this supposedly tough new Charles Witter Kirwan wasn't just a fraud, just a cancerous version of the old futile, daydreaming Charles Witter Kirwan.

Foolish, really.

So in preparation for the girl's next appearance I took my courage from the bottle as my stepfather so often used to do. Although I was not at my best that day I forced myself to abstain from the usual steady dose of Percodan, not sure how alcohol would mix with it, and at lunch put away almost a full bottle of wine. It worked. It laid the old Charles Witter Kirwan to rest forever.

It did not ease my physical pain. I remember that when I —

Yes.

When I started to lean back casually in my chair as a preface to what I would say I instantly discovered that this was like being stretched on the rack.

So.

So I leaned forward, resting my arms on the desk. Lorena, pencil

[30]

in hand, was using the floor as her desk, kneeling there head down, rounded buttocks high in the air.

I said, "Do you go out with boys, Lorena?"

She cocked her head toward me. So far we had exchanged no more than a dozen words altogether, and those had concerned only her make-work. Yet there was no surprise in her face at this overture, only a narrow-eyed speculation. The Bulanga instinct. The scent of oestrus coming downwind. And no fear of ole whitey either when you're twice as quick and strong as he looks to be.

"You seen me goin' with boys," she said at last. "Right outside there."

So I had. I said, "I didn't mean that way. I meant, do you sleep with any of them?"

That startled her. She slowly stood up, measuring me even more intently. "You drunk?"

"No."

"You sure smell like it."

"I'm not drunk. Just curious. Did any of your boy friends ever see you naked?"

"Hey, man ———"

"I have." I pointed at the window. "Right across the way there. Sometimes you forget to pull down your bedroom shade."

She glanced at the window, then turned back to me with curled lip. "Big deal."

"It could be, Lorena. A big money deal for you. I liked what I saw. I'm ready to pay to see more of it." I laid the money out on the desk as if I were laying out a hand of solitaire, fifty dollars in tens. I had carefully calculated the amount, calculated that if everything went well, stakes would have to be increased later and this was exactly the right bait for the start. Not too little, not too much.

Yes.

More important, I was prepared for anything going wrong at this point. For the least hint of rejection, which could mean mama would be told about all this. So, if the least trouble impended I must be ready to reach mama at once. With outrage. I am sorry to say, Mrs. Bailey, that I badly misjudged Lorena. For her to demand more money when I'm being generous as it is, and then to threaten that if I

[31]

didn't give her more she'd tell you I tried to get her clothes off and make love to her —

Oh yes.

Ole whitey—frail, gentle, pathetic, bronchial-tormented ole whitey—has the edge here. Even the toughest Bulanga mother would have more reason to put her faith in him than in a troublesome teen-age daughter.

All those fancy calculations.

And what happened?

Lorena moved toward the desk. She ran a fingertip back and forth over the money as if making sure it was real. "I git off my clothes, you git off your rocks, that it?"

Mind you, this is a fifteen-year-old child speaking.

But of course the Bulanga female matures early. In 409 Witter Street there is a mother just fourteen years older than her infant son. Mother attends a special public school for conspicuously fertile juveniles. The school is always overcrowded. It is one of life's wonders that —

No. Never mind.

Where was I?

Oh yes, Lorena.

I braced myself for the crossing of the Rubicon. Then I heard myself say, "Clothes off while you do your work here. And you get the five dollars for that work besides this big money. Every time."

"Every time? That same money?"

We were in business.

A funny aspect of it. The first few times it was plain that she didn't like my watching her undress. She would huddle in a corner while at it, a Bulanga *September Morn*. Then she became casual about it. Now she's arrived at the point where, seated on the edge of a chair, darting sidelong glances to see how I'm taking it, she sometimes performs a sort of slow striptease for me.

A long-legged, delicately curved budding beauty.

I take it very well, thank you.

My partner in felony.

Wrong? Sinful?

Not for the transformed Charles Witter Kirwan it isn't. Not a goddamned bit of it.

[32]

No.

What do you know about sexual deprivation?

Are you enjoying its blessings?

I married at forty-two. I can count on the fingers of one hand my sexual experiences before my wedding night.

My wife was a dear woman. She had many virtues, few vices.

Florence Pettengill. Clerk in the bursar's office at the college. An attractive woman. With friends who also happened to be among my friends. Insistent, nagging, well-meaning, matchmaking friends.

Florence and I liked each other before our marriage. We became used to each other afterward.

My wife was a gracious woman. Everyone who reads this and knew her will testify to that.

She consented to sex graciously. She tolerated it patiently.

Think that over.

I masturbated almost every day of my life from pubescence to marriage. Is it any wonder that I masturbated almost every day of my life after my marriage?

Did my wife know? I've wondered about that sometimes. If she did, she would have graciously preferred it that way.

And now that I

A hiatus.

While I was dictating into this machine I could hear Mrs. Bailey wielding the vacuum cleaner downstairs. It suddenly stopped, so I did. I think the lady has an ear made for pressing against closed doors.


Mrs. Bailey has now been paid her money and taken herself off. She asked how Lorena was doing, I said she was doing very nicely.

That reminds me. When I warned Lorena against any careless display of her newfound wealth before her family she looked at me blankly and said with apparent puzzlement, "What money, man? I don't know about any money."

She actually put me off balance for the moment.

Bulanga wise.

# John Milano

TUESDAY, THE LID BLEW OFF AT WATROUS ASSOCIATES. No big surprise for Milano: it blew off whenever the pressure rose above boiling level, something of an annual event in recent years. One trouble, as Milano saw it, was that Willie had always been a son of a bitch, and old age, senility, whatever, seemed to be making him a bigger one every time you looked at him. The other trouble was that the pair of them, like an old married couple, knew each other's weak spots too well. If there was an old married couple somewhere who could refrain from shoving the needle into each other's weak spots, they hadn't stood up to be counted.

Yet the day had started nicely. On impulse, a phone call to Mama and fifteen minutes of her on the subject of her evil daughter Angie. This evened things up, because it was no secret that when Mama talked to Angie her favorite subject was her evil son Johnny. But at least the call had been made. Chalk that up on the board.

At breakfast prepared by himself, Milano went through the *Daily News* and the *Times* with an eye out for any item suggesting a possible client for the agency. In the middle of breakfast — tomato juice, single scrambled egg, single piece of unbuttered toast, black coffee, no sugar — it struck him that he had somehow slipped into a diet during the past two days, a realization which filled him with a glow of virtue.

The glow lasted until he was at his desk and called in Shirley Glass. "A bank messenger job, beautiful. I'll need three thousand expense money. In hundreds." Shirley seemed to whimper in response, and he looked at her appraisingly. "What's wrong with you?"

"Not me. Helen Monahan. Willie fired her at quitting time yesterday."

Helen Monahan had been one of the first typists hired by Watrous Associates back in antediluvian times. Grotesquely fat, already middle-aged, she had plainly hungered for the job in contrast to the shapely young things who took their time deciding whether or not it was worth their trouble. Over the years since getting it, she demonstrated gratitude, not by efficiency, but by such an eager effort to be efficient that it made Milano nervous to deal with her.

But fired?

"Why'd he fire her?" Milano asked.

"She was coming in late sometimes, going home early sometimes. She couldn't help it. She's got a very sick husband she's trying to keep at home instead of sending away somewhere for nursing. That's not easy."

"Then there's no problem. Get her on the phone right now and hire her back."

Shirley shook her head. "Willie said if you tried that he'd fire her again as soon as she showed up. You can't kick her back and forth between you like that. Willie has to do the hiring."

Milano said grimly, "I need this kind of soap opera like a hole in

[35]

the head," and walked across the carpeted hallway into Willie's office loaded for bear.

Willie sat hunched over his desk, hands clasped before him. He promptly said, "If it's about Monahan, Johnny boy, forget it."

"Willie, you don't fire people that way."

"I didn't. I retired her. She made sixty last month. That's retirement age around here."

"Since when?"

"Since right now."

"If sixty is the deadline," said Milano, "where does that leave you?"

"I'm still the boss. Monahan was hired help."

"Ah, come on, Willie, we're making more money than we ever dreamed of. What the hell would it hurt to carry her? She's like family after all these years."

"Yours maybe. Not mine." Willie dropped the cape and showed the sword. "But I'll tell you what, Johnny boy. There's ten thousand dollars worth of pictures on your wall across the way. That the company paid for. And not even real pictures, for chrissake. Copies."

"They're quality Rouault prints, you ignorant bastard. Right now they're worth twice what we paid for them."

"Twenty thousand? Are they now?" said Willie sweetly. "Then I'll tell you what you can do with them, you smartass guinea. You can sell them and give half the take to Monahan. The other half you can give back to the company. That way we'll all be happy, won't we?"

Milano tried slowly counting to ten. A thousand wouldn't have done it. "Well, see you around, killer. Sooner or later."

Willie came to his feet, forefinger aimed at Milano's nose. "Don't you give me that sooner or later shit! Not if it means you now head for the hills because your fucking tender feelings are hurt. Oh no, not this time!"

Leaving, Milano slammed the door behind him so hard that the knob came off in his hand. He laid the knob on his desk, and Shirley looked at it. "You beat him to death with that?" she said.

"Not yet."

"But he wouldn't change his mind about Helen?"

"No. Look, I'm taking off from the job for a stretch. Hy can keep that chair warm meanwhile. Just give him whatever pointers he needs."

"Hy Greenwald? Johnny, outside of all the routine here you've got a couple of big ones on the burner. Especially that Pacifica thing. Hy's not up to that."

True. But the routine and the rare coin job could be left to simmer on the burner, no harm done.

Which left a pair of lovely helpless Boudins heading underground somewhere like lovely helpless Persephone. And once underground, never to be seen again. Hell, never even to be listed in any catalogue again.

Milano said, "All right, I'll see what I can do about Pacifica. That's all. For starters, send a messenger over to the apartment with the three thousand. I'll be waiting for it there around noon."

"And how do I tell Willie about you?"

"I have a feeling he already knows," said Milano.

Instead of going straight back to the apartment he walked full-tilt into the park as far as the zoo. A mistake. Except for the Prospect Park Zoo which had to be the absolute bottom, this concrete detention center was undeniably one of the most depressing zoos in the world. He lingered for awhile in front of the cages penning the big cats. In one cage a tiger contentedly dozed, eyelids half shut, sunlight toasting its belly. In the next an edgy leopard restlessly padded back and forth covering the small distance between walls. If neither of them was faking it, this proved, philosophically speaking, that it took all kinds.

In the apartment he hesitated between a low-calorie Perrier and a high-calorie Jack Daniels and compromised by mixing a half-and-half. He put the Maria Caniglia *Tosca* on the player, then stretched out on the couch. He stayed with *Tosca* to Scarpia's booming solo which brought down the first-act curtain and felt a little better. He shifted over to Billie Holiday and drifted into a pleasantly mournful stupor.

At twelve-thirty, the messenger arrived with the money. At one o'clock the phone rang. Hy Greenwald.

"*Que pasa*, Johnny? You really cutting out just like that? What're you doing there?"

"Like meditating, sonny."

"Good. Then I'll give you something heavy to meditate on. A phone call from a guy who wants to meet with you about those Boudins. Not Rammaert. This one says his name is Irv and you know him. He gave me a number to call back."

"Irv Saltzman. In the trade. Lives under a rock."

"But is there any chance that —?"

"There's always a thin chance. What you do now is ask him to give you the exact head count on how many women in each painting are carrying parasols. Exact. You can get the count from those two photos."

"I'll do that. But if he doesn't have the paintings, what his angle?"

"Dreams of glory. Trying to weasel into the deal as our agent. Anyhow, call him back now and see what happens."

Three minutes later, the phone rang again. "Looks like he's not the one," Hy reported. "Not from what he had to say."

"What was that? Wrong count?"

"No, he just said to tell you to take a flying fuck. That's all. Then he hung up."

"So it goes," said Milano. "And you could hear from others like him. Give them all the same treatment. If anyone looks kosher, call me fast."

"You mean the woods are full of hyenas like that?"

"Along with the Rolls-Royce type hyenas who manipulate the art market and eat up all the little lambs that come in to shop. Those you'll find listed in *Who's Who*."

"Very informative. They never had seminars on that in Cornell. Say, when do you expect to be back here?"

"I'll let you know when the countdown starts," Milano said.

According to its brochure, the Rammaert Gallery closed at six. Milano timed himself for a five-thirty arrival. Carnegie Hall on the corner, the Russian Tea Room, and, a few doors farther along, the gallery, street level in an unobtrusive four-story building. Despite heavy homegoing pedestrian traffic which occasionally bounced off his shoulder, he braced himself in front of the display window for a view of its contents. Very discreet. A single painting and a plasticized blow-up of a New York *Times* review. The painting was of a swirling nebula which pretty well covered the range of Grumbacher's color charts, surrounding a rectangular white core. The review was the usual cotton candy whipped up in these cases. The artist was Archbold. No other name offered, just Archbold. Like Rembrandt.

There was more Archbold to be seen in the gallery's long, narrow front room, about a dozen nebulae on each wall. Also a desk at the head of the room near the display window. On the desk a phone and on the phone's base the army of buttons marking this as a mini-switchboard.

A young woman sat behind the desk.

Christine Bailey?

From Hy's awed description, Christine Bailey.

Black. Both-sides-of-the-family black. Frizzy hair in a modified Afro. And, Milano had to admit to himself, Hy hadn't exaggerated. Any healthy male dropping in here would have a hard time trying to focus on the finest of fine art with that showpiece in view. Matter of fact, you could hear some client in a burnoose and with a sack of petrodollars — or the ranchero with the gaucho gold — telling Rammaert to forget the prime Picasso, just wrap up the lady there for quick delivery.

The lady glanced up at Milano, gave him the briefest of pro-fessional smiles, and went back to reading the book before her. He tried to make out its title and couldn't, helped himself to a descrip-tive flier on Archbold from the stack there, and went for a stroll among the nebulae. A couple bore unobtrusive red stars indicating that they were already sold. Maybe they were. On the other hand, as any operator like Rammaert could tell you, boxes of little red stars were easily available at your local stationer's for just one dollar a box.

There was a smaller room behind the main one. Here, under more subdued lighting, was hung an assortment of Nineteenth Century French academic stuff. Milano stopped to scrutinize a Gérome closely. Probably authentic. Géromes were now being feverishly hauled out of attics and dusted off for the chicken-headed market, but their prices, while rising, still hadn't hit that level which might tempt a world-class forger to try his hand at one. Glossy stuff, not too hard to imitate, but mind-numbing in its detail.

At the far end of the room was a door, a light shining under it, a voice within audible in the phone conversationalist's grumble. Rammaert's office. No doubt, Rammaert's voice.

[39]

Milano looked at his watch. A few minutes before six. Despite powerful temptation, he managed to refrain from considering the lady at the desk and, instead, considered the layout of the premises. A simple-minded alarm system conspicuous over the front door. No uniformed man on duty. All adding up to third-rate security for third-rate merchandise.

He had not really — not directly, at least — lied to Hy Greenwald. Thanks to the agency's vast accumulation of indexed information, the evidence pretty much tallied up to Rammaert. And if he was the one, the Boudins would very likely wind up right here in his shop on their way through. Not even hidden. Just left crated in a storeroom. Or even in a corner of that back office.

Because, contrary to amateur logic, that was the place for them if the cops miraculously pinned the job on the right man. That was what gave the right man room to be a terribly innocent victim wrongly accused. My God, officer, these paintings were taken on consignment in all good faith. Here's the correspondence to prove it. And to think they're stolen goods! Horrifying. Unbelievable.

Check out the West Coast end of the correspondence and nobody's there. Had been, but not any more. Is that the fault of this honest New York art dealer? The defense rests.

So going by the odds, as Hy had been advised, the Boudins could be here or, more likely, on their way here. No guarantee, but that was the smart bet. And with solid evidence that Rammaert had possession of the goods, you could then approach him, ransom money in hand.

What Hy hadn't been told was that there was an option to weigh before the Q.E.D. Just as the paintings had been lifted from tycoon Grassie, they could be lifted from art dealer Rammaert. Surreptitiously removed by experts in that line of work for shipment back home to daddy as soon as Pacifica made full payment to the agency for them.

Nothing Rammaert could do about it afterward. Not a thing.

Couldn't go to the law, couldn't raise a howl, couldn't even risk a stifled moan about it. The biter bit.

A little grand larceny? Well, yes. But consider the poetic justice of it. And the results.

But that was Willie's end of it, the larceny. After thirty years of

Safe, Loft and Truck, and Special Frauds, and Riverfront, and God knows what else on the Force, Willie had contacts who'd hit Fort Knox if the price was right. For a place like Rammaert's you could line up a team who might do the job for five thousand. You could also line up a team who'd guarantee a flawless job for fifteen or twenty. And this was the only kind of marketing where Willie — give the miserable little bastard credit — didn't go bargain-hunting.

Milano cast an eye at his watch: a few minutes after six. The place to wait for Christine Bailey was outside the foyer, clear of the display window. Then, depending on the play of cards, it could be the bar of the Russian Tea Room or that coffee shop on the corner of Seventh Avenue for the warmup pitches. Right now, there was still a chance of getting a look into the office behind him.

He tried to, but the view was instantly obscured by the man emerging through the office door. Big-bellied, jowly, and with the Flemish high color. The russet hairpiece over the graying sideburns was transparently a hairpiece. Had to be Rammaert. Then the door was pulled almost shut.

"I'm sorry" — the hint of a guttural — "but we are closing now."

"Yes, of course," Milano said, but bided his time as Hairpiece ponderously made his way into the front room. That office door was tempting. An inch of opening allowed a narrow view of the office.

He heard the front door bang, then the outside door, and wheeled around. Hairpiece was at his desk, Christine Bailey wasn't. She must have shot out of there like a bat out of hell. "Goddam," Milano told the Gérome between his teeth.

He left the gallery at a brisk pace, nodding pleasantly to the proprietor as he went by, then stood on the street looking up and down for any glimpse of that Afro hairdo and ebony swan-neck among all the commonplace heads and necks in view.

Lost her.

Even Hy Greenwald could have done better.

[41]

# Charles Witter Kirwan

Hᴀᴠᴇ ʏᴏᴜ ᴇᴠᴇʀ ʜᴇᴀʀᴅ ᴏғ ᴛʜᴇ Mᴏᴏɴʟɪɢʜᴛ Mᴏᴠɪɴɢ Cᴏᴍᴘᴀɴʏ? A Bulanga term. Sometimes the Bulanga, despite their limited vocabulary, come up with an image of surprising acuity.

The Moonlight Moving Company consists of a rented U-Haul truck which appears between midnight and dawn to be loaded with unpaid-for furniture by unpaid-for tenants on the move. It is the creation of our town's political messiahs who, brimming over with Christian and Jewish charity and avid for the Bulanga vote, decided on a scenario where those who rent the Bulanga their living space must always emerge as the villains of the piece. The bad ones. The whiteys. Instructed to cosset their tenants, tend their quarters, pay property taxes on schedule, and always acknowledge that they themselves are the worms in the Big Apple.

And the Bulanga? A regally proud people, never mind the public charity that droppeth on them like the gentle rain from heaven. After all, as the scenario has it, charity won by extortion and menace is not charity, it is dues.

Does it surprise you to learn that my prideful, dues-collecting tenants have better things to spend their money on than their rent?

To be absolutely fair, not all of them. At any given time no more than half are in arrears beyond two months. Just enough to have the building drain away what money I have left instead of providing for its own maintenance.

This comes up because last night, a little after midnight, I watched the Moonlight Moving Company in action next door. The Mitchells this time, four months in arrears, were decamping. In my records, their apartment was occupied by one mother, two children. On the street before 409, loading furniture and furnishings into the U-Haul, were two females, five children, and four adult males. I recognized two of the males; I had seen them in and out of the building sometimes. As a gentleman, I will assume that the other two were friends of the family in a Boy Scout mood.

I make such assumptions now and then for my private entertainment.

So.

For the first time, I could, with death's firm and friendly grip on my shoulder, watch this kind of event dispassionately. I must make clear I was not on the lookout for it. Not in the tower room to do any spying. But in the way of the Bulanga culture, when the Moonlight Moving Company is on the job there is no secrecy about it, no hush-hushing, no tiptoeing. There is thud, bang, and clatter; there is unrestrained badinage and laughter. The uninhibited Bulanga cackle and whinny. All more than enough to have me part the window curtains a bit and view the action.

Dispassionately.

Caliban upon Setebos.

Yes.

> "Let twenty pass, and stone the twenty-first,
> Loving not, hating not, just choosing so."

[43]

Know that one?

Robert Browning. Too long a poem—smothering in its own luxuriant verbiage at times—but these lines

The Victorian poets? Possibly too fluent? I've sometimes wondered if they

Never mind.

But these lines of Caliban strike sparks.

You see, Mrs. Mitchell and her spawn and her dear friends will not be part of the grand event. They will only learn about it afterward, from a distance. They will sit popeyed before their television sets viewing the devastation and trying to comprehend the goodness of de Lawd. They will feed on it all the rest of their lives like the people who cancelled their passage aboard the *Titanic* as it prepared to sail on its first and last voyage. They will be the cynosure of all Bulanga eyes for their uncanny prescience, and if Mrs. Mitchell is shrewd enough to seize opportunity, she can wind up reading the cards for fun and profit, as do Madam Dora and Madam Clarissa around the corner here on the avenue.

Charles Witter Kirwan. Caliban upon Setebos. In his own fashion.

I watched the U-Haul laden, I watched it depart. In farewell, one of the party tossed an empty beer can—or soft-drink can—over the high railing of my front yard to land among the rest of the evening's deposit in the grass. It could have been a comment on the landlord, it could have been the usual Bulanga method of trash disposal. Impossible to say.

What was I doing in the study at that hour?

I was supposed to get an urgent phone call early in the evening. When there was no phone call I was disturbed and angry. And, inevitably, sleepless. At such times I usually take refuge in the study and its distractions.

Yes.

An intensely urgent phone call.

I have my six dozen sticks of dynamite. I still do not have the blasting caps containing the necessary primers for them, nor the length of wire fuse needed to set off the explosion from a single detonator, nor the detonator itself.

And in view of my physical condition, time grows short.

[44]

I have estimated as accurately as possible. I'll be working under difficult conditions, but if I can put in between two and three hours a day, I should be able to position and wire the dynamite within two weeks. If I have the necessary materials at hand.

For the information of the police, this depends on a gentleman named Swanson—I don't know his given name—who is right now night watchman for the Passarini Demolition Company of Sutton Falls, New York, a few miles above Kingston on Route 32.

I'm afraid Mr. Swanson is not quite the devoted employee that his employer may think he is. He is the one who sold me my dynamite from his company's stores without its knowledge, and, as if to prove that his felonious nature knows no bias, he cheated me thoroughly in the process. For the agreed-on price of one thousand dollars—which I paid in cash—he was to supply one gross of dynamite sticks, one hundred yards of wire, and a detonator.

When I made my count of the dynamite in his watchman's shanty and found only half the promised order, he had his excuse all ready. Inventory had just been taken by the boss, so this was all he could risk of the stock. Refund half the money? Well, he no longer had any of the money to refund. Anyhow, he had been paid by me to do his best, to stick his neck way out, and that was what he had done.

Oh yes.

And the wire and detonator? And blasting caps?

Well, now —

A shabby, boozy, threatening Viking, but the Lowland Witters never took kindly to intimidation.

"Mr. Swanson," said I, "If I tell your boss what's happening to his supplies and offer to return what I already have of them, I have nothing at all to lose. You have a great deal."

It took courage I didn't know I had, and that was a pleasant discovery. He could have split my skull and buried me under that shanty without anyone the wiser.

He didn't. Instead, I was given solemn assurance that in exactly a week—Wednesday—today—he'd call me collect at home after dinner and let me know when to make the pickup.

And there was no call.

And, inevitably, no sleep for me.

On the face of it, it was reckless of me to do my shopping this way.

[45]

On the face of it.

But in practical terms, I had small choice in the matter. There are no shops I know of where you just walk in and order several cases of high explosive. And any authorized supplier would certainly be curious about why someone like myself was in the market for his dangerous wares. Identification and some form of license could be necessary. A check-up by the authorities might follow.

Not for me, thank you.

There is another reason for depending on the undependable Mr. Swanson.

Let it be entered into the record now that I did not plan the grand event and then search for the means to execute it.

Not at all.

In fact, it was the witnessing of a purposeful and controlled explosion that inspired the plan. And I must make clear—I must make absolutely clear—that it was not a scene presented by television or in a movie, those media so often blamed for the aberrant acts of some lunatic members of their audience.

My mental balance is just fine, thank you.

And that explosion I witnessed

No.

I must place the matter in its proper context.

I have—I had an elderly aunt. Maggie. Margaretha. Some time ago, I took it on myself

Sorry.

That long silence was simply because I forgot to turn off this machine while I got my thoughts in order. I believe this can be corrected by cutting and splicing the tape, but I won't attempt it. I'm not that sure of myself when it comes to handling this equipment.

Now where was I?

Yes. To start at the proper starting point, my grandfather had two children, a daughter and a son three years her junior. The daughter was my Aunt Maggie—always Margaretha to my grandfather—and the son eventually became my father. From all accounts, Aunt Maggie was the apple of my grandfather's eye, a rather plain-featured girl but, in my grandfather's words, always mannerly and dutiful, which, I assume, meant that she always did as he told her to do.

[46]

Don't get the impression from this that he was some sort of family tyrant. Far from it. He made a formidable appearance, yes; rather short but broad-shouldered and powerfully built, and with a square jaw and unusual pale gray eyes that enforced respect at a glance.

Yes indeed.

But contrary to appearance he was in no way the bully. Never raised his voice in anger, a marvelous trait in any human being, one I've spent a lifetime trying to cultivate. Never threatening. Always in calm, certain control of himself. Rarely given to demonstrations of affection, but, in fact, they weren't needed. Weren't needed at all. The affection was there, and his family knew it. And I, the one and only grandchild, came to know it very well.

So.

Disaster, as they used to put it in those ancient melodramas, lurked in the wings. At eighteen, Aunt Maggie spent her summer at the farm of some people who provided fruit for Witter and Sons, ships' suppliers of Fulton Street, Brooklyn. Founded, may I say, in the year 1830. At the foot of Fulton Street, and provisioning ships of every type, not only with their edibles, but with every possible article needed for the voyage.

Enormously prosperous during the Civil War. Never again that prosperous.

Rise and Decline. Not to quick extinction, but to a slow downhill ride until it was finished off by the Great Depression. My grandfather inherited the company at the age of twenty, and in his half-century of management couldn't raise it to its glory days again. A scrupulous, capable businessman, but at a time when huckster aggressiveness became the hallmark of the successful businessman he lacked it. No Jew in him, as he put it.

Placed whatever profits there were into safe and sound investment elsewhere. And into this house. His treasure and prize. Every inch of it from foundation to spire built under his close supervision. Every bit of material handpicked.

Can you build for the ages out of wood?

Yes. If you build right. If you maintain properly.

The company's brick and stone building at the foot of Fulton Street long gone. The wooden house remains.

Witter and Sons of Fulton Street.

[47]

Strange and wonderful smells in that old building.

Grandfather pointing across the river. "Do you know that our Fulton Street in Brooklyn continues that Fulton there in Manhattan? One long street with a river crossing it?"

Then walking to Brooklyn Heights nearby to see where Washington embarked his army for Manhattan in their flight from the British. And grandfather pointing here and there, and somehow William of Orange came into it. William sailing from the Netherlands to become King of England. And with him a trusted secretary, Piet Uitter.

And then our trip back to Flatbush on foot. Miles and miles of hard pavement where I — nine years old? ten years old? — sometimes walked and more often trotted to keep up along Flatbush Avenue, the finger pointing that this was once the old Flatbush Road, pointing out the past here and there, while the tempting trolley-cars rolled by me one after another.

And home, dear God, home at last, with my mother working my shoes off my swollen feet and saying, "Oh, Papa, what were you thinking of?" and grandfather, who lived not for business but for his Gibbon and Motley and Prescott and Guizot — all still ranged right around me here on these bookshelves, each volume with his signed nameplate in it — yes, grandfather saying, "He was learning history. I think the boy has a head for it."

A head for it. If not the feet for it that memorable day.

Yes.

His very last letter to the American Historical Journal

No.

I seem to have lost my thread. That isn't what I was getting at.

What was it?

Oh yes, my Aunt Maggie.

So my Aunt Maggie spent that summer at the farm upstate and fell madly in love with the young handyman there. Came home and announced the news to her father. A handyman. And he loved her as madly as she loved him. And since they couldn't bear to be apart she wanted to marry him right now.

Oh dear, oh dear.

A handyman. For bed and board and five dollars a week in cash. When my grandfather digested this there was no *sturm und drang* in the house, no stormy weather, that was not his way. But there was a deep freeze. My Aunt Maggie weeping the days away in her room. My grandmother, already close to death though no one knew it yet, weeping in hers, the nurse along with her. My father, the teen-age brother, carefully keeping out of sight as much as possible.

Aunt Maggie won the battle and lost the war. Married Curtis Hayes, her handyman, and was disinherited. On my grandfather's death — my father having predeceased him — Aunt Maggie got nothing, I got it all. Not much money left by then, but there was the family home and the apartment house next door. Lucky for the family home I was the one.

So my Aunt Maggie and my Uncle Curtis — a big, strong, perpetually smiling fool — lived outside Sutton Falls upstate on their little dairy farm as dependent on my grandfather's ongoing charity as they were on their few pathetic Holsteins. My uncle died, and charity had to be increased. My grandfather asked Aunt Maggie to share this house with us; she refused. Had a need, she said, to tend to her husband's grave every day. Perhaps she did. In her old age she was a great one for table-tapping, horoscopes, and communicating with the dead.

However, not to digress

No.

I was leading up to something here.

On the tip of my tongue.

Infuriating. Really infuriating.

# John
# Milano

Too early Thursday morning he woke up mysteriously guilt-ridden, the voice of the radio weatherman jubilantly advising him to expect cloudy skies with occasional rain. This was followed by Aretha who tunefully presented much the same message about life in general. It took him awhile, with Aretha providing background music, to pin down that guilt.

The poker game. Betty. The Staten Island *Zeitgeist*.

He had come back to the apartment last evening with his head full of Christine Bailey and her magic disappearing act. No room left in it to remember that Betty, after leaving her office, was to have her hair done and then come over to whip up dinner and settle in for the night.

So, with considerable effort, he had put together a poker game for the night. Couldn't get all six regulars but finally did line up four of them, including Maxie Rovinsky who operated the building's garage and who, against strict co-op rules about parking being limited to one car per resident, allowed Milano to maintain both his cars there; and Gracie MacFadden who, all liver spots, blue-white hair, and arthritic claws, occupied the building's duplex — top floor and penthouse — with what appeared to be two husbands simultaneously. Gracie dripped heavyweight diamonds, a large number of them recovered by Milano after a very nasty physical heist in the penthouse, and in return for this job well done, Gracie guaranteed — and delivered — house seats for any show in town on one day's notice. Gracie had theater connections like no one else in New York had theater connections.

The point is that these were friends to be cherished. Not in any way to be put out of countenance.

The troops were to rally at nine. At seven-thirty, there was Betty at the door, all smiles and dimples and fresh hairdo.

The smiles and dimples disappeared as she sized up Milano's rigor mortis. "You know," she said with devastating accuracy, "I don't think you even remembered I was coming."

It went from bad to worse. From Patient Griselda to Katharina of Verona. Prettier than ever in a cute little Bloomie's apron, she laid out dinner. He picked at it, one brain cell counting calories, another wondering how best to break the news of the poker game.

Betty was narrowly watching. "Are you on a diet or something?"

"No." Hell, no big deal about dieting. But admitting to it somehow presented the picture of a pathetic hulk desperately fending off middle-aged flab.

"Then," said Betty, "there must be something wrong with you because you did the same thing Sunday. Your mother spent a whole day cooking all that food and you hardly touched it. Is there something wrong with you?"

"Well —" said Milano, and since it was getting that close to nine o'clock, he told her about the game.

She didn't go off with a bang, more like a string of those small Chinese firecrackers. The smoke hadn't completely dissipated when the company arrived, but since Betty was obviously programmed for

[51]

good manners under whatever conditions she bore up bravely under the impact of these rambunctious strangers, closing her ears to Gracie's truckdriver language, and even doing yeoman duty as barmaid and snack dispenser, beyond which she made herself generally inconspicuous.

In brief, as Milano took note through the smoke of the lovely contraband Havana that Maxie had supplied, the girl was handling herself very well indeed in very rough waters, and he could feel sister Angie's matchmaking elbow pointedly digging him in the ribs.

No use smiling to oneself about it. For all he knew, given time he might find out that Angie was making good sense. He was, at that moment a little before midnight, ahead of the game by a euphoric hard-won fifteen hundred dollars.

At midnight, Betty motioned him into the kitchen and he followed her there.

"I have to be up at seven," she said. "I have a job to go to. As I'm sure you know. What do I do now?"

"Just go to bed," Milano said reasonably.

"Now? With everyone still here?"

"You don't have to undress in front of them. Use the bedroom."

"Very funny. But it seems to me you've won more than enough for one night. There's no reason you can't just tell them the party's over, is there?"

"Sure there is. They're playing at my invitation, and, as you say for yourself, I'm the big winner right now."

"That's ridiculous."

"No more than your impression that we're holding a meeting of the Holy Name Society in there. Look, baby, I'm sorry about this whole mixup. I really am. But all I can do if you won't stay is call a limousine service to get you home. They'll have a car here right away."

"No. Oh, no. I'm not being driven up to my house at this hour in any chauffeured limousine. I'm supposed to be spending the night with a girl friend. Just how would I explain a limousine to my father and mother?"

"Explain?" said Milano. "Jesus Christ, at your age you should really——" and was struck dumb right there by the expression on her face.

[52]

So, after being turned down by the first half-dozen cabs the doorman hailed, he had finally managed to send her on her way by cab. The bribe required to have the driver head in the direction of that terra incognita called Staten Island could have bought a trip by limousine to Chicago. After which he had gone upstairs and dropped not only his fifteen hundred win money but another five hundred. And most of it to Gracie. Who was both an obnoxiously triumphant winner and a too frequent one.

The good part was that he had hardly given Willie a thought the whole night.

The bad part was that Betty, as she got into the cab, was distinctly red-eyed. Not crying, but on the verge. Probably spent the whole trip in tears, then had to put on a bright smile for mommy and daddy who apparently waited up for her by candlelight any night she spent away from the nest.

Idiotic, as Milano plainly saw. Bad comedy. Nonetheless there was this dismal early morning guilt, a sort of psychic hangover.

Odds were that she hadn't left for her office yet. He switched off Aretha, looked up the Staten Island number and touchtoned it. Betty answered.

"Look," Milano said, "I want to apologize for last night. No fancy explanations, no excuses. Just an abject apology."

"Thank you." Very cool. Very controlled.

"I want you to know I mean that."

"Yes." A long pause. "Well, I think there's something you ought to know. I told my mother and father about us. I mean, I told them very plainly that you and I were having an affair."

"You did?"

"Very plainly. I mean, after what happened last night — after what you said —— " She seemed willing to let it go at that.

"And how did they take it?"

"Mother took it very well. Father didn't. But he'll survive. I asked him if he wanted me to move out and he said absolutely not. But I probably will. If I find a place I can afford near the office."

"Makes sense," Milano said. The original guilt had somehow been transformed into another variety of guilt which he couldn't clearly identify. "Meanwhile, how about lunch with me today?"

"No. Not today."

[53]

"Now look——"

"Goodbye," said Betty, and hung up.

Milano suddenly recognized that new variety of guilt. Just before their initial roll in the hay, she had answered his common sense question with yes, she was on the pill. And, with some hemming and hawing, had let him know that he would not be the first to bed her. From the evidence, this was certainly the truth.

Then why was he now weighted down with this feeling that he had been the one in her life to deflower her?

No answer. None really expected.

At eight-thirty he walked over to the Rammaert Gallery and made the best of a steady drizzle in the shelter of a neighboring doorway. A few minutes before nine, Christine Bailey appeared from the direction of Sixth Avenue and entered the gallery. Very nice. No umbrella, no hat, the cap of wiry hair gleaming with droplets.

So far, so good.

The drizzle became a driving rain as Milano set course for the Midtown Athletic Club on Fifty-third Street. He used it infrequently but his level of tipping made for instant and effusive recognition. He turned his suit over to the valet for drying and pressing, then, allowing plenty of time in between each operation to get his wind back, did twenty laps on the track, twenty in the pool, and wound up in a wild three-on-three basketball game with some muscular and humorless members of the younger generation. His man featured mugging as a defensive maneuver until Milano hipped him with a bang into the wall, after which junior was openly hostile but highly respectful.

Then there was a sweat, a long, luxurious rubdown, hot and cold water, and a trip to the scale which provided good news. Four days of starvation plus one workout came out to minus six pounds, never mind the bald spot. One-ninety for his big-boned, better than six foot height—all right, call it an even six foot—would be gratifying, but meanwhile he could live with two hundred. He stretched out on the rubbing table again and fell asleep feeling macho as hell.

The rain had stopped at five o'clock when he went back to Fifty-seventh Street. There he had a slow vodka and tonic at the bar of the Russian Tea Room to ease newly discovered muscles in shoulders and legs, and booked a table for two for six-fifteen. He returned to his post near the gallery, and when Christine Bailey emerged from it he fell in step with her. "Miss Bailey."

She continued on another couple of steps, then pulled up short in a sort of pedestrian double-take. She frowned at him, calling on memory. "You were in the gallery today."

"Yesterday." Seen across the desk she was eye-filling. Seen this close up she provided powerful impact. "Milano's the name. John Milano. Private investigator. On business that might involve the Rammaert Gallery. And I'm risking a hell of a lot when I level with you about it like this, but I think it's the only way to do it."

"Do what? Mister, if you want to talk gallery business, just talk to the boss. He's there right now."

"No way, Miss Bailey." With a hand on her elbow he eased her against a store window clear of passing foot traffic. "I'm under strict instructions from my client not to talk to Rammaert. That means if I do I can blow this case and all the money that goes with it. Including your own large payment for helping out. And you have my word for it, it's clean money. A California divorce case where let's call him Mr. Smith is trying to put the boot to Mrs. Smith by getting away with part of the estate before the settlement, you know what I mean. Some fine art that's being shipped out when nobody's looking. And I think Rammaert's been made agent for it. Given the job of converting it into cash. And that's it."

"Is it? Do you want to know what I think?"

"Gladly. But first let me ask you something. Do you like borscht? Shashlik? You know, those skewer jobs. The best in town."

"What?"

"Because," said Milano, "if you do, we ought to be working out this question and answer thing in that restaurant down the block. On the expense account. My client Mrs. Smith is a very rich lady. Vindictive, you may say, but very rich. So I'm not only in line for a heavy payment if I can tell her where her paintings are, I am also on what amounts to an unlimited expense account meanwhile."

"Oh, man," said Christine Bailey wonderingly.

"Well?"

"Forget it, mister. If I want to believe this isn't your freaked-out idea of an easy pickup ——"

[55]

"Believe it, Miss Bailey. I play for money, not pickups. Easy or otherwise."

"If I want to believe that, what I think is that you people got some kind of divorce hassle you're looking to dump on Rammaert. Only, he and I get on fine. I like him, I like my job, and the only favor I'll do you is not tell him about this come-on. And the only reason I'll do you that favor, Mr. Milano — it is Milano, right?"

"Right."

" — is so I can walk down the street at night without wondering if some Mafia brothers of yours are waiting for me around the corner. See? You leveled with me, I am leveling with you."

"Miss Bailey — "

"I don't have time for this. I have other business I'm already late for."

"Miss Bailey," Milano said with elaborate patience, "I am an investigator working out of this office." He lifted her hand and pressed the Watrous Associates card into it. "It's three minutes away from here. Tomorrow, just drop in, look around, ask any questions you want to about me. Right now, let's talk money." He drew the envelope from his breast pocket and offered it to her. When she made no move to take it he held it up, flipped through its contents. "Five hundred cash up front, Miss Bailey. A lot more if we make the client happy."

She was briefly tempted, no question about it. Then she shook her head vigorously. "No dice, mister. And when I move off I don't want you tagging along. I won't like that."

"You've got it backwards. I'll take you wherever you're going. Just say where."

"You're the big detective, you can try to find out where all by yourself. Just keep off my tail, understand? Now and for good."

She walked off toward Sixth Avenue, and Milano, after giving her a fair lead, followed at the proper angle. Righthanded was the way she had started to reach for the envelope, and it was Willie who long ago pointed out that righthanded people tended to look back over their left shoulders. Obviously a textbook case she did that once, then headed into the subway entrance on the corner and took a D train downtown, Milano one car behind.

Rush hour over now, not much of a crowd, so he had a good view

[56]

of her through the windows at the head of his car and tail of hers. Although not as good a view, he saw, as that provided the male customers facing her across the aisle who were plainly gratified by the scenery. She took notice of this and responded with a sharp little downward tug of her skirt, symbolic of the contemptuously curled lip.

Up and out at Fourth Street, Milano giving her plenty of room to maneuver in. Along Sixth Avenue, down Cornelia Street where the early evening Greenwich Village crowd made it a case of broken-field running, and so to Bleecker Street. There, Christine Bailey joined a huddle of others, mixed black and white, before a theater which looked like an abandoned gypsy tea room, curtained display windows and all, and which bore overhead a poster announcing *Two Stops Before The End Of The Line.*

Not even Off-Off-Broadway. Off-Off the map altogether.

Milano bided his time, then as the huddle broke up he strolled over, taking notice that on the billboard beside the door was posted, among other names comprising the cast of the play, the name of Christine Bailey. "Evening, Miss Bailey," he said to that shapely back.

She turned and confronted him narrow-eyed. Simmering. "Man, I warned you."

"No, you didn't. You challenged me."

An exasperated shake of the head. But was there the suggestion of an involuntary smile in that quirk of the lips? "I can see that was my mistake," Christine Bailey said.

"A small one. The big one is the way you give away money."

"Oh yeah, money. You do have it on the brain, don't you?" She looked him over. "Those threads never came off the rack. What kind of car you drive? When you do drive. Caddie?"

"Mercedes. This year's."

"Not much like those late-night movies, are you?"

"No, I'm up to date and for real. Now, can we meet after the show, Miss Bailey, and talk things over? With my assurance that nobody suffers the least pain from this deal except possibly my client's husband?"

"I have to see somebody tonight. Maybe tomorrow night after the show. Maybe."

[57]

"And final curtain's down?"

"About ten. Just remember the maybe. It's a big one."

"I'll keep that in mind," said Milano.

Back in the apartment he phoned Shirley at home and was answered by the lord of the manor, sometimes acidly referred to by Willie as Mister Shirley Glass. Sam Glass said, "She's not here. She's out visiting the daughter. Want to leave a message?"

"Yes. Tell her this is Pacifica Inland business. A girl named Bailey might check me out at the office tomorrow, and I want Shirley to give her my four-star treatment. And to keep Greenwald out of sight all day. Got that?"

"Sure. Pacifica Inland. Bailey. Greenwald. Four stars. Say, I hear you and Willie are at it again."

"Yes," said Milano.

# Charles Witter Kirwan

A TEST OF ENDURANCE TODAY.

Now feeling acute pain in chest and spine, but that is balanced by an excitement—a rejoicing—that I've discovered a reserve of strength in me which will certainly carry me to my goal. A marvelous feeling. High as a kite, as my grandfather used to say of my stepfather, although I haven't allowed myself one drop of alcohol all day.

And at this moment—eleven-thirty this memorable Thursday night—I still feel no need for any such stimulant.

I now have in hand

I now have in the trunk of my car the last of the materials

necessary for the grand event. The wire. The detonator. Both manifestly brand new, guaranteed to do the job.

Our Mr. Swanson who was supposed to phone me last evening never did, a stupidity that cost me most of my night's sleep. But he did phone early this morning with a rambling, unbelievable excuse for the stupidity which I

Never mind that. He phoned to say that the materials were ready and that I was to pick them up at seven in the evening. The drive up the Hudson to Sutton Falls ordinarily takes about two and a half hours. Considering my physical condition — impossible to find a position behind the wheel that doesn't cause misery — I allowed an additional half hour, and then barely made it on schedule. The return trip, where I had to pull off the road several times and leave the car to ease incessant pains, took four nightmarish hours. No resorting to the Percodan either. That, I could not risk on the public highways with a load of high explosives in my possession.

The nightmare isn't completely over either. When I tried to lift the coil of wire from the car's trunk I found it too much for me. It will have to be dragged into the basement of 409. I'll attend to that in an hour or so, this time fortified by my dosage. And with no bright Bulanga eyes tracking me from those still lit windows.

Or in front of my headlights.

Oh yes.

Wheeled into the driveway and there like the doe at the crossing, Christine Bailey. A rare visitor in these parts lately. Black as the night itself, wearing some sort of dark dress, almost invisible until my lights hit her. She jumped, I stamped on the brake.

"I'm sorry, Miss Bailey."

"That's all right, Mr. Kirwan." And off she wiggled to 409, each movement free, as the poet happily put it.

Yes indeed.

So.

Sleepless last night, troubled by yesterday's taping of a narrative whose point and purpose I lost in digressions. I replayed a lengthy section of it just now. I've done that once before, and evidently to good effect: the sound of my coughing is almost completely eliminated. But in this replaying — is it the machine itself? — my voice sometimes emerges as denasalized and too high-pitched.

[60]

Those records played on our old wind-up Victrola

My professorial voice? Is this what my blankfaced, contemptuous classes heard? The Bulanga among them openly stretching and yawning so that you could see right down to the quivering pink uvula in the midst of all that blackness?

Disturbing in a way.

Well.

I did, however, determine where my yesterday's narrative was intended to lead. The explanation of how the grand event was conceived. A vital matter, not to leave this explanation to those psycho-academicians who practise historical divination according to the gospel of Doctor Fraud.

This is not a case history, doctors. This is — and you must forgive my use of an archaic, dirty, despicable phrase — a social history.

Starting with the death of my aunt, Mrs. Margaretha Gretchen Witter Hayes. My Aunt Maggie. Who, having spent the final years of her life in the exclusive Sutton Falls Memorial Home, died there at age ninety-five, demanding, ungrateful, and quarrelsome to the end. Childless. A record of long ago stillborn deliveries. Which was good luck for the stillborn, bad luck for me.

It is possible that someone somewhere may be in possession of those notes I addressed to her now and then over recent years. Notes very affectionate in tone. It's more than possible that some people close to her — certainly some attendants at the Home — may recall my visits to her every few months, my patience in dealing with her, my apparent regard for her.

Understand this now. If such notes and such recollections are made public they must be dealt with as entirely false and misleading. I detested the woman and I detest her memory. But my grandfather out of concern for her made a coward and a liar out of me in this regard. He asked me near his death to assure him I would continue providing for her what he had: understanding, sympathy, money.

Money, money, money.

Out of the little that was left. The scrapings of the barrel. The remnants of ancient investments. Retirement funds. With insane inflation to contend with. And my wife's lingering death. And that blood-sucking Bulanga resort next door to maintain and pay taxes on. And this house, this family home, to keep in the condition it requires.

[61]

And yet the money, money, money draining into that fine room in the Sutton Falls Memorial Home, and into all those diamond-studded medical services needed to keep the old bitch alive and whining.

If

Yes, a coward and a liar. But not any more.

If I had it to do over, I'd take whatever oath my grandfather asked of me and as soon as he drew his last breath I'd put it right out of my mind. Turn the goddamned case over to the County, where it belonged. Because this Charles Witter Kirwan is no longer bound by the social graces of cowardice and deception.

Shocking, isn't it?

Is it?

Listen, I want to read you something I have right here before me. One line from Pasternak's *Zhivago*, courtesy of critic V. S. Pritchett. Right here. Listen.

"Health is ruined by the systemic duplicity forced on people if you say the opposite of what you feel, if you grovel before what you dislike and rejoice at what brings you nothing but misfortune."

There it is. One line.

Systemic duplicity.

Oh dear, the roaches are on my plate eating my hard-earned dinner. I will let them eat all they want and when they are done I will thankfully finish what they leave.

Love thy neighbor.

Love thy roaches.

One line. Systemic sweetscented liberal duplicity.

And systemic duplicity means sickness and rot. Cancer. As long as society demands that duplicity. As long as in its craven fears, its political opportunism it has us meet the Bulanga with hypocritical welcoming smiles on our whitey faces?

A coincidence that my love-thy-neighbor smiling wife, inwardly terrified to walk outside her own home, was cancerous?

That I am cancerous?

Let me put it this way.

Already, when I was given the news of my aunt's death, when I

[62]

drove up to Sutton Falls to attend the services and the burial, I had glimmerings of the truth about my condition. Pains, persistent cough, loss of weight—glimmerings of the bitter truth. And I don't think you can live close to cancer as I had in Florence's case—my wife's case—without being traumatized by it.

But I'm not one to go looking for trouble. No, it was my aunt's doctor who insisted on the examination. And turned it into an exploratory operation and a death warrant.

Two weeks in that hospital. Two weeks at the bottom of the pit. Nagged by those solemn salesmen with their M.D. degrees to buy further operations, to buy futile nauseating treatments. No guarantees of success, naturally. Oh no. No easing of pain promised. Just a profitable experiment in the raising of the dead.

Charles Witter Kirwan, invited to be a second Lazarus.

If we could speak to some member of your immediate family, Mr. Kirwan.

Doctor, I just buried my last relative. You were there at the services, remember?

Nightmares—wide-awake nightmares—of my home and what happens to it now. Flawless. Pristine. And then the Bulanga occupation. The last outpost fallen.

The racketing of the Bulanga stereos in the night announcing the triumph.

Right now coming across the courtyard from 409.

Tum-tum-tum and tum-tum. And tum-tum-tum and tum-tum.

No Lazarus for me, thank you. Better to be the sick old hound who drags himself home and dies on the familiar doorstep.

That was my emotional state when I started to drive back to New York from the hospital. Not the Street called Straight although a miracle was waiting for me on it, but that twisting road—McClain Road—which follows close beside the river a couple of miles then enters Route 32 below Saugerties.

Miracles may be announced in strange ways. For example, a man with a warning sign holding up the few cars that made up traffic at that moment. Trotting up to me. Cut your motor, please, they're setting off some charges over there.

Over there on the river's edge was the McClain brickyard, long abandoned. Sheds fallen down exposing rows of huge kilns. Five minutes went by with the miracle waiting to happen. Then a sudden flash of red and orange light along a row of kilns, a thundering reverberation. Smoke and dust billowing up. And through that cloud the sight of the kilns dissolving into rubble.

That was it.

The miracle.

The revelation.

In my mind the image of Witter Street struck by that flash and reverberation, crumbling in on itself. Under the smoke and dust only the house remains. Only the house. Nothing more.

Silence.

Then a Bulanga voice crying out from under the destruction. "Oowah oowah oowah, whitey? Ooowah?"

Why did you do it, whitey? Why?

I would be glad to explain.

The sign along McClain Road said Passarini Demolition Company, and the company plainly had its work cut out for it. Those other rows of kilns. Windowless, roofless office buildings to dispose of. Passarini would be here for awhile.

How did I understand my mission? No, not as an attempt on a whole block of housing, but only one building of it, a building I own and am free to deal with. How did I understand my mission? I'll put it this way. One instant I was a pain-racked, despairing, dying lump. The next instant I was, incredibly, in an ecstatic state, sweating with excitement, my mind blazing with the creative impulse, my emotions centered only on the need to live just long enough to answer that impulse.

Yes, yes, yes.

All despair gone, ideas raced through my mind like pieces of a puzzle being locked into place at lightning speed.

The grand event.

Not an act of nihilistic destruction. Not a mystery to be wondered about afterward and theorized over.

None of that.

A lesson. A guide. A warning. If—if its explanation in full was there and waiting.

More.

That explanation would not be a kindly gift to the public. Why

[64]

should it be when it would make a document worth hundreds of thousands of dollars? Millions of dollars. The best-seller lists are waiting for it. So-called newspapers — I exclude the *Times*, a monument itself to a dead and decent past — are slavering for such documents. A movie production. A television showing. Money from all sides.

And out of this, the salvation of the house.

The Witter Foundation. Well-endowed. Luxuriously endowed. Providing for proper maintenance. Providing for a handpicked couple in residence. Caretakers of the property, guides for the curious public.

The Witter Foundation.

The following is addressed directly to my lawyer, my friend George Grant Davis — no less my friend because I have not lately been open to his kind invitations — who will attend to my estate.

Dear friend, in our last phone conversation you expressed puzzlement as to where the money would come from for any such Foundation. And I'm afraid my evasiveness led you to believe the worst: that I was distrustful of you and was concealing information from you about my finances.

Now that you're hearing this — reading it — you'll see why I couldn't let you know my secret.

As you will find out in handling the estate, there is very little cash left in it. But this taped record will be worth a great deal — I estimate in the millions — and my sealed instructions left with you explain the administration of that money by the Witter Foundation.

Of which you are designated pro tem director.

I also rely on you in all dealings with the authorities and the press to make plain to them that I am — was — emotionally stable, mentally sound, through our entire acquaintance.

Also

Also I can only hope you won't be shocked by the frank discussions of my sexuality in this record. I know you always felt that Florence and I had made an ideal marriage, and in some ways we had. Please consider that no hurt can be inflicted on her by anything I choose to reveal after her death.

You must understand.

# John Milano

A PLEASANT RAMBLE UP BROADWAY FROM Columbus Circle to Lincoln Center brought Milano to the library of theater arts, that haven for the show biz freak, and not unknown here he was soon provided with the material he sought. There turned out to be very little of it. Three skimpy reviews of Pearl Byum's play *Two Stops Before The End Of The Line*, directed by Lenardo Hanna, presented by The Birdbath Theater Company. And a single-page program which listed, besides this information, its cast of four.

The reviews—from *Variety*, *Village Voice*, and *New York* magazine —were uniformly negative, indicating that what we have here is a muddled exploration of lesbian attachments, with the issues of racism and feminism tossed in for good measure and contributing to the muddle. All, however, commended a Tamar McBride for the skilful handling of her supporting role. And one added the information that lead performer Christine Bailey was dazzling to behold, but. . .

Back at the apartment Milano kept half an eye on the time until sure enough at about twelve-thirty Shirley Glass phoned to say that a Christine Bailey had just dropped in to ask some questions about him and had been given the full treatment. A tribute to John Anthony Milano whose word was his bond.

"Did she get a look at my office?" Milano asked.

"She did. I'd say your credit rating with her is triple-A right now. And considering this is one gorgeous *schvartzeh*, Johnny, I trust you're all strictly business?"

"Strictly. How's Hy Greenwald making out? Steering clear of Willie?"

"No," said Shirley, rounding the word out, drawing it out. "More like cozying up to him. Listening to every word with his mouth open, you know what I mean? Willie seems to like it."

"And Hy's getting paid way below scale too," said Milano. "Obviously the boy's got everything going for him."

He put in the rest of the afternoon at the Midtown Athletic Club, this time eschewing any basketball game. Near eight o'clock, curtain time, he presented himself at the box office of the Birdbath Theater, a battered kitchen table with an open cash box on it, and bought a ticket for the evening's performance.

Seating here, he was informed by the wraithlike, foggy-eyed lassie who took his money, was a matter of first come, first served. Since seating consisted of about a dozen rows of slatbacked wooden folding chairs, maybe half of them occupied, he readily located a place with a fair sight line behind this sparse audience. From what he had put together about the play, the nature of the audience was no surprise. Predominantly female, it appeared to be all thrift shop chic and hardbreathing intensity.

But just as the Diamond Horseshoe — name your opera house — provided the necessary ambience for bejeweled and perfumed lovelies, so the Birdbath Theater provided the necessary ambience for these cases. A long, narrow room with a jerrybuilt stage at its far end exposing a set obviously furnished by the Salvation Army. Cracked and flaking walls. Worn linoleum underfoot. And overhead, dependent from a ceiling which looked dangerously unable to sustain it, a complex of track lighting. Dressing rooms — more likely dressing space — had to be behind that flat at stage rear on which was sketchily painted the suggestion of a couple of windowframes.

Never mind those reviews, *Two Stops Before The End Of The Line* had its moments. A garrulous replay of an increasingly popular theme — boy meets girl, boy loses girl, girl gets girl — it presented a black couple, united in unwedded bliss, acquainted with a white couple, in this case both female, whose dominant partner smitten by the beautiful black lady sets out to seduce her and for the big finish of the first act succeeds in doing so.

In act two, the black beauty, however beset by the chauvinistic threats of her erstwhile male lover, enters more and more spiritedly into this new affair, discovering along the way not only a sexual gratification she had hitherto been deprived of but an innate racial superiority to her fairskinned seductress. For the climactic scene she contemptuously dismisses both male and female from her life forever and lets it be known that somewhere out there must be a woman of her color and nature fit to be her true mate.

Somewhere waiting.

Blackout. Except for the red glow of the emergency *Exit* sign at one side of the stage which spectrally illuminated Christine Bailey's crouching departure behind the flat.

A round of applause, a curtain call, house-lights up. The audience moved toward the street door, and Milano, holding his seat, had a feeling that as the well-dressed, over-aged embodiment of the oppressor male he was getting the icy eye from quite a few. Or maybe he was being evaluated as one of those uptown voyeur types who gets his jollies from very brief theatrical displays of full frontal nudity. Because two such displays had been offered during the show, both times involving Christine Bailey who succeeded in looking even better unclothed than clothed. No use denying the charge in this case because get his jollies he did at each exposure, until those unveiled wonders were quickly veiled by the embrace of the tall, blonde, handsome Tamar McBride, a powerful stage presence. The embrace each time had Milano's hackles rising, but what the hell, he assured himself, it was all make-believe, wasn't it?

Most likely.

But most likely didn't seem altogether satisfactory.

He made his way behind the stage which turned out to be, as he had estimated, a dressing area. Once a kitchen, it was now the beat-up remnant of a kitchen, rust, dust, and cracked wall tiles predominating. Most of it was occupied by a couple of spraddle-legged bridge tables placed together in the middle of the room and buckling under the weight of several face mirrors and an immense disorder of makeup tubes, bottles, and jars.

The cast, each with a well-smeared towel over the shoulders, was seated at the mirrors working off greasepaint. A couple of super-numeraries, black male, black female — the director and the play-wright? — were dipping into yogurt containers by a museum piece of a refrigerator in a corner, the refrigerator rattling away merrily.

Milano leaned over Christina Bailey's mirror, and she said to it accusingly, "I saw you out there," all the while applying a wad of tissues to forehead and cheeks.

"I paid my way in," said Milano. He held up his watch to the mirror. "Ten o'clock. Matter of fact, five after ten."

"Sure it is," said Christine Bailey. "So you just back off a little, and I'll be right there." She didn't seem called on to offer introductions to the others, who were now giving him the once-over. The voluptuous Tamar McBride, topless except for the towel, smiled at him, and Milano, gratified by what might be evidence of heterosexuality and courteously trying not to goggle at the view — it was an exceedingly skimpy towel — smiled back at her, and that was as far as the social-izing went. Not that the lady's smile and exposure really guaranteed anything, so he reflected following Christine Bailey out to the street. Not with the tangle western civilization, God bless it, had lately gotten itself into in sorting out the sexes.

They wound up in a café off Sheridan Square, a room apparently dedicated to the breeding of spider plants which overflowed pots dangling everywhere from the ceiling and brushed green tentacles over passing scalps. Christine ordered a cappuccino, Milano ordered an Irish coffee and, on being informed that the house did not purvey distilled liquors, settled for a cappuccino. It had its own magic when if finally arrived. Somehow, while the cup itself was blistering hot to the touch its contents were tepid.

So far Christine hadn't spoken a word since their departure from the theater. Sullen, troubled, reflective, that was about how it shaped up. Now, slowly weaving a mound of whipped cream into her coffee with rhythmic figure-eights of her spoon, she looked at him squarely. She said, "You know I was in your office today, don't you? That I talked to the woman there about you?"

"Yes."

"You're full of surprises, aren't you?"

"Well," said Milano, "not quite as much, let's say, as some very dignified young lady who keeps a very dignified shop daytimes, and then nighttime pops up on a stage down in the Village stripped to the buff."

"I see. That bother you any? That stripped to the buff part?"

"No. What bothers me is the way your director screwed things up. It's supposed to be your show, but it's been handed over to that big Tamar girl. Now it's her show. Which throws it all out of kilter."

"I don't think that you —"

"Look. She steps on your lines, she upstages you so half the time you're talking to the backdrop, she does everything but wave a hanky at the customers when you're into one of those heavy speeches. Isn't that so?"

Eyes veiled, Christine appeared to consider this. Milano considered that face and decided that on any scale from Warhol up to Vermeer it had to rate Vermeer. At last, after due consideration, she came out with it. "Maybe," she said.

"No maybe. The only question is why it's so. You're no amateur. You don't move like one on the stage, you don't sound like one. So why give Tamar a free ride?"

"You looking to be my agent, mister, along with your other line of work?"

"You're ducking the question. Is it possible that Tamar really is Papa Bear when you two are away from the footlights?"

Christine gaped at him. "Man, you are pushy, aren't you? I mean total bulldozer."

"You're still ducking the question."

"All right, my tastes don't run that way, if you're so fucking

[70]

curious about it. Not that those bare-ass scenes on stage don't get both of us heated up some, because we are nice, normal, healthy people. But Tamar's daddy is McBride of McBride and Wheelock, the ad agency. Ever hear of it?"

"Yes."

"Yes. So daddy is very big money. And what money it took to get this show on the road and keep it there is mostly his. So Nardo — Lenardo Hanna's the director — knows which side his bread is buttered on because Tamara told him which side was which. Happy, now that you know all about life behind the footlights?"

Yes, Milano thought, with her sexual identity thus established he was indeed happy about it.

At the same time, a little uneasy.

Race.

Granted now there was no obstacle posed because he happened to be male. But white male? White? She had already pushed the warning button with that Mafia crack on their first encounter. She could have been putting down Italians with that crack, but no matter how you looked at it, it was Italian white. Hard to figure. The fact was that in his varied acquaintance with women none could be listed on a census form as black. And this one didn't go in for hair-straightener, either.

As for himself, was J. Milano somewhat to his own surprise really color-blind, or was he seeing her as a heart-stopping ebony *objet d'art* posed against the oyster-white walls of J. Milano's apartment? That this kind of surmise should even enter into the reckoning of the future spelled trouble in itself. If she wasn't psyched out on race, how would you know it?

And if she was, what the hell, he had to acknowledge on her behalf, black as such had no more reason to cherish white than white had to cherish black, never mind Brotherhood Week. The best you could hope for was polite. When everybody settled for polite, New York City would have it made.

Matter of fact, given another two or three hundred years even tight-assed, white-assed paisano Bath Beach and Canarsie and Mill Basin might settle for polite, not that he was ready to bet on it.

The real deep-down trouble right now while he watched her drinking her tepid cappuccino which left a faint white trim on

[71]

that marvelously curved upper lip was that he had no intention of settling for polite.

She put down the cup and licked away the white trim with the tip of her tongue. She said, "Those paintings you think Rammaert might be handling. What am I supposed to do about them? If I want to do something about them."

"Oh that." It took him a moment to switch over to this track. "Well, there's a thin chance they're in the gallery right now, and I'd need verification of that. Or, more likely, they could be on their way there, and I'd want to know when they arrive. I pass the word along to my client, and she arranges with Rammaert for their return. Meaning she's ready to cover his commission without his even having to sell them. As I said, my client, Mrs. Smith, is very vindictive and very rich. If she can prevent her husband from cashing in on those paintings, it'll make her day."

"Whose paintings are they? I mean, who painted them?"

"Boudin. You know Boudin?"

"Yes," said Christine, then thought better of it. "No, not really. I'm just catching up on that stuff. I was High School of Performing Arts, not Music and Arts."

"You know the French Impressionist school?"

"Yes. Those I did catch up on. Some, anyhow."

"All right, Boudin was a precursor and then sort of fellow traveler to the Impressionists. These two paintings are both beach scenes — people fully dressed strolling on the beach — on fourteen inch by seven inch panels with the signature very clear. Eugene Louis Boudin. You can't miss them even across the room. There's an exceptional use of sky over the scene. Seen anything like that around the gallery?"

"Not that I know."

"There's Rammaert's office. And there must be a storeroom. I don't think he'd hang those paintings, so they could be in crates. Smallish. With a West Coast shipping address. You have the run of the place, don't you?"

"Uh-huh."

"And the apartment upstairs where the Rammaerts live?"

"I'm in and out there. Mornings when the housecleaning service comes in I'm up there laying out the job for them."

"Good. And you handle all incoming phone calls? And the mail?"

"Uh-huh."

"Then I'll give you the names of some people who could be middlemen for those paintings. Any of those names pop up, all you have to do is let me know." Milano reached into his breast pocket and withdrew the envelope with the five hundred in it. He placed it on the table before her. "As I said, this is just a down payment."

Christine shook her head in a firm negative. "No money."

"But I thought we just —— "

"No money. A trade-off."

"A trade-off?"

"That's right. I help you do your homework, man, you help me do mine. From what I've put together between you and your secretary —— "

"Mrs. Glass. She's office manager there."

"Whatever. And if any fat little old lady with gray hair could have hot pants, she's got hot pants for you. But even allowing for that, I get the feeling you're real good at your job. Like tailing somebody to find out what she's up to."

"She?"

Christine said as if unwilling to say it, "My kid sister. Really a kid. Won't make sixteen until next month. A good kid. A pain in the ass forty different ways, but up to now nothing that couldn't be handled. Now we don't know."

"Who's we?"

"Family. My mother and my two brothers. One of them's college, one's finishing up high school. Honor high school. Brooklyn Tech. And you better know these are strictly no-foolin'-around people. Lorena — my sister — lives with them out in Brooklyn. And naturally she's the baby, everybody's little prize package. Now she's scaring the shit out of them. And me."

"Drugs?"

"No. I guess she smokes a joint now and then but who doesn't? No, it's not that. It's stealing, possibly. Shoplifting. Not nickel and dime either. She makes fifteen dollars a week doing some part-time office work, and that's supposed to take care of lunch money and movies. Meanwhile she's piling up stuff in her closet that takes a lot more than fifteen a week to buy. Designer jeans. Fancy-label shirts.

[73]

Top quality shoes. She's got a pair of joggers that goes at least eighty or ninety dollars. Get the picture?"

"Yes. But you folks must have given her some hard questions to answer about that. What's her story?"

"She lays it on about some mysterious character named Jimmy. No other name, just Jimmy. He's crazy in love with her, he looks to marry her, he buys her things just to make her happy. She's lying. My brothers went into that and while there's some Jimmys around, they couldn't turn up any Jimmy like that."

Milano thought it over. "Is it possible that while she's not into drugs or pills or acid herself — or at least not showing signs of it — she might be dealing in them?"

"No. I don't believe she's dealing any more than she's making out with some invisible Jimmy. What she does mostly with her free time is head down to those stores on Fulton Street and come back loaded. You figure it out yourself. Possibles don't mean anything here. It's probables that count."

"Could be. By the way, where does your family live?"

"East Flatbush. Witter Street. Near Erasmus. She goes there."

"I gather you don't live with the family?"

"No, I've got a room over on Sixth Avenue. Are you listening to me? Or just looking?"

"Listening and thinking," Milano said, not quite lying about it. "You understand I'd have to see Lorena. Clearly identify her. No photos either. A live close-up."

"And afterward suppose she identifies you away from home and starts wondering?"

"My worry. Leave it to me."

"Not altogether," Christine said grimly. "The family's got a great big worry about this. Lorena's real uptight now about the pressure on her. Last blow-up about it, she said if there's any more of these question and answer games, she just takes off where nobody'll bother her. This is not just loose talk, man. She did it twice last year. Almost sent my mother to the hospital with a heart attack. You let that kid find out who put you on to her, you will wind up with real trouble on your hands. For starters, I'll let Rammaert know what you're up to. That's why this is a no-money deal. This way I keep my options wide open."

"Fair enough. Where'd Lorena wind up those two times?"

"First time, the Port Authority bus terminal. Lucky the cops moved in when some mean stud started bothering her. Second time she made it out to New Jersey. Friend of a friend there. The mother had sense to turn her in to us after three days. Trouble is, now Lorena knows you don't trust friends of friends to hide you out. Next time it'll have to be strangers."

"Scary," said Milano, and meant it.

"Very. Enough so I'm getting into a deal with you I don't even like that much. But you have got to move fast. Like, you want to see Lorena? Tomorrow's the time."

"You don't work Saturdays? I'll need you along first time out."

"I'm off from the gallery Saturdays, but I've got a matinee at two, then the evening show. So it has to be tomorrow morning. Now tell me what happens tomorrow morning about getting to see her and all. What's your moves?"

"Your mother rent or own?" Milano asked.

"Own?" Christine looked startled at the idea. "It's rent. A beat-up apartment house."

"For sale?"

Christine shrugged. "Could be. The owner's the old man next door Lorena does some office work for. Can't say he comes on all that happy about owning. Why?"

"Because I might be interested in buying. Maybe that building, maybe others like it in the neighborhood. I'm very high on urban redevelopment. Buy up some of those old buildings, get some long term, low interest government funding to help polish them up, help out the neighborhood. So it makes sense if I'm here and there around the neighborhood, doesn't it?"

Christine regarded him curiously. "You just come up with that?"

"Well, it's not all that original as a cover. Now, suppose I pick you up tomorrow morning and drive you out to Witter Street so I can size up properties. Maybe ring your mother's bell while you happen to be there, so I can get the tenant's slant. Nine o'clock all right?"

"To get a look at Lorena?"

"That's what it's all about, isn't it?"

"Uh-huh. But maybe you don't know how smooth you come on,

mister. I was beginning to wonder if you didn't look to buy that building."

"No chance. Nine o'clock?"

"All right with me." She pushed the envelope back across the table toward him. "That's all yours. Better put it away before somebody picks it up for a tip."

"Are you sure you wouldn't rather —"

"No," said Christine, "I'm not all that sure. But for cash I might feel I'm selling out Rammaert. This way I don't have to feel that."

A nice point, thought Milano. Proving that the Jesuits didn't have any monopoly on casuistry.

He gave her a handshake farewell at her address, Sixth Avenue near Tenth Street just a few doors away from Balducci's Market, that fantasyland for the well-heeled fatso, and took a cab to the office. Not altogether deserted despite the hour. Lights showed beneath a couple of doors along the corridor, and there was the clacking of a typewriter being pecked at. No use dropping in to say hello; odds were he couldn't even identify these midnight laborers in the vineyard. Couldn't keep count of the payroll any more — fifty, sixty, whatever. Personnel came and went but somehow, like rabbits, kept multiplying. Willie loved numbers, so that was Willie's business, keeping count.

Milano pulled the photos of the Boudins from his files and Xeroxed a couple of them. Then he phoned the car service and set up a date for the morning. David's car, David at the wheel. No trouble there getting exactly what was asked for. The service was a sideline of Maxie Rovinsky, operator of the co-op's garage, and David was Maxie's nephew in from Israel to make his fortune in American dollars.

Or, since Uncle Maxie was an old bachelor, at least to inherit it.

## Charles Witter Kirwan

A WEEK OF SMALL DEFEATS, LARGE TRIUMPHS.
Yes.

Precisely a week ago — last Saturday — when I recorded my opening statement on these tapes I had a schedule for the grand event fixed in mind but I was not all that sure I'd be able to meet the date. A Thursday night that was to be, allowing a full three weeks for preparation.

Now, after yesterday's very large triumph, I believe I can reduce that schedule by a few days. Under any conditions, the event will take place on a week day. Weekends are out. Some of my Bulanga tenants wander afield weekends. But on midweek nights most tend to gather in the kraal, so to speak, for sessions with the deafeningly electronic tom-tom. Or to squat before whitey's marvelous glass-eyed box, its volume also turned up sufficient to make my own windows across the courtyard rattle. Home is the hustler, home from the hill, the racket of his entertainment punctuated only now and then by the crash of a bottle or the clatter of a can in the courtyard, the handiest disposal system when one moves toward the end of the sixpack.

But at the very end—however briefly—one ten-thousandth of a second?—they will hear a clap of doom that will out-thunder all the collective noise they ever manufactured since they seized this territory.

When he wants to, my friends, whitey can make a noise to deafen this entire planet.

Oh yes.

Yesterday's triumph.

To explain it I must explain the method of destruction planned for 409 Witter Street in some detail. Bear with me.

Dumbwaiters.

Are they still in use in any residential buildings in our fair city? Anybody remember them? Remember their use?

The aged possibly. My uncherished tenants, the Friedmans, most certainly. When the dumbwaiter door in their kitchen was permanently sealed up they went into Semitic convulsions. Why must two such deserving cases be condemned to lug their daily garbage downstairs to those cans in the courtyard just because *They* made filth in the dumbwaiters? Because *They* were the ones who threw unwrapped scraps down the shaft. And *They* were the ones who left the disgusting remnants of their stew meat and chicken bones and fish heads soaking through flimsy paper bags in the dumbwaiter overnight. And so *They* were the ones who bred the vermin over-running the building. If I lived right here in the building instead of in that fancy house next door, would I have even thought of renting to *Them*?

*They? Them?*

The Bulanga.

The Friedmans—like my pharmacist, Irving Saphir, like the scattering of other ancient Israelites still afloat on this dark tide

—use *They* and *Them* in shuddersome reference to the Bulanga.
"You know how *They* are."
"You know what *They* do."
"Do I have to tell you about *Them*?"
And there is a body language involved. A casting up of the eyes to a merciless God, a wrinkling of the nose as if one could actually smell a reek of pomade and beer and frying fish emanating from those magic pronouns.

The dumbwaiters.

Midway between floor and ceiling of each kitchen wall of 409 Witter is what appears to be a large steel-jacketed pantry door. At one time, if you slid back its bolt and opened it, you would find yourself looking at the naked brickwork of a shaft that extended from basement to roof of the building. Under the skylight of the shaft was a pulley from which was suspended a long rope. The rope was attached to a four-sided box—front and back exposed. The dumb-waiter.

Pull on the rope—the janitor in the basement attended to that every evening after pushing a buzzer warning you of it—and when you opened that door you would find the box rising to your level and waiting there for you to deposit your garbage in it.

Yes indeed.

Four dumbwaiter shafts provided for eight series of kitchens, ground floor to top floor. Donkey work for the janitor.

Who was glad to get it for a few dollars a week and free rental. And whose wife would lend a callused hand to that prickly rope without complaint.

Irish mostly. But I remember a Polish couple. And a Ukrainian couple.

But it takes a certain minimal intelligence to occupy an apartment with a working dumbwaiter and not to convert that simple machine into a pollutant. Not to heap that box any time of day with sodden and stinking filth. Not to bury the bottom of the shaft under it. I imagine a chimpanzee might display such intelligence after having been advised on the rules.

But the Bulanga?

Let me put it this way. The gods of the Bulanga detest a clean and orderly area as nature abhors a vacuum. So it is a necessary appeasement of the gods to cast filth — to pollute — any clean and orderly area. Fortunately, whitey's civilization with all its wrappings and containers and whitey's food stamps which provide cheap and readily wasted edibles offer the devout tribesman all the materials needed for offerings anywhere he roosts, everywhere he goes.

Brown-bagging.

Have any of you wide-eyed whiteys ever observed the desperate need of the Bulanga on the move to absorb enormous amounts of fluid along the way? Have you ever witnessed that fascinating scene where a Bulanga orders a bottled or canned drink at the counter, has it placed in a brown bag, straw included, and then leaves the store to down its contents outside?

Where he then drops bag and emptied bottle to mark his trail?

I can see a grand banquet celebrated by the Bulanga. A magnificent room. A lavish table. More than lavish. There is a bottle of champagne at every setting. A full bottle, mind you, for each celebrant. And each bottle is, of course, in a brown paper bag.

Not one drop is consumed during the banquet. Not a drop. But when the tribe leaves, each member carries his bottle to the street and only then does he consume it.

And leave bag and bottle there to the greater glory of his gods.

So.

So, as the Bulanga came to occupy 409 Witter Street, its dumb-waiter came to be their altar to those gods.

That clean, scrubbed, deodorized wooden box — obscene really — but how much improved now with the sodden, reeking filth bestowed on it at any hour of day or night. Shoved into it, flung down on it, so that the mice and roaches rejoiced, and at last the dumbwaiter, vestige of whitey's chauvinistic ways, had to be taken out of service. Seal the doors, advise all tenants that henceforth they must carry their deposits direct to the courtyard and place them in that array of cans there.

Oh yes.

The bus

The bus stops at the corner here before those brownstones which adjoin this house. It is a transfer point, it draws a heavy Bulanga traffic. And by mid-morning every day of the week one needs an alpenstock to make his way over the litter of bottles and cans on this

[80]

sidewalk. At noon almost every day, Perez, the superintendent of the brownstones, makes an effort to thin out this midden heap. Sometimes when I am cleaning up the residue from my own lawn he and I exchange sympathetic shrugs of the shoulder.

My lawn costs in money and effort

Never mind

The dumbwaiter. That is the point here.

I long ago sealed the dumbwaiter skylights with metal plates. Sealed what was left of them, because the Bulanga young with free entry to the roof had a game called Smash The Glass Of The Dumb-waiter Skylights.

A nuisance when I had to do it. Now a blessing.

Because no one on the roof can possibly see the activity going on in those shafts. My activity.

My ah vee. Vee. Vee

A hiatus.

Blackout?

A few minutes. All well again. Weak though.

A blackout. Amazing experience. Bewildering.

I was leaning forward addressing this microphone. That was it. Leaning forward addressing the microphone.

Then I was opening my eyes. Sprawled over the side of this swivel chair a distance from the microphone on the desk. No sense of time elapsed. No sense of entering or emerging from coma.

Not frightening. Aware that it

Aware that it is the result of extraordinary physical strain and emotionalism. Thoughts and feelings running away with me. Galloped me right into a tunnel. Also codeine plus Percodan plus half bottle of wine.

Curiously, pains in chest and side which were acute during previous narrative — pre-blackout narrative — now are less acute.

Sensory brain cells somehow permanently affected?

No chance of that. Clearsighted and clearheaded now. Can recall my exact thoughts and words.

My activity. In the dumbwaiter shaft. Out of anyone's sight.

Yes.

To resume.

[81]

The grand event will be the explosion of seventy-two sticks of dynamite planted within those shafts. Two of those shafts. Those servicing the — those which used to service the interior apartments. Implosion. The caving in, not the flying out.

To that end, the necessary wiring must be run from bottom to top of each shaft, the sticks of dynamite, capped and wired, attached to the dumbwaiter doors. Decreasing number of sticks from bottom to top. Twelve for the ground floor, ten for the second, eight for the third, six for the fourth. Severest impact centered at the lowest levels.

The basement is now privileged territory. The door reinforced, bolted from the inside when necessary. The windows on the sidewalk level sealed with concrete block. That, five years ago after a series of raids and depredations.

So

The basement is my private cave — series of caves — and now with the gas and electric meter readers not scheduled to reappear until next month, there is no reason for anyone to ask entrance. It was those meter readings which determined my own schedule for the grand event. Once they were out of the way I could mark my calendar accordingly.

Pain in chest and side suddenly as bad as ever now. A good sign after blackout? Or could blackout signal a very small stroke?

Bah bee bo. Bahbeebo. Bah bee bo.

No stroke.

Tongue and lips completely under control. All limbs

All limbs flex on demand. Mind crystal clear.

Make a note of that, you psychology whizzbangs. Mind crystal clear.

Well.

Digression, said Professor Morton Shapiro, Department of Psychology and saintly Bulanga-fancier, is creativity.

In which case, friends, pardon my creativity.

And to return to flat, uncreative exposition, yesterday I used chisel and hammer to open the sealed door of the first dumbwaiter shaft. Basement door. I then dismantled the dumbwaiter itself, giving me clearance to enter the shaft. I mounted it by way of those small angle irons driven as footholds into one side of the shaft, bringing up the first set of wires with me.

A hellish vertical tunnel, dank, smelly, still thick with the vermin crawling its walls. Lit only by my flashlight propped on the floor, the beam directed upward. Unlit, one might say, my body constantly cutting off the light every time I moved.

That ascent alone was the cruellest of tests, but hauling myself up one careful step at a time, resting to ease the pains, I rejoiced in it. I was afraid only of making noise. Coughing. Thus an extremely heavy dose of the codeine compound to help control it. And most difficult to bear with, a section of clean handkerchief wadded in my mouth and a handkerchief tied over my mouth like a gag.

Two trips up. The wire first, then the six dynamite sticks. The process of capping and wiring them. I then made the mistake of trying to tape the assemblage to the dumbwaiter door there, but it was too heavy. Finally, I placed it on the narrow ledge at the base of the door, taped it to the door that way.

Coughed only infrequently. Tried to contain each spasm so that I thought my head would explode. In the end not contained but certainly muffled.

Total time required for the operation two hours, twenty minutes.

Returned home in time to admit Lorena Bailey to her unclothed duties. More about that.

Not now.

# John Milano

S ATURDAY MORNING. Double order of sit-ups and push-ups, single cup of black coffee with artificial sweetener, single scrambled egg, half a tomato — the tomato had to be non-fattening because it seemed to be made of plastic anyhow — and a quick scanning of the *News* and the *Times*. After some weighing of pros and cons Milano guiltily ate the remaining half of the tomato. He had just gotten it down when the announcement came on the intercom that his chauffeur — to put it kindly — was waiting.

That was David, Maxie Rovinsky's Israeli-American heir-apparent, who, a faded twenty-five-year old, always managed to look as if he had just crawled out of bed after a hard night and put on whatever he found in the laundry bag. The car itself was the plebian number in Maxie's mini-fleet, a dented, always dusty Granada, once seen never remembered, and thus highly suitable for Milano's occasional purposes.

When it pulled up to Christine Bailey's doorway the lady herself was visible at her open window on the third floor apparently keeping lookout. Still, Milano had to hail her a couple of times to start her downstairs. As she got into the rear seat beside him she remarked in explanation, "I thought you said something about a Mercedes."

So it goes, Milano told himself, not without satisfaction. The Queen of Sheba might have been strung out on Solomon's wisdom, but that kingly, gold-plated chariot sent to pick her up at the station didn't hurt one bit.

"The Mercedes is mine," he said. "This is hired. It comes with David there. It's tough keeping people under surveillance when you're behind the wheel yourself wondering about parking spots." He said to David, "Brooklyn. Manhattan Bridge. Right down Flatbush Avenue to Witter Street."

"Witter Street?" said David who nested in Queens.

"I'll tell you when you hit it."

Christine yelped as the car, with horn blasting, made a wide U-turn through the thick of Sixth Avenue traffic and headed south.

"You'll get used to it," Milano assured her. He handed her the tightly rolled-up papers he had waiting. "Your half of the trade-off. Photos of those two Boudins, and inside there's a list of names. You see or hear any of them in the gallery, you pass the word to me quick. Try my home phone first — the number's in here — and if it's no dice, call Mrs. Glass at the office. Right now you can tuck that package away in your bag and go over it in private. Monday you start checking out the gallery and upstairs there for any sign of those paintings. Any questions?"

"Uh-huh. But not to do with this. I want to know what's supposed to happen when I walk into the house right now."

"A little performance. I'll give you a head start to say hello to the folks, then ten, fifteen minutes later I'll ring your bell. Community-minded stranger in town looking for some redevelopment action. Want to see what this typical apartment is like. Once I get a good

[85]

look at little sister I'll take off and lay low outside. When she leaves the house I'll just tag along. No sweat."

Christine shook her head. "I'm still not so sure. When you get a good look at her she gets a good look at you. Then if she spots you tagging along —"

"Look —" said Milano. "Say, do you mind if I call you Christine?"

"It's my name."

"All right, Christine." Mark it as one small step in the right direction for mankind. "You leave the worries to me and just tell me who I'll be meeting up with when I walk into the apartment now."

"Mama. Lorena. My kid brother Vern. My older brother Odell, but I think he took off for the weekend."

"No papa."

Christine's eyes narrowed. "What's that supposed to mean?"

"Just what it sounds like. What do you think?"

"You ask me, man, I think it sounds like oh sure papa took off long ago. You know how these blackie papas are. Love 'em and leave 'em and let Welfare do the mopping up. So it's just another of these black mama families I'm walking in on."

Milano ran through astonishment and outrage. With an effort he shifted over to reflection. The female had lately taken to bushwhacking the male. The Libbers for sure. Even a seemingly stable element like Betty Cronin, right off the cover of *Woman's Day*, had suddenly gone split personality. The response? You just moved out of range until they either did or did not come knocking at your door again. One way or the other you were in control. But with this Queen of Sheba and her sudden knee to the groin anti-white tactics, control seemed to be a serious problem.

Be smart. Give up.

Like hell, give up.

He finally said the kindest thing he could think of saying. "You're a flake, Christine."

"Or a mind-reader?"

"You'd starve to death in that line of work. Another thing. When you turn on this race crap your voice changes somehow. Deep and mellow, know what I mean? Real Carolina cotton-pickin'. Tell me something. You ever pick any cotton in your young life?"

"My goodness gracious, listen to the man. Art lessons. Stagecraft. How to be Sherlock Holmes. Now it's elocution for the minorities."

"And now you're talking straight midtown New York."

"Don't kick it around too hard, mister. You could sprain a toe."

"I'm John. Or, even better, Johnny. And Italian. I thought Italian rated minority too."

"Does it? You want to hear in detail, John-or-even-better-Johnny, just how fucking tired I am of hearing all that Italian and Jew talk about their minority miseries? While who the hell do you think they hire to clean out their dirty toilets?"

"My mother," said Milano, trying to make it light but not too light, "always cleans her own."

"Well, mine cleans other people's. And my father used to call himself a railroad man. That meant a diner waiter on the old New York Central. He died ten years ago from a bad appendix. We didn't see much of him what with those runs between here and Chicago, but take it from me, man, what we saw was very good."

Score a point for her, thought Milano. But score a point for him, because she was handing him all this in straight midtown New York. Just like real people talking to each other.

Manhattan Bridge. No heavy traffic in Brooklyn this time of Saturday, so clear sailing all the way. Empire Boulevard, and those high-rises there were once Ebbett's Field. Among others, Robinson, Newcombe, Campanella. Milano was about to comment on this sweet recollection, then thought better of it. This volatile Queen of Sheba was likely to take any such reference as condescension. It was a case of think twice before you even open your mouth about the weather. Milano had a feeling that his consciousness was suddenly being raised so high that it made his head ache.

Past Empire Boulevard, Flatbush Avenue showed signs of government money at work. A new roadbed instead of the old washboard. New sidewalks with a handsome brick trim. Saplings planted at regular intervals, each wired between a pair of upright two-by-twos for protection. With the help of God those saplings might yet become trees. The stores, however, once a class act, now added up to shlock alley. Second-hand Sams had taken over, and funky clothes shops, and Korean vegetable markets with their

[87]

loaded bins blocking off most of the sidewalk, and hole-in-the-wall take-out food joints. Saturday was a heavy shopping day around here. A lot of folks out with full shopping bags; a lot of small fry being nudged along.

At Witter Street, Milano gave David the signal for the left turn and then had him pull over into the space decreed by a hydrant. That four-story number down the block, said Christine, was 409. As she opened the car door, Milano asked, "Your mother know about me?"

"Yes. Just her."

"She a good poker player?"

"She's mad enough and scared enough to play this hand just fine."

When she was on her way down the block David sourly addressed the rearview mirror. "You mind me saying something, Mr. Milano?"

"I might, sonny. So don't say it."

From the car window Milano had a clear view of the three tired-looking brownstones on the corner and the brick façade of 409 which fronted directly on the sidewalk. He had only a partial, but fascinating, view of the building between, mostly of the shingled octagon cone of a tower rising above a gabled roof and surmounted by a gilded weathervane.

With ten minutes clocked off, he followed Christine's course, taking his time in front of that curious structure to get the full view of it. A view to make any fancier of pure, mind-boggling Victorian — American Victorian, of course — weep for joy. A great big bay windowed, leaded-glass windowed, stained-glass windowed job, the octagon tower rounding out its corner toward 409, a wide three-stacker chimney crowning it all. A spacious colonnaded porch on a fieldstone foundation. A massive double-doored entrance in front, and on the tower side a porte-cochere. Delicate fretsaw trim wherever there was room for it, from the roof overhanging the porch to the eaves over the attic. And every inch of the building looking as freshly painted and polished as if it had been hauled here from a century ago by an oversized time machine.

Even the color of that paint job — too many eager beavers who picked up these classics nowadays immediately laid on the white paint, the Colonial bug having bitten them. But this baby was, as were all proper models in the Gilded Age, exactly the right chestnut brown.

At the far end of the driveway, partly hidden by the house — house? mansion? demi-mansion? — what must have been the carriage house in the good old days was now a garage with a carriage house look.

And that sweep of lawn around the whole works, except for some casually disposed of empty bottles and soiled newspapers, had the closecropped lustrous texture of a golf green. All of this guarded by a high, wrought-iron fence which, although showing some dents here and there — that knee-high series was most likely made by a car bumper whamming into it — was still in respectable shape.

Number 407. No doubt the domicile of the old character who gave little sister her few hours of paid employment each week. A black squire? Had to be. No sane white property holder would still be living on this block to start with. And if he did, for whatever whacked-out reason, he wouldn't keep up his property this way, he'd look to dump it for what he could get. Presentable would be the best he'd offer, not this kind of high-cost perfection.

Those shingles alone — slate shingles, no less — looked like they were laid down last week.

The apartment building next door was a different story. A good solid Jazz Age survivor, but now on the way down and out. The pavement-level cellar windows sealed with concrete block. Graffiti. A taped up crack in the glass of the front door. Inside, a cavernous terrazzo-floored lobby stripped of all furnishings. A chandelier reduced to one naked light bulb. Flaking paint everywhere. Some kindergarten-sized kids loudly having a tricycle race in the emptiness.

The building was divided into two units, front and back, sort of a squared-off exercise weight in design, with the lobby as the handle of the weight. The Bailey apartment was one flight up the front stairway. Milano rang the bell and Christine answered it. Holding the door open behind her, she asked with a straight face, "Yes?" and, after Milano had jovially explained his redevelopment mission in tones that had to carry through the door, she motioned him in and made introductions to the kinfolk: mama, short, stout, and maybe a little too falsely welcoming to be rated a first-class poker player;

[89]

brother Vern, a razor-thin six-four in warmup pants, neon jacket and sneakers, evidently itching to get to his basketball game; and sister Lorena, a leggy kid just on the interesting side of nubile, as those skintight jeans and T-shirt plainly signalled. Pretty, but would have been a lot prettier if that face wasn't unrelieved sullen.

She didn't feature Christine's kind of Afro hairdo either. Her hair was a silky-smooth ebony cap, a pageboy right out of King Arthur's court. In terms of surveillance, definitely an easy mark. While Milano went through his community-minded rote again, carefully not selling too hard, he caught the girl from several angles, sprawling, sitting, standing, and, under mama's orders, heading into the kitchen for breakfast. Meanwhile, Vern took just enough interest in the rote to point out that all this redevelopment jive only meant tenants getting shoved out of the building, and if they weren't shoved out, man, it was only because they would be hustled for a lot more rent, and wasn't that the truth?

After which he took off to his game, and because Lorena was now back on the scene, a cup of coffee in hand and a transistor to her ear, but casually curious about these goings-ons, Milano played it cozy by asking for a tour of the premises. Two bedrooms, twin beds in each, and from the window of what was obviously the ladies' quarters he had a fine view of the Victorian beauty next door, especially that noble tower right up to its weathervane which, gratifyingly, twitched south to southeast and back again as he watched.

In white territory the apartment would have been rated a find. Two bedrooms, living room, kitchen, and bathroom. All right, the dingy walls showed leakage stains here and there, and for want of any floor coverings — except for the kitchen lineoleum — the bare hardwood floors showed rough wear. But this was a well-crafted old building, and who, nowadays, was planning cheap apartments with nine-foot-high ceilings, solid doors, and honest-to-God eat-in kitchens like this one, big enough to seat six around the table? In his own super de luxe co-op, a man had to suffer what was politely called a galley, for Jesus sake. Bend over to look into the refrigerator and you found your butt in the oven right across the narrow aisle from it.

Interesting on a different score was that ornately framed,

hand-tinted photo on the living room wall over the stereo set. Father of the family. Easy to see where his female offspring got their enticing looks. A strikingly handsome man, caught in his prime, staring grimly at the camera as if defying it to do its worst. No nonsense. And, Milano wondered, how would he have handled daughter Lorena? Laid her over his knee, strap in hand, taking the chance she wouldn't be listed next day in the runaway files? Or come on as one of those doting, more or less unconsciously incestuous daddies who'd never admit that their suddenly curvy little girls could be rambling out of legal bounds?

Christine led him outside the apartment and let the door shut behind her. She said in a low voice, "When do I hear from you?"

"Right after the show tonight."

"No. Not there. But you can call me at home any time after, say, midnight."

Milano jotted down the number she gave him. "Sure I won't be bothering anybody there?" he asked, putting it about as subtly as he could. Which, as he knew — and he had a feeling she knew — wasn't all that subtle.

Christine chose to overlook any nuances. "Lenardo and Pearl have the bedroom. I have the parlor couch. Phone's next to the couch. You call as late as you want."

Pearl the playwright, Lenardo the director. All right. And while the couch might possibly open into one of those double-bed jobs, the way it was put suggested — wish-fulfillment? — that it was serving solo duty.

"One other thing," Milano said. "If Security in some store jumps the kid, do I let nature take its course, or do I step in and blow my cover? Not that blowing my cover means much in that case. You'll have whatever evidence against her you need right then and there."

Christine looked like she was fighting off a qualm of nausea. "It'll kill Mama if she has to go down to the station house for anything like that. But what could you do about it?"

"Trade secret. Leave it to me."

"All right," Christine said unhappily, "I'm leaving it to you."

Marking time outside the building, he took inventory of the block. Not too bad. Tree-lined, old Brooklyn style. Some graystones and brownstones in fair shape. Apartment houses needing work. The closer you got, the more work you could see they needed. In the middle of the block across the street a real loser. Abandoned, sealed up, every window shattered. Looking up through the empty frame of a top-floor window, Milano could see the gaping emptiness of what used to be the roof there. Probably a torch job. Hit a loser with torch hard enough and collect full insurance.

One job like this on the block wounded the block. A couple more could kill it. "Want to wet down those torches?" Willie had once said. "Knock off those fucking crooked insurance agents who sell policies to the mob. And while you're at it, knock off those fucking crooked claims adjustors who okay the claims."

Willie, of course, was always powerfully set against anybody else's corruption.

Kids were whooping it up and down the street in some kind of space-wars game. A couple closed in on Milano. "You the City, man?" one asked. He might have been eight years old.

"Private," Milano answered man to man. "Wondering how much that pile would cost to buy."

The kids gaped and giggled. Then number one said, "Man, you give me a dime, it's all yours."

Tempting to work up this comedy act, but there was Lorena Bailey, ballasted by a swollen shoulder-bag, coming out of 409.

Back to the job.

As anticipated, it was an easy, uncomplicated job. David, who seemed to take a disdainful pleasure in this kind of chauffeuring, maintained precisely the right distance behind the girl as she moved along, stopping to pick up a pair of girl friends on her way. And managed to neatly tailgate the Flatbush Avenue bus the trio took all the way to downtown Brooklyn. When they disembarked at the Livingston Street entrance of the Abraham and Straus department store Milano said goodbye to his chauffeur and resigned himself to tedious footwork.

And, after he got his bearings in the store, to some worrisome considerations.

It was a big place, A and S, a whopper, and saturated with uniformed security, not to mention the plainclothes variety. A light-fingered pro might get by them, but Lorena didn't have that pro look. So the sensible play would be to spot any wrong move, then come on as fast as possible. Beat the uniforms to her. Or, if it was a tie, make immediate payment as required and get her out from under. The worrisome part would be her reaction to him under these conditions. Not really him. The family.

If there was a loud bust-up with them, and she did take off—

By the time they were done with A and S, Milano didn't believe for a moment that there had ever been any shoplifting. Lorena bought—after much conference with her two chums—and paid cash. A couple of blouses upstairs, some items at the junk jewelry counter on the main floor. Lunch at a stand on Fulton Street, a pair of shoes in a shop nearby, a couple of purchases in the Albee Mall, and all paid for with Lorena's green folding money.

Mid-afternoon, the party moved along to the Loew's movie house, and was there joined by a couple of boys. Callow, noisy, good-natured kids, no hard edges to them. Most to the point was that Lorena was the one who bought the tickets for the whole crew, boys included.

Once he saw them through the theater doors Milano treated himself to a hot dog at a corner stand, used a men's room at A and S, then seated himself on a bench down the block from the theater to wait it out. Government money had gone into this Fulton Mall thing too. The roadway had been narrowed down for bus traffic only, the walks on either side had been expanded to boulevard width. For trimmings, these semicircular benches had been planted at intervals along the way; as a test for the spine they were backless. Ranged along the street robed and skullcapped black Muslims pushed Islamic reading matter, bric-a-brac, and punk from folding tables. Burning samples of the punk scented the air not unpleasantly. And the passing show provided fair entertainment value. The largest part of it was colored, a good proportion Hispanic. No one among the younger women was up there in Christine Bailey's class, but quite a few added considerable charm to the scene.

It interested Milano that, of course, these were the same black and brown women, men, kids as ever, but he seemed to be getting a subtly different view of them.

A magic bench?

Christine?

Hunger pangs?

[93]

Lorena and chums emerged from the theater, made their way across the street to a music shop. One hour and twenty minutes going through the stock there. Outside, the party broke up, the boys going off one way, the girls back to Livingston Street and the bus. There were cabs in sight, but Milano let them go by. His accounts with both Christine Bailey and Eugene Louis Boudin were balanced for the day, and tomorrow was another day.

Besides, his feet hurt, his back ached, and some energy had to be reserved for the evening's program.

Timing it to a nicety, he paid his way into the Birdbath Theater a few minutes after the action had started. More audience than last night, enough so that he could logically and inconspicuously seat himself in the last row, in the corner away from the entrance.

At first, what he saw might have been interpreted as a bad night for all concerned. A spasmodic, bumpy, jumpy set of performances, none of the gears seeming to mesh. Unbelievably, even for this level of theater, during a scene in two between Christine and Tamar McBride the spotlight lost both players and had to go prowling around to relocate them. Amateur night all right, until it dawned on Milano that what he was viewing here was no series of accidents. Christine Bailey, so pliant to the wily machinations of her co-star in her last night's performance, had given up on pliant. Tamar was trying the same old scene-stealing tricks, but this time they were backfiring.

What d'ya know!

Milano slipped out of the theater a few minutes before intermission, and what he knew was that there would be hell to pay backstage during intermission. What he wondered about when he returned—he wouldn't have missed the payoff for anything—was who the second act would declare the winner. He didn't have long to wonder. Tamar was having her hands full and not liking it. Christine was cutting loose and sending those previously muted vibrations right to the back row. Awkward timing, weird lighting and all, *Two Stops Before The End Of The Line* now gave loud, clear signs of what it could be. Not bad. Not bad at all.

Regretfully, Milano ducked out before Christine's final lines. His feet had long ago ceased to hurt, his back felt just fine.

Midnight, she had said. Phone any time after midnight.

He killed two hours at O. Henry's working on a steak—no trimmings at all—a salad, and a couple of Perriers with lime, and the New York *Post*, then wended his way along Sixth, up three flights of narrow, loudly creaking stairs, and knocked on Christine Bailey's door.

She asked who it was; he told her. She opened the door and stood there wrapped in a blanket. From the look of those bare shoulders and bare legs up to mid-thigh she had nothing on under the blanket.

"I told you to phone," she said.

"I don't like phoning when I don't have to." True. "And I happened to be in the neighborhood." Nearly true.

She still stood there blocking the doorway. A good actress, especially, it seemed, when she didn't intend to be, it was all there on her face. Concern, wariness, irritation. All three in one.

"Well, what happened?" she asked. "What did you find out?"

He could plainly see that the room behind her was empty, that the couch was just a cushioned couch with a sheet tucked around the cushions. Still, she didn't invite him in. His feet and back suddenly started to hurt again, and his temper started to rise. In a nutshell, who the hell did she think she was?

"Do you always talk over your family troubles out here in the hall?" he asked.

She grudgingly stood aside. "All right, come on in."

"No need. I can give you the word right here."

"Look, I am asking you to come in. I don't know why you're making a case of it."

Milano remained where he was. "The word is," he said, "that there's no shoplifting. The kid did some buying in a few places, treated a couple of girl friends to eats, treated the girls plus a couple of boys to the movies. Paid cash all the way. She seems to have that pocketbook stuffed with cash. And neither of these boys is a Jimmy-type buying her favors. Both are wet behind the ears. That's it."

"What do you mean, that's it? Then where's she getting that money?"

"An interesting question. If you want to discuss it further, just phone me at home any time tomorrow morning."

He started down those creaking stairs, and Christine leaned over the bannister. "What's wrong with right now?"

[95]

A panicky note there? Good. "I'm off duty now," said Milano, going his way.

In the lobby of the co-op the night man hailed him. "Message for you, Mr. Milano. Mrs. MacFadden said that if and when you showed up, there's a little party in the penthouse."

Gracie's Saturday night little parties were like Ringling Brother's little circuses. On the other hand, to go up to the apartment and walk the floor mentally snarling at the image of the blanket-clad Christine Bailey—

"Tell Mrs. MacFadden I'm on my way up," said Milano.

# Charles Witter Kirwan

SUNDAY.

Sunday afternoon.

I withstood an impulse to attend church this morning.

The Dutch Reformed Church, that is, over on Flatbush Avenue. Worth the few blocks extra walk if and when you come to view what will be listed in the guide books as The Witter House.

The Witter House.

Funded — richly funded — by The Hendrick Witter Foundation.

What I was about to

Oh yes, that churchgoing impulse. It was not an impulse born of any need to atone for the splendidly perverse sexual experience to which I finally introduced Lorena Bailey late Friday afternoon.

Most certainly not that.

Nor did the impulse come from any need to sit through lugubrious hymns and a watered-down sermon. In this libertarian society, Calvinism, a once powerful brew for my ancestors, has become so much sugar water. As have so many once proud and potent faiths, excluding, of course, that raucous, high-profit evangelicalism nowadays completely addling the wits of the already half-addled.

So

In point of fact, my impulse was to attend services this morning as Quakers do their meetings. That most curious and foolish of sects — with its remaining handful of beatific, traditionally Bulanga-loving ninnies — holds meetings for worship without any pastor in charge. The congregation just sits there speechless until God, who obviously has nothing better to do with his time, plants words in someone's mouth, and these words are then solemnly declaimed to the faithful.

Well, not altogether a bad way of giving the taxpayer a chance to speak his mind, if only that mind isn't petrified into a lump of cant. Mine is not, thank you. Whatever my record of politely speaking cant to the issues, it is not. Now listen to this. Psalm 32, 3.

"For while I held my tongue, my bones consumed away through my daily complaining."

Lines of fire.

I politely kept my tongue from speaking the bitter truth and so my bones are being agonizingly consumed. Bones and lungs and guts.

Therefore I would attend church and would rise like Jeremiah to deliver that truth to this captive audience.

I did not.

Too much to lose. I would be marked as eccentric, to say the least. Mentally out of gear.

Why lay all this before you — the impulse and its restraint?

To give proof that I am, as I always have been, entirely clear-minded, precisely understanding the nature and consequences of the grand event I'm designing.

If the psycho-quacks will forgive the expression — totally sane.

I must also make plain that I'm no churchgoer. Florence — my wife — was. Liked the singing, liked the saccharine sociability, dozed

[98]

through the sermons. Your good average churchgoer. I am not, and since my youth I never have been. My grandfather was not. I suspect his passion for historical study soured him on organized religion. When I handed him the draft of my doctoral thesis on Alva's occupation of Flanders and The Netherlands during their struggle for freedom—where it was Roman Catholic against Lutheran and Calvinist, during which butchery Lutheran and Calvinist turned to butchering each other—he first said, "Very sound work," which was what I wanted from him. Then he added drily, "On three of our dear Lord's churches who'll never be able to wipe each other's blood off their hands."

True.

One danger in studying history is the contempt it can breed for mankind's most cherished institutions in their unending stupidity.

But our Bulanga have found a way to beat that game. Too dull-witted in their African grass huts to ever invent a written language and come up with a recorded history of their tribe's arid past, they are now busily conjuring up glowing accounts of its imaginary glories. Using whitey's alphabet and whitey's printing press of course.

And pundits nod approval of this make-believe, and publishers pour out good gold for it, and television audiences sit goggle-eyed at gaudy dramatizations of it. And courses in Bulanga hagiology are instituted in my college so that the tribe can rejoice in its made-to-order past.

The Bulanga witch-doctor as Thucydides.

Dear God.

Where was I?

Church. Church-going. Yes.

While I'm at it, since this is uninhibited family history, I may as well complete the roll call.

My mother. Hattie—Harriet Sprague Witter that was—one of the most god-fearing. Locked horns with my grandfather a few times during my puberty about my freedom of choice and finally gave up.

My father. Henry Witter. Sorry. Too much of a blank there. A lieutenant in the infantry during the First World War—a volunteer —he died of influenza in a hospital in Brest in 1918. Survived combat in the Argonne campaign. Died of influenza.

[99]

I was five years old the last time I ever saw him. I have a favorable memory of him. I don't know if it's accurate.

Sorry.

But

But his replacement in my life

A different story.

Daniel Kirwan, stepfather.

Daniel Kirwan, born Roman Catholic, became a devoted Protestant. Devoted, remember. I did not say devout. Devoted to the Witter house, to the Witter Packard which he proudly drove to church each Sunday, to the Witter money, and possibly—as much as he could squeeze out that kind of devotion—to my widowed mother whom he married two years after my father's death.

Stupid. Burly red-faced, red-haired Hibernian, loud in his affections, his good intentions, his stupidity.

A go-getter. His own words. A common idiom in my childhood. Go-getter. Someone on the rise, using elbows and knees however he had to.

A heavy drinker. Sometimes a self-accusatory, weeping drinker. I owe him one small favor for that. I was newly enlisted in the army, still in basic training at Camp Gordon, Georgia, miserably homesick, when he died of cirrhosis of the liver and I was given a few blessed days leave to attend the funeral.

Unfertile.

Yes he was. This man of muscle, this mighty hunter before the Lord—at least each fall, with scarlet jacket and shiny rifle and shotgun—could not produce a child of his own.

That hurt him terribly, my mother confided to me near her own end. He drank because of that.

Did he?

No, he didn't.

He drank because he was a sot.

And, unable to produce a little Kirwan of his own, he did me the glorious honor of legally adopting me. Of making me his own little Kirwan on my tenth birthday. I had no voice in this. My grandfather's protesting voice was not listened to.

Did I feel stange about my new identity?

Yes. But I think at ten you feel strange about everything. This was just one more thing to feel strange about. And I was an amiable child. Kept my nose clean, my thoughts to myself, and did as I was told.

However

However, this tenth birthday gift of mine, which was announced to me by my mother with much smiling and petting, was nothing as compared to the really great event of my childhood exactly one week later.

The completion of 409 Witter Street. The first apartment house on the block. The very first. Daniel Kirwan's project. Daniel Kirwan's dearest dream come true.

The go-getter had gone and gotten.

The one-time foreman of Witter and Son's stockrooms could now claim ownership — at least his name was below my grandfather's on the mortgage — of a magnificent apartment building. Magnificent especially in the way it bulked over everything in sight, seemed to devour the block, distorted its perspective, made a strange new world of it.

What tune did the British fifes tootle as Cornwallis surrendered the old world to the Yankee upstarts at Yorktown?

*The World Turned Upside Down.*

And that memorable day a week after I became Charles Witter Kirwan we had music on our block too. Music. Lights strung overhead. Tables — planks on sawhorses — heaped with food and drink. A brass band right there in the middle of the roadway. Barricades against motor traffic at each end of the block, courtesy of our local police precinct. A block party.

Music and dancing and bright-colored balloons. And plenty of surreptitious boozing — remember Prohibition? — in the garage of 407. Everybody came, the neighborhood came, the architects and bricklayers of the new wonder came.

My grandfather came out of good manners. Wheedled, cajoled, bullied, pushed beyond endurance to invest a large share of his diminishing wealth into this future, he must have carried to his dying day the memory of that spacious lawn with its oaks and maples and cherry trees that 409 had engulfed.

But the Good Steward cannot hide his money in his mattress. Nor can he invest it only in repairing and preserving his own fine home.

[101]

He must also invest it in the profitable destruction of his world. Must, in the end, bow to the go-getter who knows a good thing when he smells it and leaves as his inheritance the destruction.

Oh yes.

The new wonder rented well. Very well.

And having demonstrated its success, it was followed by facsimiles which sprang up along this block as if sown from dragon's teeth.

And not only fine old trees went crashing down now to make room for them but fine old homes. The spacious homes of the clean and quiet and civilized. Why not? With their paradise defiled why should the civilized remain in it?

It was go-getter time, and the banner of Daniel Kirwan flew high above all others.

Listen. Listen closely.

Destruction need not be wreaked by explosion. It can come about in much more insidious form. Infiltration. Infiltration by waves of the less clean and quiet and civilized. Less and less, each wave. For Witter Street? A wave of Hibernians came and receded. A wave of Italians. A wave of Jews. Oh yes, the Children of Israel knew they had again found their Land of Canaan.

And in the darkness of the night, the campfires of the waiting Bulanga twinkled all around the margins of this land.

The brave Israelites fled like rabbits at the sight of the first Bulanga invader.

The end.

It was over that quickly. Our city of New York made the rules to assure it would be over that quickly.

The final wave.

Ooze and muck.

Are you listening closely? If you're consumed with curiosity about how I came to design the grand event — to execute it against all odds — you must be.

I am vengeance.

Futile vengeance?

Yes. I admit that. I admit it.

But I am what vengeance there is or will ever be.

My own salvation. I feel acute physical pain now. But this is the salvation: That I feel pain as if it were being suffered by someone else. Cold remote pain dimmed by heated triumph. An anesthesia that comes from not merely reading the future but of shaping it.

As for the past

That is, the episode of Friday afternoon involving Lorena Bailey. Wait.

I must first reiterate here a vital instruction included with the sealed will I placed in the hands of my executor. My estate's executor. That is, nothing in all these tapes — absolutely nothing — is to be in any way deleted or censored when this material is published as a book.

Not a word.

Allowance is made for necessary deletions when it comes to magazine and newspaper publication. I bow to that necessity. Magazines and newspapers face the problem of limited space. They must also tone down explicit descriptions of sexual activity. The danger there is that portions of an original, meaningful text may thus be reduced to mere titillation, but I accept this unpleasant possibility. I can only hope that the reader will then be moved to buy the original book itself and read the work in its entirety.

Incidentally, reproduction and sale of these tapes themselves — as tapes — is absolutely forbidden. The pirating of printed matter is unusual. The pirating of tapes however, as I have learned, is now an industry in itself, not a penny in royalties going to the rightful proprietor of them. Or his estate.

Fair warning. The Hendrick Witter Foundation is not to be cheated this way.

So.

The events of late Friday afternoon.

By three o'clock Friday afternoon I had planted the first charge of high explosive in 409. A dirty and exhausting job. I emerged from it at what I thought was my physical nadir. Emotionally high though, drunk with a sense of achievement.

I dragged myself home, and no sooner was I inside the house than Lorena Bailey presented herself there. I opened the door to her, and the way she looked at me made me aware of my filthy and disheveled appearance. I explained that I had been repairing the boiler at 409. I was also on the verge of adding that I didn't feel well enough for company, that we'd have to put off this session until Monday.

[103]

On the verge. But I didn't say it. I was exhausted enough to drop to the floor as I stood there, but I was in a wildly exhilarated mood. Celebratory. Obviously, the mind does not always respond directly to the body's signals.

Nothing new in that. I know because I have lived with sexual fantasies all my life from puberty. Muddled at first—the romantic and sadistic and masochistic all muddled together—but more and more I learned to organize them properly, seek a theme for a little one-act play, time its performance so that its climax came simultaneously with the spurt of semen from an engorged penis.

In high school, wisdom was provided by helpful agencies. The friend whose father owned the works of Havelock Ellis. Impotent, pseudo-scientific Havelock Ellis, whose italicized little case histories were each a heated little one-act play.

And the schoolmate who came into the possession of those few raggedy, grossly pornographic, marvelous pages of *The Story of Josephine Mutzenbacher* by Felix Salten.

Felix Salten? No, it can't be the same Felix Salten who wrote that virginal classic *Bambi*. Never.

But it is. The very same.

Fantasies.

All in the mind. A distortion of the body's signals that the time has come, that there are females available, that the reality of them will be better than any dreams.

I was a virgin until at Camp Gordon I was led by some platoon mates—forcibly steered—into bed with a stout, bucktoothed, businesslike Georgia belle whose home on weekends served as a makeshift brothel.

My sexual adventures through all the years following until my marriage could be counted on the fingers of one hand, and you'd still have two fingers to spare.

The body signalled for action. The panicky mind settled for yet more lurid fantasy.

Variations of it were later woven into my marriage. Through the act itself, with my patient, awkwardly accommodating, unimaginative wife. Born middle-aged, dear soul. Never liked to be called Flo.

A Flo might have been tempted to enjoy playtime in bed. Not a Florence. Not even wise enough to pretend enjoyment.

So there was Lorena Bailey, my part-time naked Bulanga nymph, standing before me. No fantasy either. The living descendant of those naked black maidens who stood chained on the slave blocks terrified into mute, wide-eyed obedience. Quivering under the poking and pinching and sampling of the crafty bidder's hand.

Secretly excited by that hand. Ashamed of the secret.

Bought and paid for. The only difference was that there was no middleman involved here; I was making payment direct.

And

And in a way I was being cheated. Not by her. By myself. Familiarity takes the edge off any experience. What I was buying for my money was the display of that body, and that body—every curve of it—was now too familiar. In this little peep-show arrangement I was no longer getting value for my money.

I think I've already said

Yes, I did say it. That while at that moment my body felt as if it had just been lifted off Torquemada's rack, my mood was triumphant.

Celebratory, that was the word.

So there would be a celebration. Long-planned. A party whose time had come.

Yes.

I said to Lorena, "You can go to work without me. I want to clean myself up first."

I unlocked the door of the tower room for her. I went to the bathroom down the hall for the necessary cleaning up. Shower and soap, a courtesy to her. Then into a robe. Unglamorous. Terrycloth. But the right costume for this party. In the bedroom I counted out the necessary money and stuffed it into my pocket.

When I entered the study she was sprawled in an armchair still fully clothed. I frowned at that, she frowned at my robe. "You gonna sit aroun' like that?" she asked warily.

"Any reason why I shouldn't?"

From her expression she was probably thinking of a few, but after

[105]

a moment's hesitation she simply shrugged them away. Harmless broken-down ole voyeuristic whitey, all eyes and nothing else. I sat behind the desk and watched as she kicked off her shoes and then indifferently pulled off her clothing.

By now

Well, a surmise.

But by now she may have found her own interest in this game dulled by familiarity. More often than not she liked to enliven it with what amounted to a clever parody of striptease. Now she was altogether perfunctory.

I took out the wad of money and motioned her toward the desk with it. A little change of routine. Except for our first time around, payment had always closed the proceedings. Distinctly wary now, she moved to the desk, taking her time about it. But money, money, money was an irresistible lure. The look of it spread across the desk. The feel of it each time as she would gather it together, fold it carefully, and thrust it, not into a pocket of those jeans, but under the elastic of her panties, her hand going out of sight as I watched, centering the treasure down there as if shielding those maidenly lips with it.

A sensible hiding place of course. Of course. But what a web of psycho-theory the great Sigmund, the begetter of all wisdom, could weave out of that bit of common sense, couldn't he?

Yes indeed.

The money.

I slowly laid it out on the desk like a hand of solitaire. One two three four five ten-dollar bills. Then one five-dollar bill in payment for her Stepin Fetchit imitation of a librarian.

Her hand moved toward the desk and I waved it back. She narrowed her eyes as I laid out still another hand of this expensive solitaire.

One hundred and ten dollars altogether. Marguerite's chest of jewels.

Lorena was no fool. She pointed. "What's that extra?"

I told her. Incredibly mawkish, the way I put it, I realize that. But the word fellatio would mean nothing to any Bulanga of Witter Street. And while I'm familiar with a couple of the gutter phrases for the act I couldn't bring myself to speak them, even at that overheated moment. Mawkish it had to be. I said, "I'll put it very plainly, girl. I want you to make love to me with your mouth."

She seemed stunned. No performance there. Genuinely stunned. This didn't give me any qualms. The time was long past when she might announce my depravity to the world.

It took her time to get her wits together. Then she said, "Man, you want me to give you head?"

I indicated the money. "It means double pay each time, Lorena."

Curious.

Very curious, now that I think of it, but it never entered my mind during this passage that I might be incapable of performance.

If Lorena was willing, I was ready. Rotting lungs? Cancerous everything else? No connection with Priapus.

Incongruously, Lorena stood there stark naked, all parts showing, and made a case for high morality. "Man," she said, "I don't eat nobody. I don't even eat my boy friend. I sure don't eat you, old man."

"Do you know how much money you're looking at, Lorena? Do you know how much it'll add up to in just one week? Three days of it?"

She betrayed herself by glancing down at the money. She knew how much it was all right. Then she looked at me, plainly wrestling with temptation.

Writhing under it. Tortured by it.

"Never done it," she said sulkily. "How'm I s'posed to know what to do?"

I had never done it before either, but I knew what she had to do.

She did it.

On her knees — that view between my splayed legs was enough to send Saint Anthony himself straight to hell — and with lips, salivating mouth, hardworking tongue.

She didn't like it.

Her hands

She kept her hands away, fingers delicately curled, pink palms showing. Intriguing. Mouth yes, but no hand contact.

She didn't like it, so I did not discharge in her mouth. Might draw too violent a reaction. When the moment came I pushed her away roughly. Caught her by surprise and she almost went over backward. Even then, semen spattered on her shoulder, on one breast.

Fifty years—fifty-five years of fantasy, all jetted away in one instant.

She looked down at herself, saw what had happened and snarled something intelligible. Scampered to the bathroom. After a long while returned angry. Refused to meet my eyes. Took the money and dressed, face stony and averted.

Then—Bulanga unpredictable—she stopped before the desk on her way out and with one wild motion of the arm swept everything on it to the floor. Telephone, papers, penholder, ancient brass lamp, its bulb shattering as it hit the floor.

She glared at me, challenging me.

A bad moment. Yes. Once, Charles Witter Kirwan would have quailed in the face of that nasty little tempest. Not now. Not the almost dead Charles Witter Kirwan.

I said with absolute calm, "I'll do you a favor, Lorena, and not take that from your pay. And I'll see you Monday. The usual time."

It surprised her, ole whitey's cool authority. I think it really shocked her.

I believe I will see her Monday at the usual time. Tomorrow. I'm sure of it.

That's all.

No.

Nature. The natural order in human society

Never mind.

# John Milano

G<small>RACIE</small> M<small>AC</small>F<small>ADDEN</small>'s <small>OCCASIONAL</small> S<small>ATURDAY</small> <small>NIGHT</small> <small>BASHES</small> started late and, as far as Milano could ever determine, kept rolling until Monday dawn, just in time for the last of the Hollywood contingent to catch the reverse red-eye back to the Coast for late breakfast there.

Always a big crowd and a hectic one, but the sprawl of rooms on the co-op's top floor, and the penthouse above, absorbed it easily. Broadway and Beverly Hills predominated, slob-chic was the preferred costume. A cornucopia of mediocre food, oceans of excellent bottled goods, plentiful good quality grass, and even a coke corner hidden away in Gracie's dressing room. Two resident hosts in attendance: a baggy-eyed, snowy-thatched Colonel Blimp in yachting jacket and ascot, and a considerably younger and more hard-featured Hispanic type. Both were addressed by Gracie in her gracious moods as Mac, in her other moods as MacFadden. Touch on the subject of her relationship to them and she'd tell you it was none of your fucking business.

True.

Disco was the big thing, the naked floor of the penthouse literally made to order for it, but in the deeply carpeted quarters down below, aside from some low visibility sex, poker and backgammon were the featured attractions. Milano, bone-tired and irritable, took a seat among the barracudas at Gracie's poker table, found himself playing a stupidly reckless game, knew he was doing so, and couldn't work up the willpower to change tactics and go smart. The nourishment he was getting from slices of tired roast beef rolled in wilted lettuce leaves and washed down by puritanical Perrier and lime, didn't help either. By sheer wild luck — otherwise flabby hands he held seemed magnetized to the draw that would make them all muscle — he got away with his life. At four a.m. when he cashed in his chips and registered just about even-steven, he had the feeling Gracie was glad to see him go. You can beat smart, as she put it in her farewell, but you can't beat dumb luck.

Also true.

He heard his phone as he was unlocking his apartment door.

Christine Bailey said, "I've been calling you every half hour."

"Didn't I say to call in the morning?" Milano asked.

"This is morning. You think I could get to sleep after what you said? After what happened?"

Cotton-pickin' or midtown, that was quite a voice. Milano sat down in his number one armchair, pulled off his shoes, and settled back the better to enjoy it. "Said what?" he asked. "And what did happen?"

"That whole business about Lorena you didn't finish telling me. Meaning that because I didn't drag you right into the house, you got pissed off and ran."

That was accurate enough to bruise. "Well," Milano said, "I know a grudging hostess when I meet one."

"Uh-huh. So let's skip all the funny dialogue in between and get

[110]

right to the meaningful stuff. I am not part of this trade-off, Milano. Not personally. No way. You read that?"

"You mean I look that menacing?"

"Come on, Milano, don't turn it on for me. Just talk business. Like about Lorena. And that money she spent. Where do you think it came from? How much did it look to be anyhow?"

He did some sketchy mental arithmetic. "Oh, maybe one-fifty, maybe two hundred. But like I said, there was no shoplifting, and she had some easy shots at it, too. You don't want to hear it, Bailey, but that kid must be selling something. Something high profit."

He didn't have to spell it out. Christine said, "Look, she doesn't show any sign — the least sign — "

Milano cut in: "I didn't say she uses the stuff, did I? As you put it, maybe a joint now and then at the most. But what's that got to do with the price of pills? Or whatever."

Silence. Then Christine said, "God damn." More silence. When she finally spoke she really did sound as if she was up against the wall. "You know we can't let it go at that, Milano."

We.

But from the way she sounded, this was no time for smart-ass repartee.

"What's her school schedule?" Milano asked. "And home and job schedule?"

"My mother would know that."

"Would she know about her school friends, club activities, neighborhood bunch — all that?"

"A lot of it. Mama always likes to know what's going on with us. That's what's killing her now. That she can't — "

"Right. So I want to talk to her in private. Away from the kids, that is. Any chance of setting it up quick?"

"Well, the kids have tickets for a Palladium show tonight, so they'll be lining up for it around noon. And Mama can be home from church around then if I phone her to. That leaves the rest of the day there for any private talking."

"All right, I'll pick you up at noon," Milano said, then couldn't resist saying, "I won't come upstairs. I know that hall already. I'll just ring from downstairs."

She laughed.

[111]

Yes she did. Just a brief involuntary hoot out of all the misery but an honest laugh nevertheless.

Heavy points there.

Then a thought struck Milano. "I forgot," he said. "You've got Sunday matinee, don't you?"

"No performances today. Maybe none at all any more. Period."

"The show fold just like that?"

"Not exactly. Look, what matters now —— "

"I know," said Milano. There was no indication that she had spotted him taking in her act last night, so what the hell. "But let me try one of my educated guesses. You got fed up with what's-her-name — Tamar — steamrollering the show, so you cut loose about that. And since it's Tamar's ball, she won't let anybody play with it unless you say you're oh so sorry."

There was another of those Christine Bailey silences, then finally: "Were you there last night, Milano?"

"No, I was not. Why?"

"Because I — no, never mind. But you're not a bad guesser. Now let it go at that."

"Sure. Are you going to tell them you're sorry?"

"That's my problem, isn't it? I'll see you around noon."

Smart girl. Woman. Person. Girl. Smart girl, but she was up against a man who had, one hour before, filled a flush against a pat king-high straight on one side and three bullets on the other. Obviously, the Force was with him.

At eleven-thirty, he tucked away two thousand dollars worth of Pacifica's money into his pocket and went down to the garage below the co-op to pick up his Mercedes. A lovely thing — a 450SLC in royal blue — that Maxie Rovinsky kept parked in a special area of the garage among some other regal numbers, including Gracie Mac-fadden's Rolls. On the other hand, the Milano second car, a work-aday Toyota, was relegated to inner darkness. Milano got into the Mercedes, then after some reflection abandoned it for the Toyota. He had the uneasy feeling that rolling up to the lady's door right now in the big one would be making it show-off time. The peacock strut. Material values, something like that, when focus should be concentrated on the suspect in the case, not the private-eye. At least, that was the way Christine might view it.

[112]

Matter of fact, he was warming up to this case of the pain-in-the-ass kid sister and her mysterious wealth. Definitely, if not stealing, then dealing. But it was uncomfortable to think of a wrong number in that family after what he had seen of it and put together about it. And the kid herself under observation hadn't showed any signs of street smarts at all. And why, since she was obviously living right under the money tree, would she take on even a few hours a week boring work next door for pennies?

Annoying.

As it happened, when Christine got into the car she had no comment to make about it. Or about anything. Just hunched down as if afflicted with an inner chill and kept her thoughts to herself. Milano let it go at that until they were well on their way, then remarked, "*Two Stops Before The End Of The Line.*"

"What?"

"The play. Will they really fold it?"

"Maybe. Or get someone to replace me. It's up in the air for the next few days. And I'm not being asked to say I'm sorry. The last from Tamar was that it's her or me. Simple. One or the other. So if it reopens, I guess it'll reopen without me."

"I see. How much has it been costing to carry it?"

"Oh, four, five hundred a week. Good weeks."

"All from Tamar's daddy?"

"She's his great big golden girl," said Christine. A little acid there.

"And," said Milano, working through this very carefully, "this playwright — this Pearl — and your director don't like the set-up any more than you do, but that's the way it has to be, right?"

Christine looked at him suspiciously. "What about it?"

"Good question. Because I'd like to buy into that show. Say, a couple of thousand to start with. That's four or five weeks' worth. If it builds at all, more to come. Of course, Tamar's daddy is out. Possibly Tamar too, if she doesn't know what's good for her." He slapped his pocket. "The investment is right here waiting."

"Forget it."

"Jesus," said Milano, "there's a knee-jerk negative if I ever heard one. Now consider. When I told you what I thought about that production —"

"You didn't incite any mutiny, Milano. All you did was say out

[113]

loud what's been bothering me since first rehearsal. You don't owe me anything for what happened."

No question, she did have some good moves.

"All right," Milano said, "look at it this way. The show might fold. I think it should keep running. What's wrong with me backing my judgment with cash?"

"Because I'll handle my end of our trade-off without your cash. Look, man, you suddenly start to bankroll this production now, nobody'll have to wonder why. They'll know fucking well I must be putting out for you. I wouldn't even try to tell them they're wrong, that's how useless it would be. And I don't want to live with those opinions. Simple?"

"Maybe not," said Milano. "Suppose it was some black money-man from Harlem or Bed-Stuy who told you he wanted to bankroll that production? Could you live with that?"

No answer. Not until two blocks and one red light later when Christine said, "Believe me, Milano, if I give you an honest answer to that one, you won't like it."

Milano couldn't quite throttle rising temper. "You mind if I tell you I'm getting a little weary of this racist comedy bit? Black, white, and everything in between?"

"Do you mind if I tell you I've got twenty-three years head start on you in that?" said Christine.

Another one of those deft moves for which the heartfelt and proper response would be a swift boot in the tail.

Then think what a case the NAACP could bring to court.

Despite the assurance that Lorena's mama kept close tabs on her, Milano wasn't surprised to find that the tabs weren't as close as advertised. But the essentials were there. Lorena left for school every morning at eight-thirty, and she was doing all right in school. She had to be home in the house — no fooling around on those steps out there neither — every night at eleven sharp, same as it had been with Christine and the boys in their turn, and she didn't give much trouble about that. Not too much.

And yes, there was a classroom schedule pasted right in front of Lorena's school copybook. Milano, borrowing a sheet of Lorena's looseleaf paper, made his own copy of the schedule while mama dredged up a residue of essentials along with some interesting non-essentials. Lorena ate supper mostly with the family. In fact she had to get that supper on the stove when her mama had late days doing domestic. Sometimes she ate out with girl friends at one of them Chinee or maybe Jamaica beef-patty places on Flatbush Avenue and Lord knows what junk she was stuffing into herself then.

No, for all the child told about a Jimmy who bought her things, there was never any sign of any such Jimmy. Try to pin her down about it, she'd get real tensed up. Threaten to just take off and never show up again. She could do it too. Done it twice already. Now with all this money on her she could do it even easier. Her daddy's spoiled baby until he died, always Miss Uppity once she got over the hurt of his dying.

Not that Christine there had been any little woolly lamb.

"Man's not asking about me, Mama," said Christine. "I am not the one giving you that high blood pressure. You just tell him what you can about Lorena."

What else was there to tell? Oh yes, Monday and Wednesday and Friday she did an hour's work for old Doctor Kirwan next door. Landlord here, but lived in the old family home there.

"Doctor?" said Milano.

"Ph.D.," Christine said. "Doctor Charles Kirwan. Used to teach over at Borough College. Retired now."

"A nice man," said Mrs. Bailey. "Real nice."

"Mama," Christine said, "he is a cheap son of a bitch. You look what's happening to this building. He's too cheap to even have a super in here any more. And then you look at that great big fancy place of his next door and see what your rent money goes into."

"Man's got troubles," said Mrs. Bailey uncowed. "Sick old man. Got misery in every bone. And the way that Miz Florence died so hard——"

"God damn," Christine said loudly, "it was not Miz Florence! It was Mrs. Kirwan! You don't have to come on like Butterfly McQueen just because you ran and fetched for her all those years cut-rate!"

"Don't you curse like that, Christine, 'specially Sunday. And that old man's got nothing now except that house. Family's all gone, friends don't show up. You curse like that, it'll happen to you some day, girl."

"Anyhow," said Milano the peacemaker, "that means Lorena'll go next door from school tomorrow. About what time?"

"Half past three," said Mrs. Bailey. "Home first to get neatened up, then over there till four-thirty."

"She seems to like him," Milano said. "Otherwise, why would she put in any working time for him, what with all that other money she's got?"

"Because he is a nice old man," said Mrs. Bailey. "You listen to Christine about this one and that one, you are listening to the lemon juice lady."

Christine leaned back in her chair, closed her eyes, and growled deep in her throat.

Milano hated to cut this short, but there was the domino effect to move on. Lorena Bailey, Wim Rammaert, Pacifica, and at the end of the effect about a quarter of a million dollars. "Can I use your phone?" he asked.

"In the bedroom," said Mrs. Bailey. "The one that side of the hall."

The ladies' bedroom it was, providing a view through its open window of the landlord's domain across the courtyard, the windows of the tower close curtained. At least a dozen rooms in that building and one sick old man rattling around in their emptiness.

He dialed Shirley Glass's home number.

"Johnny," she said, "no office today. Please. I've got the whole family here."

"You can handle this from home. I need somebody on a sur- veillance first thing tomorrow morning. Somebody"—he lowered his voice—"black, you what what I mean?"

"There's Lee Meecham."

"Too old. I need somebody young. I seem to remember somebody like that around the office. Chunky kid with the earring. Is he just clerical or does he know his way around?"

"DeLong Heywood. He knows his way around."

"And another one, same age, same caliber," Milano said. "Not much travel, but it'll be double shift for a couple of days."

"Same color?" asked Shirley.

"Same."

"No other men, Johnny. But I've got a girl in the steno pool who's itching to get into investigation. Gracella Smith. Smart, twenty-six, could pass for maybe eighteen. But you know Willie."

"Never mind Willie. And a female is even better. Just get those two together and have them meet me eight a.m. at the Church Avenue station of the D train. I'll be outside there. Got that?"

"Yes. Charge to Pacifica?"

"What did you think?"

"I think that if I tell Willie it's Pacifica he'll buy anything right now. That Grassie — the one who owns those paintings — called him personally Friday and gave him the needle about them. Also let him know the San Francisco P.D. is convinced the paintings are going through New York like some others did from a museum burglary out there last year. And if the New York police — "

"Not to knock the New York police, beautiful, but we're still a long way ahead of them at this reading. But let Willie sweat it out. It'll do him good."

"But not me." Shirley's tone changed. "Johnny, there's one other thing. You mind? Helen Monahan."

Ah yes. Monahan, the sad, toadlike secretary lately canned. "What about her?" Milano said cautiously.

"She thought she could get office temporary jobs a few hours a day, but she can't. And she can't leave her husband alone all day, he's that helpless now. So if you could line up somebody who needed occasional help — "

"Line up who? Look, Shirl, there's all kinds of social welfare programs we're paying taxes for."

"Johnny — "

"All right, all right. What you do is draw another three thousand Pacifica expense money for me and give it to her. Just tell her not to make the mistake of thanking Willie for it."

"Johnny, you are one hell of a nice guy, and I — oh, gee, I almost forgot again. Your birthday last week. What with all — "

"Never mind my birthday," Milano cut in. "Now get this part. You might — "

Blink

Blink

A flash of light from the second-story window of that tower across the way. The briefest dazzle of reflected sunlight followed almost instantaneously by another dazzle of reflected sunlight. Then nothing. The curtain there was closed, but it seemed to be still in motion, settling down.

"Johnny?" said Shirley Glass.

"Yeah. Sorry. Anyhow, you might be getting a follow-up call from Erasmus High about a Lorena Bailey this week, and I — "

"Another Bailey?"

"The kid sister. And I want you to cover my cover. She's being considered as an applicant to the Watrous Associates summer training program for deserving youth. I'm in charge of the program. That's all you need. And, Shirl, just make sure your Heywood and Smith team get to church on time tomorrow morning."

He put down the phone, squinted at the tower window.

Binoculars? He looked around the bedroom. Lighting not too good but sufficient. Lorena there by the window, mama here, going by these pill bottles on the night table. Not long ago most likely, Christine had used that bed by the window and mama had the privilege of a sleeper in the living room.

Milano went back to the living room. Something had gone on between the ladies, because mama now looked weary and Christine looked on the edge of distrait. Vulnerable. First time she had exposed that side of herself. She looked very appealing vulnerable.

Milano said, "I've just arranged for the kid to be under surveillance full-time for a couple of days. Maybe more if it's necessary. And you two'll have to back this up by being smart about it. Meaning you won't tip Lorena off in any way. Understood?"

"Yes," said Christine, and looked at her mother who nodded woefully.

"One more thing," said Milano. "I want you to let her know that you asked me about office work for her next summer. Like in a summer training program for youngsters my company runs."

Christine frowned. "Why that?"

"Oh, let's say it's to add verisimilitude to an otherwise bald and unconvincing narrative."

"Lend verisimilitude," Christine corrected mechanically, and

[118]

when Milano gave her a split-second double-take she said, "Yeah, I played in *The Mikado*. Slant-eyed was easy. Never got a chance at Ophelia though."

Vulnerable certainly didn't last long with her.

String along with this one long enough, Milano advised himself, and you'll wind up picketing something.

He said, "Anyhow, just tell her that. Now there's a couple of things I'd like to know about your landlord. Does he make a habit of checking out his tenants through a pair of binoculars?"

"Binoculars?" said Christine.

"Field glasses." Milano mimed them sweeping the room.

Mrs. Bailey looked shocked. "I never see any such thing. And Christine never see it either else she would have told me." She turned to her daughter. "Wouldn't you?"

"I guess," said Christine. She said to Milano, "You catch him at it?"

"Maybe, but I couldn't swear to it. Meanwhile, there's one other item. You work there, Mrs. Bailey, don't you?"

"Tuesday every week. Do what I can. He's neat as a pin, that man, so it's mostly just dusting and bathroom and kitchen."

"Whatever. But all the time you've known him, did you ever get the impression he keeps a lot of money around? Right there in the house?"

"In the house? No——" Mrs. Bailey's eyes opened wide. "You think maybe Lorena——"

"Stealing from him?" said Christine unbelievingly.

"I didn't say that," Milano protested.

"Oh, don't play dumb, Milano. The way you put it—what else were you getting at?"

"Well, the thin chance. She's working for him right there and might have the run of the house. He comes on eccentric. It's something to think about."

"The way he is about money?" said Christine. "He is so tacky cheap he'd know if a nickel was missing. Much less a couple of hundred dollars every week."

"All right," said Milano, "I asked, you answered." He glanced at his watch without noting the time. "Can I give you a lift back to the city?"

She hesitated. "No, now that I'm here I guess I'll stay awhile."

You didn't push at a moment like this. And both she and her mother looked like they could use some of each other's company for awhile.

"I'll keep in touch," Milano said. "And remember you go on the job tomorrow."

"Yes." She sounded vague, her thoughts on their own track.

"Boudin," he reminded her. "Eugéne Louis Boudin. Remember?"

"Oh yes. Sure." She opened the door for him. "And thanks for everything. I guess."

He stopped at the almost deserted office on the way home and hunted through Shirley's desk until he came up with a job application form. He typed Lorena Bailey's name, address, and school on this and under *Nature of Employment* put down *Special Youth Training Summer Program*. Looked good and, when he read it aloud, sounded good. He folded it into a company envelope, but on second thought removed it and stamped it *Confidential* in bright red warning. With that and a couple of the company's embossed business cards, the jokers imprinted *Watrous Associates, Research Consultants*, he was in business.

Monday morning, the team of Heywood and Smith beat him to the draw and were already waiting outside the Church Avenue station when he pulled up in the Toyota. DeLong Heywood, moonfaced, chunky, solemn and still sporting that single gold earring, was identifiable at sight. Gracella Smith, small, skinny, totally unpretty, had a pert, sharp-eyed quality and the wound-up look of a sprinter just waiting to get her feet against the starting blocks.

Milano gave Heywood the copy of Lorena's classroom schedule and laid down the ground rules. Close surveillance from the time the subject left her home until she was in it for the night, probably around eleven. That meant inside and outside the school — Erasmus — and if there was security trouble at the gate, head right for the principal's office and come on as an investigator for Watrous Associates, checking out a job candidate. If no security trouble, save that visit to the office for afternoon. Trick there was to pump all sources for whatever could be brought up on the subject. And "confidential" was the key word to use on school staff. Confidential. Lower the voice when you speak the sacred word. Any questions?

"Yeah," DeLong said. "We looking for something special along the way?"

"Selling maybe. Anything from grass on up." Milano nodded at Gracella. "That makes the girls' toilet your territory any time the kid walks into it. No problem inside the building as long as you both stay inconspicuous during classes. Outside the building you figure it out. I mean when and where you team together or just cover for each other." He handed DeLong his own card. "Midnight tonight you phone me a detailed report at that number. Now hop in the car and I'll finger the subject for you."

"Oh my," said the perky Gracella. "Finger the subject. Real private-eye talk, man."

They caught the subject coming out of her apartment building, tracked her along Bedford to Church Avenue where Milano pulled up and let his passengers out. "Remember," he told DeLong, "a detailed report. You got your little notebook?"

DeLong slapped his pocket. "Big one," he said.

But when it came, the midnight report made it plain that a little one would have done. No security problems for the team in school or out. No signs of Lorena selling, buying, or trading. Company she kept, matter of fact, seemed kind of straight arrow. Also, assistant principal put the team on to her counselor regarding that job application, and it seemed Lorena, aside from occasional fits of big mouth and hot temper, had a fair scholastic record.

"Where'd she go after school?" Milano asked.

Delong seemed to be flipping notebook pages at the other end of the line. "That big house next door to her place. Three-thirty to four-twenty. Then back to her own place."

Milano thought it over. "All right, you two pick it up again tomorrow. And report to me same time tomorrow night. By the way, how'd Gracella make out?"

"Sharp chick," said DeLong. "But she says her legs hurt."

"Professional pains," said Milano.

He got a busy signal the first two times he dialed Christine, and then to teach her a lesson she wouldn't even know she was being taught he angrily piped in a promising film on the WHT channel — nudity and vulgar language — and while the language was certainly vulgar, although not down to Gracie MacFadden's level, the nudity, mistily poetic, appeared to be shot through a bath towel. Milano shut off the set as soon as the phone rang.

"What happened?" Christine asked without preface. "Did you find out anything?"

"No," said Milano, "but it's only one day. We'll take another crack at it tomorrow."

"You sure she didn't know she was being followed?"

"I'm sure. Why?"

"Because Mama just phoned to say Lorena was really in a mood tonight. Way down. Not a word. Just sat around hating everybody."

"I thought that was standard procedure for teen-agers."

"Sometimes. But this time she got around to locking herself in the bathroom for a couple of hours and wouldn't answer anybody until my brother busted the door in. Then she tried to take his eyes out. That's a lot more than standard procedure."

"Could be. Did you tell her about her name being put in for a summer job at my place?"

"My mother did."

"Then even if somebody in school tipped her off she was being investigated, that would cover it. And I don't believe anybody did tip her off or she would have laid that on you. No reason for her not to."

From the sound of it, Christine was blowing a long slow breath into the mouthpiece. She finally said, "I guess not."

"So there we are. And tomorrow's another day. That is, today's another day. Meanwhile, were you able to move on those paintings at all?"

"Yes. There are a couple of packing crates in the office, some in the storeroom. But no West Coast labels. I'm also going through the

files on that list of names you gave me. That'll take a little while. I
don't like to be at those files every time Rammaert or his wife walks
in."

"Smart," said Milano.

"Sure, man," said Christine. "We're both smart. Only a fifteen-
year-old kid comes up even smarter."

# Charles Witter Kirwan

Our Mrs. Bailey has just left.

Aunt Jemima. With just a touch of larceny.

Done her work. Collected her pay. Departed.

Confusing.

Not Wednesday. I've been living Wednesday in my mind these past few hours, but it is not Wednesday, because Mrs. Bailey comes on Tuesdays.

Tuesday.

Definitely Tuesday.

Strange. But understandable. The tolerance for Percodan increases. An excess of Percodan fortified by wine and you may lose a few hours. An error easily corrected, the mind in this case hardly the ordinary instrument.

Meanwhile, the pain is held in abeyance. Knocking at the door but can't come in. And that spasmodic, gut wrenching cough is held in abeyance. I sense the rising of it, brace myself against it, but no cough.

A bad sign? Nothing left of the lungs now but a mass of putrefaction? Time running out too fast, trying to cheat me — cheat the world — of the grand event? No. I'm on schedule. The second charge was planted this morning in the dumbwaiter shaft of 409. Two out of eight. Agonizingly tedious and difficult work. I watched my hands at it. Braced up there in that filth-ridden stinking dimness, the cockroaches nauseating me as they scurried close to my face, I watched my fingers and wondered why they were so slow and clumsy. A stranger's fingers. A roach ran along the taped sticks of dynamite, was almost on my fingers before I shook it off.

Roaches. If one believed in the transmigration of the Bulanga soul, it would explain that multitude of roaches.

Where

Oh yes, Mrs. Bailey. Today.

I let her in to do her work as I was on my way out to 409 to attend to mine. I said to her, "More repairs next door." She clucked her tongue. Just clucked. Fat black hen who lays eggs for gentlemen. Cluck, cluck. Ordinarily she would comment at length, given that opening. Shame about that old building, Dr. Kirwan. Shame you have to do all that fussin' with it. Use up what strength you got. Given any opening, talk and talk.

Not this time. Furtive. I could meet her eye boldly, she couldn't seem to meet mine. It should have been the other way around. It wasn't.

And on my return from my job storing up the grapes of wrath, the same. Furtive. Avoiding me. Applying herself passionately to the vacuum cleaner and mop and dust cloth. Paid her due, mumbled something, waddled off.

Lorena's secret out? Hardly.

Her brothers in some trouble? Odell? Vern? From my view of them, no.

Christine? Showing up so often lately? Possibly. Lost her job?

[125]

Pregnant? Making arrangements for a new little Bulanga to be delivered—as happens with so many new little Bulangas in 409— into grandma's care when the time comes?

Possibly Christine. Christine has affectations. Nose in the air. An actress. The Bulanga answer to Katherine Cornell. When she made application to the High School for Performing Arts I wrote straight-faced a stirring recommendation of her. Fine girl. Noble character. Yes. And now? Don' act all that much, Dr. Kirwan, but she got herself a good steady job at a place downtown sells them fancy pictures. Painted pictures. Says folks pay real big money for one of them pictures. Sometimes five, ten thousand dollars, you believe that?

Affectations, yes, but Christine is pure Bulanga. Could have been unloaded from the slave-ship yesterday, stood naked on that platform down there in tobacco-land, hands chained behind her. House stuff, while the lady of the plantation simmered.

Yes.

Possibly Christine is the

But not Lorena. Nothing about Lorena from her mother. No charges. No policemen at the door. Lorena knows her place now. House stuff. Bed stuff.

Oh yes.

Yesterday I was already in my robe when she arrived. She stood in the doorway and looked. Lost heart. "Just wanna tell you I'm not comin' in today. Don' feel good."

Oh ho.

"Don't be stupid, Lorena. Your money's waiting."

She hesitated. I motioned her in. She came in.

No improvisation this time. A bed, not a battered old swivel chair. Her clothes on, mine off. On my back, hands clasped under my head, her mouth the milking machine. No mercy this time, no warning. Hard work dispelling a numbness in the organ, then I came when I had to into the milking machine.

She squawked and gagged and fluttered. Into the bathroom full-tilt noisily making repairs. Came back, her expression making plain that she had just ingested a mouthful of lemon juice. The out-stretched hand took the money I had waiting under my pillow.

[126]

For the first time she didn't even count it. Just went.
She

A hiatus.
Forgivable under the circumstances.
I was under the misapprehension that my supply of Percodan was sufficient, but it must have been a bad weekend. While I was speaking into this machine the pain broke through. Bad. Very bad. And I found very few of those tablets rattling around in the bottom of the bottle.
So
Not to digress, do you know what a controlled substance is?
A controlled substance is any substance which our benign, libertarian government — Big Brother — thinks may do us harm.
And since every substance under creation may do us harm under certain circumstances, Big Brother has a lot to play with. To control. To protect all his infantile little brothers and sisters from.
A drug which may even briefly ease the pains of a dying human being must of necessity be a controlled substance, God forbid that anyone ever be allowed to die in peace.
Controlled.
Legally allowed this moribund specimen in just sufficient amount so that he may barely survive the pain.
Controlled.
I will now
Yes.
I will now put on the record information of special interest to the authorities. Big Brother's eager beavers. I will preface it by stating as a fact that the owner of the pharmacy in question, Irving Saphir, Nostrand Avenue, has no part in this matter. No knowledge of it. More Jew-cowardly than Jew-greedy he was openly alarmed when I suggested he augment the meager amount of Percodan allowed me by prescription.
This, after I had dealt with him for more than twenty years.
Now forget him. Forget the name.
The name of significance is Jennings. Whether that is his given name or family name I don't know.

[127]

Jennings.

He replaces his employer at five-thirty, keeping the shop open until midnight. All other local pharmacies close at five or six, so there is evening trade to be had.

Jennings is a Bulanga educated beyond his station, as the fine old phrase goes, and ready to take advantage of that. He heard me discuss my problem with Saphir, and that evening phoned me to meet him at closing time, because he might have a solution to the problem. I suspected from his tone during the call, from the heavy-handed humor and broad innuendo of his language, what he was getting at, and of course I was right. He could supply my needs for a price. The source of supply was his own. It had nothing to do with any of the shop's wholesalers.

Big Brother controls. Jennings decontrols.

The price? Three hundred dollars for one hundred tablets the first time I dealt with him. It was four hundred dollars the second time. Cash. I have just now, within the hour, met friend Jennings at the shop's closing time and paid him five hundred dollars cash for his merchandise. A seller's market, and this canny Bulanga knows it.

A formidable-looking creature, a cur in a lion's hide, our friend. He wears the mask so many of our Bulanga tribesmen in these parts favor.

The mask. Not the ancestral colored mud and the bone through the nostrils. Now it's composed of a fierce beard and mustache, a towering shock of untrimmed frizzy hair, menacing dark glasses. Or instead of that haystack of hair, there may be oiled and braided locks of it draped around the face and head. Dreadlocks, the Bulanga call them.

Clever word. Clever disguise for a cur. Pass it in the street and shrink from it involuntarily. Strip it away and there is the cur under the lion's mane.

Secure only in packs, these tribesmen. Their youth jeeringly brave only in packs. Over the centuries, sold cheap by their own brave chiefs in Bulangaland.

Five hundred dollars. One hundred pills.

The residue of my cash goes fast.

Household expenses minimal, but Lorena. And Jennings.

Time is on my side, of course. And sufficient unto the day is the cost thereof.

Yes.

If I could place the dynamite charges each day, only six more days would be needed. Too much effort that way though. My store of energy must determine my schedule. Use energy near dinnertime to climb three flights of stairs in 409 to repair a badly abused refrigerator, and I am cheated out of that much strength tomorrow.

Yes.

Well

The mask.

The image of it seems stuck in my mind now. Good. Determination may lag under physical weakness; that image fortifies it with hatred. All those masks blown apart at the instant of the grand event. All those dark glasses blown away, the eyesockets emptied by concussion. All those whining, yelping, howling curs dead.

That mask suddenly appeared on campus, courtesy of our city's Open Admissions policy. Open Admissions. If the applicant's pulse could be detected, he was welcome to share in higher education at public expense. Somewhere along the way might even learn to read and write. But the natives grew restless in their futile pursuit of the diploma, that magic piece of paper. The Bulanga rose. The intellectual demands were too great; ease up on them demands for readin' and writing' and 'rithmetic, whitey.

The masks suddenly appeared on those old enough to cultivate facial hair and fierce scowls. Well-feigned anger. Fire and sword. The citadel was taken. Easily taken. It had been a distinguished institution in its own curious, mass-production fashion. It became a bad joke overnight, fountainhead of hypocrisy, the liberal's delight.

It was

I was

Yes, I will say it here and now. I, Charles Witter Kirwan, apparently fearless in military combat — under Lieutenant-Colonel Willis Crittenberger of the IV Corps through the Italian campaign — I who managed to play the brave company commander through that horror became a coward, a liar, a dissembler in the face of a moral

[129]

issue. Knew hatred, had every good reason for it, and didn't have the guts to stand up and proclaim it.

Overwhelmed by my liberal colleagues who, in the privacy of their locked bedrooms, must have cursed the day while they publicly rejoiced in it. I could not believe — I still cannot believe — that in their secret hearts they yearned for that mad degradation of all standards. It had to be opportunism, that pedagogical disease, a yielding to the political tide, a readiness to yield all issues rather than have our buildings leveled by the invading Bulanga.

The liberals who finally saw the consequences of their political folly must have shuddered at it. I, who could have predicted those consequences, stood with those betrayers as their ally. A greater coward than any because so much less a fool.

In the end, early retirement. This one and that one and the other one. And myself.

*Sauve qui peut.*

Well.

Refuge elsewhere? A job elsewhere? Too late. Retirement was almost due anyhow. And my college

Very much my college. I entered it while it was still only a fresh addition to the city's free system, was still without its own identity. I obtained one of its rare fellowships five years later in the depths of the Depression. I have served it all my working life. Home, sweet home.

Except for those years in the military.

But

In my youth I was intended for very private Princeton, not any public institution. My grandfather was Princeton. My father was Princeton. My grandfather with honors, my father spasmodically brilliant.

Then, as the silent movie captions would have put it, came the crash. October, 1929. And all the king's horses and all the king's men couldn't put together my grandfather's portfolio again.

His in name.

Dapper Dan Kirwan's in spirit. My high-flying stepfather with one trophy already in hand. Four-oh-nine Witter Street. Money coming from it as proof of his sagacity. Be smart, Hendrick, the stock market's going right through the ceiling. Get in now. Never

mind that Witter and Son is barely turning a profit. Up up up.
Ninety percent margin. Get in now now now.

Crash.

Acceptance from Princeton in hand, I entered college in September 1930 and it wasn't Princeton. It was Makeshift College, far from Princeton Junction, New Jersey.

But in time it did find an identity and — yes — a distinction. Yes. And I will say it myself, I served it well as those years. Served it very well.

And, in the end, betrayed it, betrayed myself, betrayed all decency. Kissed those plump liberal asses. Sat silent in the face of Open Admissions. More than that, manufactured excuses for it.

Did not even exercise the instincts of those geese who cackled a warning to the Romans that the barbarians with torch and sword were moving in to sack their city.

Utter betrayal.

And now, absolute atonement.

# John Milano

Two swings of the bat, two strikes. When DeLong Heywood, a sobersided lad never mind that golden earring, made his midnight call it was to report that the Tuesday Lorena was as pristine as the Monday Lorena.

"No action at all?" Milano asked.

"None. I got the notes here covers her from school right through to lights out. Want a run-through?"

"Not now." Notes droned over the phone drew no picture in depth. "Tomorrow morning you and Gracella meet me for breakfast that place across from the office. Eight sharp."

"No more Lorena?"

"Not tomorrow," Milano said. "After that we'll see."

He got Christine first ring of the phone, and she took the news—or absence of it—dispiritedly. "Good one way, bad the other," she said. "I guess the question is how bad."

"We could know more after I meet with the troops in the morning. Meanwhile, how about Eugene Louis Boudin?"

"Oh, yes. That. I started checking through the files with that list of names you gave me, and so far nothing. But if it's crates you want, Milano, we just got some great big ones in the gallery."

"Only great big ones?"

"Four of them, all big. You said those Boudins went fourteen by seven inches; these things look more like fourteen by seven feet. And no West Coast. All Miami."

"You mean Archbold's being replaced by some new non-talent?"

"A Raoul Barquin. From Cuba, now lives in Miami. Rammaert's very high on him."

Barquin. Milano ran through the mental index and drew a blank. "Never heard of him."

"This is his first major show. Anyhow, Archbold comes down tomorrow, and Barquin goes up. Opening's Saturday."

"I see. Now how about telling me all about it at lunch tomorrow? Some place out of the boss's range?"

"No way." It was decisive, but not hostile. "Tomorrow's picture-hanging time right through."

Since it had been decisive but not hostile Milano took his chances. "Dinner?"

"Well—"

"I could have more on Lorena. And you might be able to offer more on her too."

"Man, that is clumsy of you, that approach."

"Pathetic. I know. Dinner? I'll be outside the shop in the car any time you name."

"It'll be overtime tomorrow—that's really today, isn't it?—so you can make it about seven o'clock. And just dinner, Milano. Got that? Steak and potatoes and good night, that's the program. Read me?"

"Loud and clear," said Milano cheerfully.

The good news Wednesday wake-up time was that there was suddenly slack in the waistband of his trousers, at least enough room for a couple of thumbs inserted in it to wiggle freely. The full-length profile in the mirror still didn't show concave, but it was definitely no longer convex. Straight up and down was how it read right now, even without straining to suck in the gut.

The bad news was that when, full of self-congratulation, he joined the stolid DeLong Heywood and the pert Gracella Smith at the breakfast table in Sudie's coffee shop across from the office he found he was in the company of a pair of World Class eaters. Bacon, eggs, and toast for openers; double order of wheatcakes, heavy on the syrup, as an entree. Milano, single scrambled and black coffee, sustained himself with the hope that sooner or later in their young lives both his guests would wind up permanently bloated beyond recognition. DeLong already suggested a metabolism in that direction. Gracella, however, maybe a hundred pounds soaking wet, had the look of one of those blessed who turned every calorie into instant energy.

They went through DeLong's notes of yesterday, Gracella adding footnotes. He was exact and methodical, she was sharp-eyed and perceptive. A good team, Milano saw. For instance, it was Gracella who had gotten to the home-room teacher — strictly confidential, you know — and put together the picture of a change in Lorena lately. Last few weeks that is. Had been sociable, talkative, even if hot-tempered and with a tendency to flare up at teachers she felt were putting her down. Now in her classes she was withdrawn, uncommunicative. The silent one.

"And outside classes?" Milano asked.

"Well," said Gracella, "pretty much the same. At least that's how she came on yesterday. Steered clear of everybody. The action boys — older stuff, you know — they go for her all right, but she sure don't go for them. Across the street — you know in front of that church there — one of them kind of put an arm around her, and, man, she reacted like a big snake dropped out of a tree on her. I mean she really landed on that dude. Landed that hand across his face as hard as she could."

"Really shook him up," said DeLong. He sounded as if he disapproved. "What do you expect? She walks around waving that butt at people —— "

"Fact," said Gracella. "But the way she turned off, that was the weird thing. I mean, too much of a turn-off."

Milano said, "Anybody at all she seemed close to?"

"Not yesterday," said DeLong. "School, then straight home alone. Into the house and stayed in."

So they went back to Monday's input. Monday, the subject's mood had been a little brighter. Socialized with some kids. A couple of the girls walked her up Bedford Avenue to Witter Street where she turned off toward 409. Into the building, then out again and into that big house next door. Out of there at four-fifteen and back home for keeps.

"A loner," said Milano.

"But didn't used to be," Gracella reminded him. "That homeroom teacher said she used to be kind of a ringmaster for that circus there. You know, watching her I had a thought."

"Yes?"

"Pregnant. Doesn't show yet, but there's that look about her, you know? I've seen it too much. The whole world on those skinny shoulders. And not letting anybody know why."

And that, thought Milano, was all Christine and her mama needed. But it made painful sense. Knocked up, given abortion money by the stud, and using the money to dress herself up with instead of for the doctor.

Milano's hackles rose. The old intuition.

Doctor.

But hell no. This one was a Ph.D., not an M.D.

Retired Ph. D. A widower living alone.

With binoculars.

Enjoying a Zeiss superview of a bedroom not fifty feet away.

And this was where you cooled it. Gracella had said pregnant, he had thought Peeping Tom, and all of a sudden he was drafting a presentment for the grand jury. But, in fact, he hadn't actually seen binoculars any more than Gracella had seen a bulge in the subject's belly.

He said to Gracella, "When the kid went next door did she

[135]

just open the door there herself? Did she have a key to the place?"

"Didn't have to. She pushed the bell, the man opened the door for her."

"What's he look like? Black or white?"

"White," said DeLong. He flipped through the notebook. "About six foot. Skinny. White hair. Bathrobe."

"Bathrobe?" said Milano.

"That's what it was," said DeLong. "Couldn't get much of a look at him, but it was a bathrobe all right. Kind of tacky-looking, too. Seemed to me he was probably sick in bed and had to get out of it to answer that door."

The bright-eyed Gracella cocked her head at Milano. "Seem like more than that to you?"

He dissembled. "No reason why he has to dress up for his hired help. But he is the only one we know so far who's a connection between the kid and any cash money." He turned to DeLong. "So now we do a little fishing. This subject's name is Charles Kirwan, Ph.D. Used to teach at Borough College. Retired a few years ago."

DeLong was scribbling in his notebook. "Backtrack him?"

"Start with the college, and handle with kid gloves. They must have a public file of yearbooks, college newspapers, faculty indexes. That could be a couple of day's work right there."

"Am I in on this?" Gracella said.

"Well, this kind of investigation — "

"Research. That's just another word for research, Mr. Milano, sir. And in case you don't know it, I've got a Master's degree from N.Y.U."

The tone was light, but she wasn't putting him on, Milano saw. And experience with touchy Christine warned him not to ask why, with a Master's, she was down there in the steno pool at Watrous Associates. But of course, as his high-achiever sister Angie liked to point out on occasion, he himself had kissed off three years of Fordham to go gumshoeing for a notorious shit like W. Watrous.

Kind of classy gumshoeing, but gumshoeing nevertheless.

So much for all the hard-earned money she had invested in him.

"I think," Milano said to Gracella, "you just got yourself an assignment."

[136]

"Well, all right. And after this one? Any chance of moving over to investigations for good?"

"It's Mr. Watrous who——"

"Oh yeah. I already spoke to him about it. You want to know what he said?"

"I can imagine. So I'll do what I can when the time comes." He cut this off before it got really heavy and said to DeLong, "First thing now, stop off at the office and give Mrs. Glass this stuff so far on Kirwan. Tell her it's a million to one shot, but if there's any P.D. record on him, I want a copy of it."

"Police record?" said Gracella. "You mean the police department'll just hand you over something like that?"

"Not the department," said Milano. "Some dear old friends of Mr. Watrous in the department. You see, he can come in handy now and then."

Seven o'clock, Christine had said. Steak and potatoes. No problem.

He had half a dozen first-class steakhouses on his list; it was just a case of picking the right one for suitable ambiance and maximum impact.

But late afternoon, robustly giving *Vesti la giubba* the full treatment while soaping himself in the shower, Milano began to see problems, all named Christine Bailey. By richly pleasurable examination, most often covert, sometimes unblushingly open, he had, as the song goes, become accustomed to her face. Was even growing accustomed to her charms for that matter, a process which Daniel might have undergone with his feline companions in the lion's den. But it was a vivid image of that face being introduced to the restaurant of choice that stirred uneasiness.

He had the list down to three possibles: Peter Luger, great old-fashioned style under the bridge in Brooklyn; Christ Cella, East Side luxurious; Gallagher's, Broadway, but old Broadway. Now the vision of that face, lip curled, had him mentally tripping over the doorstep to each one.

The vision had a way with words too.

*Brooklyn slumming, man? Just so's I can feel at home?*

*East Side de luxe, man? You itching to show all these beautiful Caucasian-type people the black person you are making it with?*

*Fifty-second and Broadway, man? With all those soul-sister hookers outside that window to let me know how lucky I am?*

Ridiculous, for chrissake, to emotionally revert to sideburned, leather-jacketed, New Utrecht High Johnny Milano who, surprisingly accepted by the dazzling Esther Hershkowitz as her Senior Prom date, was then unnerved by the thought that he'd have two thousand years of religious misunderstanding to contend with that night, misunderstanding being the polite word for it.

Really ridiculous for any mature, well-seasoned male to develop adolescent qualms. Next thing he'd be digging through the medicine chest for a tube of Clearasil.

Proving, if nothing else, that it takes a paranoid to make a paranoid. The bottom line? The Bailey person wanted steak, potatoes, and goodbye, and that was what she'd get. A strictly business dinner. No subtle working around to the question of your place or mine. Afterward, let her wonder why.

Which, of course, saved him the trouble of finding a hideout for some-intimate garments of the recent Betty Cronin, now stashed in his dresser. Another case, Betty. Had landed on him with both feet for inadequate cause, given him troubled conscience, and had cut out just like that. No doubt, now forgiven her indiscretions by her doting dad, she was making novenas in Staten Island to shorten the sentence in purgatory.

Milano struck Peter Luger's off the list and, with admiration for his own sensitivity in the matter—Christine in workaday garb might not relish being ushered into high-fashion company without warning—he struck Christ Cella off the list. So Gallagher's it would be.

As it turned out, Christine, in workaday garb and bone-weary from a day's work wrestling with Raoul Barquin's oversized oeuvre, liked the Mercedes, liked the wood-paneled, sporting-life look of Gallagher's, liked her steak and potatoes, and seemed oblivious to the white middle class theater-bound throng around her. She was also amused by her host's having taken her steak-and-potatoes order literally when it was intended as hyperbole, and was openly curious about whether this spread was his treat or was being charged to Mrs. Smith, his rich and vindictive client. When Milano, weighing his response in one second flat, told her it was the client's treat, she said, somewhat deflatingly, that she had certainly hoped as much.

No paranoia at all. Not even later on when Milano wondering about her long-term schedule — hers and his, that is — brought up the question of *Two Stops Before The End Of The Line*.

"Any chance it'll reopen?" he asked. "With you?"

"Not with anybody," Christine said. Bad part was, she went on, that playwright Pearl and director Lenardo had really been reamed by the situation, and to make it worse they were so goddam forgiving to her about it that it made her teeth ache. Getting a little hard to live with these last few days.

"Too bad," said Milano soberly.

The sobriety might have been overdone. Christine gave him a hard look and said warningly, "All the same, that does not mean you now come up with any envelope full of green."

"No envelope. But just talking about acting jobs, there's a lady lives right upstairs from me got heavy theater clout. Off and on Broadway. If I got you two together — "

There went that curled lip. "Somebody I'd know about?"

"Could be. Since you're in the business. Name's Grace Mac-Fadden."

The lip instantly uncurled. "*The* Grace MacFadden? You putting me on, man?"

"Nope. But she'll ask you to call her Gracie."

"And she lives right upstairs from you? Where do you live anyhow, Milano?"

"Right downstairs from Gracie MacFadden."

"Very funny. But you want to know something. I believe you. Man, I do want to believe you. But what's she got to do with casting? She backs shows, Milano, she doesn't produce them."

"It's Johnny."

"All right, it's Johnny. Which does not answer the question."

"Figure it out for yourself. You show a check for a hundred thousand to a producer, and he goes all over friendly. She's no star-maker, Gracie, but she'll get talent a chance at a part. And in case of a tie, she's the tiebreaker. When it comes to casting a musical — "

"Oh?" Christine cut in. She opened her eyes very wide and held both clenched hands up high, forefingers aimed at the ceiling. "You mean like, hey man, it's dat oldtime Harlem again. Just hear dem saxophones and watch dem flyin' feet."

It could be, Milano told himself without conviction, those two Jack Daniels she had put down. "Come on," he said, "you know what I meant."

"I did. You didn't. So I'll enlighten you, man. What you meant was that if I don't sing and I don't shake that thing, I could have career trouble." She rested a dark-skinned hand on the table before him, the fingers finely tapered, the nails cut very short. "See that? Hardly pays to answer any casting calls around Shubert Alley because I just seem to be the wrong shade of blonde."

"You finished?" asked Milano.

"Yes. You pissed off?"

"Yes."

"You'll get over it," said Christine. "And when you do I'd still like to meet that Grace MacFadden."

"Baby, the way you come on——"

"With the understanding," said Christine, "that I do not sing and I do not dance. I just act. And I do not act maids in Art Deco revivals."

"You'll have a chance to tell her that yourself. Meanwhile, if this party's on the expense account, how about switching over to company business? Like Lorena."

"Something turn up since you called?"

"No. But one of my people on her came up with the idea—what with her emotional state and all—that she might be pregnant. How about it?"

"She isn't. We thought about it along the way. Then it turned out a couple of weeks ago she wasn't."

"You're sure?"

"Total sure. Mama's right there on the spot. She got all the evidence she needed. You don't mind me being a little indelicate, Lorena's not the neatest girl in the world when it comes to that kind of evidence. So. Emotional yes, pregnant no. Is she the whole business?"

"Well, there's also that landlord of yours next door. Kirwan."

"Charles Witter Kirwan," said Christine, nicely rounding out each word of it. "He says the street's named after his folks from way back.

Could be." She frowned. "You mean about Lorena stealing that money from him? But I told you I really don't think —— "

"Let me ask the questions. Like, when your mother said she liked him you made it plain you don't. Said he's one of those real crummy tightwad landlords. But is that the only reason?"

"Isn't being a crummy tightwad landlord enough?"

"But your mother does seem to like him."

"Oh yeah. Mama did domestic work for him and his wife a long time. Took care of that woman night and day too, when she was hit with cancer. Real care, the kind you cannot just go out and buy. Now Mama's all teary and grateful about it. You see, Mama's got the idea you should be real grateful to people who let you do favors for them."

"Not all mamas," said Milano.

"Yours?"

"Mean. And comes up a little meaner every day."

"Well, I guess I'll settle for Mama's style over that. And to lean all the way backwards, I'll admit Kirwan isn't so unlikable when it comes to just talking to him. Nice and polite. Keeps the voice down. Makes no waves. Kids around that building could make you crazy, he goes easy on them. And he did give Lorena a break when she needed it."

"How does she get along with him on the job?"

"No complaints. What is it, Johnny? He bother you some way?"

"I don't know. He housebound most of the time?"

"Pretty much, I guess. Except for fussing around our building trying to fix up leaky pipes with Band-Aids. You own what used to be a nice apartment house, you keep it up or give it up, man. You do not put everybody's rent money in your own private, freaky house next door. Fire our super so you can put his pay into landscape gardeners all over your place. That is really shoving it up."

"Kind of an interesting old house though."

"Freaky. And one old man living all alone in a place like that. But it does make him king of the shitpile, doesn't it?"

"Depends," said Milano. "Suppose I wanted to drop in on him? Talk about my interest in his beat-up property next door. How do you think he'd take it?"

"I told you he's got his all-right side." Christine frowned. "What's on your mind, Johnny?"

[141]

"Oh, eccentric neighbors for one thing. Mixed-up kids like Lorena for another. Isn't your mother ever tempted to just take that kid over her knee and use a strap on her until she comes up with the truth? I mean about what the hell she is up to?"

"Sure. And so am I. And so are Odell and Vern who are a very square set of big brothers. But Lorena's not lying about turning runaway again if she gets leaned on too hard, so we are all her hostages right now. And she knows it."

"Which," said Milano, "makes her sound like a winner. But she's not coming on like a winner. I think that kid is unhappy as hell about whatever she's got herself into. There's a good chance that if you all got together and had a real confrontation with her — crisis time, no way out — she'd be glad to get it out of her system."

Christine shook her head. "She has got a very stiff backbone, my little sister. And a lot of money somehow. We try any real hard line with her, and next day you could have a job hunting her up somewhere between here and California. Are you volunteering for that?"

"Well, I'm not your natural-born volunteering type."

"Except sometimes," Christine said pointedly. "Seems to me you just volunteered to have me meet a friend of yours."

"Gracie MacFadden. Right."

"Glad you didn't forget. So now it's just a question of when, isn't it?"

Actress, thought Milano. Black. Woman's lib. Actress.

Put 'em all together, and they spelled complications to make the mind reel. It brought to mind that old porcupine joke. How do you make love to a porcupine? Very carefully.

Milano said very carefully, "I'll get you together with Gracie as soon as possible. Meanwhile, since we now seem to have finished dining, and it's only nine o'clock — "

"Home," said Christine, rattling her quills prettily. "Big day tomorrow getting Mr. Raoul Barquin's pictures on the wall. So you just drop me off home now, and I'll say thank you for a very nice evening. Which it was."

True.

At least, what there had been of it.

# Charles Witter Kirwan

I HAD IT ON THE TIP OF MY TONGUE.

That word. That word. That

Ah yes. *Todessüchtigkeit*.

German. Compact and potent.

*Todessüchtigkeit*.

A yearning for death.

The last agonizing breath exhaled. The eyes blind. The ears deaf.

Peace forevermore.

My wife knew that. Poor creature who managed to whisper in her final throes: "The only good medicine. Sleep, and never wake up."

Consolation for me? Consolation for herself? Either way, the truth.

[143]

My grandfather
Hendrick Witter, born 1857, died 1951.

My grandfather knew that truth. Rejected the savagery of Calvinism, his heritage. A gnome at the end. Shrunken down. Passages of senility. But so often clear-eyed, clear-headed. Believed that the mind was the soul, the light, the meaning. When the mind ceased nothing was left. Meat. Feed it to the dogs. Would do them good, would do the dead no harm.

Tough-minded. Obsessive. Amateur historians are always obsessive. Evangelists of information retrieval. Tough-minded, obsessive old man. Made me a historian. Made me believe I was born to be a historian. Student of—instructor in—mankind's endless record of self-destruction. Over and over, the lesson never learnt. Build a fine nest and shit in it. Build a civilization and invite the ignorant, the incapable, the envious outsider to turn it to shit.

Never had the courage to show the old man the stories I wrote. That novel. Half a novel. The rejections came to my mailbox at the college. Half a novel. All about the loud, drunken, greedy Irish invader—Dapper Dan Snopes of Kings County—polluting the Witter nest. Rejected rejected rejected. Half a novel—all the sad truth—scrapped in the garbage can.

The garbage that day. Coffee grounds, orange peels, eggshells, three empty pint bottles of Calvert's. Three bottles, less than a day's ration for Dapper Dan. Loud, reeking, backslapping family optimist. Not afraid of the old man any more. At the dinner table, fat red face with the stubble of red beard flecked with gray. Infertile—childless—and called me son.

Oh yes. I was my grandfather's made-to-order historian, my stepfather's made-to-order son.

So

Thursday.

Thursday?

Yes, now Thursday night. Thursday an empty bedridden day, the price of Wednesday. Yesterday. A triumph yesterday, and a failure. Put together they drained all strength.

For your instruction, my friends, first the triumph.

Yesterday, half my work of setting the explosive charges was completed. One entire dumbwaiter shaft now ready and waiting.

[144]

That means charges were attached to the dumbwaiter doors of both the second floor and the ground floor. Working my way from top to bottom, I attended to the second floor, then discovered I had strength left to attach the charge to the ground floor door as well. Two in one long brutal morning's work, all wired and ready. The basement itself will not be done. The building to be leveled at the ground floor.

Halfway home.

Implosion, remember?

Captain Kirwan, demolitions. Was artillery. Happy in his new job. Artillery pieces crash in the ears, demolition charges crash at a distance. Less deafness, less buzzing in the brain. Good at the job too. Six blockhouses, four rows of Italian slum flats, one church. Shattered Jesus crunching underfoot afterward. The fortunes of war providing cheap symbolism.

Implosion. Inward.

Explosion outward. Guy Fawkes and his merry men prepared for explosion outward with those barrels of gunpowder under the Houses of Parliament. Covert consent of His Holiness to blow those cursed Anglicans all straight to hell. Once served with bloody Alva in the Lowlands, Guy Fawkes. Fanatic R.C. Blow all King James's bloody heretic Protestants to the devil, then ascend to the grateful arms of gentle Jesus and tender Mary.

But explosion outward of Dapper Dan's 409 Witter Street next door could jeopardize this building. Too near. Bricks and mortar like cannon fire through these wooden walls.

Still troublesome.

Yes.

Now listen.

With implosion you create a core of nothing in the heart of the structure. An instantaneous nothing. The base of the supporting walls suddenly become nothing. The walls collapse on this nothing. Rubble heaps high within that perimeter, no damage done outside it.

How best done? Timed discharges. Delicately timed. Each packet of explosive going off in the smallest fraction of a second after the other. Split split-seconds. Length of leads from the detonator help, but not enough. Scaling my dynamite charges from greater to less —

most on the ground floor, least on the top floor — will help, but no assurance of how much.

So

The element of risk is there. Not much, but there. Some masonry flung against these wooden walls here. A Bulanga head rolling across this floor, eyes astonished.

Some risk. A little damage. Depend on Captain Kirwan, sir, to make it very little. And then repaired — flawlessly repaired — with Witter Foundation funds. As good as new.

As good as old.

So

The triumph today. On this day my job half done. And enough left of me to do the other half.

But not enough

Not quite enough any more, my avid, dirty-minded dear friends

So, dear friends, the failure. *In puris naturalibis*, I will tell you about the failure.

Lorena Bailey.

My dutiful Bulanga maiden.

She came to the door on schedule, and robed and ready I admitted her. No instructions needed any more, she followed me to my bedroom. Impassive. No heat in her. One would think there would be some heat in the face of this adventure.

And

None in me. None. A remoteness, a vagueness, a feeling of all muscles turned to jello. Slack. Unrobed, I lay on my back and offered her my slackness. No hands again. Just the mouth.

Dutiful, futile mouth.

Nothing.

Circled lips, closed eyes, furrowed black brow. Nothing. A tickle. Mark Twain said it. The kind of tickle a corpse might feel when electricity is applied to it.

Nothing.

Bulanga spittle wetting the graying pubic hair. Bewildered, impatient, she raised her head and looked at me. Returned to her labors.

Remote, lethargic, I suffered them with growing disgust.

Yes. Disgust.

[146]

A sense of degradation. Bulanga spittle on me. Bulanga spittle on my world. My impotent world.

I said, "That's enough," and she gave up. But worried. "My money?" I gave it to her. I said, "Close the door on your way out. You don't have to bother to come back Friday."

She looked at me. Opaque. Hard to tell what they're thinking. They live by instinct, not intellect. Soul, they call it. Her mother, openfaced, all joviality, wondering where my loose change is kept so that she can steal it.

I said to Lorena, "You heard me, girl." If she was challenging me, that challenge had to be met directly.

She suddenly turned and went down the stairs full-tilt. I waited for the front door to slam shut but it didn't. A warning in that silence Her way of telling me that she's not giving up her profligate income that easily. I will predict now that Friday — tomorrow — she will be here, mouthful of saliva ready.

Mistress of the household, so she thinks.

No matter.

I am the high priest in her life, making her sacrificial altar ready for the grand event.

*Satis verborum.*

# John Milano

THURSDAY'S DAWN WAS LOUD WITH the sound of rain spattering against half-open windows. Hanging on to sleep, eyes closed, Milano crawled out of bed, banged down the windows, and crawled back into bed. Too late. All mental circuits were now tuned in to the persistently recycling images of screwed-up Christine Bailey, her even more screwed-up kid sister, and a pair of magnificent Boudin beach scenes wandering across these United States in search of their destination. By all odds, in search of Mister Hairpiece himself, Wim Rammaert, who, the word having gone out over the grapevine that Watrous Associates was in the mood for a deal, still hadn't showed his hand.

[148]

Peculiar.

But with every shred of evidence pointing straight at Rammaert, he was the go-between for those paintings. Had to be. To reinforce that logic, consider that no other candidate had popped to the surface either, at least none with proper credentials.

Two Boudins.

And binoculars?

Professional landscape gardeners manicuring a lawn on a beatup block in East Flatbush?

Doctor Kirwan, I presume?

Bailey-Bailey-Rammaert-Kirwan. Milano did some calculation and found, surprisingly, that it added up to only twelve days since he had taken on Pacifica's case. He had a feeling he'd gone through a lot more of the calendar than that on the case. And its complications. Of which the most complicated was certainly Christine Bailey, fit subject for a Velasquez. Or a Rubens. A small, highly personal Rubens. Or—

After enough of this mental exercise Milano gave up on any hopes of sleep, switched on the TV to catch a six a.m. zoo show featuring a bevy of immobile Galapagos tortoises, and when it was over padded into the kitchen to finish off a container of cottage cheese, one of a half-dozen he had stored away in the refrigerator as a guilt-free nosh. By now the *Times* and *News* were on the doorstep, and he took them back to bed with him. He fell asleep, the Op-Ed pages of the *Times* across his chest, just in time to be brought wide awake again by the phone.

"Did I wake you up?" asked Betty.

Betty. At seven-ten a.m.

Milano braced himself. "It's all right."

"I'm sorry. But you have that phone-recorder thing, don't you, Johnny? I wish you'd leave it on. I tried on and off all day yesterday to reach you."

The tone was affectionately chiding. Warm, where that last call from her—whenever it had been—registered thirty-two degrees Fahrenheit, zero Celcius. Milano forbore from explaining that during his last year's mutiny against his business partner the message tapes had come up at every reading with some very loud and virulent messages from the partner.

[149]

"That gimmick's out of order," he said. Betty. Neat, sweet, pretty, and always—well, almost always—the soul of amiability. And with a key to the best computer bank east of the Mississippi. And now living proof that absence could at least make the female heart grow fonder. This, considering the inspiring image of ebony Christine Bailey posed against these stark white walls, might make a serious problem. Feeling his way, Milano said politely, "Everything all right?"

"I don't know. Look, I have to see you Johnny. Right away."

"But if you're going to work now——"

"I'm not. I'm taking off today. And I took off yesterday. I moved out of the house yesterday. I'm at the Prince Albert down on Twenty-seventh Street here. That's what I want to get together about."

"I see. You moved out on the family. Permanently?"

"Yes, of course." The tone was a feeble attempt at irony. "After all, how could a fallen woman live with such a pure and holy father? Oh, it's permanent all right."

Jesus. Fallen woman. Staten Island father with a horsewhip. How did Staten Island ever come to be part of New York City in the first place when it was strictly backwoods New Jersey from any angle?

But there was no question that the get-together its most recent emigrant had in mind was supposed to take place right here in this apartment. And that, if not deterred, she'd soon be ringing its doorbell, suitcase in hand and some long-range plans in mind. After all, intimate items of her wardrobe already occupied that bottom dresser drawer.

"I'll be right over," Milano said.

"Well, I thought that——"

"No trouble at all. Right away. Just stand by."

The Prince Albert Hotel down on 27th Street was what anyone with a good architectural eye might weep over in its decay. A big one all right, a massive baroque beauty dating from that era when Herald Square was way uptown. The grime on it seemed to have been accumulating since those days, and, like the yet unopened shops surrounding it, wholesale outlets mostly, the building had a dismal cut-rate look. Steady rain didn't brighten the scene either.

The lobby however was in decent repair and, as evidence of

respectability, the desk clerk phoned Miss Cronin's room before passing along its number. The room itself turned out to be small, in need of some serious plastering and painting, and offering a claustrophobic view of an airshaft through its murky window. There was not one suitcase here, Milano took note, but four of them. And two bulky cartons still corded around. And a couple of bulging shopping bags.

All the earmarks of a permanent resettlement.

Go figure. A week ago, the last word you'd use in describing the lady was impulsive, but what other word better described the way she had suddenly confided her sins to her daddy and now, just as suddenly, had taken off from the nest? So far in his experience, Milano reflected, impulsiveness, as demonstrated by the female in a sort of "You know what let's do now?" role-playing, could have its charms. Betty's exercise of it, however, seemed more like a variation of Russian roulette.

She was plainly scared by this herself. The strain of playing it bright and chipper showed. "Not much, is it?" she said, indicating the room. "I seem to be full of surprises, don't I?" Then frowning as she looked him over, she dropped the act. "You've lost weight. What are you doing, starving yourself to death?"

Better if she had expressed admiration rather than concern, but even so, considering the ongoing martyrdom involved, it was nice of her to take notice. A nice observant concerned girl, and what the hell were you supposed to do about it? There were women you could let down with a thud, but this was definitely not one of them.

"Just counting calories," Milano said. "What happened with your father anyhow? How'd you wind up here?"

"I'd just as soon not talk about my father. And I wound up here because it's the cheapest place I could find on one day's notice. I mean, where I wouldn't be afraid to walk out in the hall. Even so, you know what it costs, Johnny? It's really murder."

"I can imagine," Milano said. He poised on the brink, then took the plunge. "But if you can dig up some girl who's looking to split apartment rent——"

Her expression cut him short. Bewildered. Stricken. "Is that how you feel about it, Johnny?"

"It?"

[151]

"Us."

So here it was. The us part. Milano started to sit down on the edge of the bed, realized his raincoat was sodden, and, rather than take it off, stood up. He said gently, "If what you're getting at, baby, is that we set up housekeeping together, it would never work. It wouldn't last long enough to be worth trying. Believe me, I know we've been getting along fine with each other——"

She cut right across his bow full speed. "You know it's been a lot more than that, Johnny. I'd say we definitely arrived at a very meaningful relationship. And you know I'm not talking marriage. I'm just saying that when two people have something so good to share why share it just weekends and holidays? We're happy with each other then, aren't we? So why not make it every day of the week?"

"Because maybe I'm only happy weekends and holidays." A mistake. She was shakily trying to hang tight, and cheap repartee was no help in that direction. Milano said quickly, "I'm sorry. But I am also confused, baby. Last time we were together we had a very loud blowup. Remember why? I suggested you stay overnight in the apartment what with the trouble you'd have getting home at that hour, and you wouldn't do it because my friends there might take notice. Now you're proposing an arrangement where practically everybody in town would have to take notice."

"Yes. But I was being stupid that night. And when you said — you know — I was too old for such nonsense I thought I was angry at you for it. But I wasn't. Afterward, I realized I was really being angry at my father. And my mother too, because she is just like an echo in that house. Look at me. At my age. And with a good job. And with you——"

"A different father."

"What?"

"Think it over, Betty. You're saying you finally broke loose, you're your own woman now. But all you're really doing — call it symbolically — is trying to switch fathers. And what you call a meaningful relationship looks made to order for the switch."

"Oh no, Johnny, I never——"

"Oh yes." Amazing. That nickel and dime analysis was supposed to be just evasive action, and suddenly here it was providing insight into some painful facts of life. Forty years old. The father image. And what were the odds on Christine Bailey settling for any father image? But this wasn't Christine here, it was a bird of a very different disposition. Milano said, "We have to be honest about this, baby. You move in with me, it'll only be a change of address for you, nothing else. You'll take all the signals from me, you'll make all the adjustments, and in the end you'll be as scared of me coming on mean-tempered as you ever were of your father. And you won't know what to do about it this time around. For that matter, neither would I."

Betty frowned, trying to work it out. "I don't see that. You make it sound like we were always at each other. But we weren't."

"Because you've always been just as weak-kneed with me as you were with your father." He pushed ahead fast before she could offer more than a hesitant shake of the head. "Look, you're still mixed-up about all this, and that's natural. And this room here isn't helping any; it is depressing as hell, baby. That brings up a practical concern. Moving into something civilized. Happens I'm owed a couple of favors by the manager of a very civilized apartment hotel uptown on Fifth. Bedroom, sitting room, and a kitchen layout where you won't bankrupt yourself eating out. Not easy to get in there short-term, but it can be done. Meanwhile——"

"Uptown on Fifth? I've got some money put away, Johnny, but not that kind of money. And my paycheck would never——"

"Right. So meanwhile, just to make me feel better about such items as your comfort and security, you will kindly let me finance the deal until you make your own arrangements."

"You mean, pay my rent?"

"Only until you make your own arrangements. Now relax. Obviously I am not trying to buy your favors. All I'm doing is offering a helping hand when you need one. If you turn it down out of some whacked-out principle, I'll go along with that. But I can tell you one thing, baby, I won't be happy about it."

When you've taken a hotel manager off the hook for the looting of his safe-deposit boxes by speedily nailing the looters and recovering most of the loot, you have a large reserve of gratitude to draw on. Mr. Francona-Nerisi, manager of the Wardour, was ready to bend all rules in his gratitude. More than that, whatever private doubts

[153]

he had about Mr. Milano's apparently well-bred and undeniably very pretty country cousin and her curious assortment of luggage, he was positively courtly in his welcome to her.

So at ten a.m. the country cousin took possession of her new apartment and set to work storing away her belongings—the procedure seeming to firm her resolution about this adventure as she gained momentum—while Milano, after surveying the scene outside the sitting room window—a Childe Hassam Fifth Avenue below, the noble bulk of the Metropolitan Museum a couple of blocks north—ran the Mercedes downtown to lay in a store of provender from Balducci's. He couldn't eat most of this wonderful stuff, especially now that his new figure had been given public recognition, but he could sure as hell take a bitter satisfaction in buying it.

Back again, he was relieved of his cartons by Betty who, making protesting noises at such extravagance, loaded up the refrigerator and kitchen shelves. With everything done that could be done, she joined him in the sitting room. She confronted him, face flushed, arms akimbo, like Joan of Arc getting ready to address the troops.

"Well, all right," she said.

"Except for those hunting prints on that wall," Milano said. "And those School of Fragonard teasers in the bedroom."

"I'm not talking about any pictures. I'm talking about this situation. It just takes some time to get used to, that's all. Even if it is only for the time being."

"Good. Got any ideas on how to celebrate the occasion?"

"Don't you have to go to work?"

Milano shook his head. "Today is all celebration." No use hinting that the Met was only a short walk away. At best she was a dutiful museum-goer, dim of eye, polarized to the obvious, always a step behind him, waiting to get his reaction before coming up with her own. Skip the Met. And Velasquez. And that small Rubens. "So," said Milano, "how about Atlantic City?"

"A casino? Now?" She had made this expedition with him once before, had been alarmed and baffled by any table action, but had discovered the slots with rapture. He had observed at the time that where she was shy about his providing her original stake she popped up at his table regularly after that for an added twenty or fifty. The reason, of course, was that she had been almost instantly brainwashed by the spirit of the place. This wasn't real money. There was no real money in Cloud-Cuckooland. The picture of those rows of slots, jackpots heating up for her in each one, must have inspired her now. "All right," she said, answering her own question. "Why not?"

A small hitch developed in the expedition when Milano stopped at his bank downtown to raise necessary funds. His bank balance, it appeared, couldn't cover a check for ten thousand. Sorry, but would eight thousand do?

His instant heated reaction, uncontrollable as a hiccup, was that Shirley Glass who saw to the direct deposit of his hefty Watrous drawing account each week had somehow gone and skipped a week. But of course she hadn't. She never did. It was just a case of the four M's again, he knew — mortgage, maintenance, Mercedes, and Mama. Mama's house, that is, which sister Angie had somehow laid off on him when the bills for keeping it livable first started to pile up. And then there were all those handy credit cards, whose statements the bank electronically attended to behind his back. Personal merchandise and travel and entertainment and such, not to be weaseled into the company expense account, because if he was going to ream Willie, it wouldn't be by any soft-core swindling.

Come to think of it, there was now another item for the list, Betty's gilded cage in the Wardour.

Oh yeah. It was beginning to look like that almost quarter of a million of Pacifica's money he'd be splitting with Willie was definitely needed to recharge the money machine.

Any chance of not delivering the goods to Pacifica?

Yes. But minimal if Rammert and the buyer's representative had arranged for the classic procedure of swapping paintings for cash, face to face. Across the table, one examining the paintings, the other counting the cash, neither trusting the other the length of a pinkie-nail. C.O.D. and probably a couple of custom-tailored hired guns standing around making sure the figures balanced.

Milano settled for the eight thousand the bank teller had offered and in his first two hours at blackjack almost doubled it while Betty at her slots was getting just enough return now and then to put the roses in her cheeks. When she finally did tap out, he planted her in his lucky seat to nervously hold the fort with small bets while he phoned Shirley at the office.

[155]

Her report was irritating. Yes, Willie had gotten on his P.D. buddies first thing, and no, Charles Kirwan had no priors, no police record of any kind, no nothing. All very negative. Who was this Kirwan anyhow?

"Somebody who bothers me," Milano said. "Is that Heywood and Smith team in touch with you?"

"Uh-huh. DeLong called in this morning from the college. He'll call again before closing time here."

"Good. Tell him to meet me for breakfast tomorrow morning. Same place, same time. And to bring whatever he's got on Kirwan so far."

"Sure," said Shirley. "By the way, I also took a message for you yesterday. Four times. A Betty Cronin wants you to get in touch with her as soon as possible. I'd appreciate it, Johnny, if you'd—"

"I'll take care of it right now," said Milano.

Back to the table then, where he staked Betty to her next try at the giant jackpot and where the dealer was openly relieved to see him replace his lady friend. The dealer must have known something, because his concentration was now definitely blown. The cards were far away; up front was that nagging Bailey-Bailey-Rammaert-Kirwan cycle again, so after losing back his winnings he shifted over to a crap table where the dice might do some reverse magic for him. No use. By dinnertime he was down to about a thousand, Betty was down to a cupful of half-dollars, and that was what they took back to New York with them. Not good, but better than nothing.

Could have been worth it too, considering that Betty, despite some battle scars—a badly swollen hand and sore feet—appeared to be dreamily content with her lot. Romantically disposed, too.

But there was no romantic interlude at the Wardour. Parked at its entrance, Milano remarked that he was sorry to say—really sorry to say, sweetheart—that as of this moment he was officially back on the job, a heavy case that would probably tie him up into the small hours.

"Oh," said Betty. "Well, I'll call you tomorrow then."

"No, better let me do any calling. For one thing, I'll be short of sleep as it is, I'd just as soon not have the phone breaking it up. For another thing, you've got message service, and I don't."

"That's right," said Betty. She leaned over, locked her arms tight around his neck and gave him a lingering, heated kiss. Smelt good, felt good. But—

He watched her walk a few steps toward the doorway. Then she stopped and shaded her eyes against a fine drizzle, her head going back, back, back as she took in the height of the building, its façade studded here and there with a glow of light from picture windows. The way she did it, the contemplative shake of that head, suggested that what she was viewing here was improbable, it was no more real than casino money.

Which, come to think of it, was all to the good.

Of course he should have phoned Christine Bailey before making a useless trip down to the Village. To simply assume she'd be home and ready for a little chat over a glass at, let's say, O. Henry's was stupid. Smart would have been to assume that right now the girl was having a lot more than a little chat with some fucking black Adonis of a pro-ball carrier who, of course, got added exposure in fucking glamorous TV commercials.

No response to the bell, to the persistent knocking at the door?

The hell with her.

He changed his mind about that first thing in the morning. A fair night's sleep helped, the sunshiny Friday morning was calculated to settle turbulent emotions, and, of course, J. Milano could provide what even the smoothest running back couldn't: the job of hauling little sister out of whatever deep and dangerous hole she was digging herself into.

A troubled kid all right. Definitely not happy down there at the bottom of that hole.

He had invited DeLong Heywood to attend breakfast with him solo; it was no big surprise to find that the sprightly Gracella was, without apology, a member of the party. And exceedingly tender toward her working partner who showed no resentment of the motherly ministrations — the straightening of his jacket collar, plucking of a minute bit of lint from his sleeve — delivered his way in public.

No resentment at all. In fact, when he handed Milano the Kirwan dossier — a folder with a stack of Xeroxed sheets — he motioned at Gracella and said, "Most of this is hers. Girl really knows her away around this kind of stuff."

[157]

She did. The pages were obviously lifted from every type of printed medium, of every size and shape, and wherever Kirwan's name appeared it was highlighted by colored marker. There was a cover sheet too, a sort of index categorizing the folder's contents under the headings of *Family History, Military, Academic* and so on.

"Nice," said Milano. He risked treading on DeLong's toes by addressing Gracella. "How do you figure him?"

"Kirwan?" She made a face. "Kind of the last of the dinosaurs."

"How?"

"Oh, old family. Old, old. Way back to Dutch times. Funny thing is his real name is Witter — I mean his father's name — but when his mother married again he took the new father's name. That's the Kirwan. Anyhow, the family's been there since the beginning of Brooklyn. That street is named after them."

"How about more up-to-date?" Milano said. "Why did he give up teaching at the college? Any little difficulties? Aberrations? Anything at all in that line?"

Gracella shook her head broadly. "No way. Just retirement, that's all. With honors. Big farewell dinner and such."

"And," said DeLong, taking time off from his pancakes, "he got a big writeup in the student paper about it." He pointed at the folder. "It's all there. When they were having those troubles a few years back — "

"Ethnic troubles," Gracella put in wickedly.

"Those troubles," said DeLong, "about, you know, open admissions and black studies and all, he came out for ethnic. Big man on the faculty, graduated from the college himself, snow white" — he shrugged in apology — "you know what I mean."

"I know," said Milano.

"Yeah, well — so that did good for ethnic in newspaper and TV interviews where he could have scored for the other side. So the student paper gave him heavy credits. Also that now he was retiring he didn't look to go Sun Belt like a lot of other retired teachers but would be staying right there in the family house and keep on being part of the changing community."

"Very touching," said Milano. "And what about before all this? The military stuff. That would be World War II, I take it."

"Uh-huh," said DeLong.

[158]

"Anything about what kind of discharge he got?"

DeLong looked at Gracella. She did some thinking and then shook her head. "But it had to be an all-right one."

"Why?" asked Milano.

She ticked it off on her fingers. "Captain in the army. A lot of combat action. Medal for a special mission. I mean, what kind of discharge would he get? Anyhow, you go through these papers you will see we really did a job. And if anybody ever came through like a total Mister Clean, he is the one."

"Total," said Milano.

"You don't want to believe that?"

"Well," said Milano, "I was once at a dinner for another total like that. Pillar of the community, model citizen, saint of the year. The only guest who didn't show up was him, because he got caught by the cops grabbing some teen-age kid's prick in the airport toilet on his way in."

"Happens," said DeLong equably. He frowned at Milano. "You got something on this Kirwan we don't know?"

"Not that way. But look at it this way. That girl's come up with cash money amounting to at least a thousand dollars so far, maybe more. Possibly she got it all in one bundle, but I don't think so because her spending pattern is too even and regular. Which means most likely the money comes in installments. And Kirwan's the one regular contact we know she has in private. Behind locked doors. And there's nothing to say that Mister Clean isn't a user, and that this kid isn't the smartest kind of connection he could set up for himself."

"Makes some sense," DeLong acknowledged. "Except where's her connection at the other end? Who's supplying her? I watched that girl making her moves. Nothing there. No fancy footwork, no hide-and-seek at all."

"Still, said MIlano, "you have to work with what makes sense. And wondering what Kirwan's got going with that kid is the only thing that makes sense."

"Q.E.D.," said Gracella. She raised her eyebrows at Milano. "Now what?"

"From your angle, nothing. You two want the rest of the day off with pay, you've got it."

[159]

"All right," said Gracella. "But how about something else? Remember? I did my thing, you saw how I did it, how about a little changeover from secretarial to investigations? Kind of a permanent changeover."

She was poised and ready, Milano saw, but for what? He said, "You told me you had a Master's degree, didn't you? In what?"

"Education."

It would be. "Didn't you ever think of teaching?"

"I did teach, Mr. Milano sir. Two years in junior high. You want my opinion of New York City's junior high schools in twenty-five words or less?"

"I'm reading it between the lines," Milano said. "All right, I'll tell Mr. Watrous we've got a hidden talent in the office we can't afford to waste. Won't be tomorrow or next week though. You want to wait it out, fine."

Gracella opened her mouth, and Milano held up a hand. "That's it," he said.

He made the trip to Witter Street in the Mercedes — the car providing built-in bona fides — and, alternate-side parking rules holding good only until eleven a.m., he found at eleven-ten that there was still a space left near the driveway of 407. But no one answered the doorbell of the Victorian 407. Timing was essential, too. Lorena would be passing here a little after three on her way home from school; she'd be ringing this same bell around three-thirty. So it had to be curtains down on any interface with Kirwan well before three.

Bedridden? No, not completely if at all. Sleeping it off? Milano was meditating this when he was hailed from the sidewalk. "Hey, mister."

An elderly couple — white — the man behind a shopping cart, the woman vigorously gesturing. "Mister."

Milano joined them on the sidewalk. The woman, a withered crone in space shoes, said reprovingly, "He's not home."

"Kirwan?"

"He's not home." She narrowed her eyes. "You the inspector?"

"No. Just here on business. I thought he'd be in."

"He's next door." She pointed at 409. "In the cellar. Fixing something. You're not the inspector?"

[160]

"Not me," said Milano.

The old man said sternly, "There was supposed to be an inspector a week ago."

"A month ago," said the old woman. She thrust a knotty forefinger into Milano's chest. "Mister, you're gonna see the fine Mr. Kirwan, may he rot in hell, you do me a favor. Tell him it's Friedman, he'll know. Tell him the toilet still leaks and the vershtoonkeneh icebox still don't make cold. You tell him that."

"If I find him," said Milano.

"In the cellar there," the old man said. "Remember, it's Friedman. He'll know."

You'd have to be a fool to bet he wouldn't, thought Milano.

The way to 409's cellar was down a few stone steps and through a dank tunnel which opened on a large courtyard below street level. The cellar door was steel-jacketed and double-locked, the cellar windows were all sealed shut with concrete block, and door, windows, and every inch of wall around the courtyard were so dizzyingly thick with graffiti there didn't seem to be room for even one more drop of spray-can inspiration.

There was company here. In a far corner, a half-dozen boys were squatting, kneeling, standing over a card game, posed for a photo of youth playing hookey from high school. They froze at the sight of this stranger, warily eying him from the distance. In proletarian contrast was a burly, grayhaired black man attending to a row of battered garbage containers ranged against the wall. The containers overflowed with garbage, it was sloppily underfoot all around them, and the man was shoveling the excess into one of those reinforced black plastic bags. A couple of filled bags were already ranged against the wall beyond the containers. The man gave Milano a gap-toothed smile. "Lookin' for somebody?"

"The landlord," said Milano. "I was told he's in the cellar."

"Uh-huh. But that door's locked solid and no use skinnin' knuckles on it. When he's workin' in there either he don't hear or he don't want to hear."

"I see," said Milano. "You the super?" According to all reports Kirwan was supposed to be his own super.

"I super across the street. Just help out here. Al Bunting." He cocked an inquiring eye. "You on building business?"

[161]

"Not an inspector. Private business. John Milano." It was a cue for the card players to quit focusing on him and get back to their game, which they did. Al Bunting, however, seemed willing to be sociable. Milano said to him, "How long will he be in there?"

"Don't know. Been doin' a job there most of the day already, so he got to come out soon, I guess, get a bite to eat. Like that every day. Told me coupla weeks ago he got to fix up them boiler pipes once and for all, been at it since then. Wastin' time, man. You need new iron in there, not clamps over all them leaks." He showed that smile. "Most of them pipes is older than me and even rustier."

"You seem to be doing all right," Milano said in honest compliment. He looked around. "Building itself looks pretty solid too. Needs work," he said thoughtfully, planting the seed, "but it could be worth it."

Bunting seemed doubtful. "Could be. Trouble is, you put in the work and right away somebody fucks it up. Some messy people here. And" — he motioned with his head at the card players — "some mean ones. Rip off what ain't nailed down, bust up what is. Know what I mean?"

"Oh yeah." Milano gave it a couple of beats. "But that big house next door is Kirwan's too, isn't it? Fine old house. And wide open for rip-off and bust-up. How come that one looks so good? Connections in the neighborhood take care of him maybe? Send out word to lay off?"

Bunting grinned broadly. "Could put it that way."

"Could I?"

"Uh-huh." Bunting motioned at the card players. "Most of them dudes lives right here. Way I hear, their mamas put it to them that they tangle with that man he gonna come right back with that eviction paper. Rent control building here, too. You get yourself rousted out of here, any other place like it you will pay maybe double the money. See? That kinda makes mama the connection you talkin' about, don't it? Also — "

"Yes."

Bunting scratched his forehead reflectively. "Well, you could say he is an easygoin' man. Peaceable, you know? He don't hassle them uglies about what goes on with this building, they don't hassle his house. That is how you got to do it, man. I super that Number

Four-sixteen across the street, I give them uglies there space, they give me space. Control. Keep that temper nice and cool. Makes livin' a lot easier for one and all."

"Turn the other cheek," said Milano.

"Most times. But one of them ever lays a finger on me personal, I bust his fuckin' arm. Outside of that, peaceable is the word, man. You ask Mr. Kirwan, he'll give you a whole talk on it. Says it works, and he the proof. Sure seems to be."

"Sure does," said Milano, "but it's a little hard to ask him anything this way."

"He'll be out. Could be soon."

It was soon. A few minutes after Milano had posted himself on the street at the head of the stairs there was a scraping of footsteps in the passageway below. Funereal dragging footsteps. Milano moved to the head of the stairway and saw Father Time himself making it up the first step with an effort. The yellowish ten-watt bulb in its cage overhead dimly illuminated a tall cadaverous figure moving with an arthritic hitch of the hip, a face in chiaroscuro all sharp angles and deep hollows under an unkempt head of white hair.

The first step up was hard for Kirwan. The second was murder. He needed to grip the iron railing on either side to give himself leverage, but a weighted plastic shopping bag in one hand made this tricky. Milano moved down a couple of steps. "Can I help you?"

Kirwan squinted up at him. "I think you can. Yes." The enunciation was precise, the voice pleasant, but it sounded like the lungs were being charged with air just to propel the words any distance. A cough followed them. Not outward. A sudden wheeze and crackle in the chest. Must have been an eruption of mucus into the mouth too, from Kirwan's suddenly tight-lipped and wrinkle-nosed expression. And where anyone else in this situation and this place would simply have spat it out, Kirwan showed his gentlemanly colors. Dragged out a handkerchief from his hip pocket and deposited the load into it. He carefully folded the handkerchief before putting it away. "I've been doing a job of plumbing," he said apologetically. "I'm afraid I've overdone it. Now if you'll just relieve me of this bag — "

Milano reached down and took the shopping bag inside of which something clinked metallically. Even free of this burden Kirwan had to work hard to make it up to street level. He finally reached it and stood there struggling for breath. Under the sunlight he didn't come off as ancient as he had in the dimness of the passageway, but sickness was more plainly stamped on him. Grayish complexion, purplish tone to the lips. Not what you'd call your average prepossessing landlord figure. Coarse dust-bunnies clung to the back of the frayed cardigan, the trousers were paint-stained ruins with more dust-bunnies adhering to the cuffs, the footwear was grimy sneakers. But the manner was courtly. "I thank you, sir. I believe you're the one my handyman told me wanted to see me."

"Yes. Hoped you wouldn't mind talking over some business." Milano handed over the engraved card, and Kirwan closed one eye to squint at it with the other. The card, one of an assorted dozen or so, was Willie's brainstorm, and not a bad one at that. Under the *John A. Milano* was inscribed the all-purpose *Properties Consultant* which, if you nailed John A. Milano to the wall, he could truthfully describe as consultant in handling security problems for the property owner. Otherwise, it invited the broadest interpretation. The kind Kirwan was now apparently leaning toward.

"And what properties do you have in mind, Mr. Milano?"

"Matter of fact, could be this one. I represent some investors — well, I don't want to make it sound like a philanthropic project — but these are people who are interested in neighborhood redevelopment. A neighborhood like this, say. Marginal right now, could go up, could go down, population heavily ethnic — "

"You don't have to qualify that, Mr. Milano. You can just say population ethnic."

It was hard to tell if Kirwan was being cute about this. The face remained expressionless, no flicker of humor showed in the glassy eyes.

"All right," said Milano, "population ethnic. That means your average investor stays away. We don't."

"I see. Are you saying you're interested in buying this building, Mr. Milano?"

"At least interested in discussing possibilities."

"You've seen that abandoned apartment building down the block, I'm sure. Do you know you could probably pick it up for back taxes?"

"Yes," said Milano. "And then have to lay out maybe a couple of hundred thousand to make it viable."

"Ah yes. Viable."

The old man was being cute.

"Livable," said Milano. "For the occupants." Cute old bastard, all right. And glancing at his wristwatch now, getting ready to sign off. That door into 407 fifty feet away began to look like fifty miles away. Condescending cute. But house-proud. Could be an Achilles heel, that house-proud. Milano took careful aim at it. "Of course, if I were sole investor, if it were my money alone — you own this property next door, too, don't you?"

"Yes."

"Well, that's what I'd be itching to buy. An architectural gem. I've seen others in this class but none in this condition. About eighteen-eighty, isn't it?"

"Just about." Bull's-eye. Kirwan now looked as if oxygen was being pumped into those bronchial or asthmatic or whatever lungs. He regarded his home tenderly, running his fingers slowly back and forth across his mouth. "But most definitely not for sale, Mr. Milano."

"I can't blame you for that," Milano said soberly. He switched his attention to the house again. "Classic American Queen Anne. And that paint job. You've held to the original color, haven't you?"

"Chestnut. Oh yes. You appear to know your architectural history."

"Kind of an avocation. Along with historical interior decoration." When you've got the subject wondering, baby, lay it on thick and move it fast. Milano wrinkled his brow. "By any chance, is the interior authentic too?"

"Oh yes. Yes indeed. Allowing for some inevitable improvements. No gas mantels now, I'm afraid. And comparatively modern kitchens and bathrooms. And some repair of furniture, but never reconstruction of them or the interior woodwork. Never."

"Unbelievable." Milano hoped he was looking properly awe-struck. "You know, Mr. Kirwan, if it isn't an imposition——"

Kirwan glanced at his watch again. "Well——"

"I'll gladly settle for the express tour. And no talk about business. Plenty of time for that another day."

Bull's-eye again.

Milano carried the plastic bag, and as Kirwan worked his key into the lock of the front door he managed to take surreptitious inventory of the bag's contents. Thermos bottle, flashlight, large pair of shears, some kind of round-nosed pincers busted into detached halves, nothing at all to suggest that an acid factory or pill plant was being operated out of 409's cellar. It would have been nice to come up with a dozen unlabeled bottles of capsules, although this would have dented logic by making Kirwan the inside man and Lorena his connection to the outside. Not that there was much logic in the idea that Kirwan would casually turn over to this stranger a bag containing felonious merchandise, but logic itself, good old-fashioned police procedural logic, didn't seem to offer much of a handle for Lorena's goings-on.

Or, for that matter, Kirwan's. Eccentric was the word for it if you were rich, loony if you weren't, but how to figure this moneyed landlord with the expensive obsession for High Victorian, and the painful hip condition, and that gut-tearing cough which made him look apoplectic as he fought it now and again—how to figure this character crawling around the fouled-up boiler pipes of a fouled-up apartment building day after day doing hopeless repair work, unless you wrote him off as an authentic crackpot? That, as the Bard had put it, was the question.

Crackpot? But there were those quick-minded, sharp-edged flashes that seemed to indicate otherwise.

And, as it turned out, the interior of the house provided evidence that Kirwan didn't suffer Collyer brothers' syndrome, that packrat hoarding and piling up of decaying junk which, as clear a signal as any, signals galloping senility. Far from it. This place, marooned here in the middle of beat-up Ethnicville, was a treasure chest. Oak-panelled walls, sculpted inglenooks, arched and curving ceilings, superb Gilded Age naif floral designs on hallway windows. And the furnishings. A Victorian crowding and clutter, organized for a formidable coziness. Some superlative Duncan Phyfe plus Biedermeier and Morris pieces to make those polished floorboards creak under their weight. Everything mahogany, oak, walnut, ebony. Brussels carpets, the real goods, the colors showing true around threadbare patches. A dazzling show of Morris glass. Predictably, the art on the walls was a dead loss. Original Germanic pastorals along with copies of Alma-Tadema, Millais, Landseer and company, all — originals and copies — ornately framed. Front parlor, interior sitting room, library, dining room, pantry and maid's room off the kitchen, and finally the kitchen itself, big enough to hold a ball in. Milano blinked at the table there, the trim chairs, the severe Mondrian lines of the wallracks.

"Authentic Shaker?" he asked, and "Oh yes," wheezed the proprietor of the works. "Authentic Shaker."

Reversing course, Milano did sketchy arithmetic, starting with that kitchen layout, picking up with the massive Biedermeier cabinet at the head of the dining room. Cherrywood? Had to be natural cherrywood and with a fine ebony inlay like lace trim decorating each panel. Adding it up all the way, room by room, the furnishings in sight would call for a reserve price of at least two or three hundred thousand. And that would be strictly reserve price, no telling what the competitive prices on the auction floor could hit, considering the skyrocketing market. And the army of moneyed meatheads ready to ride the rocket still higher.

No price at all, of course, for that bronze urn on the shelf over the tiled fireplace, each tile alone — Dutch motif — now a red-hot item on the market. Engraved on the urn in florid script was *Hendrick Jan Cornelius Witter — 1857–1951,* and in a tone that suggested he was removing a hat and holding it over his heart Kirwan said, "My grandfather's remains. A remarkable man."

"This was his home?"

"He built it. And furnished it. A remarkable man. A successful merchant, a brilliant scholar. Of history. Such qualities weren't incompatible in that era, Mr. Milano."

In the nick of time, Milano remembered he wasn't supposed to know Witter history offhand. "Witter," he said. "Witter Street."

"Yes. The family was among the original estate holders in Flatbush here. You might say that his house represented its high water mark. Unfortunately, I represent the end of the line."

"I see. And that apartment house next door — "

"Talking business again, Mr. Milano?"

"No, just talking out of curiosity. If you don't mind." Odds were the old man wouldn't. He had been handed — honestly — the right reactions to the guided tour, the right knowing and admiring comments. No reason for him to pull up short now.

He didn't. "That apartment building. Yes. Built in the early 'twenties, the very first of its kind on this block. It was regarded as a sound investment when it was built."

"But now that the neighborhood's changed——"

"Opened!" Kirwan's voice was suddenly sharp. "Human beings are human beings, Mr. Milano, no matter their color. And an oppressed people trying to overcome a bitter and degrading past deserve more than the kind of contempt invested in that word 'changed,' the way you're using it."

Jesus.

Milano said, "Wrong, Mr. Kirwan. All I was getting at—no prejudice intended—was that since this neighborhood isn't what it was a hundred years ago——"

"Or a dozen."

"Or a dozen, what happens to this house in the long run?"

"You mean, of course, when I'm dead."

"It comes to all of us," said Milano.

"So it does. In any event, this house will remain exactly as you see it. A family foundation—the Hendrick Witter Foundation—has been richly funded to that end. So if you have any worry—or hope—that my estate may some day be reduced to job lots for the market, Mr. Milano, forget it."

Sharp as the proverbial tack when he wanted to be. And in the mood for some kind of game-playing, too. It was there in the amused twist of those thin lips. Which brought up unfinished business.

Milano said, "If you knew me better, you'd know I'm the last one to want something like this reduced to job lots. What it comes to is, I see a lot of properties in my business but this is one I never imagined seeing in the city here. Everything about it——"

"Yes. Well, now that you have seen it——"

"That tower, for instance," Milano interposed before this nudge could become a push. "Octagon inside as well as outside?"

"Yes."

"I've wondered about that kind of interior design. If you could spare just a few more minutes——"

It was touch and go while the old man weighed this, but in the end, as Milano had calculated, it was like asking a doting parent to have his kid play just one more violin solo for the company. And it took better than just a few minutes for Kirwan to make it up those stairs, stopping for a breather every couple of steps. So, one might ask, why hadn't he rigged up sleeping quarters on the ground floor, thus saving himself this misery at least a couple of times a day? Of course, it would spoil that decor downstairs, now frozen in time. And then grandpa's spirit, peaceful in its urn over that marvelously tiled fireplace, might haunt the place. Although, come to think of it, it seemed to be doing a fair job of haunting right now.

The stairway mounted to a broad corridor, all doors along it closed, and at the end of the corridor was the tower room. A true octagon all right, larger in area than one would guess viewing it from the street. Four of its eight walls were windowed, between two of the windows was a closed cabinet and over it were open shelves containing odds and ends, a trio of plaster busts, some scrimshaw, two ship's models, a fishing boat and an instantly recognizable New York ferry.

And binoculars.

Uncased. In open view. Well-worn, possibly army issue.

Milano looked once and turned away. So he had been right about Kirwan's hobby; from the convenient location of the glasses it was an active hobby; and its exposure, Milano thought, meant that what we had here was not merely an eccentric old coot but a dirty old man.

Taking in the view all around the room—turn of the century furniture—big flat-topped oak desk, swivel chair, classic old iron safe with *Witter & Son* gilt-inscribed on it, Naval Observatory clock over the door, Milano drifted along the walls, which except for the cabinet section, were tightly packed bookshelves from floor to ceiling, until he stood at the window facing the apartment house next door. The shades were up here, the curtains were transparent enough to get a gauzy view through them of whatever was to be seen, and what was to be seen across the way were the windows of the Bailey apartment, exactly on the second-floor level of this room. The ladies' bedroom window there was angled off a bit, but still, with shade drawn up, provided plenty of interior exposure.

And, unless Kirwan was some kind of fat-lady freak who'd get turned on by such as Ma Bailey, Lorena had to be the object of interest. In the nymphet class, she didn't have much more to show than a starter set, but that would probably be enough for Father Time.

Christine.

The thought popped to the surface. It had been down below, tangled in the subconscious since that first flicker of binocular lenses glimpsed from the Bailey apartment. Now it was a queasy thought breaking the surface like a bubble in an oil slick. If Kirwan's hobby dated back any time, it would have been Christine, not the weedy Lorena, who was its original inspiration. And Christine could have been just as careless about pulling down window-shades as her kid sister.

Or would it have been indifference, not carelessness, considering that naked view of herself she had lately presented onstage? Goddam irritating quality in a woman, too, not being able to predict her response if you told her the landlord used to enjoy a peepshow of her free of charge. Another woman would react with outrage, calculated or not. This one was just as likely to shrug it off and remark that, after all, what could you expect of the lascivious, exploiting white male of any age, any condition. The fact that in sexual terms Kirwan barely had strength enough to pick up those binoculars might even amuse her.

It didn't amuse him.

Milano drifted away from the window. Kirwan had some points to score. Those books. The old man drew a couple of them a little way out of a shelf. "My works." A shit-kicking tone, making light of his works. Hard to believe he really was, though. "History. But not much on architecture and interior decoration. More on the movers and shakers."

He was plainly inviting close inspection of the works. Milano drew one from the shelf, a heavy number with a textbook look to it. *Alva: Imperial Power and Politics In the Netherlands.* The printed inscription on the reverse of the title page read *For Hendrick Jan Cornelius Witter, Inspiration and Invaluable Source.* Grandpa's ghost rides again.

"A lot of work in this," said Milano.

"Oh yes. Yes indeed. You're Roman Catholic, I take it?"

This, coming out of left field, momentarily handcuffed Milano. "I suppose so. Although hardly a pillar of the Church."

"Hardly an Alva." The tone indicated that the game-playing was on again. "You've heard of him?"

"Yes." You couldn't go very deep into Flemish art without running into the Duke of Alva, the Spanish hatchetman sent to put the Dutch in their place. But what was this? Testing time? Put-down time?

Seemed to be. "And," said Kirwan, "of one of his most devoted henchmen, Guy Fawkes?"

"Vaguely. But he was English, wasn't he? Not Spanish."

"Oh yes." Kirwan held up a bony forefinger and chanted, "'Please to remember the Fifth of November, gunpowder, treason, and plot. Guy Fawkes, Guy; hang him on high——' A merry requiem for a bungling conspirator, Mr. Milano. Bungling is something no conspirator can really afford."

"One of your favorite historical interests?"

"Bungling conspirators?" Kirwan seemed tickled by the question. "Lately, yes. In the past, no. But lately? Oh yes."

From the sound of it, a private joke somewhere in there.

And from the sound of it, the goombah—Professor Peeping Tom—was laying it on the lowly paisan. Still with those dust-bunnies attached to the rear of those raggedy poor-mouth clothes.

While Lorena Bailey was out shopping for fifty dollars a pair designer jeans and ninety dollars a pair super joggers with whose money?

Who else than the professor's?

It was now Milano's turn to check the time. A little after one. Getaway time. A shame to break up whatever game the professor was playing, but there was other investigating to do. So, putting his best manners forward, he thanked Kirwan for the tour, remarked that there was no need to show him to the door, and left his host watching him from the head of the staircase as he trotted down. Getting into the car he glanced up and saw that the curtain of the second story tower window overlooking the street was now pulled aside. He couldn't make out the old man's face behind the window, but he didn't have to see it to know it was there.

A few blocks away on Bedford he parked at a hydrant while he called Betty's number at the Intercontinental Credit Bureau office on the car phone. Betty said, "I was wondering when you'd call. I mean, I'm not really clear about the weekend. About your plans for it."

"Very iffy. I'm stuck in this big one and can't seem to get unstuck. How are you making out?"

"Well, I've got a notice on the office bulletin board about sharing an apartment, and a couple of the girls told me the *Village Voice* had listings for that kind of thing. But it could take time. That's what worries me."

"Don't let it."

"Well, it does. And I'd feel a lot better if we could have this weekend together. Just be together. You know it's really weird, Johnny. I woke up this morning, and I just couldn't get myself together on where I was and what I was doing there. And making breakfast in that fantastic kitchen. And taking the Fifth Avenue bus down to work. All the same, I'm not used to being this much alone, you know what I mean?"

"I can guess. Hell or high water, baby, we'll work out something for the weekend. Some part of the weekend at least. But right now I need a favor. Some dollars and cents input that can speed up this case I'm on. And I can use it by closing time today."

"Is there a social security number?"

"No, but he's a property owner and I have the address of the property, so there must be an employer's I.D. to work from. Think you can make it before you lock up there?"

"I can try."

Greater love hath no woman, thought Milano, since she must suspect that if Intercontinental ever caught on to these handouts, it could amount to felony, even though polite, white-collar felony. He gave her Kirwan's full name and address and then the address of the apartment building. "Oh yes," he added. "One more item. The Hendrick Witter Foundation. Probably incorporated in New York State, but you'd be programmed to foundations all over, wouldn't you?"

"That's right."

'Good. Then I can use whatever you get on it. The Hendrick Witter Foundation. I'll phone you six o'clock at the hotel. Or is that too early?"

"No. And, Johnny, our weekend — "

"Top priority. I'll have something worked out for us when I call."

Never mind that some youthful locals of the female persuasion were now gathered on the sidewalk taking a giggling interest in his operation of the car phone. He called the Rammaert Gallery and got a pleasant jolt from the sound of that warm, husky, professional receptionist-type greeting. On the other hand, annoyingly, Christine Bailey didn't even know yet who the hell was at the other end of her line. Did she have to sound that warmly inviting to every unknown?

"I was at your place last night," Milano said. "Pretty late. You weren't there."

"That's right, sir."

"I'd like to see you tonight. How about it?"

"I'm sorry, sir, From four to nine the gallery is holding a reception in advance of the Raoul Barquin opening tomorrow. Some critics will be here and some guests from a closed list."

Of course. Stupid of him not to have picked up her signal at once. The boss, his wife, maybe Barquin himself must be cluttering up that space around her.

"I get it," Milano said. "You're not alone there right now, are you?"

"Yes, I am, sir."

"You are? Then what's this whole line of talk? This sir business?"

"My way, sir," said Christine sweetly, "of handling the Milano accusatory. And exactly what am I being accused of? Going out with an old friend?"

"Hey, I'm sorry. I didn't realize I was coming on like that."

"Well, you were. Why were you at my place anyhow? Something turn up about Lorena?"

"No."

Silence.

A long silence. Milano felt it humming in his ears as it went on and on.

Then Christine said in a changed voice, "It really was an old handshake friend, Johnny. And just some disco. That's all."

Offered gratuitous, mind you. Unsolicited. You're arm-wrestling a toughie, your arm is going down under the pressure, suddenly there is no pressure. For the moment at least.

Milano found himself driven to seize the moment. "Baby," he said sincerely, "I hope you had a perfectly lousy time."

"Wasn't much of a time. And you don't call me, baby, man, and I won't call you man, baby."

[173]

"Chris."

"That'll do fine. But no use counting on tonight. After closing time here the Rammaerts are giving a very fancy dinner right upstairs. Catered. Champagne will flow and caviar will be supplied to all them who does like fish eggs. Very select company. And I'm supposed to be there so that I can be nice to some drunk critics."

"How nice?"

"Oh, neckline down to here and skirt slit up to there, that's about how nice. Now how about Lorena? Didn't you turn up anything yet?"

Milano rerouted his thoughts. "I don't know. I made pals today with your landlord. Your mother's landlord. While shopping for properties to develop. He interests me."

"Him? You're wrong, Johnny. I think."

"Maybe. But he's some kind of case all right, only I'm not sure what kind. How about tomorrow for us?"

"Work day. The Barquin opening." She sounded regretful about it, too.

"As it happens," Milano said, "I'm crazy about his work. Can't wait to see his latest. Any objection?"

"Not if you stick to Barquin while you're here," said Christine.

He put away the phone and waved goodbye to his sidewalk audience as he got the car into motion, Manhattan-bound. And along the way did some stock-taking of J. Milano. Suddenly jealous. Hypersensitive to nuances. Asking for trouble, because this Bailey woman — on the basis of race, age, condition, and temperament — certainly spelled trouble. As for himself — on the basis of an astonishing regression to moony high adolescence — he had the feeling that what he was moving toward was not intended by fate to be just another score. In a nutshell, he had it bad, and, as the song went, that ain't good. But it felt very good.

Back home he turned the car over to the doorman and with the assurance that yes, sir, Mrs. MacFadden is right upstairs, he took the elevator to Gracie's apartment. The Colonel Blimp, glassy-eyed and redolent of juniperberry juice, let him in and told him that the lady was getting her treatment in her bedroom. And so she was, belly down in that polo-field-sized bed with an instrument panel like a jumbo jet's in its headboard, while a Doctor Feelgood number inserted a murderous-looking needle into an exposed buttock. When the Feelgood and the Colonel Blimp were gone and Gracie arranged in queenly respectability against the pillows she deigned to take notice of her visitor. "Enjoy the show?" she asked him.

Milano shrugged. "I'm not into S and M."

"Well, you look like the kind who should be." She held up her arms and surveyed them with distaste. "'Age cannot wither——'," she said. "Shit on that. It withers all right. If they ever peeled my skin off and smoothed it out, there'd be enough to carpet this goddam room. And why the visit, Mr. Milano, during what should be your working hours?"

"A favor. From me to you."

"Some hot jewelry for sale? Going into that end of the business now?"

"Not yet. You setting up one of those weekend orgies tomorrow night?"

"No. I'm supposed to be stuck here in bed for awhile. Avoiding all sinfulness."

"No objection to my bringing somebody up to meet you tomorrow evening?"

"Somebody is very vague language."

"Well, it's a kid I saw give a real hair-raising performance in a show down in the Village. The Birdbath Theater. Ever hear of it?"

"No, thank God. A female kid just possibly?"

"Definitely. With talent. Lights up the stage, as the saying goes."

Gracie raised an eyebrow. "Now just how much wattage would it take to light up something called the Birdbath Theater? By any chance, you wouldn't be making me your personal casting couch, would you, Johnny?"

Milano considered this. "No, I don't think so. Not really."

"No you don't think so not really? Now you interest me. All right, we'll make it tomorrow evening after dinner. Right now you'll find a deck of cards and a rack of chips in that cabinet there. I'll bank a few hands of blackjack. Ten dollar minimum, no limit."

"I thought you were supposed to be getting bed rest. Avoiding all sinfulness."

"There's nothing sinful about booting you right in your guinea machismo, buster. And on your way back with that stuff lock that

[175]

door. If anybody on the other side of it thinks we're fucking in here, I'll thank him for the compliment."

At about five-thirty, when the Colonel Blimp on the other side of the door announced with his knuckles that the session had to be concluded, Milano handed over a check for exactly seven hundred and twenty dollars to his hostess, reminded her of the salon she'd be holding next evening, and took the elevator down to his quarters to mark time until six. At six on the dot he dialed Betty at the Wardour.

"This Kirwan," she reported, "is a college professor. Was a college professor."

"I know. What about his financial set-up right now?"

Betty had a special voice for this routine. Very brisk. "Well, there's one known checking account, balance for last quarter under required minimum. No other banking account, no brokerage account. One known domicile, eight months' tax arrears. One known rental property, three years' tax arrears. Also its present value is negative, maintenance costs exceeding income. One known car, 1972 Skylark, value negative. Only known income here on the printout is from pension and social security. No other known assets listed either. That's it."

"All negative," Milano said.

"Uh-huh. At least under Kirwan's name and I.D. Of course, if he's got a lot of gold stuck away somewhere —— "

In a way, thought Milano, he did have. Maybe not in gold, but in room after room of goodies calculated to make any treasure hunter reach for his checkbook. No problem at all about converting negative to positive by just going to market with a few of those items. A reminder there. "Wait a second," Milano said. "The Hendrick Witter Foundation. What about that?"

"Nothing. It didn't show up at all, Johnny. No way."

No way. So much for that, the foundation that could be screening a hidden cash flow. And could maintain Kirwan's Victorian memorial in the style to which it was certainly accustomed. Yet, Kirwan had been goddam convincing about preserving grandpa's home for the ages.

Betty said, "Still there, Johnny?"

"Yep."

"A retired old professor?" Something in her voice suggested more than just casual reflection. "Funny how you have to put in so much time on him."

"I know. But there are some retired old professors who might just possibly be up to something illegal when no one's looking."

"Oh. So what about Sunday then? I know you're working all hours now, but how about breakfast? A great big old-fashioned one. Say ten o'clock."

"Fine."

"Sunday, ten o'clock then," said Betty. "And just try to make sure it doesn't rain." She hung up.

Charles Witter Kirwan. Scraping the bottom of the financial barrel.

What with one thing and another, it looked like Lorena Bailey had more pocket money to spend than her employer.

# Charles Witter Kirwan

MIDDAY SATURDAY. A brief quiet time among the kraals. A break in the usual Bulanga weekend festival.

The Socratic mode.

I tell you, dear dead Socrates, that in fact you were an agent of corruption.

I tell you, dear self-righteous liberal idiots, dear do-good institutions dedicated to the glorification of the Bulanga, that the ruins all around us are the ruins you made.

My grand event will leave a ruin too.

Rubble dripping with ooze from pulped black flesh.

Oh yes.

Catharsis? No. Catharsis invokes pity and terror, and you and your generation cowering before the occupying tribesmen have already spent enough tears on their sad plight. Enough to drown the world in brine.

Yesterday

Yesterday evening, the heralding of the weekend by the Bulanga in all their glory. Partying by my tenants and their kraal-mates indoors and out.

Inside the apartments of Dapper Dan's folly they gather, windows open the better to share their festival. On the sidewalk before my home they gather. For sustenance, foods packed in greasy wrappers and cardboards. For the total stupefaction of already dull wits, every mode of cheap alcohol in bottle and can. And the holy weed marijuana, so that the night air curling up from my lawn is thick and sick with it. In the morning that stink is gone, replaced by the stench of piss on my sidewalk and garden wall. And both sidewalk and lawn are instant midden heaps of greasy wrappers and cardboards and broken bottles and empty cans.

For entertainment, whitey's own diabolical invention, the electronic music player, turned against him. From the apartments, rent paid or not, the thud-and-thud-and-thump-and-thump on and on and on and on through the endless hours to dawn, the Bulanga water torture, the boiling drops of water rhythmically pounding against the oversensitized whitey skull.

Oh yes.

And there are electronic voices too, raised in tribal song. The caterwauling of the Bulanga female wailing for her demon lover. The bellow of the Bulanga troubador chanting over and over the baby-baby-baby he has managed to memorize.

So

What was left for old whitey through it all last night was a drugged and sweaty and broken sleep, the little there was of it.

Exhaustion in the end, not of pain but of rage.

Yet, one needs

I need that rage.

Dulls the gnawing physical pains. Fires the will.

I need five more days of it. Five. The grand event will take place this coming Thursday at seven in the evening. As full a house as

[179]

possible then, before the weekend. The close of dinner hour. The heating up of those television sets and those stereos.

Then the moment.

The instant end of my pain, the beginning of your wisdom.

Yesterday I set the explosive charge at the top floor of the other dumbwaiter shaft. The western wing of the building. Only three of these jobs remain now, a few hours each for tomorrow and Tuesday and Thursday. Alternate days. Days between will be needed for me to muster my strength.

Good that there is no photograph showing the scarecrow Charles Witter Kirwan of this moment. Old pictures will have to be used by those newspapers and magazines and book publishers and television and motion picture producers to make even more profitably vivid my narrative of the grand event.

Mine.

For which they must pay and pay and pay because it is all mine alone.

An endowment to make this house inviolate. To staff it and secure it and make it a treasure for all time. To celebrate the

The

Where was I?

The photographs. A photograph. None to show me as I see myself in the mirror now. Show what's left of me. Failing flesh, potent spirit. Leader of the *Tötentanz*, lacking only the scythe.

That last photograph of me taken at my retirement dinner. Sage and smiling, full of years and honors. Full of hate for myself. And for all those smiling bleeding-heart faculty faces around me. Cowards who had incited my own cowardly surrender to the Bulanga.

My own hypocrisy.

So

Yesterday.

A hard morning, braced there at the top of that shaft. Suffocating dust. And flaccid muscles now which can lift a little weight but not sustain it. Maddening. You tell your fingers to close tight around a tool. You watch them as they slowly move—doubtfully —as if deciding among themselves whether to do it. They suddenly give up, and you climb all the way down to retrieve the tool. Once, twice, three times. and all the way up again, the last time with

[180]

legs buckling as they carry you rung by rung to the top of Everest.
But
But as long as the raging spirit does not fail, the body will not fail.
So
Only three more days of this trial. Five days altogether.

Now a message to the authorities. And to the executor of my estate. Attention, please.

Believe me, I am not indulging in the macabre when I say bluntly that my own remains will be hard to detect. If they can be detected at all. One stick of dynamite is being withheld from its planned location on the top floor. It is being reserved for my personal use. For my personal instantaneous destruction. Against my chest. The shortest lead to the detonator. The first to go. Instantaneous.

This information is urgent. Pay close attention to it, please.

It is formal assurance that I will be dead — I will be totally dispatched at the moment of explosion — detectable remains or not. So there must be no foolish legal questions brought up about it. No red tape to delay the immediate execution of my will and final instructions. The papers establishing the Witter Foundation must be filed at once by my estate. The very first money coming to the estate from the media must be applied to the Foundation.

The very first.
Yes.
So
What was I about to
Yesterday.

A curious episode. Inevitable in a society with a fatal *nostalgie de la boue*. With a wild yearning to kiss the shiny black ass of the Bulanga.

An enlightening episode. It must be told. Bear with me.

Arson. Arson for profit. Inevitable. Under sentimentalist liberal law, the landlord, worse comes to worst, must house the Bulanga at his own expense. Make sure they're snug and secure. And make sure you buy a large bottle of red ink for your bookkeeping. The landlord's options? Abandon the property or sell at a loss to someone who has his own way of making a profit from it.

A profit? How?

Oh, by way of a large insurance policy, a few gallons of gasoline, and a match.

[181]

That's it. A fat profit and a burned-out building. To be then sealed up by the city of New York so that drunk and derelict Bulanga can't make a home of it and perhaps bruise their tender hides falling through its charred floorboards.

Oh yes.

We already have one such monument on this block. No secret about it, the work of a professional arsonist. The top floor going up with a roar, bringing down the roof, making the building uninhabitable. Full insurance paid, every penny of it.

And behind that professional? The unsentimental gangster. The new generation of whatever it is that's called the Mafia, the Syndicate, Cosa Nostra. That smart new businessman who really does make the doomed landlord an offer he can't refuse.

No sensationalizing in this. No imagining. I met one yesterday.

Smooth. Obviously designated by the family for the college finish, the cultural veneer, the ingratiating manner. No plug-ugly, but a veritable Borgia. Beautifully clothed, well-spoken, driving fifty or sixty thousand dollars' worth of imported car. Middle-aged—plenty of time to progress from rhinestone in the rought to polished rhinestone—and yet, despite those choirboy eyes, plainly stamped with the inherited family ruthlessness, the bent for pimping and arson and murder.

Italian, of course. For our police officials—for what good it may do them—the name is John A. Milano, the address the Sunderland Towers, Central Park South.

Smooth. He came to buy my wretched Kirwan legacy next door, and at my first sign of refusal he demonstrated an instant passion for my Witter legacy, this house. Not to buy, of course. Oh no, not to buy, but simply because it overwhelmed him with its magnificence. Anything, you understand, to charm, to ingratiate, to get me in a selling mood.

And, in fact, he displayed enough shrewd judgment of this house and its furnishings to intrigue me despite myself. To actually gain a foothold in it and a sort of tour of it. But he was up against something new to him. Someone whose life is now being measured out in minutes and so wasn't in the least afraid of him.

An amusing episode. A visitor symptomatic of these obscene

times. Dapper Dan Kirwan would have found him admirable. Impressive. His idea of quality folk. Not quite as desirably flashy as our family bootlegger had been, this Mister Milano, but he would do. High style. But tough. In charge. Capable of beating you to death if you trod on his handsome shoe.

Italian? Well, Dapper Dan never forgave that in those new neighbors from Palermo and Naples who first settled on our block, but he did forgive it in his bootlegger. He would forgive it in our Mister Milano, too.

Here, I should

I must make clear that I am not deprecating the Italian or the Italianate style. No witness to the Bulanga invasion should do anything but admire it.

Yes.

Instructive.

It is

A moment, please.

Not a seizure.

No.

The mind remained clear. In control. Always in balance.

A sort of strangulation. Sudden shortness of breath, then no breath. Agonizing pain extending from throat to right hip.

My fault. I had delayed in taking the increased dosage of Percodan now required. Knew it was required, thought to put it off until I had dictated today's installment. Afraid of drowsiness, so invited disaster.

Never mind.

Today's installment. The bitter truth. No surprise in this since absolute truth is always gall and wormwood. Those history texts which Professor Charles Witter Kirwan researched but never had the courage to write. Our idols, our shining beacons, always driven by fanatic self-interest. The catering to the populace. Elitism made a dirty word by my secretly elitist colleagues.

They will read this narrative, and oh dear me, oh gracious, oh horrors.

Outwardly. For public consumption.

And inwardly? They will never let you know. Too much at stake. Tenure. Honors. The esteem of their masters, the high-intellectual liberal press.

So

Here is a dose of gall and wormwood to constrict their impacted bowels.

There are two bodies of unrelenting resistance to the Bulanga in this Borough of Brooklyn, City of New York, United States of America. Unreconstructed and unrelenting. Our native Italian-Americans, our native Hasidic-Jew-Americans. Sons of the sons of Sicily. And sons of the sons of Polish ghetto ecstatics centuries ago. They live in enclaves, all whiteys so to speak, ferocious in their hatred of the Bulanga.

Oh yes.

Primitives in their way, deaf to sweet socio-political songs about brotherhood, they are wise enough to know their brothers, and their brothers are not the Bulanga. The Bulanga is the enemy and must keep his distance or suffer the consequences.

Your history lesson for today. Your sociology lesson for today.

So

Whatever repugnance I feel toward this Mister John A. Milano as predator — and scavenger — I must — this dying, truth-telling Charles Witter Kirwan must — defer to him as one of that breed staunchly committed to holding their gates against the Bulanga.

Thus ends the

No.

One more item. A non-event.

Lorena Bailey did not make an appearance yesterday. I had not told her to, but I believed that her money hunger would lead her to defy orders. Have her intrude on me. Blackmail perhaps.

I was wrong.

It is a curious fact that with some

# John Milano

Saturdays apparently being newsprint conservation days for the New York *Times*, this morning's Saturday *Times* was inevitably skimpy, but, as Milano flicked through it, there the ad was anyhow, a small, tasteful job among a few others of its kind on the fine arts page.

Neo-Cubist Constructivist works by Raoul Barquin. Opening today at the Rammaert Gallery. Ten a.m. to five p.m.

Milano put aside the paper and attacked his three-minute egg and patented Swedish Rye-Bites. Neo-Cubist Constructivist. Jesus, art hustlers had to have some freak locked in an attic somewhere just cooking up names for these passing—and profitable—fancies. Our Mister Bananas, Director of the Trendy Department.

On the serious side however, he warned himself, helping open the gallery at ten a.m. could be overdoing it. Eleven would be about right. Just drop in casually. See if she still looked like that. Moved like that. Sounded like that. A clandestine lunch together maybe, during her noon break. See if she could still pack it away like that, the miracle being that a large helping of everything obviously had no effect at all on that mind-boggling figure.

This reminded him to do some lover's calculation. Nourishment presented no problem. The co-op's doorman, its Numero Uno hustler, could, on amazingly short notice, come up with anything from the lowly pizza to the regal caviar on toast any time of day or night. As for liquid refreshment, Milano decided, since there was a sufficient variety of bottled high-proof in the wet bar to cover any request, it was just a case of whipping up a pitcher of dynamite martinis and stashing it in the refrigerator for the occasion. He did this, and as an afterthought planted in the vegetable bin of the refrigerator — its higher temperature zone — his last half-dozen bottles of John Courage beer, that lovely evidence that the British, whatever their other deficiencies, could manage to brew a veritable wine from malt and hops.

Music. *Musica*.

He squatted before the stereo cabinet considering political implications. Thus, if out of personal preference you laid on Bessie and Billie and Aretha, would it be tantamount to offering this edgy love object fried chicken and watermelon for dinner? For that matter, who the hell knew how she even felt about fried chicken and watermelon? Would she casually eat it, wisely smile at it, or bounce it off your skull?

All right, let her pick the goddam music. Open herself to his judgment for a change.

He carefully checked out the apartment which, no surprise, was about as pristine as the housecleaning service had left it earlier in the week. The living room maybe a little too pristine, so some careful disarrangement of a cushion here, a couple of magazines on the coffee table there, was in order. The bedroom okay, with a change of bed linen. The bathroom, after he had finished using it, got closest consideration. Luxurious all right — the Emperor Caracalla couldn't have had it much better — but just one of these long black hairs decorating the sink basin could turn any female stomach. At least, so sister Angie had caustically informed him on her maiden visit to the apartment, and while resemblance in any way between Angie and Chris Bailey appeared to be slight who could tell?

Standing before the mirror like that, he let himself do the schizophrenia bit, a hopeful, heated seventeen-year-old Milano looking at his mirrored forty-year-old face. He pulled out of it fast. Fascinating all right, but heading straight for the macabre.

Cool it, man. You're an Earthling, Chris Bailey is a Venusian, and you have no idea what kind of circuit those Venusians operate on. So cool it.

Easier said than done.


When he entered the gallery it was evident that the public was not breaking down the doors to get a look at Raoul Barquin's works. Three youthful floaters solemnly pondered the works. The bulky Rammaert, russet hairpiece aglow, was holding a low-voiced conversation with a prosperous-looking middle-aged couple. Chris was at her desk. When Milano strolled over to she gave him the quick professional smile and a little extra.

Milano leaned over the desk. "Lunch at twelve?" he whispered.

She offered a barely perceptible negative shake of the head and whispered back, "Sandwich and coffee for me in the office. Rammaert wants me on the floor so he can come and go. It has to be after five."

Milano raised his voice. "Thank you. I'll look around."

He helped himself to a brochure from the desk and moved away to dutifully read it. Raoul Barquin. Cuban refugee, now residing in Florida. Having fled oppression in his homeland, he found that in his art he could and so on and so on. Represented in distinguished private collections in Buenos Aires, Santiago, Rio de Janiero. Four major works exhibited here: *Surface Number Eight*, *Surface Number Ten*, *Surface Number Eleven*, *Surface Number Twelve*.

It was, reflected Milano, a neat little Baked Alaska of a brochure. Spoon it up and get a mouthful of foam. Distinguished private collections without their distinguished private collectors being identified. And major works in whose judgment? Well, the artist's for sure. Maybe his doting mother's.

[187]

A close look at the works, however, suggested that they were certainly major in one regard: physical heft. Two on each display wall of the front room, facing each other. Tondos, all of them, cartwheel shape and size. Viewed from the side, they were nearly as thick as cartwheels too, solid wood all the way. Their Neo-Cubist Constructivist faces were canvas over wood. The canvas was untreated and just drawn tight over various solid geometric forms — cubes, cones, cylinders — and, as Milano observed when he looked still closer, it had been stapled around the base of each form to anchor it firmly. Seen from a distance, the color and texture of the canvas gave these productions the unlikely effect of bas reliefs made of wet sand.

And if that wasn't what the artist intended, it sure as hell would be as soon as some hyperventilating art critic put him wise to it.

As Milano started a slow, meditative stock-taking of the merchandise he saw that Rammaert was taking surreptitious stock of him. No big deal, this indication that here was a somehow familiar face which couldn't be placed. Milano soberly nodded a greeting, Rammaert returned the nod and gave his attention again to the couple addressing him. A good eye for faces all right. They had had a split second encounter almost two weeks before, but it had registered.

And, apparently, at least as good an eye for the muttonhead market. Low down near the rim of *Surface Number Ten*, one of those telltale red stars was stuck to the canvas. Sold. Or, since the show had opened just an hour ago, pre-sold. Or — the thought was inescapable when it came to such as Mister Hairpiece — this item was as unsold as the others but had been picked to shill for them. Of course, this had to be done with the connivance of the artist, and, come to think of it, where was the artist on this, the opening day of his exhibition?

But Milano had the feeling that it wasn't the red star or the absence of the artist which troubled him as he made the circuit of the other *Surfaces*. It was something about *Number Ten*. Now why was that when it offered no more or less than its companion pieces? A stirring of *déja vu*? No. Had Raoul Barquin come up with something mysteriously potent in this one case? No chance.

From midway in the room Milano took in the collective show.

The jolt hit him flush in the diaphragm.

Rectangles.

Every tondo displayed an assortment of cubes, cones, cylinders in canvas-covered bas relief. So did *Surface Number Ten*. But it also presented something all its own, something not visible on the others. Rectangles. Identical rectangular forms. Two of them, one southwest about waist high, the other northeast about shoulder high.

Eugene Louis Boudin. *La Plage*, panel fourteen by seven inches. *La Plage, Trouville*, panel, fourteen by seven inches.

Here? Arrived at last?

Only if each of that pair of rectangles measured at least fourteen by seven inches. Or maybe a shade more, allowing for some kind of sheath protecting them. In that case, it would explain why *Number Ten* wore its red star. It meant that nobody, but nobody, could lay claim to it except its consignee.

With the observant Rammaert only a few steps away Milano realized he was concentrating too hard on *Number Ten*. He shifted his attention to another number, eyed it blankly while meshing his mental gears.

What it came down to, if these were the Boudins, was that Win Rammaert, fat face, tacky hairpiece and all, rated top scores in planning the transport of stolen art to foreign shores. Package it inside some clunker that rated as a work of art itself, and then how does anyone get at it without damaging the container? Without desecrating a great big masterpiece by artist Raoul Barquin?

Beautiful.

Because without evidence of a felony there wasn't any customs inspector or law man privileged to slice up this masterpiece to see what was nesting within. Try to X-ray it? A courtroom comedy. Unless its owner agreed, no X-raying would get judicial approval without that evidence to justify it. And where's the evidence unless you do X-ray it? Let the good guys figure that one out.

So much for the good guys.

Willie Watrous, on the other hand, with the sweet scent of Pacifica's near quarter of a million payoff in his hairy nostrils, would not be concerned with judicial process. Definitely not, as he once put it succinctly, when it came to making a crook eat a plate of his own turd. So an easy breaking and entering by Willie's midnight associates, two minutes' work on *Surface Number Ten* with a razor blade, and all Wim Rammaert could do on discovering his loss would be to eat the turd and cook up an outraged and weepy story for the media about art-hating vandals.

Right now, however, the magic numbers were fourteen and seven.

The couple talking to Rammaert finally ran out of conversation and departed. Milano moved into their spot. "You'd be the proprietor."

"Yes. Wim Rammaert. I thought I recognized you. You were at the Archbold showing, weren't you?" The Teutonic-flavored basso was a tuneful growl.

"I was there. I'm sorry, I didn't find it too impressive. This work, however——" Milano made a gesture that took in the collective *Surfaces*. "Will the artist be here?"

"Barquin? Unfortunately, no. Too ill to travel. A sad business for him, missing the occasion."

"I'm sure. But you'd be his agent, I believe?"

"Yes." Rammaert was warming up now, the puffy eyelids starting to droop a little over the bulging eyes.

"In a way," said Milano disarmingly, "I'm something of an agent myself." He lowered his voice. "Representing several novice collectors. Substantial people interested in enlarging their cultural horizons. With a special concern for market appreciability. Comparatively short term appreciability. I think you know what I mean."

Rammaert's expression might be veiled as he weighed this, but he damn well knew what was meant. And that was the approach you used on a Rammaert. Go into raptures over Barquin's wall-coverings, and he might wonder about you. Get right down to business—your clients are out to beat inflation by buying fad art cheap today and selling dear tomorrow, or by donating it to some helpless museum after bribing its curator to appraise it for tax purposes at a wildly unrealistic figure—and this, Rammaert would understand. And even cherish.

Even so, he took his time coming out with it. "My first sale for Barquin indicates he will be highly marketable. And as to the rate of appreciation——" He cast his eyes upward, awed by the possibilities.

"What's his price?"

"For each of those three remaining works the same price. Naturally, it must meet the price fixed by the initial sale."

"Naturally. How much?"

"Sixty thousand dollars. Each."

Milano smiled. "I said my clients were novice collectors. Obviously they are not the Guggenheim and the Whitney."

"Of course. But——" Rammaert let the eyelids droop almost shut. He seemed to be absent-mindedly addressing someone over Milano's shoulder. "—if this concerns your acquisition of all three available works, I would say that anyone so helpful to an artist is certainly entitled to some personal reward for it. Some token of the gallery's esteem."

"I couldn't agree more," said Milano.

"Ah. In that case, if there is a deposit paid——"

"Not yet. I have some hardheaded people to deal with. A little consortium of medical doctors. I'll start with a few phone calls right now. I'm sure you'll be seeing me around."

"I look forward to it."

Foxy grandpa, thought Milano as he walked to the door, deliberately not even glancing in Chris's direction. Bright-eyed, bushy-tailed, and ravenously hungry as only a proper art dealer or casino operator can be.

Near the subway entrance on Sixth Avenue was a newsstand, and there Milano picked up a New York *Post*. The world in tabloid. In Lamston's variety store a block away, he located a stationery department offering a selection of rulers. He paid for an eighteen-incher, waited patiently while the girl at the register tediously found a bag for it, bagged it, stapled the sales receipt to the bag to seal it, and handed the finished job to him, then, while the girl looked uncertain as to whether this was criminal activity or not, he pulled open the bag, extracted the ruler and measured the *Post*, length and width. Fourteen and a half inches long—obviously sent from heaven—but about twelve and a half wide. Using the ruler, he measured off a seven-inch width at the top of the cover page and folded the entire paper to that width. He dropped ruler and bag into a trash barrel at the store's entrance and headed back to the gallery with the fourteen by seven inches of New York *Post* displayed under his arm.

[191]

When he entered the gallery it was with his memo pad pressed hard against the folded newspaper and with pen in hand. Rammaert, engaged in talk with a newcomer, took notice of him, Milano displayed pad and pencil, and Rammaert, the friend co-conspirator, nodded wisely. Note-taking time. Some hard-sell description of the oeuvre for the clientele.

Buddies already. It was enough to make Milano wonder how much of a kickback foxy grandpa had in mind for him, if those three *Surfaces* were picked up in one load.

It was also a problem to maintain a tight control at this moment and not aim straight for *Number Ten*. It was a case of studiously making the rounds of the others, giving Rammaert a view of him jotting down something now and then. And finally, drymouthed and with a churning in the gut, of delaying momentarily in front of *Number Ten*, just long enough, with body concealing the motion as much as possible, to pass the folded newspaper over that southwest rectangle before moving on. Legerdemain. That one pass did it. No need to try another on the northeast rectangle; it was obviously a twin in measurement.

A shade over fourteen by seven.

Jesus, talk about your bargains. A pair of Boudins sealed inside this cruddy construction would add almost a million dollars to its twenty dollars worth of lumber and canvas.

And as the records had it, Milano reflected sourly, when down-and-out Monsieur Boudin finished a beach scene he would wander along the sand trying to find a cash customer for it among all those dull-eyed slobs sunning themselves there. And, put in today's American money, how much did Monsieur Boudin ask for his little painting? Two dollars.

But this was no time to get all heated up about those slobs or about that vast company of them who today had learned to make an international crap game out of authentic art. Now was the time to concentrate on Rammaert. A gifted hustler, yes, but how gifted? Enough so that those two rectangles might be red herrings? In that case, making your moves as if they were the real thing could mean all kinds of disaster.

And the possibility was there.

Milano found Rammaert at his shoulder. "A phone call was made?" Rammaert inquired casually. "Some difficulties ensued?"

Milano slipped pad and pencil into his pocket, released the newspaper into its natural fold. "As expected. Who is this artist? Where is he? What's his reputation so far? What makes the work unique? The usual thing."

"Familiar music." Rammaert shrugged understandingly. "Just give assurance that the artist is a victim of Fidel Castro—a tribute to him right there. And that he's a resident of Miami Beach, which offers cachet of respectability and solvency. Something of a recluse, natural for one so passionately devoted to his art. As for the rest—"

"A modern master," said Milano unblushingly. "The works are powerfully immediate but enduring. Would they be shown by the Rammaert Gallery if they weren't?"

"Would they indeed?" said Rammaert, just as unblushing. "The gallery is closed tomorrow, but my personal phone number is in the book." He gave Milano a friendly clap on the arm and moved off.

Very, very shrewd, Milano thought, watching him go. No pressure. No suggestion of hard sell. Of any sell. Not even to the point of asking for the name, much less any credentials. A case of one fox instantly recognizing another and making a pact with him in foxy talk.

Chris at the desk looked up, face a mask of polite inquiry, as Milano helped himself to a few more brochures and said to her, sotto voce, "You know Richoux a block over on Sixth?"

"Yes. But what was—?"

"I'll be waiting there at five. In the back room. Afterwards it's Gracie MacFadden time."

Leaving her to digest this, he walked out to the street at an easy pace and, since everybody in town seemed to be gathered on boulevard-wide Fifty-seventh Street this pleasant Saturday afternoon, he had to work his way against the crowds at an angle to get to the row of public phones at the corner. Obviously, this was his lucky day on all counts, because the first phone he picked up was a winner. Not vandalized, all parts working. Charging it to the company credit card, he got the Miami area information lady, then, through her, the necessary number.

[193]

Sullie's number. Sullivan had been on the force with Willie, had retired at the same time, and, in fact, had been an inside man for newborn Watrous Associates for a few months until he finally had all he could take of Willie and went down to the Sun Belt to open his own one-man agency. A small-timer, but competent and comparatively honest. And he knew the Miami territory like the back of his hand. The highest tribute that could be paid him was that Willie referred to him as a fucking Boy Scout and almost trusted him.

When you run a one-man agency you're usually there to take a call, and Sullie was there.

"What it comes down to," Milano told him, "is a quick profile. No surveillance. Just get together with the guy somehow, size him up, report back what you make of him. An artist. Miami Beach. Raoul Barquin. You know how to spell that name?"

"By now," said Sullie, "I can spell every goddam Spanish name in the deck. This is Havana North, John, or didn't you hear?"

"Whatever. The joker is that I want word by tonight, I don't care how late. I'll be home waiting."

"If I locate him by then. And meet up with him. But it's five hundred, John, whether I can or I can't."

"Double or nothing. A thousand if you can, forget it if you can't."

"Well now. You sure Willie'll okay that?"

"He'll okay it. And for cozying up to this Barquin, you just tell him a rich, no-name friend of yours saw his art show in New York and wants to know if he's got other works for sale besides the ones in the show. That's all. Simple?"

"Maybe. I'll call you tonight, one way or the other. And," said Sullie in farewell, "don't bother to give my love to Willie."

It was well after five when Chris showed up at Richoux — British soul food, cozy corners, and not likely to be one of Rammaert's haunts — and Milano, watching the reactions of the clientele as she made her way toward him, observed with mixed pride and irritation that she was, indeed, a real head-turner and eye-opener. But something was cooking. Her face was clouded, and when she seated herself you could feel those minor-key vibrations in the air.

His expression must have told her he was getting those vibrations. She grimaced at him.

"Let me guess," he said. "Something happened at the shop."

"At home. Made a duty call to Mama closing time and caught a real earful."

"Baby sister?"

"A baby all right, whatever she thinks. Seems like she woke up Mama in the middle of the night, throwing up all over the bed. Half an hour after that, same thing in the toilet. Then even with nothing left in her, it kept happening. In between she was having some kind of hysterics."

"Pills," Milano said with assurance.

"No pills. What happened then, about six a.m. Odell borrowed a car from the folks upstairs and he and Mama practically dragged that kid to the emergency room over at Kings County. All cleaned out by then and still heaving up. She couldn't hold down any sedative to stop it either. The doctor there finally stopped it by shoving a rectal suppository into her with the sedative in it. And he said it wasn't pills or such, it wasn't junk food, forget it. Reverse peristalsis. Allergy maybe."

"How about a bad case of nerves?" Milano said. "I've been thinking that whatever the kid is doing for her money she doesn't like it. Where is she now?"

"Back home. In bed. And not talking to anybody."

"Nailed down. You want my advice, now's the time to try a bluff. Figure that even if she isn't using anything, she's moving it. Get her eyeball to eyeball and tell her you know about the deal Kirwan has with her, you just want her to come clean about it. Tell her you even have a lawyer lined up who'll get her off without a scratch. Watch her reaction when you say it. That can be the giveaway."

"Uh-uh. She'll just stonewall, Johnny. I know her and you don't. She'll stonewall, and then first chance she gets she'll head right out of town somewhere. Then it'll be Mama's turn for the emergency room. And why do you keep saying Kirwan? Just because there's nobody else you can point at?"

"Want to order?" Milano said. "How about a drink?"

"No. I want to hear about Kirwan. You said you met him. What about him?"

"Well, I think he could be a user. Maybe a mainliner. Far gone."

"Him?" Chris's astonishment was genuine.

[195]

"Him. He looks like it, he sounds like it. Got just enough grip on himself yet to come on shrewd, but the holes keep showing."

"That's what you think. Not what you know."

"Jesus," Milano said, "what are you, witness for the defense? You were the one who told me he rated zero in your book. What did you do, change your mind about that?"

"No, not about him being a cheap, chiseling landlord. Or the way he plays good old plantation boss with Mama. But I told you he had his plus side. Maybe it don't mean anything to you, but in college he was one of those who did all right by minority kids. Always stood up for them. And when I put in for Performing Arts Mama got me a very heavy recommendation from him. Know how hard it is to get into Performing Arts?"

"Now I do," Milano said. "Tell me something. When you lived at home you shared that bedroom with Lorena, didn't you?"

Chris looked puzzled. "What about it?"

"Because Kirwan sure knew exactly what he was recommending. He does keep a pair of binoculars handy for any opportunity that's offered."

"I never saw him try anything like that."

"No but circumstantial evidence is usually what hangs people. One more thing. How would you rate Kirwan financially? You can make it rich, medium, or poor. What about it?"

"How would I know? And what difference — ?"

"Just give it your best shot."

Chris squinted at a wall decoration. She finally said, "Rich. Maybe between rich and medium."

"Furniture rich. He's got stuff in that house worth plenty, but it is not for sale. Nohow. For the rest, that apartment house is a dead loss, taxes way overdue. And there's no cash. Fact. He is on a day to day basis right now. And one way you can get down to that is by having a habit that costs you all the cash you keep scraping together. I started off by figuring Lorena was delivering something from him to the kids at school. Didn't add up though, not after the surveillance reports on her. But switch it around, say she's delivering something *to* him, and it does add up. That's why I say it's time to bear down on the kid. Better you than some narc looking for an easy kill."

Chris picked up a spoon and abstractedly traced a spiral on the tablecloth, starting from its center, carefully working outward in tight loops. "Trouble," she said at last.

"I'll split it down the middle with you," Milano said. He though wistfully of the apartment, the refrigerator humming away, the music box waiting, then said, "I mean that. We can run over to Brooklyn right now, try to get the kid unscrambled before she has a total breakdown."

Chris studied him. "You do mean it, don't you?"

"And about the lawyer too. My sister. Used to be with Legal Aid — one of their best — now in business for herself. Knows every angle. And no charge."

"I'm not looking for any handout, Johnny." No resentment there, Milano took notice. It was the gentlest of reproofs. "Anyhow, it's too dicey that way."

"Only in your mind." He had to wonder why he was pushing it like this when it looked like the evening could be salvaged after all. John A. Milano, obviously built to self-destruct.

But virtue, once or twice in a lifetime, may be its own reward. Chris put aside the spoon and rested her hand on his. She said, "I can't help it, Johnny. I hate to think what could happen if it doesn't turn out the way you think. Like, I'd have to live with it afterward. You wouldn't."

"All right, then how about just getting her to give up that cataloguing job for Kirwan. Or alleged cataloguing job. Help keep her clear of him that way. You've got a handy excuse. No reason for her to hold down a job after school when she's not feeling well."

"I don't know. I guess I could get Mama to try that."

"Good. Now how about you trying some dinner? And a drink."

Chris still had her hand resting on his. Very pleasant. She squeezed his hand, then released it. Even more pleasant, that brief pressure. She said, "You did arrange it about Grace MacFadden tonight, didn't you?"

"Oh, yes."

"Then I'd rather not do any eating or drinking at all right now. Stomach is real jumpy about it."

"Runs in the family?" asked Milano, the interest transparently false.

[197]

"Cheap shot. No, that's just how I am. Casting calls, tryouts, same thing. What do I say to her anyhow?"

"To Gracie? Whatever you feel like saying. As I remember it, you were going to tell her you don't sing, you don't dance, you don't play maids in Art Deco revivals. Why not start with that and see what happens?"

Chris raised her eyebrows. "Maybe I will."

And, thought Milano, maybe she would. It would depend on which part of her tilted the balance when the moment came, the black part or the actress part. He had a feeling she wasn't too sure about it herself right now.

A waitress — pretty enough to make that floor-length Victorian maid's gown and ruffled mobcap highly decorative — was hovering over the table. "Would you care to order now?"

Milano glanced at his watch, then looked up at the girl. "I'm terribly sorry, dear. It seems that the idiot who invited us here has forgotten all about it. We'll be leaving now."

The waitress looked sympathetic. "Well, there is a phone over — "

"No, dear. He will have to do the phoning."

He made up for the idiot's amnesia with a profligate tip, and Chris waited until they were out on the avenue before saying, "Don't shake this off because I mean it. You could have told her I was the one. I mean, taking up her table, and then no order. But you didn't."

"Why should I?"

"Men do. They like to do it. That's all." She made a gesture indicating that the subject was now closed. "When do we meet your lady friend?"

"About eight. It's near Columbus Circle, so if you want to head there now and freshen up at my place first — "

"No, I'd just as soon do some walking around. Getting hefty in the tail sitting on the job most of the time. And the park's right over there. I never do get to it somehow."

A long walk in the park, Milano realized as darkness set in and street lamps went on, had its advantages, especially when it was Central Park where the lamps didn't do much to warn of uncertain footing on untended pathways. And his partner's high heels made the going that much trickier. After her first stumble she slipped her arm through his and hung on tight in bumpy terrain. Tall and

[198]

free-striding, she imposed no burden on him this way. And when his imprisoned arm occasionally made contact with that swell of flagrantly unharnessed breast, she didn't shy away from it.

Definitely prom night again, Milano thought, marveling at his restored innocence.

But, he found, the innocence was fragile stuff. It took just two jolts to fragment it, one little, one big. The little one came when, as they walked into a patch of almost total darkness, Chris slowed their progress and, features barely distinguishable, showed him her teeth set in a broad smile. "Just to let you know I'm still here," she said.

It rattled him. "What call is there for a gag like that?"

"Hey, man, it's a good old Harlem joke."

"Also a good old Bath Beach joke. Only I've heard a lot better."

"Maybe." She wasn't fired up, he saw, just seemed to be interested. "Bath Beach your turf?"

"Was."

"Glad you made it out of there, Mr. Milano."

Happy ending. It almost made that small jolt worthwhile. The big one came after they reached the Bethesda Fountain and parked themselves on a bench there. The area was almost deserted, and, allowing for the sounds of jet traffic overhead, a kind of quiet prevailed.

Peace.

Not for long. A couple of kids drifted over. About seventeen or eighteen, Milano calculated, one black, one white, both street stuff. Equal Opportunity assholes. Moving close, they gave off a fragrance of piss and fried potato grease.

Milano glanced at Chris and saw that she wasn't liking this. He detached his arm from hers and leaned back lazily against the bench thus giving himself leg room for a proper heel to the groin. Traitor to his class or not, he thought, he was grateful that when white stopped in front of him, black pulled up a step behind. With Chris as observer, it meant at least that it wouldn't be the ethnic minority who got that heel planted on him.

White scratched his chest while sizing up the trade. "Man, you lookin' for a good high?"

"Fuck off, sonny," Milano said amiably.

"Oh, hey. Hey." White was amused. Behind him, black was

amused. "Dirty talk, man. Dirty. Right in front of that lady."

"Sonny," Milano said, "if you don't know a cop when you are looking right at him, you are in the wrong business. This is now last call. Fuck off."

They went. Slowly. Making it plain that if they didn't want to they wouldn't, but it just so happened that they were in a mood to.

Chris released a long breath and replaced her arm in Milano's. "Cool, papa."

"Anyhow convincing."

"Seems so. Were you on the cops?"

"No, my agency partner used to be. That's where I learned the subtle techniques."

"Then how'd you get started in the business?"

"Oh, security for one of those fancy Fifth Avenue hotels. Did all right, so then it was free-lance detecting for a whole lot of fancy hotels. Did all right, so this retired cop I helped out on some cases asked me to go partners with him in an agency. His money, my brains. And here I am."

"Still doing all right. Oh yeah, what was all that with Rammaert today? You weren't telling him about the Boudins, were you? I thought that was supposed to wait until they show up."

The end of innocence.

Bad.

Made all the worse, Milano realized, by the compulsion boiling up in him to pull out the plug right now. Tell her what was going on. More than that, give her the combination to John A. Milano. Make her know that along the way all these years he had never thought of offering that combination to anyone else. What is Johnny like inside? Listen —

Not yet.

As things shaped up, it was going to be done sooner or later, but not yet.

There had to be absolute assurance that those were the Boudins. And if they were, she had to be kept clear of the action until it was all over. For everybody's good.

Now what was her question? Rammaert.

"No," Milano said, "nothing to do with Boudin. I just asked him how much an original, handcrafted Raoul Barquin would cost, and he told me."

"Sixty thousand," said Chris wonderingly.

"Right. Then he really laid it on me about buying one. He was so damn convincing that I found myself coming back later to make some notes about the whys and why-nots."

"Mostly why-nots from the way you sound," said Chris.

"You think different?"

"Well," said Chris, "Picasso and Braque dissolved the representational into its cubistic elements. Barquin is now isolating those elements again. Purifying them."

Milano looked at her long and hard, and she laughed. "Rammaert. That's what he told me when he saw me wondering about them."

"And I was just starting to wonder about you. So that leaves one fascinating question. What kind of turkey would lay out sixty thousand for that *Number Ten*? Got an easy answer to that?"

"Sure. Some gallery in Zurich. Switzerland. Anyhow, that's what the consignment order says. Hey, isn't it time to get moving?"

It sure as hell could be, thought Milano. Switzerland. According to what Hy Greenwald had dug out of the files, home base of Gerard Ost and what's-his-name Fountas, prime art hustlers now in jail there. And Ost was Wim Rammaert's cousin. Along with a few other wheeling and dealing Osts operating out of Zurich and Basel. And Rammaert himself had an address in Basel.

So now it could only be Sullie's phone call that might hold things up. Maybe assurance of a highly respectable Raoul Barquin, one-time political prisoner of Fidel. Maybe kudos from that dandy little Norton Gallery in Palm Beach or from the curator of the Miami U. collection. Troublesome evidence that those fourteen by seven rectangles could be red herrings. Or—even though the odds were a thousand to one against it—a thundering coincidence.

Useless and itchy speculation was cut short by a nudge in the ribs. Chris said, "It's getting near Grace MacFadden time, Johnny. How about it?"

First things first.

Gracie's housekeeper let them in. Gracie, prettily negligéed, hair freshly blued, and fingers aglitter with assorted sapphire and diamond, was in bed attended by both Macs, the Colonel Blimp Mac and the Argentinian polo-playing type Mac. When Milano made introductions, he observed that Gracie couldn't seem to keep her eyes off this mystery guest. He had expected surprise when the moment came—probably pleased surprise, at the very least interested surprise—and it was disconcerting that Gracie, a great little poker player, now chose to put on that impossible-to-read poker-face.

And, naturally, there was Chris matching it in ebony.

Hell.

No chance to loosen things up either. Gracie waved an arm at the male contingent. "Out."

"Oh, come on, baby," said Milano, and that was as far as he got.

"Out," said Gracie. "Girl talk. Don't call me, I'll call you."

Outside the closed door, the Colonel Blimp said, "Difficult woman sometimes."

"I suppose," said Milano.

"Beautiful girl, that," said the Colonel Blimp.

"That she is," said Milano.

The Colonel Blimp went his way. The other Mac tuned in the TV to a soccer game, courtesy of some Mexican channel, and Milano stood watching. After awhile he sat down to watch. When the housekeeper came in to take orders for refreshment he realized he hadn't eaten since around noon and still had no appetite. That was something the Old Testament left out, the part where Solomon took one look at the Queen of Sheba and developed anorexia nervosa. And instant madness. Instant total possessiveness. It was one thing to get hit that way by a Vermeer; you knew you couldn't have it so you then suffered instant logic and went your way. But it was, without question, different with people. No need for consoling logic, so the condition spread through the system and into the brain like a dose of encephalitis.

Girl talk. She had a real way with words, did Gracie.

Milano ordered a vodka and tonic, extra large, please, and it was brought to him in a crystal container of not quite hogshead capacity.

When he got it down he felt a little better. The vodka—it must have been hundred-proof—had just about reached all extremities, and the soccer game was on its way to half-time when Chris finally appeared. "Ready?" she asked Milano, and he heard a rumble of metaphoric thunder overhead.

Neither of them said anything as he led the way out and along the corridor to the elevator. Since the elevator men knew Milano's floor, nothing had to be said there. It continued this way to the apartment and through its door. The only good part of it, Milano thought, was that this mute and impassive being from outer space hadn't questioned their destination. Getting into the elevator he had half expected her to say, "All the way down, please." Or even omit the please.

She looked around the living room, spotted the bar and headed straight for it. She hoisted herself on a stool. "I'd like a drink."

"You skipped supper," Milano reminded her. "I thought that first—"

"I would like a drink, please."

Milano went behind the bar. He said doubtfully, "There's martinis all ready. Could be dangerous on an empty stomach."

"Make it Jack Daniels. Straight. Water on the side."

Milano obliged. He watched her down the J.D. chug-a-lug and ease the impact with half a glass of water. He leaned on the bar, everybody's friendly bartender. "Well?" he said.

"You didn't tell her about me, did you?" Chris said sweetly.

"Tell her what?"

"That I was black as the fucking ace of spades, did you?"

"Why the hell do you have to talk like that? If anyone else did it—"

"Never you mind anyone else. You did not tell her."

It wasn't exactly rage mounting in him, Milano knew, it was a kind of wild frustration that had no place to go. He said, "No, all I told her was you had talent and needed a break. But I will now tell you something. Half the big-name black performers between here and L.A. are always in and out of that place upstairs. They know her, they like her, they get along fine with her."

"Well, good for them."

"Because none of them are suffering from a galloping case of paranoia, that's for sure."

[203]

"None of them?" Chris looked at him, it could have been pityingly. "Man, do you know how stupid that sounds?"

"Do you know how freaked out on this race crap you sound?" He struggled to get control of himself. He had a feeling that what with the Stolichnaya now circulating through all capillaries and this awesome emotional case to contend with, his face must be bright red and his eyes popping like Wim Rammaert's. This was not the image planned on while he was whipping up that crock of martinis and disarranging those cushions. He took a deep breath. "Chris. Look. If I thought for one second — one split second — that she'd turn you off like this, I wouldn't have let you near her. You must know that."

Her turn to take a deep breath. "I didn't say you were evil. I said you sounded stupid."

"All right, educate me. Something happened up there, but all I get of it is a Raoul Barquin production. Neo-Cubist Constructivist. How about we try Gérome? You know. All the details down to the last shiny little button."

He waited. At last Chris said, "All right, one big detail. Your friend thinks I'm a high-class hooker."

"She said that?"

"No. But she let it be known. You don't come right out with things like that to a high-class hooker. You just let it be known how you rate them."

"Or," said Milano, "is it possible that's your reading of her?"

"Oh, shit. Look, you really want to be educated, Johnny? Then listen close. This is not the first time it happened to me with people that color. Want to know why? Because I am a real foxy lady. Great-looking and with a lot of style. And very black."

"For chrissake," Milano protested, but she wasn't letting him off the hook that easy.

"Want some more education, Johnny? You know my mother? Grayhair, fat old lady? She goes to an apartment to do domestic and there's the husband and wife. Caucasian, you know? The wife takes off for the supermarket meanwhile, and next thing, my grayhair, fat old mother with three grownup kids feels a hand on her rear end. Because it is a black rear end. Has to do some heavy wrestling sometimes before she can get back to the floor-scrubbing."

A lot of style all right, Milano thought. Sugar Ray Robinson had that style. Jab, jab, hook off the jab, right cross. Bang.

He said, "That's the big detail. What about all the little ones? Exactly what did happen up there?"

Chris held up her glass. "Refill."

"Not yet. You are not going to hang me up like this, foxy lady, and then go all incoherent on me. No chance."

"No? Do you believe what I just told you? Do you understand it?"

"Yes."

"Hurt?"

"You must know goddam well it does."

"If you say so. All right then. First your lady friend asked about me and I told her. I think she bought maybe ten percent of it. Then she asked about you. Real tough exam paper she handed out. Highly personal."

"What's that mean?"

"Oh——" said Chris. She scrutinized his face as if searching out blemishes. "You do have a way with bitchy old ladies, don't you? The one runs your office, this one upstairs——"

"You were with her an hour," Milano cut in. "You weren't talking about me most of it."

"Just some. Then she told me to get cards and chips from that cabinet there and she'd deal some blackjack, dollar a hand. So I told her I did not have the money to be a loser with, and the way she looked, that was one of the things about me she did not believe."

"So you didn't——"

"Yes, we did. She said all right, not to worry, she'd bill you for anything I lost. Only I didn't lose. I took her for thirty-two dollars."

"You took Gracie MacFadden for thirty-two dollars at blackjack?"

"Only on paper." Chris smiled wickedly. "She said to collect from you. Said if you were going to pay for me losing, you could just as well pay for me winning."

That thundercloud over her, Milano saw gratefully, was starting to dissolve. An edge of silvery moonlight was showing through. Thirty-two dollars, thirty-two hundred, name your figure, it was worth it to get that change in the weather.

He drew out his wallet, and Chris clapped a hand down on it

pinning it to the bar counter. "No. I already told you that, Johnny. Never lay money on me."

"It's her money. Don't worry, I'll collect from her."

"No. You just let her know I wouldn't take it from you. Then anybody asks me about her, I can tell them all I know is Mrs. Grace MacFadden personally owes me thirty-two dollars. And when they ask how come, I will be happy to tell them. Including, you know, the media. If they ever get around to me."

"Some day they will."

"Oh yeah." It came out half sardonic, half mournful, and the sound of it reminded Milano that two fingers of Jack Daniels in that wide-bottomed glass made a lot of Jack Daniels. "Only trouble is," Chris said, "no singing, dancing, or Art Deco maids. And I do not do windows. You know what? I'm hungry. You have a kitchen around here, don't you?"

"The doorman offers better. Quick delivery, too."

"No, all I want right now is something to stop my stomach from talking."

In the kitchen he watched her take inventory of the barren refrigerator. "Old Mother Hubbard," she commented and helped herself to a tomato. She quartered it and ate it drippingly over the sink. She paper-toweled her face and hands. "Better," she said. She leaned back against the sink. The way she regarded Milano, a faintly puzzled expression on her face, tongue out, the tip of it touching her upper lip, gave him the feeling that doctor was working out a troublesome diagnosis. At last she said, "I guess I'm sorry I dumped on you like that."

"So am I," said Milano. "But you know my intentions were good."

"Talk about wooden dialogue. But I know. What I liked was the way you took it when I told you about my mother on the job. You looked real sick."

"Anything to brighten up your day."

"You know what I mean."

She moved back to the living room and Milano followed. The existential life, all right, instant by instant, where the decisions were hers to make, and unless he was willing to have everything suddenly come apart, where all he could do was stand ready to deliver the response called for. And, if it wasn't too paradoxical a thought, to keep himself braced for the unpredictable.

Fascinating, if that was the word for it.

Half his ancestors were Brescia Lombards from the far north, the other half Catania Sicilianos from the deep south. Right now, he told himself, every dead and buried male of at least the Siciliano half had to be spinning in his grave with outrage.

He stood by as Chris appraised the living room. "Nice," she decided at last. "But kind of bare, isn't it?"

"All the essentials are here."

"Hmm." Forefinger pressed to her chin, she did some more appraisal. "That's what it is. Nothing on the walls. On purpose?"

"Uh-huh."

"But for somebody like you? No paintings, no prints, nothing? The way you are about art?"

"I know. But what I want on those walls I cannot afford. So it's better this way."

"Poor-mouthing? You could always trade in that Mercedes."

"Yeah, but it wouldn't help much, not even for a small down payment."

"On what?"

"Oh, the three Degas portraits I've got on the shopping list. And Seurat's *Grande Jatte*. You know it?"

"I know that much. It was mostly scenic design at Performing Arts, but we got into a lot of art history that way."

"Well, *La Grande Jatte* centers on the wall right there. And my two Turners go right over there. Late Turners that fit the Impressionist ambience. One Renoir. Trouble is it's a vertical seventy by thirty-eight, so those bookshelves have to be cleared away. And that's all temporary. Because after a couple of months we switch over to some of my Spanish school biggies. Featuring Velasquez, El Greco, Goya. Then the Italian show. The primitives are in the bedroom, but here we've got Caravaggio. Two of them. One way we save room, no Raphael. Do you know what it would have to feel like to stick a finger into one of Raphael's people?"

"You tell me."

"Like sticking a finger into the Pillsbury Doughboy." Milano

[207]

pulled up short. "Does all this strike you as being a little weird?"

"Sure. Isn't it?"

"I guess. So just keep it to yourself. I mean, not make table-talk of it with anybody."

"Trust me," Chris said. She reached out a finger and traced a small circle in the middle of his forehead. "Nothing more recent in there? Like, not even Jackson Pollock and Franz Kline and such?"

"No room. Anyone breaks completely with representational is just giving me a close-up of his brain cells. Artists don't have much in the way of brain cells."

"Your opinion."

"I'm the one doing the collecting," Milano pointed out.

She was looking at him speculatively. In silence. She had a way of turning on these long silences which hummed in the ears. She said, "Sometimes you find things out backwards, know what I mean?"

"No."

"No. Well, when you told me in the gallery about meeting Grace MacFadden tonight, that was a real high. But I was also pissed off some, because I could see what was coming. You both lived in the same building, we'd visit her, then we'd drop into your place and I'd be owing you a big one, and there would be the bed waiting. Your way of operating. Kind of simple-minded but, like, highly workable. You still with me?"

"Yes."

"You don't have to get uptight like that. Because while I was thinking just how hard to put you down when you tried aiming me at that bed, it came to me that I was all ready to hop into it with you. And if we didn't make it together somehow after Grace MacFadden, I would really be pissed off."

"I'm simple-minded?" said Milano

"Some ways. That's all right." She languorously draped her arms around his neck, and he, with the feeling that he was about two steps behind the parade and running to catch up, found his arms around her waist.

Then, during the exploratory meeting of lips and teeth and tongue, he moved one arm high, the other low, and there was a straining together as tight as possible of every square inch of body surface. She finally drew her head back. "In case you don't know," she said, "you got my timer all set and ticking."

In bed, it was the same exploratory trip to start with, a long, voluptuous exploration, and then a series of variations on the old basic theme, none especially inventive, but all, as far as Milano was concerned, dazzling. The noisy, rampaging finale left him replete and thoroughly winded. His partner, he was pleased to see, appeared to be just as replete and just as thoroughly winded.

After awhile she sat up, drew her legs under her, and used a corner of the sheet to wipe the sweat from her face and chest, so that he had the pleasure, from just about the right distance, of studying that gleaming back from the roundness of the buttocks resting on her heels to the narrowness of waist and width of smoothly curved shoulder. That skin, he saw as he slowly drew his thumb up along the arc of spine, was not black. It was the whole palette under a sheen of blackness. The crisp hair was black — soot black — but alive with a glitter of pinpoint lights seemingly woven into it.

He worked his fingers deep into that glittering crispness, and between the fingers it seemed as magically alive as Medusa's serpents.

"Brillo-head," said Chris.

Milano gripped the hair and pulled her head back. She didn't resist.

"Bailey," he said, "don't ever pull that kind of crack again."

"What kind?"

"You know goddam well what kind. That putting yourself down clown kind."

"Oh yeah?" She dropped her head farther back and looked at him upside down. "Well, it is like Brillo, didn't you notice? And down here" — she reached around for his other hand and planted it against the dampness of her mound " — it is just like watchsprings. Little tiny watchsprings."

He could feel that familiar frustration building up in him again. And that upside-down face was making him dizzy. He released her almost roughly. "Let's talk about the weather," he said.

She pivoted around on her knees to face him. "You have got to get one thing straight, Johnny. I never put myself down."

"No? Then why that kind of talk?"

"Because I felt — you made me feel — like doing you kind of a favor. I was taking you inside, so you could look outside with me."

It took Milano a few seconds to get a handle on this. "I see. And outsiders are all those terrible white people. And their buzz word is Brillo-head."

"Oh, do not play word games, man. I said I'm trying to do you a favor. Could be I'm trying to do me a favor, too, because this does not look to be any one-night stand. Or does it?"

"No, it does not."

"I thought not. But you still do not know what favor I'm talking about, so I'll make it real simple. You have got a mother and a sister, right? You know hypothetical? Well, this is hypothetical. What happens if you feel like showing me off to your mother and sister?"

Oh yeah, Milano told himself. On a scale of one to ten for conversation stoppers, we have just come up with an authentic number ten.

*Melanzana.* The Bath Beach, Mulberry Street, paisan word for her division of sad humanity. *Melanzana.* Eggplant.

Hey, did you hear about Johnny's *melanzana*?

Chris said, "And they're not terrible people, are they, Johnny? Or the people in your office? Or your friends? Just people, right? Only when you see them from inside where I am there is something about them, you know? And if you can't see it that way when we're together with them, you could come off stupid and I could come off hurt. And maybe you can live with stupid, man, but I will not live with hurt."

Milano carefully did not reach out a hand toward her. "Are you hurting now?"

"No."

"Well," said Milano, "that's not a bad start, is it?"

They had shared the last remaining tomato and container of cottage cheese and were on the floor of the living room sorting out record albums when the collect call came. Sullie, on the line from Miami.

Milano took the call in the bedroom, closing its door behind him.

Sullie started right off with, "You know that double or nothing deal, John? No dice. We'll have to make it the regular five hundred."

"Couldn't you get close to Barquin?"

"Let me tell it my own way, John. What happened, there's no Raoul Barquin listed anywhere on the Beach. So I tackled what Barquins there were, all by doorbell, no phone. About an hour ago, I hit pay dirt. Guy name of Adolfo Barquin. Runs a carpenter shop way downtown in the low rent section here. South Beach. Almost solid Cubano now. And this Adolfo lives upstairs over the shop.

"Anyhow, he's Raoul's uncle, and he was ready to spill his guts to anybody who said hello. Seems Raoul came over in that big Mariel boat-lift, and it was Adolfo and some others in the family sponsored him here. Guaranteed the government they'd take care of him, even get him a job. So Adolfo took him into the shop where it turned out he was no use with the hammer and nails, but he was one hell of a salesman. Went out and got a lot of business, plenty of it fancy, high-price jobs."

"A salesman," Milano said. "Not an artist."

"No way. But a lot more than a salesman. Three days ago, the cops walked into the shop with a warrant for him and Adolfo and a search order. Seems Raoul is a hot connection to the cocaine cowboys here, and when some of those high-price jobs went out of the shop they were loaded with coke. Picture frames, little wood statues, stuff like that, and all loaded up. And it turns out he was never any political prisoner in Cuba, the way he claimed to be. He was just one of those scummy jailbirds Castro dumped on us here."

"Where is he now?"

"Nobody knows. Or is saying. He must have been tipped off, because he got away clean. That's why Adolfo is so talky. His story is that he never knew what was going on, that Raoul doublecrossed him by involving him in the racket after all he did for Raoul, and he'd like to find the guy himself and beat the truth out of him."

"You believe that?" Milano asked.

"Nah. He's lying all the way. But what other story could he tell? He's out on bail himself right now. And that's it."

"It's plenty, Sullie. Just bill the office for that double-or-nothing thousand and address it to Shirley. By the way, what's Adlofo's address?"

"Two-ninety Jefferson Court, right near the marina down there. You're all right, John. Drop in whenever you're in town. Don't forget your Spanish dictionary."

Milano put down the phone.

Home free.

No, he warned himself, not yet.

Two Boudins waiting, lowgrade security, Rammaert nailed to the wall no matter how you looked at it. But time was now of the essence. The L.A. police might have kissed off those paintings, but if the Miami police were scouring through Barquin's shipping orders, they could wind up at Rammaert's door ironically checking out cocaine connections. It still wouldn't be a case of ripping open those canvases, not with some smart lawyers yelling desecration of art, but sooner or later there would be X-raying, what with the evidence on hand. And Pacifica — and collector Henry Grassie — would sooner or later get their paintings back without any obligation at all to Watrous Associates.

Lucky it was the weekend. It meant a little head start.

Unlucky that there was no way to move alone on it any further.

Like it or not, it was Willie Watrous time again.

Milano picked up the phone distastefully, touchtoned the number, and was both irritated and relieved when there was no answer. He tried Shirley Glass's number, and her immediate response was, "If it isn't a fire drill, it must be John Milano."

"Good guess. I can't raise Willie, Shirl. Where is he?"

She had to know from his tone that this was serious business. She said, "Chicago, Johnny. That retired cops organization he belongs to. What is it, Pacifica?"

"On the stove and boiling over. You know where to reach him in Chicago?"

"Yes, of course."

"All right. Call the airlines now, book him for a flight back here tomorrow morning. Then call him about it and tell him we meet in the office as soon as he gets in. What time would that be about?"

"Should be before noon, Johnny. You want to play it safe, make it noon. Am I expected, too?"

"No need. Oh yeah, and when you get a bill from Miami — Sullie's

[212]

office—that's on Pacifica, too. Make it quick pay. And make sure about Willie, Shirl."

Milano put down the phone again and sat for awhile considering the coming bloody bout with Willie. Then he went back to the living room where Chris, naked and enticing, was sprawled on the floor on her belly reading the jacket copy of an old album.

"Business call," Milano explained.

"You don't have to apologize," she said. She handed him a record. "I pick one to start, then you pick one. This is my pick."

Bessie Smith.

"Mine, too," said Milano. "So you also get the next pick."

At about four o'clock, he got out the Toyota and they drove through dark, almost empty New York to Sarge's all-night deli over on Third Avenue for a combination dinner and breakfast. Afterward, since they agreed it would obviously be graceless of her to risk waking roomies Pearl and Lenardo by coming in at this hour, they headed back to the apartment and this time had one of those languorous, almost slow-motion sessions which, however, produced the same rapid-fire M-G-M fireworks for the big finish.

When Milano finally got around to turning off the light he discovered that there was sunshine filtering through the blinds. He closed them tight, pulled the phone jack—with phones disconnected there could be no communication from reality out there—and set the alarm clock.

"Busy little beaver, aren't you?" Chris commented sleepily.

"Meeting with my partner at noon. I'll be gone before you're up, but you just wait here for me. Any objections?"

"No. One, maybe. What do I do if I crave some nourishment meanwhile? Fry up a pan of ice cubes?"

"You use the kitchen intercom and tell the doorman all about it. And when delivery is made remember it's all on my tab. Hey, are you listening or are you asleep?"

"Both," said Chris.

She was still sound asleep, twenty fathoms under and far gone, when Milano took his departure, and when on the way out he

[213]

stopped to remove the Sunday papers from the doorstep and lay them on the bed beside her as his replacement, she didn't twitch.

Willie, on the other hand, was wide awake and ready to go. A little pouchy-eyed and the worse for wear after the high old time at his antique cops' convention and the quick flight home, but in, what was for Willie, a good mood. If there was any such thing as a happy ferret, Milano reflected, his partner was giving a first class imitation of it.

It wasn't going to last long, but it was nice while it lasted.

They met in Milano's office, and Milano, seated at his desk, took note of subtle changes on its surface. Some of Hy Greenwald's personal effects were there including Hy's own appointment calendar, pretty heavily loaded. Evidence in a way that the protegé might be the ball of fire he had been estimated to be.

By way of a sociable warmup Milano remarked on this, and Willie, lighting his cigar in the armchair across the desk, grunted affirmation. When he had the cigar properly fuming, he said, "Greenwald told me you two figured out it was this guy Rammaert over on Fifty-seventh. It is him, isn't it?"

"Nobody else."

"Shows you. I dropped in there myself to size him up, and that fat son of a bitch don't look like he has the brains for any such operation. Looks like he runs a funeral parlor. Great front. And that shop, too. You spotted those Boudin pictures? You know where he's got them?"

"Come on, Willie, would you be here if you thought I didn't?"

Willie had the grace to wink broadly. "My partner. A real wildman. But when it counts — "

"Sure," said Milano.

"Look, Johnny boy, you think you're easy to live with? But I never said you didn't earn your keep. All those fat cat connections, glamor people, show biz screwballs, art crazy characters like that Grassie — I never said we don't put money in the bank from your side of it. But you forget sometimes there is a beat-up old man with his nose to the grindstone across the hall. Doing all that boring nine-to-five paperwork that has got to be done."

"Finished?" said Milano.

"I'm letting bygones be bygones. Now what about those pictures? From what I saw in that shop, the security is strictly nothing. So it's just a case of lining up the two guys I want on this and timing their moves right. You give me that floor plan with the little old *X* marked on it —— "

"How do you know I can?"

Willie froze for an instant, then warmed again. "Johnny boy, if you know where those pictures are, you saw them. I mean, with your own big brown eyes. You did not just see a paper bag with a string around it and *Boudin pictures* marked on it. If you did, you'd know it was just goddam bait, wouldn't you?"

"Whatever I saw, Willie, we're playing this one legit. We're buying those paintings from Rammaert."

Chris Bailey could produce silences that hummed in the ears. Willie now produced one that roared in the ears. He finally found his voice. "We are what?"

"Buying them," said Milano equably, "and fast. Now cool off and listen. Those paintings made it from the Coast to Miami, probably by car. They were shipped to Rammaert from Miami, and he's got them ready now for delivery to Europe. Probably by plane. And if they're on that plane when it gets off the ground at Kennedy, we have blown the deal."

"You still don't —— "

"Keep listening. There was kind of a screw-up at the Miami end, so the cops there might wind up with Rammaert's name and address. He doesn't know about that, because if he did he wouldn't have those paintings so close to him right now. That's why we have to move fast, make it legit, not take any chances. And I guarantee Rammaert'll sell me the goods for a bargain price."

Willie was fast recovering himself. "The Miami cops? For chris-sake, if there was ever a small town, redneck, meatball department, you just named it. Whoever's handling this case for them, you just show him a twenty dollar bill and watch how fast that folder gets lost."

"Stop dreaming and talk sense, Willie."

Willie was now back in balance. To prove it, he held the cigar at arm's length and carefully tapped its ash to the carpet. He said in friendly fashion, "First let's get straight what we mean by sense. What would you call a bargain price?"

"Sixty thousand for both. He'll want a lot more. He'll settle for sixty."

[215]

"Sixty." Willie pursed his lips and nodded solemnly. "Very reasonable." Milano waited. He didn't have to wait long. Willie removed the cigar from his mouth and leaned forward. "You really think we will pay that thief sixty thousand bucks for those goods — stolen goods — when we don't have to? For that matter, if you got the gun to his head the way you say, why not just pay him off by telling him we'll keep out mouths shut? And what can he do about that?"

"You never push a rat up against the wall, Willie. He must have sunk plenty into the deal so far. We cover that so he won't go dangerous on us. We get too greedy and the agency license could be on the line."

That touched a nerve but didn't sever it. "Sixty thousand," Willie said.

"It makes the deal a piece of cake. Pacifica said they'd have payment in our hands on forty-eight hours notice. Probably through that Hale character. So you give them notice right now and by Wednesday he'll be here with the money. The other thing you do right now is countersign an agency check for the sixty thousand. I'll settle with Rammaert fast, and I'll have those paintings waiting for Hale when he shows up. Simple?"

Willie was taking it surprisingly well. Too well. So this was not going to be one of his apoplectic sessions, Milano saw, not this one. This would be one of those classic stonewalling jobs. An invitation to keep banging your head against that wall until you went dizzy and had to be carried to your corner.

"John," Willie said in the gentlest of tones, "my way costs only twenty thousand. At most. And Rammaert never knows what hit him."

"It's still grand larceny."

"Then all Rammaert has to do is yell for the cops. Which you and I know is the one thing he will never do. Right? So we come around to that same old question. How can you have any kind of larceny without a complaint?"

"Bullshit. The agency's loaded, Willie. We're not working out of that dump off Union Square any more. It's getting time to change old habits."

"Maybe. So you just make out that floor plan with that big $X$ — and with any helpful little notes to go along — while I think it over."

[216]

# JOHN MILANO

They looked at each other. A new comic strip featuring William Watrous, thought Milano. Granite Man.

And it was better-than-a-Vermeer Chris Bailey, he knew, who was somehow blocking his way to the usual weary surrender. A co-conspirator, but to what? Buy back the paintings, and though this would bruise Rammaert, it meant she'd be the co-conspirator to only a mild scam. Let Willie do it his way, and, Chris baby, you are co-conspirator to something you might think is real evil.

And it wouldn't matter that John Milano had chosen not to tell you what had transpired behind the scenes. Five minutes after you opened the shop on that torn and disfigured canvas next morning, you'd work it all out. Too brainy for your own good, baby, and disastrously too brainy for mine.

Milano watched Willie, an unruffled, squint-eyed owl, watching him. Settling in for a long stay.

"There's an informant involved," Milano said. "You know how we stand on that. If we do it your way, this one could be hurt bad."

"Christine Bailey?"

For two heartbeats Milano had the amazed feeling that the old bastard could actually read his mind. Those two beats were all Willie needed to settle any doubts he might have had, that was for sure.

"I thought so," Willie said. "For one thing, there I am okaying charges to Pacifica for surveillance of a Lorena Bailey. Big fat charges. By a couple of our colored help, no less. And when I put it to them, all they could tell me was it was some high school kid you had them tailing. But when I put it to Greenwald he said he didn't know about any such kid, but there was a grown-up Christine Bailey worked for Rammaert. I got a look at her in that shop, Johnny boy. Great-looking piece of dark meat all right. So she fingers those pictures for you, and you pay off by fingering her sister for something or other. I'll bet you fucked the ass off her too along the way, didn't you? Not that this bothers me any. At least, not as long as I got my own private toilet here. With my own private toilet seat."

This man is garbage, Milano thought. A lot of words came close to describing him, but here was the only one that really did it with absolute precision. Garbage.

But shrewd garbage.

[217]

"She's still an informant," Milano said.

"Knock it off," Willie said contemptuously. "This is no pro we'll ever do business with again. This is a pigeon flying by."

Milano seized the opening. "The total pigeon. In fact, she still doesn't know Rammaert's private business. Or where the hell those paintings are. But if you lift those paintings, Willie, she winds up at the bottom of the pile. I do not see it that way."

"You don't." Willie, his eyes fixed unwaveringly on this oddball across the desk, realized his cigar had gone out. He abstractedly drew the pack of matches from his pocket and then, without relighting the cigar, abstractedly put them back into the pocket. And that, thought Milano, was about as good as things were going to get. Willie said, "Let me spell it out. This piece worked the inside for you. She gave you your leads. So now you know right where those pictures are. But somehow she don't. My goodness gracious, she don't even know what Rammaert is all about, does she?"

"Believe it," Milano said.

"Yeah? Well, I believe what I can see. And what I see is that while she was doing a job for you, you were paying off by doing some kind of job for her charged to Pacifica. You scratch my back, I scratch yours, right? But of course she never had the least idea why you're scratching each other's backs like that."

"And still doesn't," Milano said. "Because I cooked up a whole beautiful story for her to go on."

"Uh-huh. And if you didn't, I'll bet you could cook it up for me right now, couldn't you?"

We are going to do it Willie's way, Milano thought.

We are going to do it Willie's way, and smartass Chris Bailey will take one long look at that pair of fourteen by seven emptinesses on *Surface Number Ten* and suddenly know all the answers.

So the logical move now would be to haul this load of Willie garbage to that window and heave it out. Thirty stories free fall, and it really would become garbage. The trouble was that whether up here or thirty stories down it would be regarded by the law as some sort of human being. Felony manslaughter at the least, not misdemeanor littering. Which shows how much the law knows.

On the other hand —

Milano centered Hy Greenwald's scratch pad on the desk, took pen in hand and wrote briefly. He tore off the slip of paper and offered it to Willie. Willie read it. He read it again. He looked at Milano. "Your I.O.U. for forty thousand?"

"My way costs sixty. Yours costs twenty. The difference is forty. I pay the forty and we do it my way."

Willie's face was screwed up into a Hieronymous Bosch study of total incomprehension. "Are you out of your fucking mind?"

"Don't push your luck, Willie. You're getting the best deal you ever had a chance at."

Total incomprehension became total suspicion. "Why?"

"Yes or no, Willie, that's all you have to say. And the way you say yes is to countersign a company check for sixty thousand right now. I cash it tomorrow and move right in on Rammaert. I'll have the paintings for you tomorrow afternoon."

"I still want to know what your angle is."

"Going once," said Milano. "Going twice. And the answer seems to be no."

"The answer is maybe." Willie studied the note again as if trying to break its code. He held it up on display. "This paper means nothing. And the way you blow your money, I know goddam well you couldn't hand me any check for forty grand that wouldn't bounce from here to Jersey City. So the big question is, if there's formal papers drawn up where you assign the forty thousand to me out of your share of the company profits this year, will you sign that?"

"Sure. Does that mean you are now saying we have a deal? Then what you do right now ——"

"Oh no," said Willie. "I'll have the papers drawn up by Tuesday morning first thing. First you sign, then you get the check for Rammaert's payoff. Don't worry, those pictures'll keep one day more. So will Rammaert. And so will that chocolate bar you and him are taking turns at. Right?"

Garbage to the end.


Walking back to the apartment, Milano put in the first long crosstown block wrestling cold fury to the mat until, while it still did some heaving and writhing, it was pinned down there.

The second block, he examined the case against John A. Milano.

[219]

Time to part from Willie once and for all. But every passing year had been the time to part from Willie once and for all. So?

Inertia. Moving along the old familiar groove you stayed in the old familiar groove.

The good life. The very good life. Half-partner in what had somehow turned out to be, as Willie had predicted it would, a money machine. You could do all right on your own, but you could not do ten or twenty times better than all right. Which is what you were doing right now.

Willie's age. Maybe not older than God, but old enough to draw social security payments along with his company take, and you had to be in a special category of old to do that. How much more time could he clock anyhow?

But getting down to the bottom line, Milano silently asked the statue of Bolivar guarding this expensive end of Central Park, can someone who voluntarily pays his partner forty thousand dollars just to claim his voting rights in the company be capable of sanely working out a heavy personal problem? Especially, as was now the case, when the problem appeared to be working him out.

What the hell, sufficient unto the day —

Milano let himself into the apartment, and Chris appeared in the bedroom doorway wearing his Sulka dressing gown over apparently nothing. She folded her arms on her chest and just stood there.

"Hi," she said.

Milano regarded his forty thousand dollar prize with a sense of profoundly pleasurable rediscovery. "Hi to you."

"Something happened here," said Chris. She hugged her arms tighter against her chest. "A little while ago."

End of announcement? Well, Milano thought, fuses will blow, and water will overflow the bathroom sink, and life will go on. He said encouragingly, "Something happened here a little while ago."

"Yes. I called the doorman on the intercom and ordered a couple of sandwiches. He said he'd be up with them in about half an hour."

"And you're still waiting."

"No," said Chris, making it a long, long no on a rising note. "About fifteen minutes after that, the doorbell here rang. I thought, well this doorman is really super service, isn't he, and I opened the door. It wasn't him."

"Chris, even in a place like this you never —"

"It was a girl. Cute blondie. Big hello there smile. Until she got a look at me."

Milano's heart sank. Literally sank, he knew, so that it was now being queasily cradled by his entrails.

He glanced at his watch.

One-twenty.

Sunday.

And ten o'clock Sunday morning was breakfast time with Betty at the Wardour.

And with the phones off here —

He said to Chris, "Did she ask who you were?"

"No. She just pushed by and went looking through every room full speed, bathroom included. Then she hauled out that bottom drawer in the dresser and pulled out nighties and such and went in the kitchen and dumped them in the garbage can. Then she took off."

"But I see you didn't."

"So far, no."

Milano started to motion at the couch, then thought better of it and motioned at an armchair. "Want to sit down while we clear the air?"

Moving wide of him, she walked to the chair, sat down well forward on it, and tugged the dressing gown over her knees.

"Drink?" said Milano.

"No. I've got that stomach again."

"Looks like you've got company this time," Milano said. "To tell the truth, I'm scared."

"To tell the truth, so am I."

Milano's heart rose a little. "She just got her own place, so we had kind of a housewarming breakfast set for this morning. I forgot all about it. Anyhow, what we had going for a few months was all low gear. Lately, there wasn't anything at all."

"She didn't think so. Until right now maybe."

"I gave her every signal I could think of," Milano protested.

"Except tell it to her right out."

"Well," said Milano, "I guess men have a problem that way. And she was getting into the orange blossom and bridal gown mood

[221]

which makes it even harder. You get the feeling you're breaking an engagement."

"There could be worse engagements," said Chris. "That is a very pretty lady."

"So my family kept telling me. Trouble was, they went for her a lot bigger than I did."

There was one of those patented Bailey silences. Then Chris rested her elbows on her knees and bent far over, head down and forehead supported by her fingertips. She finally looked up and asked, "Any other pretty ladies you're forgetting you had dates with?"

"None."

"Because there's something I never said to any man before. It has to be one-to-one between us. It is you and me and nobody else. At least that is how it has to be for me. If it's different for you, do not send out signals, just tell me right now. Is it different for you?"

"No signals," said Milano. "Nothing to tell."

"Good," said Chris. "There better not be."

"Maybe I ought to try to get her on the phone now," Milano said. "Clear up things once and for all."

"No. They're cleared up enough. What you can do now is take me out and buy me lunch."

"Those sandwiches never came?"

"They came. First I was going to heave them in the garbage on top of that see-through stuff, but I saw what they cost when I signed for them, so I couldn't. They're in the refrigerator. Do you have any idea what they cost?"

"Oh, yes," said Milano.

# Charles Witter Kirwan

Y<small>OU</small>.

You out there.

What do you know of reality?

What do you want to know of it?

Sensation-seekers, that's all. Polluters of the gift. One revelation in print as good as the next as long as both gratify your need to be lied to.

You can read and yet you are blind.

Oh yes.

And the truth-teller you scorn for your chosen liars is tormented and betrayed and would be kept from offering living witness to the testimony of his truth.

[223]

I am your truth-teller.

But I will not be kept from providing you with the grand event of your lifetime. The grand truth of your lifetime.

Today

No.

Today is Monday. Then Tuesday Wednesday Thursday. So today is doomsday minus four. Minus three.

But there must be a chronology. First the events of Sunday. Yesterday.

The task yesterday. The setting of the explosive charge on the third floor, west wing. Then tomorrow's task. Then Thursday's, the final one. Followed instantly by the grand event itself. Alternate days. A day of work, a day of rest. A schedule enforced by my condition. Powerful in spirit, increasingly weak of body. Endless pain.

Malnutrition a factor? The mind warns me to eat, I must supply myself with energy to reach the goal. But the body warns that any mouthful of food I swallow will send this serpent of pain under my breastbone writhing through me, spewing acid on every raw nerve. So I force myself to eat the way one would put a gun to his head preparing for suicide. Infant foods now. Like infant vomit. Sweetened gobbets of it in small glass jars. Nourishment, such as it is.

Mr. Saeed, my East Indian West Indian grocer on Bedford Avenue, bewildered by my purchases. Mr. Saeed purveys this stuff by the ton to food stamp Bulanga mothers. He can count their litters by the dozens of jars they cart away. But what litter does this ancient whitey Meestair Keer-wahn lay claim to?

A sudden thought. Tomorrow is Tuesday, Mrs. Bailey's house-cleaning day. I can't leave these empty jars for her to dispose of. Bulanga sly, falsely concerned, she could wonder why I am on this strange diet. Could try to become an intruder in my life as she was in my wife's life in her final days.

My wife, poor soul. Terrified to walk the streets outside her own home in the face of the glowering Bulanga, tended in her dying by their Aunt Jemima emissary. Dying of terror. The cancer of it poisoning every drop of that lymphatic fluid. Dead. Jemima provided tears and lamentations for my benefit. Away from the house, she re-

[224]

joiced as she passed the word to the tribe. Another whitey dead. Good.

So. I had to

I have to dispose of these small empty jars tonight before Mrs. Bailey time. The full ones I must hide away out of her range.

Now.

Sunday's task. The job a nightmare, the getting to it another nightmare. Waking from broken sleep to paralyzing inertia. Like waking in limbo. Knowing the day's work must be done, but unable to rouse myself to it. All thoughts and feelings seemed to have nothing to do with the Charles Witter Kirwan lying there in his bed staring at wallpaper rosebuds.

Understand. This in no way meant any unbalance of the mind. The mind as ever functioned precisely. It is functioning precisely and powerfully now. But the being was gripped by inertia. A physiological factor at work. Consequences of malnutrition possibly. Grotesque as it may sound, I am answering malnutrition by eating prepared infant food. Small jars of it which I

No. I'm sure I've already explained that.

Then what I must tell about is the job done yesterday against all obstacles. Overcoming the inertia. Improvising a tool to replace a damaged one. Running—crawling—the gauntlet of my tenants taking the Sunday morning air outside the building. Complaints. Demands. As monkeys are to a fine watch, so the Bulanga are to stoves, refrigerators, lighting fixtures, anything that might come apart in their paws. Let the rent-controlled landlord undo the damage. The whitey landlord, helpless instrument of all those soulful liberals faraway in their high-rise havens.

Oh yes.

And another gift from the soulful ones yesterday, by way of the Bulanga youth they adore. Fresh graffiti on the facade of the building, and inside its doorway, and over the courtyard wall. Spray-can art, so esteemed by our liberal art-lovers that they sometimes address rapturous paeans to it in their press. Cherish it as the purest expression of the Bulanga soul. Which knows that if you can't find the skill and patience to weave a carpet, the next best thing is to shit on your neighbor's.

[225]

I once closely examined this art on my walls. It did teach something about the Bulanga soul. The graffiti appeared to be a dashing script. Words and phrases. It is not. A letter emerges by chance here and there, but it is all an idiot's attempt to simulate writing. An attempt by the illiterate hand to imitate those strange lines and loops that the effete call words. A message of envy and hate from soul people to mind people.

That building. Dapper Dan Kirwan's folly. That courtyard. It was

Yes.

Right there on what is now that courtyard were cherry trees. Our little orchard. Eight trees, four on each side, making an aisle between them. Sourish cherries. No good for eating off the trees. Tart.

But

Jars and jars of them bubbling on the kitchen stove. Spadefuls of sugar. Some spices. My mother, sleeves rolled up, huge wooden paddle in hand. The girl — age fifteen or twenty or forty, but always the girl — always Irish fresh off the boat — lilting brogue — yes.

The girl fetching and carrying and pouring and sealing.

All those jars of cherries.

Chekhov. Was it? Yes, of course. The sound of an axe.

Eight cherry trees came down. Then other trees. The lawns gouged up.

Five frame houses and one trio of fine brownstones our side of the block. Mason. Witter. Diehl. Osterhout. Woodridge. Stevenson. James. Hooton. Six frame houses the other side. Lawson. Andrews. Vanderwink. Rutledge. Whitney. Woodridge, Junior.

Garages too. No more stables. But the garages were still like stables. No disgrace for me to be given shovel, when the occasional horsecart went by, so I could bring to the compost heap next to the garage those precious turds. Brave father at war, we would grow vegetables on those back lawns and help win the war.

Five years old. Six.

Witter Street. All gardens and lawns and trees. Serene people. Serene world. Omnipotent, all-seeing, all-serene grandfather.

And then. And then

[226]

I'll huff and I'll puff, said Dapper Dan, and I'll build you a brick house. A multiple dwelling, large and profitable.

Until then, a lovely world. Clean and quiet and mannerly.

And now our beefy Caliban with his blueprints all over the table. My grandfather's troubled face as he leaned over them.

The neighbors prescient.

Oh yes.

The gathering in the parlor. Coffee and slices of cake. The demonstration of Caliban's new radio set. Station KDKA from far away. Good evening, radio audience. Squeak, squawk.

The roomful of people, all with troubled faces.

But Mister Caliban, do you know what a multiple dwelling will do to the block?

Mister Caliban, we always thought that at least on Witter street here

Oh, Mister Caliban

Who bellows and laughs and sweats and unrolls blueprints on the floor and produces mysterious drinks for all from mysterious bottles.

The geese cackling their warning as Daniel Caliban opens the gates to the invader.

No one said to the old man in the corner, Oh, Mister Witter.

No one.

The king was dead. Long live the king.

And

In the distance, the Bulanga around their campfires scent the wind and rise to their feet and turn in the direction of King Caliban.

There will never

Courtyard. Graffiti. Trees. Those trees

Oh yes. Yes. Sunday. Yesterday. The dumbwaiter shaft, west wing, third floor. For some reason, the planting of the charge there became the most miserable and difficult of all I had undertaken till then. Airless and filthy. Dreadfully verminous. A host of roaches scurrying away from the flashlight beam. Across my hands. I had to work with them searching up my sleeves. And

A nasty little confidence for your pleasure. That old serpent of pain prodding its muzzle into my bladder. Prodding, jabbing, no escape. So for the first time since my army service—drunk and mindless in a back alley of Rome—I pissed as the male Bulanga pisses when he concludes his Saturday night festivities in front of my home. Freely, where he happens to be. Opened my fly and hosed down the wall of the shaft.

The simple pleasures of the dying.

Yesterday.

That was yesterday.

That was yesterday.

Now for today.

This Monday morning. Ten o'clock.

An obscene event. The human mind can be like the dumbwaiter shaft I toiled in. A beam of light exposes it, and you are nauseated by what you see there. The Caligula mind exposed.

Come to think of it, Caligula was the ancestral Italian.

Not to digress.

At ten o'clock this morning, a mysterious phone call.

A woman's voice. Breathless. No. Breathy. Hard-breathing. "Mr. Charles Kirwan?"

"Yes."

"Professor Charles Kirwan?"

"Yes. Who is this?"

Verbatim. That was verbatim. Now, what follows may not be the exact wording, but it will be close.

The woman: "Just listen, please. You are being secretly investigated by a private detective named John Milano. His agency is Watrous Associates on East Sixtieth Street in Manhattan. He is investigating you now. All your records, everything."

That was it.

A click, a silence, that was it.

I think that such a

No, I will make it a categorical statement.

You must go through this experience to know its shock effect. Disbelief and shock. Like resting your hands on a familiar surface and finding them caught and held there by an engulfing slime.

No pulling away. The slime is a reality. You cannot pull away from reality.

[228]

Naked and exposed — caught masturbating by a stranger staring through your keyhole.

Here, a stranger hired for the purpose.

Our Mister John Milano.

Mister John A. Milano. Alleged properties consultant. Of Sunderland Towers, Central Park South.

As I speak this now, I find the sense of shock returning. Physically. An uneven action of the heart, a sick stomach.

Unsteady hands

There must be chronology.

So

Denial at first.

A practical joke? A cruel and witless practical joke? But that could be tested.

I looked up Watrous Associates in the phone book, and the number was there. Bad news, but still not altogether defeating. I dialed the number, and a woman's voice said, "Watrous Associates."

Not the same voice. Not the same woman.

I said, "Private detective agency?" and the woman said, "Investigative agency. Who do you want, please?"

I said, "Mr. John Milano," and the woman said, "Sorry, not in. I can connect you with Mr. Greenwald, his assistant."

I hung up. Not a practical joke. A terrifying reality.

Oh yes.

Don't try to imagine yourself brave in my place.

A terrifying reality. Lorena Bailey. She had confessed her sins. Had confessed mine. Any instant there would be a banging at that door downstairs. The police.

The grand event unfulfilled. Grandeur reduced to gross comedy.

Aeschylus become Plautus.

Above all

Above all, the end of hope for the Witter Foundation. The grand event recorded here was to provide its huge assets. Without it — without the fulfillment of the event — there could be no assets.

Nothing.

But logic will prevail.

I made it prevail.

[229]

No banging on the door? No police? But if Lorena had entered charges against me, wouldn't they be here as soon as she had spoken her piece? Uniformed police? New York's Finest? For what they're worth?

A private detective. But how and why would the Bulanga Baileys come up with a private detective in this matter? And, judging from the look of him, a highly expensive one.

Do you begin to see?

No sense at all to that.

But then, what is this Milano's business with me?

Why this investigation? And, since he is only the hired hand, who is he serving? Obviously, someone who suspects me of something and now wants evidence of it. Suspects me of what?

Logic. Step by step logic. The historian's logic as opposed to the psycho-quack's. Making sure of solid ground underfoot before each step is taken.

Consider. My phone number is unlisted, but my mysterious caller knew it. Unlisted as my first line of defense against my tenantry, not altogether successfully. But strangers certainly did not have access to it. Probably someone in Milano's dirty business could obtain it, but the call was not from Milano.

A stranger.

Had I been careless enough in the recent past to give that number to some stranger? Someone who—for a logical reason—might bring about a secret investigation of me?

Yes.

Inescapably and dreadfully, yes.

A man named Swanson. Night watchman for that Passarini Demolition Company upstate. The thief and swindler who provided me with my explosives from his company's supplies. Dynamite, blasting caps, wire, detonator. Dynamite and blasting caps especially. Enough missing to panic the employer when the loss was discovered.

Oh yes.

Under fire, Swanson must have named his client, but would that name make sense to the employer when he looked it up? Doctor Charles Witter Kirwan, harmless gentle old soul? Retired scholar? Model of virtue and propriety?

So

Italian to Italian. Passarini to Milano. Private detective Milano who, if any evidence could be turned up against me, would turn it up. John A. Milano, himself such a smoothly finished model of virtue and propriety.

Awesome.

A bunkmate saying to me with awe about our commanding officer: "I never knew shit could be piled so high."

He never met our Mister Milano.

And awesomely dangerous, too. Italianate dangerous. The smiler with the knife. More of a threat to the grand event than any perverse little Bulanga slut.

One final question.

When that Passarini Company discovered the loss of its explosives why didn't it go straight to the authorities?

One obvious answer.

That company is responsible for both Swanson and the explosives. Why would it expose its mistake to the authorities at once? Why not first try to locate those explosives and get them back?

Then

With the buyer idenfified — caught with the goods — turn him in to the authorities as a sacrificial offering.

In this, Milano is the company's instrument.

An invisible presence in my life now.

The only threat to the grand event.

Not in view outside, but somewhere near.

Only three days left, but enough time for him to create disaster. To smell out my intentions and bring about that banging at the door.

Not as clever as he thinks. He doesn't know that out of someone else's kindness I have been given his secret. That I hold the advantage in this game. Ironically, he, the born Bulanga-hater, would approve the plans I must conceal from him. He and his people. Meanwhile, he makes every instant dangerous to me up to the very last instant.

I can not risk our Mister Milano's disastrous presence in my life up to its final moment.

Can not.

Will not.

[231]

# John Milano

THE RADIO-ALARM HAD BEEN SET for seven which, they agreed, would allow time for him to drive her back to the apartment in the Village where she could put herself together for the day's work, and then get her to the gallery by nine. But when the radio suddenly announced Monday morning's arrival with the tail end of a commercial Milano came awake to the realization that he was alone in bed and that no light showed beneath the bathroom door. He had an instant call-missing-persons lurch of the stomach, then saw that there was a light coming from the living room.

He made his way there. Chris, all dressed except for shoes, was stretched out supine on the couch, a cushion on her belly, one of his larger coffee-table art books propped on the cushion. She lowered the book as Milano seated himself across the room to take in the view. She said, "Woke up at five and couldn't get back to sleep. I had one of those sandwiches in the refrigerator. Bread's kind of soggy, but it wasn't too bad. I left the other one for you. Chicken with mayo."

"Later. What're you reading?"

"Reading and looking at. Raphael. You remember you said what it must feel like to poke a finger into one of his people? I still don't get it."

"Pretty packages. Not enough solid meat."

Chris shook her head. "Looks the same to me as a lot of these others from the same period."

"Well, they're not. Say, are you always this argumentative first thing in the morning?"

"Not always. Not about Caravaggio. I looked him up too, and you were right. Potent. True funky."

"That he was," said Milano. "Now let me ask you something before we work our way around to Jackson Pollock. When you told me Rammaert invited you to his catered dinner so you could be nice to the guests — "

"Yes?"

"Exactly how does he define nice?"

"Oh?" Chris raised her eyebrows. "Are you that kind of wild-eyed Italian?"

"Maybe. And there is something about the — "

"There is nothing about it, honey. I'm there as a table decoration. Look, but don't touch. Rammaert's like that himself with me. It could be because he's a foreigner. Foreigners are in and out of the place all the time, and somehow they are different. I wouldn't rate them real color-blind and female-blind, but they do know how to fake it better."

"I see," said Milano. "So Rammaert's okay in your book."

"Just about. I told you right off when you made that come-on to me about your case. That's why I'm still not too happy going through his files behind his back."

"I know," Milano said. In his mind's eye he saw calendar notations. Tomorrow morning, the payoff money from Willie. Right

[233]

after that, negotiations with Rammaert. And wherever they took place, and however speedily they were consummated, there would still be this Chris Bailey close by doing some hardheaded wondering. Milano thought, Oh, what a tangled web we weave, and said, "How about if I take this week off? Could you get off too?"

"Do not cast temptation my way, honey. I can't afford it. I get paid only for showing up."

"Just a few days? Say through Wednesday?"

"No. Rammaert gives me time off whenever I get word of a casting call or a tryout. Never makes a fuss. Or that last time Lorena disappeared and I was with Mama two days holding her hand. So I like to play fair with him. This would not go down on the chart as fair. You see that, don't you?"

A hell of a lot of good it did, thought Milano, seeing it.

After making the round trip with her and dropping her off at the corner of Fifty-seventh and Sixth, he drove back to the apartment. While parking, he remembered that the Heywood and Smith report on Kirwan was still tucked away in the Toyota's dashboard and took it along with him. But first things first. Kirwan was an increasingly large speck in the eye, but right now Rammaert rated top priority.

So in the kitchen, while getting down the chicken and mayo on soggy bread, he applied pencil to paper drafting the particulars of Wim Rammaert's modus operandi. He was at it when the phone rang.

The Wardour Hotel. Mr. Franconia-Nerisi.

"Mr. Milano? So sorry to bother you. And while I imagine Miss Cronin has discussed it with you —— "

"Discussed what?"

"Ah. Her leaving here. Her giving up the apartment. Last night."

"No," said Milano. "I've been away."

"Ah. Well, I really don't know if I should be the one —— "

"Look, what happened there?"

"Well. Last night at eleven I was called up to the apartment. A gentleman and lady were there with Miss Cronin. She appeared to have everything packed and ready to go. The gentleman, it seemed, was her father. He turned over the key to me, told me she was giving up the apartment, asked me to get a man up to carry the luggage to his car. I did that and they left very soon after."

"Just cleared out?" said Milano.

"Ah. That's where we meet a small problem. When the maid came in to do the rooms this morning she found that a very large amount of foodstuffs had been left behind. A considerable value in them. Absolutely untouched. And since the apartment is yours——"

"No," said Milano, "that's all right. Let the maid pass that stuff around. And the apartment is now all yours."

"I see. Well, I'll pro rate the rental. I'm sorry to have bothered you with this."

Not all that sorry, thought Milano as he put down the phone. Not when you consider the pleasure he must have gotten from having a front row seat at that implausible scene. Country maiden rescued from city slicker by mommy and daddy. Of course, from the city slicker's point of view what we had here was the depressing end to one of the shortest freedom marches in history. A wide U-turn, and back to the nest it went.

Painful to lose that ready entry to Intercontinental Credit Bureau's computer bank, but even more painful right now to contemplate what its pathetic keeper of the keys was letting herself in for. Crowding thirty, under daddy's thumb for good, a future sodality spinster.

Walking in like that on Christine Bailey. She must have told mommy and daddy all about it, and if she hadn't used the insulting descriptive, it was a sure bet daddy had,

Screw him and Staten Island. And you could throw in a few other tight-ass sections of town along with that.

Milano defiantly washed down the remains of the sandwich with a bottle of high-calorie John Courage, put the Rammaert papers together, and made it to the office at an amble. Vacation was over—at least postponed—but you'd have to be out of your mind to break track records getting back to the reality of Watrous Associates.

Willie, red pencil in hand, was going through a stack of expense vouchers, which he dealt with as not very well-written fictions that needed a lot of editing. He sat back and, one eye shut, regarded his partner like a bird examining a possibly indigestible worm. "I'd still like to know your angle," he said.

"Forget angles," Milano said. "What about the Rammaert payoff money?"

So far, so good. I talked to Pacifica yesterday, and that Hale fag'll be here Wednesday to make our payment and pick up the goods. Your note'll be ready for you to sign tomorrow morning first thing." The bird-beak nose twisted as Willie screwed that closed eye even tighter shut. "You still sure you want to do it this way?"

"Couldn't be surer."

"Uh-huh. You know, I can't get out of my head that somehow this Christine Bailey piece is the angle. The trouble is"—the voice was honestly querulous—"it don't add up. I mean, if it was five hundred bucks, even a thousand, what the hell, you'd be ready to toss that away for any hot number who gave you what you wanted. But forty grand? It can't be her, can it?"

"You see," said Milano. "The trouble is, Willie, you've got a dirty mind. Interesting, but dirty. Now if you don't mind — "

"Hold on. There's an extra little something we have to get straight. When you deal with Rammaert I want Greenwald there. I already told him it could happen. Now I'm telling you right out he'll be with you at the showdown."

"As supervisor?" said Milano without rancor. "Or on the way up as company snitch?"

"He's taking hold fine. It's time he learned about an operation like this. How to handle it."

"Why not?" said Milano. It was always heartwarming to throw Willie a slow curve like this and watch his bewilderment as it broke over the plate for a clean strike. "Matter of fact, I was thinking of it myself. I have to get together with Greenwald anyhow about Rammaert. I'll just fill him in on the operation while we're at it."

"Oh yeah?" said Willie in feeble challenge.

"Oh, absolutely yeah," said Milano. "And if you're working on that angle now, just figure I've got the hots for Greenwald's beard and here's the chance for me to make my move."

You didn't catch Hy Greenwald napping. The desk was littered with papers, and Hy was closely examining one, computer in hand

[236]

busily clicking away. When, peering over those granny glasses, he identified his caller he looked pleased. "Hey, man, just visiting? Or home again?"

"Hey, sonny. Looks like home again. No"—Hy was already halfway out of that super-luxurious full-leather swivel chair, and Milano waved him back into it—"just stay put." Milano made himself comfortable in the facing chair. "Willie did tell you we're ready to move in on Rammaert, didn't he? You and I?"

"Yes." Hy glanced at the door as if assuring himself there was no outline of an ear pressed against it outside. He lowered his voice. "You know what else he told me? About why I'm supposed to be there with you?"

"To keep an eye on me. Make sure I don't pocket the receipts. Report back to him any peculiar moves I might make."

Hy looked surprised. "He told it to you too? Just like that?"

"No, I read his thoughts. Willie's thoughts are always right up there over his head in big print. Don't let it bother you."

"It bothers me," Hy said. "So I tell you right now, if you don't want me around——"

"No, on this one I want you there. Otherwise, Willie could wind up cutting out paper dolls in Creedmore, and who'd sign the payroll then? Besides, you're going to start things off right now, so you should be there for the finish. It starts with you calling up Rammaert. When the girl at the switchboard——"

"Oh, yeah," Hy said wistfully.

"That's the one. When she asks for your name, give her your name, except that you are now Doctor Greenwald. Doctor. And that your representative already spoke to Mr. Rammaert about his interest in the works on display and you want to meet with Mr. Rammaert as soon as possible. Then, when she switches you over to Rammaert, just hand me the phone."

"All right. But what's been going on? How did we get this far?"

"I'll tell you as soon as we set up the meeting. You've got tomorrow evening open, I trust."

"It's open." Then Hy frowned. "Evening? Willie said it would be morning."

"Willie was wrong. Now see if you can find the phone under all that stuff."

[237]

The call went swimmingly, all in art dealer foxy talk. Yes, Dr. Greenwald was right here and had said he was interested in examining the Barquins first hand. But no, gallery hours wouldn't do; he preferred to view them privately. And yes, that was quite understandable, wasn't it?

And no, this evening wouldn't do. In fact, the only time the doctor had free this week was tomorrow evening. And no, even though Mrs. Rammaert was pleased to have guests for dinner even on short notice, that wasn't necessary. After dinner, then. Nine o'clock. Yes, that was definite. Nine o'clock.

Milano put down the phone and Hy said, "Man, that was lovely. I could just hear those violins in the background."

"Always glad to spread the sweetness and light around," said Milano. "That is one happy thief right now."

"You really know that for a fact? That thief part?"

"Yes," said Milano. "Now sit back and I'll tell you how I know it. In detail."

Omitting any mention of the co-conspirator, he told it in detail and where Willie, dean of this particular school of hard knocks, would have yawned his way through the narrative, it was gratifying that Hy, a freshman, was suitably impressed by it.

And, after some consideration, a little troubled.

He said, "But what kind of leverage does knowing all this really give us? We come out in the open with Rammaert, he stalls us, and next day that Barquin *Number Ten* is gone someplace else. With the Boudins in it. Then what?"

"Good thinking. So what we have to do is make sure he doesn't stall us."

Hy held up a hand in protest. "Johnny, if it comes to any strong-arm stuff——"

"You're getting your zoology scrambled, sonny. He's an art dealer. A hyena as you once put it. Not a tiger."

"Well——"

"Take my word for it. No fire power called for. Just a little brain power. So what you do now is get out the Rammaert file you put together with all that interesting poop about him and his connections in Belgium and Switzerland. We include the account of how those Boudins made the trip from the Coast to here—with emphasis on the

Miami stopover—and then Shirley herself will type it up for us. And run off a dozen copies of it. Remember that when it comes to an operation like this it is only Shirley who does the typing. For our eyes only."

"That makes sense," Hy said. "But twelve copies?"

"That's our fire power," said Milano. "Twelve shots."

Mid-afternoon, he called Chris at the gallery. "I've been wondering," he said. "Did you get any word about the kid today?"

"More of the same. She's in bed playing deaf and dumb. Didn't go to school, doesn't want to eat, just about sending everybody right up the wall. I told Mama I'd be there tonight, see what I could do about it."

"I'll be waiting in the car any time you're ready."

"No. Nardo and Pearl are giving a reading of her new script at seven in the flat, so I won't be ready till after nine. Anyhow, I figured to stay overnight in Brooklyn. And you don't mind me saying it, honey, I don't think you ought to be in on that family scene right now."

"All right," said Milano, "in that case I'll drive you there, wait as long as it takes you to visit, and drive back. Save you the subway trip in the morning."

"Uh-huh. Drive me back where?"

"Where do you think?"

"Well, in that case," Chris said, "I have to tell you that you are now running into the wrong time of the month. The cramps are here already, the rest is coming very soon. So for a few days——"

"Do you like opera?" Milano said.

"Opera? Some, I guess. When I know what it's about. Why?"

"Because I've got the librettos right there along with the albums. So for the soul I offer Puccini. For the cramps I offer aspirin, a heating pad, and champagne. For the rest, just talking. A lot of low-key talking. Nothing more expected."

A Christine Bailey silence. Then she said in melting tones, "Honey, remember you once told me *I* was a flake?"

"Did I? Well, that shows it takes one to know one."

"Sho' nuff, it do," said Chris. "So you just knock on the door around nine, and I'll be right out. And then we can take turns holding Mama's hand."

[239]

# Charles Witter Kirwan

**N**OW LISTEN CLOSELY.

No. I mean read this carefully. With great care.

It will provide evidence — all the evidence even the dullest psycho-quack needs rammed into his skull — of a completely rational mind. Absolute evidence which bars any court of law from dismissing the grand event as an aberrant act.

The evidence?

Yesterday, I attributed that mysterious call warning me of John Milano's true identity to the charitable nature of some stranger.

Last night I realized my mistake. A natural mistake. Caught so much off balance, entirely natural. But I had grossly underestimated the man's cleverness.

[240]

Sleepless, I wondered who could have made that warning call and for what purpose. Logic. Logic. Why would some stranger do me that favor? Why?

No convincing answers. None.

Because

Listen closely. Because I was asking myself the wrong question. I was positing a stranger out there, serving me as guardian angel.

But of course there is no such stranger. There is only Mister John Milano, Borgia devious, closing in on his intended prey.

Our Mister Milano

Who, having failed so far in his mission, resorted to a Borgia trick. Identify himself through some accomplice, and then see how the prey reacts.

Will it flee in panic? Will it speed up its preparations and become careless in them? Will its nerve suddenly crack, its courage fail? Would it actually be so mindless as to seek a confrontation just to end this game of hunter and hunted?

Because, as I learned last night, this obscene game does go on and on. While I was in this room at about ten o'clock, a car, double-parked down the block, no driver visible in it, caused a brief but noisy traffic tie-up. A truck trying to clear it swung out into the path of an oncoming bus, both stopped, neither would give way. Typical stubborn fools behind those wheels. A wild honking of horns as traffic piled up behind them in both directions. Bulanga drivers, who have replaced the assegai with the automobile. Unable to freely use this weapon now, they promised riot. The truck finally backed away, the rioters dispelled east and west.

But

But that trouble-making car under the street light seemed familiar. Through the binoculars even more certainly familiar. Oh yes. Our Mister Milano's car. Almost certainly his car.

I was careless then. Without realizing it I did the reckless thing, because conjecture alone didn't satisfy me.

Humanly careless.

I dressed and went outside, and keeping to the shadows as much as possible I moved close to verify my suspicions. And the moment I had done so I realized I was playing right into the hunter's hands. Realized how the trap had been baited by that supposedly friendly warning. Realized just a little too late the trick that had been played on me. The device that would expose me as the furtive, guilt-ridden fugitive on reconnaisance.

While he

That man. That man

Milano.

While he lay somewhere out of sight watching. Getting assurance that he was on the right trail. Closing in

Tuesday?

Tuesday today. Yes. Because this morning, Mrs. Bailey

No no no

Not Mrs. Bailey. Not today. Milano, yesterday.

Out of sight, watching. The phone call had worked, he was now sure of his man. But that was all. Ignorant of my purpose, of my schedule. But closer.

That schedule. Tuesday evening now. Almost seven o'clock. The grand event Thursday, precisely seven o'clock. First weeks, then days, then hours. Precisely forty-eight hours. Hours. Then minutes.

Almost impossible to force entry into that basement. Almost. More possible for someone like that man than others. A clever brute. Deadly up to the final minute. But the spirit to prevail is mine, so the ultimate power is mine.

And

As the life on earth of Jesus Christ had no meaning outside its sacrifice and lesson of that sacrifice, so the remaining hours of my life have no meaning outside the grand event and its lesson.

While that man. That man. That

That brute, venal, hedonistic Judas finds meaning in his life only be betrayal. Not enough to stand against my power.

The irresistible force meeting the movable body.

Oh yes.

Biding his time.

A shame.

It is possible that if he only came to me openly—not as my be-trayer—he would have understood. We might have been allies.

Not this way.

So

The schedule holds good. That is how it must be. I thought different last night after the shock of the episode. A day of work, a day of rest? I thought last night, no, I can't allow myself that day of rest. Two explosive charges remaining to be set. One Tuesday, one Thursday. Second floor. First floor. Two days work. While in the east wing I had done it in one day.

In one day.

Possessed by strength then.

Not enough of it left now. Not even enough to do without the day's rest. I found that out today, struggling against weakness to fix the explosives against the dumbwaiter door one flight up.

Leaving the last to Thursday. The same schedule.

And

Oh yes, Mrs. Bailey was on schedule this morning. Her cleaning day. But full of woe, Aunt Jemima Bailey. She would be grateful if I could do without her today. Would like to skip this week. Lorena was sick. Didn't want to leave the chile alone until the boys came home. And didn't know what the sickness was, but it was scary the way that chile is right now.

That chile.

Cunning and corrupt Lorena. Didn't come here yesterday. Understood my message to stay away. Sick now? The sickness of suddenly frustrated greed? Ravaging money hunger?

Money money money?

The hunger which had the rulers of her ancestral tribe on the Niger sell her ancestors to whitey, the slave-runner? Cash on the rum-barrel head. Ooga, ooga, take 'em away, whitey. There's more comin' from them fertile bodies every day like little black rabbits.

Black studies. Never never confide to them that it was Bulanga chiefs who sold their people to whitey for a piece of cloth and a pound of nails. Death before dishonor. Burn your fuckin' college library to the ground, whitey, does you dare tell us the truth.

And the Arab trade.

And still the hush-hush Arab trade today in Bulanga flesh. And so the Bulanga turn to Allah, put on the garb, carry the Koran to honor their loving Moslem cousins.

Dear cousins, you know how to deal with us, don't you?

Oh yes.

[243]

And dear Aunt Jemima? I tell you to dry those bloodshot eyes.
Because
In a little while Lorena's sickness will be healed forever. And all
your little troubles. And all your sly little ways.
And dear friends?
Listen to me.
Listen.
A great and terrible truth.
Omnipotence is knowing the day of your death.

# John Milano

As it turned out, her calculations that her time of the month was about to descend on her proved accurate, but when they got back to the apartment from Brooklyn Monday midnight, she rejected any opera recital or low-key Bailey-Milano dialogue, and settled for some prescription painkiller washed down by half a bottle of Dom Perignon and followed by a quick tumble into sleep. Milano settled for the other half of the bottle and the fact that in her sleep she became as ivy to his trellis.

No complaints. No complaints at all.

In the morning, however, she was herself again and full of oats. Ready, she announced, to give the Richoux breakfast menu a fair try. And she made only token objections when Milano thrust on her the keys to the Toyota. He brushed aside the objections, pointing out that it was not a gift, it was a loan.

"Neither a borrower nor a lender be," Chris advised.

"Keep pushing that line," said Milano, "and you'll wreck the national economy. What's left of it. Anyhow, as Polonius would put it, I'm not doing this for thee, I'm doing it for me. Worrying about you in that subway wrecks my concentration. In forty or fifty years when they get the bugs out of the system, okay. Not now."

Chris seemed amused and touched. "Well——"

"Good. And any time you pick up baby downstairs it'll be all gassed up and ready for you. I'll tell the boss there about it on our way out. He'll also take care of that goddam ticket."

That was another reason for cherishing this remarkable creature. After cruising Witter Street last night futilely hunting a parking space, he had at last double-parked down the block from the apartment building. She had then warned that this was a risky place for such tactics what with the buses coming through and so it had proved, for there in the windshield wiper was waiting the ticket for illegal parking, obstructing traffic, and something illegible. And heroically—there was no other word for it—Christine Bailey had refrained from even breathing an I told you so. Athena herself might not have had that wisdom.

He left her at the street entrance to the garage and found Maxie Rovinsky, boss of the works, in his glass cage doing bookkeeping. He gave the ticket to Maxie, who had a way with traffic tickets, and then explained that a Miss Bailey could have the use of the Toyota any time and that she was to be treated by all hands here like the finest and most fragile cut glass.

"Bailey?" said Maxie. "Not that zoftig blonde from the last poker game?"

"No."

"Oh. Well, whoever it is, Johnny, it's no trouble at all. And talking about poker games, can I count on you tonight? A pickup game, but I've got three hands already set."

"Including Gracie?"

"Naturally. She's into me for five thousand just this last stretch, but I got a feeling tonight is my lucky night. Tonight I'm shoveling some of that load back on my pile. Also she's been sick in bed a few days, and, like she said, this'll be the coming-out celebration."

"Sorry, Maxie, I'm working under new rules. Any time Gracie is going to be at the table count me out."

"You're kidding."

"Nope."

"But you? You come near holding her even. And you know how she is about you. I think she'd swap those two freaks of hers for you any time you say. And throw in the Rolls for bonus."

"Sorry, Maxie."

Maxie intercepted him before he could open the door. "Wait a minute. Do you mean there's something funny going on the way she handles those cards?"

This had to be sent direct from heaven, Milano thought. He froze his face. "I didn't say that, Maxie. Did you hear me say it?"

"Well, the way I read it ——"

"But I will ask one little question," Milano said. "Do you really believe that every time she takes you to the cleaner's it's because she's a smarter player than you?"

When he went outside Chris said to him, "All right?"

"Couldn't be better."

"As long I don't get any dents in baby," said Chris. "You know, honey, about that ticket. Remember last night when you parked that way? I told you then ——"

What the hell, thought Milano. Who wanted an Athena anyway when you could have someone so fallibly, marvelously human?

Willie and Hy Greenwald were keeping each other silent company in Willie's office when he arrived there, Hy slumped in a chair finger-combing his beard watching Willie painstakingly read the exposé of Wim Rammaert's life and works. Milano seated himself as well while Willie plowed his way through to the last word.

He finally looked up, "Seems to be some details left out," he said to Milano.

"There are. I'm saving them for the showdown. Now how about the check?"

"All ready. Meanwhile," said Willie, making it about as subtle as Willie could make anything, "there's some papers for you to sign."

[247]

They were four copies of the formal I.O.U. for forty thousand, and Milano went over to the desk to sign them. Then, to give Willie his due, he surrendered the check almost graciously. "Sixty thousand," he said. "Want a security man along?"

"For now and this evening both," Milano said. "Mikkelsen'll do fine."

Mikkelsen — Madman Mikkelsen — all towering two hundred and forty pounds of him, shoulder-length blond hair and that Viking mustache drooping to his jawline, had been a pro lineman for a couple of years until booze and pills had laid him out. Beating them, he had tried a comeback, but there was not enough of the old Madman left and the agency had caught him on the rebound. Not only an awesome presence but close-mouthed and pretty bright, he had worked with Milano a few times and they had gotten along nicely.

Now Willie shook his head. "I got him chauffing security for some big corporation asshole in town today."

Milano shook his head. "He's the one, Willie," he said, knowing that Mikkelsen would be the one. Because whatever edge Willie had over his partner in other workings of the agency, there could be only one captain on the ship when it cruised into these tricky waters, and Willie understood who that was.

And, thought Milano with an eye on Hy Greenwald who was watching this back and forth stuff like a worried spectator at a tennis match, it wouldn't hurt to have this apprentice understand it, too.

"You'll have to wait," Willie said. "It'll take an hour to change assignments and get Mikkelsen here."

"That'll give me more than enough time to bring the car around," Milano said.

When he and Hy brought the Mercedes around an hour later Mikkelsen, straining the seams of his chauffeur's jacket, was waiting for them. He took the attaché case Milano handed him and did the driving to the bank, his passengers at their ease in the rear seat. In the bank, when the check had been converted into packets of hundred-dollar bills, he tucked the packets into the case and led the way back to the car.

He turned to face them from the driver's seat. "The office?" he said to Milano, which was the most he had said up to now.

"The office," Milano said. "We put the loot in Willie's safe and pick it up when it's needed. Then we all take the day off together." He looked over Hy. "That gives us a chance to shape you up to Doctor Greenwald's standards. That beard, for instance."

"Strictly private property," Hy said in alarm.

"Company property right now, so it gets a dainty trim. And that outfit you're wearing makes you look like a junior member of Willie's club. We'll have to do something about it."

"Oh yeah?" said Hy. "On whose money?"

"The agency's, naturally. We bill it to your disguise."

At noon, with Hy barbered and retailored—everything was off the rack but an extremely luxurious rack—there was a light lunch, a movie over on Third Avenue, and then Milano, an eye on Hy's jitters, announced a workout at the Midtown Athletic Club.

Hy balked at this. "I might as well tell you, Johnny, athletic clubs are not my thing."

"Feeling edgy, aren't you? All wound up?"

"Why not? Remember, this is a first for me."

"In that case, a real good workout is what's called for. You might even learn to like it."

It was a real good workout, and the best part of it was a three-on-three game against a trio of tanned, sleek, but rugged basketball boys who looked like they had been freshly imported, minus surfboards, from La Jolla beach. Money talks, they said, sizing up Hy's granny glasses and Milano's bald spot, and so it did, all in favor of the good guys, as Hy often managed to feed the open man, Milano found he couldn't miss outside shots, and the Madman gallantly covered the court offensively and defensively like a company of Paul Bunyans.

Three hundred dollars total prize money, one hundred for each hero. It was enough to pick up Hy for awhile, but later in the rubbing room, with the team left to its own devices after the masseur had finished with it, he said worriedly to Milano on the next table, "Thinking about those moves tonight?"

"Something else."

"Oh sure. What else?"

Milano rolled over on his side to face Hy. "Let's say you own an apartment house——"

"That'll be the day."

"You never know," said Milano. "Anyhow, this one is a real loser. Old and tired. Taxes way overdue."

"That's more like it," said Hy.

"And," said Milano, "somebody comes up to you—somebody obviously prosperous—and says he wants to buy this pile. And you tell him to bug off, you will not sell. Absolutely not. Now why would you tell him that? And mean it."

"Are you being serious?" Hy asked cagily.

"Yes. Add to it that selling means ready cash in the bank for you, and you happen to need that cash the worst way."

"The story of my life," said Hy. "Well, maybe I don't want to sell to that somebody because I've already made a deal with somebody else."

"Not likely," Milano said.

The Madman said sleepily, "He don't want to sell because he's setting up that building for a torch job. The insurance'll pay just as good and even quicker."

Charles Witter Kirwan, thought Milano.

Setting up the building. Always working on that boiler. But what you should show after working on a cranky oil burner are oil and water stains.

Dust bunnies? Dry-as-a-bone clothes?

On the other hand, this was tight-assed old Doc Kirwan, who turned purple if you said something about his ethnic neighborhood going to seed. And was holding the fort and living his life right there to prove it.

"I don't know," Milano reflected aloud. "A torch job? This no-sell character bugging me doesn't come off as the type."

"What do you mean type?" the Madman said. "Whoever he is he's a landlord, ain't he?"

That he was.

Before dressing, they all weighed themselves, and Milano, doing some extra swaying and bouncing on the scale to make sure he wasn't being deluded by what he saw there, registered one-eighty-eight. Twelve pounds evaporated in less than three weeks. Awed by his own fitness, hobbled only a little by some three-on-three aches and pains, he led the team out for a proper celebration dinner with,

[250]

of course, one limitation. Since the Madman was hanging on to the wagon by his stubby fingertips, it was a courtesy to him — as well as a matter of self-survival — to see that no alcohol in any form was laid on.

Near nine, when Hy was starting to check his watch at thirty-second intervals, Milano steered their course back to Willie's office. Here the Madman took the attaché case in hand, and Hy, under Milano's instructions, placed in an envelope the copies of the Rammaert papers.

Watching the protegé fumble his way through this procedure, Milano was moved to ask, "Did you know that if you turned down Willie's order to join this party, you'd be canned tomorrow?"

"Sure. And if I didn't know you were on the level, I wouldn't be here to blow the whistle on you anyhow. Now what I'd like to know is when I get briefed on this O.K. Corral scene?"

"Not that much of a scene, doctor," Milano said. "You relax and enjoy the show, that's all. You say nothing and do nothing at any time."

"Hello? Goodbye?"

"Not required. You represent a furtive little band of M.D.'s with a lot of excess cash to invest and what Internal Revenue doesn't know won't hurt it. Mr. Rammaert is meeting us with that understanding. He'd be very much surprised if you came on all gabby about whys and wherefores."

"And when he finds out what we're really there for?"

"Just keep on relaxing. Our Mr. Mikkelsen has been over this course before, and he'll be covering our tails all the way."

And, in fact, for whatever comfort it was to Hy, the Madman was close on their tails, attaché case snugly in hand, visored chauffeur's cap set square on Viking skull in rinkydink style, when Rammaert came down in person to lead them upstairs to the apartment over the gallery. From what Milano could make out, Rammaert was in no way surprised to see a chauffeur bring up the rear of this very private party. Which was quite in order. An old hand in the trade, Rammaert knew a bodyguard type when he saw one, especially one this size.

The apartment, Milano observed, was what happens when a high-geared salesman's domestic yearnings and his commercial instincts take off at tangents. The furnishings were uniformly solid, gemutlich Mittel-European—in a way they bore some resemblance to Kirwan's assemblage—but the art in view was all unrelieved plastic-souled, Space Age dazzle, not a glimmer of the figurative or representational anywhere on these walls. And a couple of the pieces provided so powerful a fluorescent effect that sighting them for a couple of seconds was like staring at an unshaded light bulb.

So, Milano thought with a certain relish, while this fat, popeyed thief in the unlikely hairpiece yearned in his soul for the burgher way, he was stuck with this mind-numbing exhibition because he had to stick his customers with it. Bring them upstairs here for some personal stroking, and they saw on these walls evidence of the salesman's own passion for his product.

Whatever yearnings went on inside however, Rammaert was outwardly at ease, affable, and volubly taken with Doctor Greenwald. Success and youth together? What a happy combination. And now ready to expand horizons, the doctor and his professional colleagues. The collecting of fine art which is, after all, what civilization is about. As well as being the wisest possible investment in this troubled world today, is it not? So now to Raoul Barquin. But first a glass of wine? A good Riesling Cabinet?

Hy, who so far had been wordlessly practising a studied frown, glanced at Milano. Milano shook his head in smiling refusal so Hy dutifully shook his head. The Madman looked wistful. Rammaert, a man who had to know how nicely a bottle or two of a good Riesling Cabinet can oil the works, pursed his lips regretfully. "Well, later then. Now to the gallery."

In the gallery, all lights on, Rammaert hastened to fetch chairs from the office, two of them, the chauffeur allowed the privilege of standing at ease, his shoulders braced against the door. This furniture-moving, Milano saw gratefully, came in handy because under the lights those two raised rectangles on *Surface Number Ten* seemed magnetically compelling to Hy, and the eyeballing he was giving them could tip Rammaert off before he was properly set up. A threat to the equilibrium of the set-up.

So he jostled Hy into motion around the room, doing the steering from one *Surface* to another, foxy Rammaert a step behind and, with

[252]

the doctor's foxy mentor plainly in silent charge, wisely keeping his own mouth shut.

The round completed, Rammaert reverted to type. "Amazing work. Genius? I would say yes. Unquestionably."

"Unquestionably," Milano said. He motioned at the desk, at the receptionist's chair behind it. "If you don't mind."

Rammaert smiled his appreciation of this thoughtfulness. "Not necessary. I'm comfortable."

"If you don't mind." Milano winked at him, suggesting God knows what eccentricities in this client had to be catered to.

Rammaert, catering to them good-naturedly, moved around the desk and seated himself. He watched with interest as Milano removed the envelope from Hy's tense grip, drew out stapled pages, and laid them on the desk.

"Before we enter negotiations," Milano said, "please read this document very carefully."

Against all salesman's wisdom, Rammaert looked annoyed. "My dear sir, any contract that we —"

"Please read it."

Rammaert was good, Milano saw. Really good. He started reading with a sort of amused disdain, he somehow managed to maintain that expression to the bitter end. The only small giveaway was that when he finally raised his head that ruddy complexion was not quite so ruddy. "Fascinating," he said.

"Yes," said Milano.

"And this signature is yours? John Milano? Representing this Watrous Agency?"

"Watrous Associates Agency. Yes."

"I believe I've heard of it." Rammaert aimed a finger at Hy. "And that young man is not a doctor, of course. Only a very poor imitation of one."

"You can say that about a lot of doctors," Milano pointed out. "And now can we assume that the preliminaries are over and we're ready for business?"

"An attempt at blackmail?" Rammaert shrugged. "But, my dear friend, it won't work, you know. To my knowledge — and I can only judge by these pieces around us — Raoul Barquin is an authentic talent whatever his character. And if he and I have been victimized by some drug dealers, well, that's something he and I must work out. And I assure you we will. With an absolutely clear conscience."

"I see," said Milano. "Then I gather you don't know the Miami police have just moved in on Raoul and company. And while he's disappeared, Adolfo is right there talking as fast as he can. I'll admit one thing, Rammaert, regarding that absolutely clear conscience. The fact that you didn't know the joint was raided suggests you really weren't that close to the boys. Or involved in their real business. Now all you have to do is convince the Miami cops of that if they come knocking at your door."

"Really?" said Rammaert with the mildest of interest. But the hand resting on the papers curled into a fist, the hairy knuckles bearing down hard.

"I'll go even further," Milano said. "I don't even think you picked that Barquin team to do your fancy work. I'd say you were stuck with them by somebody else — probably your Boudin collector — who knew them in a business way. That leads me to offer a small bet that this collector is South American — Bolivian or Colombian probably, but right now settled down in Spain or France for la dolce vita — big in the cocaine trade, with an eye for art, and with all the money in the world to spend on it." Milano raised his eyebrows in polite inquiry. "Do I collect on that bet?"

Rammaert shook his head, layers of jowl wobbling. "I don't know what you're talking about, Mr. Milano. In any case, I neglected to make an urgent phone call after dinner. If you don't mind, I'll attend to it now." He pointed at the office door. "In private."

He pulled himself out of the chair and made his way to the office, eyes straight ahead, mouth set. Hy watched this progress uneasily, and when the door closed he turned to Milano. "He could be calling the cops, couldn't he?"

"If you were in his shoes right now," Milano said, "would you be calling the cops?"

"I don't know. But blackmail? Is it blackmail?"

"No," said Milano, "it's the fine-art business. And he's calling Miami now to confirm the bad news. When he gets back he'll be a lot tamer. Even shiftier, but a lot tamer."

[254]

"Blackmail," Hy said, testing the sound of it. He moved over to *Number Ten* and studied it. "You sure those are the Boudins?"

"I'm sure. Not that he didn't nearly suck me in by having four of these Barquin cheeses hung around the room. Smart investment, four of them. His mistake was in not camouflaging the shape of those Boudins, but I figure that's because he wanted to know where they were all the time. So you make one little slip and blow the game."

"Not yet," Hy said. "Not as far as I can see."

Which, Milano knew, was true in a way. Under ordinary rules it wouldn't be, but ordinary rules didn't take Christine Bailey into account. Didn't add to the usual complications the biggest one of all: that this job must be handled so that Christine Bailey never got a glimmer of it. Would never know who or what or why.

Or maybe never. That, in the faraway future, remained to be seen.

You faced a tangle like this, and you almost had to admire Willie for his way of cutting Gordian knots. A couple of pros by flashlight and with straight-edged razor—a straight-edged grand-daddy razor was the instrument for canvas—would slice through this Gordian knot in two minutes flat. You took for granted, of course, that Willie and his pros didn't have a Christine Bailey addling their brains.

Love at forty, Milano thought bemused. Who would believe it?

Come to think of it, maybe Gracie MacFadden.

Milano realized his back hurt. He seated himself, stretched his legs out and carefully refrained from planning too many moves ahead in the game. Hy nervously prowled the room examining *Surfaces*. The Madman, leaning against the door, looked ready to fall asleep on his feet.

It took Rammaert a long time to reappear. With one fist knotting and unknotting, he walked to the desk and dropped heavily into the chair. "Can we speak in private?" he asked Milano.

"Sorry."

Rammaert shrugged this off. "Your proposition?"

"I think you know it. I get the Boudins as Grassie's agent. You get the assurance that your dossier is filed and forgotten."

Rammaert shrugged this off, too. "Out of the question."

[255]

Milano drew out the other copies of the dossier from the envelope and held them up, fanned out. "One each for the police of San Francisco, Miami, and New York. One for Interpol. Maybe it would just be entertainment for them, but who knows? One each for the daily papers in San Francisco, Miami, and New York. It should be a real glamour story for them."

"If," Rammaert said heavily, "they can verify it. I think newspapers have had some experiences lately which would make them very careful about publishing libel."

"Probably. But anybody wants confirmation of the story, I'll be right there to do it."

"Do you know what you risk that way?"

"I'm thinking of what I gain. Advertising is difficult in my line of work. Since confidentiality is important, you can't go around getting testimonials from satisfied clients. But headlines in the New York *Post?*"

Rammaert sat back. He fitted his fingertips together. "Now," he said, "suppose I tell you a little secret. I had no intention of sharing it with anyone, but what other recourse is there? In brief, those works in question are forgeries. Excellent forgeries, but forgeries nevertheless. Can you see what you're letting yourself in for if you present them to your Mr. Henry Grassie as authentic?"

"And the original Boudins?" Milano asked.

"Already in the hands of the purchaser. These two forgeries here — I'll put it this way — are my attempts to capitalize on the situation. No harm done anyone. Their buyer, I assure you, will be quite happy with them in his ignorance."

Milano had a glimpse of Hy's stricken face. He smiled at Rammaert. "To tell the truth," he said, "I'll be quite happy with them too."

"You don't believe me, Mr. Milano? That's very foolish of you."

Peripherally, Hy was pulling that tennis match stuff again, his attention shifting back and forth between the adversaries. It was a distraction Milano felt he could do without. He shifted in his chair to block out the troublesome vision and said to Rammaert, "I can't even give you credit for a good try. If these Boudins are forgeries, you'd have accepted my terms on the spot. You win, here's your hat and your paintings, goodbye, Mr. Milano. So let us, as they say, cut the crap and get down to cases. You have my offer. The Boudins in return for a deep silence about your private business. What it comes down to now is yes or no."

"Then it's no. And I warn that you'll get nowhere charging me with the theft of those paintings."

"Of course," Milano said reasonably. "But I won't be charging you with theft. I'll be charging you with possession."

Rammaert glowered at him, the heavy-featured face congesting with blood. He leaned forward, hands planted on the desk. "You are a goddam blackmailing son of a bitch, mister. And the answer is still no."

Milano slowly counted to ten. "There's something on your mind besides your opinion of me, Rammaert. What is it? Painted into a corner by your associates?"

Rammaert seemed to be doing his own silent counting. Then he pushed himself to his feet and walked over to *Number Ten*. He lightly passed a hand over the outline of each rectangle — there was something almost tender in the way he did it — and said to Milano, "Do you know the investment in them? Obtaining them, transporting them, dealing with Barquin?"

"I'll let you tell me."

"A hundred thousand, Milano. And I am answerable for it."

"It's family money," Milano said. "The Ost cousins' club. And stolen art is a speculative item no matter how you look at it."

"That may be, but in this case the speculation is entirely the client's. He is not a man I'd want charging me with a swindle."

"So?"

"So it's not merely a case of your obtaining the Boudins. It becomes a case of your robbing me of a hundred thousand dollars. And however unpleasant the alternative you propose, I prefer it to being robbed of any such amount."

"I doubt that," Milano said.

"Take my word for it. And consider that whatever story you may publicize I have my own to add to it. For example, your criminal effort to become a partner to this affair by threatening to expose it."

"I see. But can I assume you'd be willing to write off this speculation if I cover that hundred thousand?"

"In cash," said Rammaert.

"No problem," said Milano. "But consider that you didn't lay out any hundred thousand for this job. By my estimate, it wouldn't be more than half that. And understand that I don't want to buy your Barquin. All I want to do is rent it."

"Rent it?"

"For an hour. It doesn't even leave the premises here. So putting everything together, I'd say fifty thousand is the right price."

Rammaert hesitated. "No," he said.

Milano stood up, suddenly feeling every one of those three-on-three twinges, and took the attaché case from the Madman. He set the case on the desk and flipped open its lid. "As you see," he said. "Cash."

Rammaert took in the view, then shook his head. "You'll have to do better than fifty."

Milano examined the Rammaert footwear. Not Swiss. The Swiss had developed a more graceful touch with leather. Belgian most likely. And Teuton Antwerp rather than half-Frenchy Brussels. With enough time measured off, Milano raised his head. "I'll make one final offer. Absolutely final. Sixty thousand."

"Sixty," Rammaert said, getting the feel of it.

Milano poised a hand over the lid of the attaché case. "It looks like we're back to yes or no, friend. Which is it?"

"It means a heavy loss. Immense difficulties. But yes, I suppose sixty would be acceptable."

Which, though Milano, made it just a little too readily acceptable for comfort. It was a relief when Rammaert, playing according to form, revealed why. He looked at his watch and seemed dismayed by what he saw there. "So late? Well then, early tomorrow morning — let us say at seven — we can meet here again and settle matters. Is seven o'clock convenient?"

"If it is for you," Milano said. "Of course, my associates will be staying right here overnight just to make sure no fanatic Barquin-lover tries to get away with one of these Neo-Cubist Constructionist gems before we do settle matters. We wouldn't want that to happen, would we?"

Rammaert, it turned out, had a wry sense of humor under all that blubber. Eyelids drooping, he studied Milano's sympathetic face at his leisure. Then he said with intense concern, "Of course, we wouldn't want that to happen. So rather than inconvenience your associates it might be better to settle matters at once." He motioned with his chin at the attaché case. "Would I be wrong in assuming there is exactly sixty thousand dollars there?"

"No," Milano said, "You'd be exactly right."

"How foresighted of you, Mr. Milano."

"Diamond cut diamond," Milano acknowledged graciously.

It was the Madman who singlehanded lifted down the dead weight of *Number Ten* from the wall and laid it on the floor. And then, as deftly as a dentist extracting loose molars, used a borrowed pliers to extract staples until the canvas could be pulled free and the Boudins removed from their mounting. Each Boudin panel was in an improvised frame of inch-wide boxwood stripping, and with a steady pressure of the thumbs the Madman worked the panels loose. Then he fitted the empty frames into their original places under the canvas and set about on a restapling job.

Milano stood the panels side by side against the attaché case on the desk, and as Rammaert and Hy joined him in silent appreciation he had that charge of gut feeling, thanks to Eugene Louis Boudin, which signalled that all was a lot better with the world than anyone really suspected. The one small irritant was that Hy seemed to be increasingly puzzled by what he was looking at, cocking his head this way and that as he studied it like one of your aficionados of the trendy who lived only to worship the gravy stains on the artist's plate. The education of the emeritus Doctor Greenwald, Milano told himself, would definitely be a high priority item in the near future.

On the other hand, Rammaert knew damn well what he was looking at. "Marvelous," he breathed. He turned to Milano. "You know his work?"

"Yes."

"Well, I have always found his larger paintings boring. He's one of those where the smaller the painting, the more restricted its dimensions, the greater its intensity. Don't you think so?"

"Yes," said Milano, and had the feeling that if you didn't watch out you could find yourself liking this slob. "He's like Rubens in that regard."

With *Number Ten* back on the wall, with the payoff on the desk in neat little stacks and the panels tucked into the attaché case, it was back to Willie's office where the panels were locked away in the safe and the Madman assigned the all-night duty of keeping them company until Willie showed up and took possession. After which Milano said to Hy, "I'm heading downtown. Want a lift somewhere?"

"No. I'm a little shook up right now. I think I'll walk it off."

"It wasn't really that bad for you, was it?"

"I don't know," Hy said. "I don't have any perspective on it yet. I'm not sure I know how I feel about it yet. Look, would you mind telling me something? When you and Rammaert were laying it on each other, how much of what you told him was the truth?"

"Just enough," said Milano

A little before midnight, and the Village was alive. Including, as Milano saw from the sidewalk, that third-floor apartment whose windows were lit up. Maybe a little too alive, because when he made it up to the apartment he heard from within a heated rise and fall of voices.

He knocked on the door and Chris, barefoot in pajamas, opened it, giving him a momentary view of what had to be her pair of co-tenants having it out. Then she stepped into the hallway closing the door behind her and moved into that familiar tight body to body pressure against him to engage him in an obscene and lingering kiss.

When they drew apart Milano motioned at the door. "Trouble in paradise?"

"Oh, man," Chris sighed. "You know, Nardo gave that reading of Pearl's new play for some of us last night. Today Pearl got the word nobody much liked it, so she's dumping on Nardo. She told him it was his lousy reading that spoiled it. Now they both want me to be referee."

"And how would you call it?"

"Well, it's got a great part for me," said Christine Bailey, true actress. "Never mind that." She led Milano to the stairway. Seating herself on the top step, she drew him down beside her. "I'm glad you're here. I phoned you a couple of times."

"I was on the job," Milano said. "How's little sister?"

"The same. This morning Mama raised a fuss over at social services about someone there coming to the house and seeing the kid, so they finally arranged it for tomorrow evening. No therapist. Just someone to see if she needs a therapist. I'll be going there after work."

"Company welcome?"

"Yours is, I guess. You can put Mama down on that list of old ladies who have a thing going for you."

Old, thought Milano. Mama could be fifty. She was probably closer to forty-five, which was just a tomorrow away from his forty.

He put an arm around Chris and she rested her head on his shoulder. From behind the door, playwright and director continued their unmelodious duet. Someone in another apartment on the floor was practising the guitar, winging it on broken pinions. A well-dressed middle-aged Caucasian quartet — two bouncy females, two professorial-looking males — appeared at the foot of the staircase, and Milano stood up to make room for them as they single-filed past, all bouncy chatter cut off until they were on their way up the next flight. Milano resumed his position, and Chris resumed hers.

After awhile he said, "You know, this stair-sitting deal is really ridiculous."

"Not from where I am."

"From where we both are. So how about getting your things together and coming along home before they even notice you're gone?"

"Your home."

"I'd say ours. Nice cozy place too."

"Maybe." She moved apart from him but tucked her arm through his. "Except when I wait for the elevator and wonder if your penthouse friend is coming down on it. Or the doorbell rings, and I wonder who else from the chorus line is coming to claim her wandering boy."

Milano felt his frustration count rising. "I thought we cleared all that up."

"Not all. Some." She sounded troubled. "Anyhow, that is not my part of town, Johnny."

"Meaning what?"

"What it sounded like. I like it down here. My friends are here. Whatever I want is here. And I am very low profile here."

"You couldn't be low profile wherever the hell you are."

"Oh yes I can. Right here, when I want to be."

He reviewed the case so far, then said, "All right, I'm not tied to that apartment. I can get my price for it any time. And there's some high-rises in the Village here that look very nice at least from the outside. Or one of those brownstones they're doctoring up. How about that?"

"No! And don't talk like that. Man, can't you see how you're putting me down with that line of talk?"

"No, I can't."

"Well, you are. I made it on my own up to now. Schools, jobs, acting, whatever came along I handled it all on my own. Now here comes the magic man. Steak dinner, car, brownstone—just make a wish and it comes true. But I do not want anyone dealing me whatever cards I call. Can you understand that much?"

"What I understand, baby, is that you are considerably coloring it in the telling."

"I'm giving it to you straight, Johnny. Like, you have me jumpy any time you mention something about the show being closed. I can just see you going behind my back to open it again. Buy a theater if you have to. Buy a whole supporting cast for me from Grace Mac-Fadden's dear friends. And that is not my style."

"In some circles," Milano said coldly, "all that would be seen as a demonstration of affection."

"True," Christine said. "And what kind of demonstration can I pay back with? You work that out, and maybe you'll begin to get the idea."

"And then again," Milano said, "maybe not," but when he rose to his feet Christine pulled him down hard.

"Oh no," she said. "You do not just walk out any time the talk doesn't go your way. Not right now for sure. Because I will shove you down this whole flight of stairs and then come to the hospital and talk you to death."

Milano laughed.

"I'm not putting you on," Chris warned, "because neither of us is ever going to blow this thing out of just plain foolishness."

"My foolishness."

"Could be mine now and then. So we make a rule. Any time the foolishness gets heavy we stop right there and talk about something else. Anything else. Just pick it out of the hat. All right?"

"All right. So this seems like the time to tell you that the case of Mrs. Smith is all washed up. Finished."

"The lady with the Boudins? Just like that?"

"Yes. Seems she got her paintings back again her own way. What I'd like you to do now is forget all about it. Especially around Rammaert. Never to mention anything to him about it. Or about me. Could hurt in a business way if you do."

"Wouldn't help me much either, would it?" Chris observed.

"I guess not." He moved his arm around her shoulders and drew her close. His hand cupped the softness of a breast, the hardness of a nipple. Prom night. Only this time his date happened to be, however frustratingly, in pajamas and barefoot.

Barefoot.

"Aren't your feet cold?" he asked.

"Believe me, honey," his date assured him, "nothing is cold right now."

# Charles Witter Kirwan

THIS IS MY FINAL MESSAGE.

My last statement.

Sacred in a way. Last statements — deathbed statements — have always been regarded as sacred to some degree. God in his infinite wilfulness lighting up the soul of the dying at their last breath. But there will be no more truth or exposure of the naked soul in what I say now than there has been in anything I have already said to you. All was the truth.

My final message? Yes. But this is Wednesday, and the grand event was scheduled for Thursday. Tomorrow.

Now there has been a change of schedule.

An enforced change of schedule.

The grand event will take place at seven o'clock this evening.

Instead of being my day of rest after yesterday's exhausting effort, this must be a day of final hard labor. And fulfillment.

Yesterday I placed the charge on the second-floor level of the shaft. The penultimate charge.

Today the ultimate charge. At five o'clock this afternoon. Two hours allowed, so at seven I can sound the Bulanga crack of doom.

No one will be allowed to interfere.

No one.

It is now

It is now precisely twenty minutes after seven this final morning. Less than twelve hours left. Too little, because I desperately need sleep to ease this exhaustion. A long sleep, not the scraps I get. Exhaustion from physical effort, yes. But from the pain too. The pain is not only the knife thrust into the body, it is now a crushing weight on the shoulders. You bow under it. There is no way of straightening up under it.

But not for long.

A change of schedule at all costs.

Why?

Ask my would-be nemesis. My personal demon.

Who for the sake of

For the money value of seventy-two sticks of dynamite, a length of fuse, and a cheap detonator would confound all plans.

His recovery of a few dollars worth of stolen property his meaning, his gratification, his madness.

Madness?

It must be. Prowling outside all night. No time to waste on sleep, food, pissing, shitting, dandifying himself. Is any avid hunter closing in on his game burdened with such small concerns?

A madman. But cunning.

I have my own cunning. Oh yes. I scent his presence. Catch glimpses of him peripherally from different windows of the house. Just glimpses before he slips out of sight again.

At three o'clock this morning I sensed him acutely. Knew, as if it were written in fiery letters on this wall, that he was attempting to get into the cellar next door. Testing the locks in the shadows of the courtyard. Skeleton keys, a wire, a blade. Testing.

Sick with panic, pouring cold sweat, I found the strength to get up, to go out, to make my way to the courtyard. Too late. Gone already. And whatever he tried to do to those locks left no marks.

But he will be back tonight in the first darkness. And tomorrow night. The worst possible time for me. Tomorrow night.

This must not happen.

Cannot be allowed to happen.

So

The grand event is now scheduled for tonight. His opportunities for mischief are cut in half.

For the rest, I know how to attend to him.

I will attend to him.

Now what else is

Notes. I had my notes here.

Yes.

That property designated in the plat book as Number 409, Witter Street.

That property afterward. After the grand event.

This is important.

In the documents covering the administration of the Hendrick Witter Fund there is an omission. I am attending to it herewith. That property, once cleared of its rubble, must be restored to what it had been, a lawn and orchard adjacent to this house.

Not too difficult.

Wait.


I have placed on my desk two photograph albums dating before the year 1922. Many of these photographs in it were taken on that property before it was built over. By using this house as location marker when you study these pictures, it should be easy to determine the kind of trees — most of them — and their location in their original setting. Especially the twin row of cherry trees.

Not difficult. And the expense does not matter. The funding will be there. The restoration must be as accurate as possible.

Accurate.

# CHARLES WITTER KIRWAN

My grandfather's favorite words. Accurate. Exact. Precise.

A comical event. I stood in kneepants under those cherry trees and told my grandfather with excitement a story—a historical event learned in school.

The trees sticky with sap, my hand sticky and blackened by it. And my grandfather saying, "George Washington never cut down a cherry tree. He was not a fool. But Parson Weems who made up that story was a liar and a fool. What can you expect from a man named Weems?"

A sense of humor? In his way, yes. And the one to go to when gospel had to be confirmed. Or denied.

A man closed to the world. Open to me. It was on that day I understood this.

I understood it, child that I was.

Oh yes.

What does a child know? He knows more than anyone thinks he does. The silent child.

I knew my stepfather drank.

I saw the bottles, I smelled his reeking breath, and from between the banister posts at the head of the staircase I observed him as the naturalist in deep cover observes the wild life around him.

I knew my stepfather and my mother did something interesting and exciting in bed late at night. The bathroom faced their room across the hallway. I lingered in the bathroom, door open a little, and was excited by the sounds from that room of the bed creaking rhythmically, of the people in the bed groaning and gasping. No dismay in me, no outrage, just the itch of curiosity.

No trauma, believe me, dear Fraudians, because I was not Prince Hamlet nor was meant to be. Just a nice little boy savoring the mysteries being suggested.

What does a child know? Like a cat in an electric storm he knows when tensions rise. Tensions rose a little, fell a little all along. But they rose high and never fell when those blueprints appeared. Blueprints. Rolls of them. And talk of building and investment and money. Not angry talk. Nagging talk. Insistent talk. My grandfather always restrained, Dapper Dan always jovial, always nagging, always insistent. But the electricity was there. Oh yes. Get too close and feel the shock.

[267]

I got too close. I felt the shock.

Not a bad man, Daniel Kirwan. Not evil.

I must do him justice.

Not evil at all.

How can I put it?

Hell must be paved with his good intentions.

Awed by my grandfather. His quality. His breeding, his manners,

Incredulous. "You really did read all these books, Hendrick?"

Awed by Hendrick's letters published in the newspapers. The *Times*. The *Tribune*. The *Morning World*. The *Sun*. The

The

No one knew it till after his death — my grandfather didn't know it — but Dapper Dan collected tearsheets of those printed letters and kept them locked away in his closet.

I came home on emergency leave from Camp Gordon for the funeral, and I was the one who found them there in the closet. A manila envelope packed with them. That envelope. Along with the dozens of pint bottles of whiskey. And the hunting guns in their leather cases. Two rifles, a shotgun. And the steel boxes of ammunition, enough to fight a battle.

His private, carefully locked closet.

Out of his depth, poor benighted soul. So money money money became his lifeline. Reckless building, reckless investment.

He would have been the first to take out that shotgun and aim it at the invading Bulanga. Never knew he was their ally, their Fifth Column. Take the cash today, never mind the disaster you're planning for tomorrow in your ignorance.

What does a child know?

I sensed all this when I was a child. Sensed the electricity generated when the ancients trying to hold the world together are confronted by the upstarts driven to smash it apart.

Oh yes.

That day

That day in this room. The door closed but the voices heard through it. Hendrick Witter and Dapper Dan Kirwan. That jovial bullying voice. "You can't keep stalling, Hendrick. Now is the time."

My grandfather: "I'm sorry, Daniel. I don't like it. No one on the block likes it."

"The hell with them. If they had the brains, they would have been the first ones to line up a deal like this."

"I'm sorry, Daniel."

"Sorry? That's all you can say? After what's gone into these plans? That's what you think of my judgment?"

"My judgment is that you don't know the elements you're inviting here when you put up an apartment building like that."

"Oh yes I do, Hendrick. People with rent money. They pay it and we collect it."

"Yes. Well, let someone else collect it, Daniel."

"No. And I'll tell you this, Hendrick. If you don't respect my judgment in this, you don't respect me. If that's how it is, I'm taking my wife and son and moving out. Get that into your head. We move out, and I handle my business on my own. You can sit here and enjoy life by yourself, Hendrick."

No answer? Yes. Finally.

"You know I won't permit any such nonsense, Daniel. My grandson deserves a little better than what you could offer him on your own. His mother chose you, God help her. He is not going to pay for her mistake."

"Your grandson? Your grandson? My son, Hendrick. Try and get that into your head. My son."

Electricity. Ten thousand volts of it in the air. Then my grandfather: "Is that why you insist on a legal adoption, Daniel? To use the child against me?"

"God damn it, don't ever say that, Hendrick. Don't ever say that again. And when we're gone — my wife and my son and me, Hendrick — don't ever come crawling and think you can apologize for it."

"Daniel."

"The hell with you."

"Daniel, listen to me. I'm apologizing now."

So

That's how the world ends. Not with a bang or a whimper. With an abject apology.

What does a child know?

[269]

He knows when he's being held hostage by a pitiful, frightened, worthless, drunken soul.

He doesn't mind.

Life goes on and grandfather is still there.

Evil will never end the world. Stupidity will.

And stupidity with its

Yes.

Stupidity with its built-in self-destruct rejoices each time it has its way.

Celebrates.

Are you listening closely?

Gaudily, extravagantly celebrates.

A block party. That evening one week after my tenth birthday. One week after the State of New York decreed I was no longer Charles Witter but Charles Kirwan.

The celebration of 409 Witter Street. Unoccupied yet, but gloriously complete, its canvas marquee handsomely inscribed with its address. A huge, shining wonder. I admired it, gloried in it, put on airs for my friends who did not have any such behemoth in their yards to show the world.

Barricades placed at both ends of the block by the kindly police, and the space between filling with neighbors, acquaintances, workers from the construction job, people from as far away as the outlands blocks distant from us. Japanese lanterns festooned on tree branches, wound around lamp posts. Tables—those long planks on sawhorses—offering endless food and drink. On a low platform in the middle of the roadway a brass band. Six pieces. Red and green and orange lights from the lanterns flickering on the brass instruments, melting together in puddles of color on them.

And bright-colored balloons floating and popping everywhere. It didn't matter if you broke one. Take another. Take a dozen.

Pop pop pop

Take another dozen. And another.

Did the Bulanga around their distant campfires—the fires lighting their stinking garbage heaps—did they hear that faraway popping of balloons and know that some day

Some day

After the Irish and the Italians and the Jews

[270]

That some day
Yes.
They wisely nodded their kinky heads at each other and settled down to wait only a little longer.
They knew.
And the band played on. All six pieces, wonderfully deafening. Stand close to the platform, plug your fingers into your ears, and the racketing of the music still found its way into your head.
And suddenly
Dapper Dan there on the platform. A bull of a man, sweatstains showing through the armpits of that jacket. And reaching down and catching me by the wrists, swinging me to his shoulder so that I sat up there, the tallest one of all, looking down on all those people who, this one and that one, and these few and those few, now turned to look up at me.
"Here it is, boys," shouted Dapper Dan to the band, and they stopped playing for an instant, and then followed the song he led them into. "Happy birthday to you —— "
He sang it, booming it into my ear, and then everyone was looking up at me singing it. Roaring it out. All the while that big hand bracing me up there, hurting me as it dug into my ribs. Dapper Dan Kirwan leading the whole world in that birthday greeting to his newly-made son.
As proud of me as I was somehow ashamed of him.
Then down to the ground again, safe away from him. He remained up there. Oh yes. He had the crowd now, and drunk on whiskey and glory he was not going to give it up that easily.
No chance of that.
He took off that handsome new hat and waved it back and forth, leading the band, leading the crowd, into a new song. "East Side, West Side —— "
They roared it out. They roared it all the louder when he held both arms wide and waved them up and up and up, exhorting thunder from them.
Thunder.

"Boys and girls together,
Me and Mamie O'Rorke,

[271]

# THE DARK FANTASTIC

Tripped the light fantastic
On the sidewalks of New York."

Roaring it out, the celebration of the end of their world.

The end.

He never knew it, poor fool. Didn't live long enough to know it.

Didn't know the most terrible truth of all: He who cannot read the past is condemned to relive it.

Vico. Libertarian democracy to chaos to autocracy.

Out of his depth.

Proud of me. Created this legacy for me out of ignorance, so I must now make penance for that ignorance.

Understand this.

I make it willingly.

That is all.

# John Milano

It REMINDED MILANO OF THE COACH who protested that his team hadn't lost the game, it had just run out of time.

The reminder was provided by the Birdbath Theater's playwright Pearl and director Lenardo who eventually took notice that they were missing their star boarder and came out on the landing to view with astonishment the pair of lovebirds roosting on the stairway. Common decency dictated that they then haul ass right out of there, and Lenardo, sensitive male, did. Pearl, after getting one look at Milano, didn't.

"You going to sit there like that all night?" she demanded of Chris with a disapproval even more chilling than the draft winding up the stairway.

That did it. The spell was abruptly broken, and Milano who, between heated embraces had been trying gentle persuasion, logical argument, and even some heavy *ad miseracordia* pleading, wound up driving home alone.

He could see that it was as funny in a way as it was frustrating, this playback of the old Senior Prom days. But it stopped being funny when the insomnia set in. He gave sleep an honest try, then surrendered to jangling nerves and aimlessly prowled the apartment trying to make the jangling coherent. For instance, there was the big score against Mister Hairpiece, the satisfaction of seeing those Boudins safely on their way home to daddy. Not the biggest score he had ever pulled off, Milano had to acknowledge, but a big one. And considering the works involved, it should have been an especially gratifying one. But it wasn't. It tasted sour in the mouth. Worse. It was likely to taste that way, Milano suspected, as long as Christine Bailey didn't know the whole scenario.

And if she was enlightened about it, what role would she feel he had cast her for? His unknowing partner? His victim? His dupe?

No matter how you looked at it, it was hard to imagine any time of such revelation however remote — she could be pushing him around the retirement colony in a wheelchair — that wasn't charged with calamity.

Jesus.

Even more depressing was the realization of the apartment's acute emptiness right now. Acute. An unnerving sense of someone acutely missing from the picture. Voluntarily, stubbornly missing. The complete flake. Wouldn't play in his yard but didn't have one of her own, so there she was fifty blocks away, curled up on her lumpy couch sleeping the sweet sleep of the self-righteous.

Maybe not. It could only be hoped that she was lying there in torment, suffering every form of guilt in the book.

Either way, how did she come to be calling all the shots?

As if he didn't know the answer, thought Milano, when the apartment really was acutely, miserably empty without her.

But she'd get around to logic, and soon. Would move in, settle down, take life as it came. And he, as he had explained to her a dozen times over on that stairway, would willingly take her as she came, God help him.

As is.

If that's how it had to be, that's how it would be.

He fell asleep trying to convince himself of it and was brought awake by the phone. Eight o'clock. He lunged for the phone, noting the time as that hour which marked Christine Bailey's surrender to logic. But when he opened with a warm "Hello there," what he seemed to have on the line was a breather who had somehow tied on to a member of the wrong sex. Or were there gay breathers now operating in town?

The breather finally found his voice. "Mr. Milano? John Milano?"

The voice sounded familiar. The hacking cough that followed it settled all questions. "Mr. Kirwan?" said Milano.

"Yes. I want to meet with you today. Here. At four o'clock."

"Meet today," echoed Milano, then got his bearings. Of course. He was John Milano, properties consultant, who had in mind to buy the decrepit 409 Witter Street. And the landlord was suddenly in a selling mood. If sufficiently stoned, he might even be in a talking mood. What's more, this Milano had arranged to drive Christine Bailey to 409 Witter to oversee a social services person dropping in this evening on little sister. The catch was that he was supposed to pick up his flakey dream girl at five. After work.

"Well, Mr. Milano?" Kirwan said sharply.

"Yes. Sorry. As it is, I expect to be in the neighborhood this evening——"

"I'm sure you do, Mr. Milano."

Sarcasm? And what the hell made him so sure?

"—so," said Milano, "if you can arrange it for the evening——"

"No. Four o'clock. Do yourself that favor. I think we understand each other perfectly."

That's what you think, buddy, thought Milano, but said, "All right then, four o'clock."

"Promptly. I'll be waiting. Oh yes, and give Mr. Passarini my compliments. Tell him for me he's done very well for himself."

Click.

Milano slowly put down the phone. The way the old burlesque routine went, it should ring again, and someone should announce himself as Mr. Passarini and ask if any compliments had been left for him. Except that with Professor Peeping Tom the humor wasn't sophomore stuff, it was strictly graduate school. Esoteric. The footnotes in print too small to read.

Passarini? Milano hauled out the Manhattan phone book from under the night table and let his fingers do the walking. Passaretti. Passarge. Passaro. Between Passarge and Passaro nothing. Screw it.

He dialed Chris's number, and when she answered he said, "Do you know what a donkey you are?"

"Honey, do not hassle me this time of day. I haven't had my coffee yet.

"Did you get a good night's sleep?"

"Fine."

"I didn't," said Milano. "Anyhow, this is a business call. I just heard from your mama's landlord. He wants to meet with me over there at four this afternoon, so I said yes."

"Why does he want to meet with you?"

"Probably to sell me his apartment house. But I'm not all that sure. He sounded far out. Past the stratosphere and still moving fast. And since he's my number one lead to what ails Lorena — "

"Honey, do you know why he's your number one lead? Do you mind me telling you why?"

"I might."

"You might. Because I think you have been down on him from the time you got the idea he sneaked a look at me bare-ass. The hot-blooded Italian outlook, you know what I mean? And I can do without that. Why don't you just lay off the man?"

"Come on," Milano said scornfully, "that's not an analysis, that's an ego trip."

"Happens to be the truth, honey."

And, thought Milano, as far as his motives went that's what it happened to be. Which still didn't leave Kirwan off the hook.

"All right," he said, "the bare-ass privilege is reserved for me. But I still want to get together with him. Can I pick you up at three instead of five?"

"I wish you could. But you can't."

He had been prepared for this. "Then you just drive out there in the Toyota. We'll get together at Mama's, and whenever you're ready you can drive me home."

"No, you can drive me back to the Village. I've still got a couple of days to go on the monthlies, so the weekend'll be better for us all around."

"For chrissake," said Milano, "I'm not even talking about sex."

"I know."

"So?"

"I'm going to have my coffee now, honey. See you at Mama's."

Milano put down the phone. Of course, she could have been lying about having a good night's sleep. The trouble was that she didn't seem to know anything about lying. And that jealous Latin lover crap. Why the hell did she have to dig up that idiotic stereotype? And, if he remembered rightly, it wasn't for the first time.

Lay off Kirwan? Because, after getting his unadvertised eyefuls of her through that window, he had patted her on the head and given her a high school recommendation? Some advice. Proof, in fact, that while in some ways this lady might be as toughminded as they come, in others she had a head full of oatmeal.

That Heywood and Smith memory book on Kirwan, Milano knew, was somewhere around the apartment. He finally located the folder on top of the refrigerator and sat down with it at his desk. A pile of stuff in the folder, but by settling for those sections highlighted by Gracella Smith's marker he made fast time through it. With a couple of exceptions, what emerged was a college level Mister Chips, American style. Portrait by Wyeth, house in the background by Hopper. The exceptions dealt with a valorous military record, and while it was hard to see Professor Peeping Tom in this light, there it was in print. Commanding officer of a special demolitions squad, decorated for the destruction of enemy strongpoints.

Talk about ancient history.

What wasn't in the folder, of course, were some items of modern history. Those porno binoculars always at the ready. Grandpa's ashes on the mantelpiece. That endless boiler repair job which produced dust instead of oil and water. Mr. Passarini.

Mr. Passarini?

Was it possible that the professor had gone so schizo that he didn't really know who he was talking to on the phone or about what? Or did he just enjoy hitting you with characters unknown to tilt you off balance? Mr. Passarini. Like Guy Fawkes. Please to remember the fifth of November Guy Fawkes.

[277]

Milano irritably closed the folder and from a drawer in the desk removed the envelope containing Pacifica Inland's front money, three thousand dollars of it. He tucked the envelope into his pocket and strolled past beckoning Central Park to the office. His room there was empty, the desk restored to normal, a pile of mail on it waiting for action. No Hy Greenwald.

In answer to his call, Shirley came in bearing still more mail for the pile. "Welcome back, stranger," she said.

"Mmm. Where's Hy?"

"He thought you'd be in for keeps today, so he moved back to his old office. Right now he and Willie and that Pacifica man and his art expert are all downstairs having a celebration brunch. If you move fast——"

"No. I gather the paintings passed inspection."

"With flying colors. Willie already gave me the Pacifica check for deposit. Quite a haul, isn't it?"

"Uh-huh." Milano reached across the desk to hand her the loaded envelope. "You can add that to it. Three thousand expense money. It wasn't needed."

"So I see." Shirley looked, if anything, reproving. "You know, Johnny, they don't give out merit badges around here for this. You could easily——"

"Don't worry about the merit badges," Milano said. "Just make sure I get a receipt." But it was the first time she had ever reacted this way to this procedure. His return of unused expense money. And she had a peculiar expression on that Jewish-mother face. Intense concern. "There's something on your mind, Shirl. What is it?"

"Well"—her face was going bright red—"when Willie gave me that check to deposit he also gave me a paper to file. Your promissory note. For forty thousand. Forty thousand, Johnny? My God, beside being in hock to him for that, do you know how much money goes through your hands? I mean——"

"I know what you mean," said Milano.

Shirley had the bit between her teeth now. "I don't think you do. And I don't want you all heated up because I have a suggestion to make about it. But you have no head at all for handling your money, Johnny. So how about putting one of those personal financial managers in charge? Somebody to take over your income, figure out expenses, see you have something to show for your work. Doesn't that make sense to you?"

Milano leaned far back in the chair and tilted it to an acute angle. "Believe it or not, Shirl, these last few weeks I've had in mind lining up someone just like that."

"Well, all right."

"Nothing settled yet, but I'll let you know when it is. Right now, what I'd like to know is if we've got any reference books on history around here somewhere."

"On history? For what?"

"I guess that's the answer," said Milano.

The nearby Donnell Library on Fifty-third, right across the street from the Museum of Modern Art — good old MOMA — supplied the necessary text. A detailed study of the early Stuart reign in England.

Guy Fawkes. The Gunpowder Plot, 1605. The attempt of England's dispossessed and persecuted Roman Catholics to blow up the Protestant James I and his Parliament. Barrels of gunpowder smuggled into the cellars of the Houses of Parliament ready to be set off on convening day. But someone sang, and a few conspirators, including ringleader Guy Fawkes, were seized. End of plot.

Not quite the end of Guy Fawkes, however, not until he could be made to confess fully and to name names.

At this point, Milano, coming up against a set of ancient woodcuts graphically illustrating the means of persuasion used on the stubborn conspirator, had the feeling that for the sake of pleasant dreams it would be smart to close the book right here and let it go at that. Morbid temptation, as he trusted it would, got the better of him. He read on with interest.

Fawkes was hauled off to the Tower of London and there chained in a kneeling position in a cage four foot square. He was force-fed regular meals — mustard for food, vinegar for drink. Incredibly, he survived this for an agonizing fifty-six days, and then his inquisitors, losing patience, laid what was left of him on the rack. The first bonecracking tug of the ropes finally broke his spirit, he confessed at length, named names.

Still not the end of Guy Fawkes. He, along with his men, was hanged, cut down while yet conscious, carefully disemboweled, and his own guts displayed to him. And that was the end. A lesson to anybody who might be tempted to play with gunpowder.

Gunpowder.

Back in the apartment, Milano opened the Kirwan dossier to the pages describing the military exploits of Captain Kirwan, demolitions expert. Two pages. One an interview, one an account of the Italian campaign in which the captain's exploits amounted to a sketchy couple of lines. In the interview, he came off as modest, self-deprecatory, ironic in his opinion of his decorations. No glory-hunter, that was for sure. No wild-eyed adventurer. Just a colorless expert for a few months in a very narrow line of work, the demolition of enemy strongholds under fire.

And, as the captain turned professor had remarked himself, with a recent interest in Guy Fawkes, who was not quite as expert in that line of work.

Of course, ancient gunpowder was one thing, modern dynamite another.

Professor Charles Witter Kirwan.

At first meeting wouldn't consider selling his white elephant apartment building. Getting it ready for the torch, said the cynical Madman, and, what with one thing and another, that was a thin possibility.

But what became of that thin possibility now that the professor had suddenly changed his mind and was ready to talk about selling?

Milano went into the kitchen, opened the refrigerator, and took out the pitcher of martinis waiting there since that memorable evening when, depending on how you looked at it, either he had seduced Christine Bailey or she had seduced him. All right, call it a joint venture. He tried a mouthful of martini, stirred the contents of the pitcher with a soup spoon, tried another mouthful, then poured the whole thing down the sink. A warning from heaven, the way the stuff tasted after aging.

He went back to the desk, went over Captain Kirwan's military history again and moved on to Professor Kirwan's record as civil libertarian. Going by that record, Milano thought, it wasn't too hard to see why his own favorite minority person, or for that matter such as Gracella Smith and DeLong Heywood and handyman Al Bunting had a soft spot for the professor. Good will and tolerance seemed to be very much the professor's thing.

And binoculars.

Milano opened the bottom drawer of the desk. Its sole contents were a sealed pack of cigarettes and a pack of matches. He had given up smoking almost a year ago—eleven months, two weeks, and three days ago by his instant calculation—and the pack of cigarettes had been planted there in that unlocked drawer as the only true test of will power. The acid test.

Binoculars.

Once, when opportunity arose, trained on Christine, naked and tempting. Then she had moved out, and it was Lorena's turn. And the kid had detected Kirwan's game. And had been blackmailing him. Of course, that five-dollar-an-hour cataloguing job was just a cover-up.

Confront Lorena with this, confront Kirwan with this, and what happens?

Nothing, when that little team had every reason to keep its mouths shut. Correction. One thing. If Kirwan is in a mood for it, John A. Milano can be held liable for slander.

Milano took out the pack of cigarettes, carefully opened it, and lit himself a cigarette. He drew in deeply, discovering sensitive areas right down to the bottom of his lungs, and exhaled the smoke luxuriously. All right, a momentary fall from grace, but it could be laid squarely on Christine Bailey who had to have a kid sister like that. A teen-age disaster area.

He had stored the ashtrays on a kitchen shelf. He went to get one and on the way back picked up the unread copy of this morning's *Times* from the foyer table. He laid it out on the desk over the Kirwan dossier and opened it to the real estate section. Sales and Rentals. Greenwich Village. Once rentals took up most of these listings; now with the co-op movement on, it seemed to be all sales. Which, considering that your rental apartment was likely to go co-op next week, made sense.

Sheridan Square. Abingdon Square. Bleecker Street. West Tenth. West Tenth? West Tenth had style. But would she regard it as true Village when funky Village it definitely was not? He took out his pen and circled the Tenth Street address, then marked off a few other possibilities. One advantage in aiming for a house rather than an apartment was that you didn't have to rush over with a deposit to nail it down. It would still be there next day when you had time to look it over.

At three o'clock, the half-empty pack of cigarettes in his pocket, he went downstairs and had the doorman hijack him a cab for the trip to Brooklyn.

It might have been Witter Street itself that put him off guard. Tree-lined, full of kids fresh home from school and more or less amiably playing an assortment of noisy games, here and there mamas and grandmas keeping an eye on baby carriages, the whole scene so charged with domesticity that it simply blocked from the brain any apprehension about what might be waiting behind the door of that house until one split second too late.

Milano had rung the bell, the door had been opened by Kirwan who stood aside to let his guest enter the vestibule, the door had closed, and that one split second later Milano felt the hard object jammed into the middle of his back.

He went rigid, knowing what it had to be before Kirwan, right behind him, spelled it out in a harsh whisper. "A shotgun, Mr. Milano. Double-barreled. Ten gauge. Both barrels loaded." Whisper and wheeze, whisper and wheeze. "Don't move. Don't speak. Just do as I tell you."

"Hey, look," Milano protested, and the pressure against his spine increased.

"Don't speak. Just do as I tell you. Clasp your hands on your head."

Milano clasped his hands on his head. The worst of it, he saw wrathfully, was that he had no one to blame but himself. Despite all kindly report about the old man along the way, he had known that this was a character way off center. Maybe dangerously off center. But comes the showdown, and here was Johnny boy with a loaded shotgun in his back and what could be a homicidal maniac at the other end of it.

God damn.

Of course, mistaken identity.

This whole act was intended for somebody named Passarini, and Johnny boy had been taken for Passarini's accomplice or whatever.

Don't speak? The hell with that.

"I tell you," Milano said, "that I don't — "

"Quiet!" The gun dug into him, and then Kirwan was seized by a spasm of coughing which had those twin barrels, their pressure unyielding, jiggle against the spinal column. Milano set his teeth hard. One cough too many, he thought, and that was it with a bang. The spasm subsided. Kirwan said, "I warned you not to speak. Just do as I say. We're going up those stairs now. Very slowly."

The inside door of the vestibule was open. Milano, hands on head, moved across the threshold of the doorway into the hall leading to the staircase, that threatening pressure still firm against his spine. Against the wall there was a full-length mirror, a wooden hatrack mounted on either side of it. From the corner of his eye, Milano caught a brief view in the mirror of the picture he and Kirwan made. Milano and a tall, skinny Quasimodo. The old man was hunched all the way over, his body twisted, one shoulder thrust forward. The gun was held low, locked against the hip by an elbow, the finger through the trigger guard.

Wheel around suddenly? Ram your shoulder back against that near shoulder, try to knock the man off balance, take it from there?

Suicide time, Milano thought. The thing to guard against right now was the temptation to make any sudden move. No matter how fast the move, it couldn't be as fast as the convulsive motion of that bony finger against the trigger. This Kirwan was not only a galloping case of paranoia but in his time a tested and proven combat man. And he was handling that ancient drill in expert style.

"Move," Kirwan said. "Very slowly."

They went up the stairs very slowly. There was a strip of carpeting, brassbound, laid on the stairs, and Milano carefully held to the center of it. Raise the left foot, place it on the step above. Raise the right foot, place it beside the left. One step. Two steps. Three steps —

"Wait," Kirwan ordered.

Milano waited. As if he held a stethoscope against that caved-in chest, he could clearly hear the wheeze and gasp of those straining lungs. Just going up these stairs unburdened, he remembered, had

[283]

been hard for the old man. Now burdened with the gun, he was being pushed to the limit of his strength.

And then, hope springing eternal, maybe past the limit?

Maybe. More likely if you're paranoid enough, that limit was highly flexible.

Captain Kirwan. That was it. Now paranoid. Reliving some wartime glory mission where he —

"Move," Kirwan said. "Slowly. Then wait."

Milano planted his left foot on the next step up. Planted the right foot beside it. Waited.

A glory mission. Captain Kirwan's foggy mind was back there on the road to Rome. The enemy all around. A prisoner taken.

That had to be it.

And then what happens upstairs? Do you plead the Geneva Convention? Ask for one phone call to the nearest Allied police precinct?

"Move," Kirwan said.

They moved that way — one step up and wait, one step up and wait — to the head of the stairs. Then down the hallway to the tower room. A delay there by the desk. The last time Milano had gotten a look at that desk its top had been almost clear, the few items on it neatly squared away. Now it was covered by a surrealist clutter. Kirwan plucked a narrow leather strap from the clutter. The muzzle of the gun nudged Milano's spine. "Across the room," Kirwan said. "By the radiator."

Flogging time? No, tying-up time.

An iron riser from floor to ceiling connected near its base to the radiator. Under orders, Milano backed up against the riser. The gun barrel clanged against the riser as it shifted position to the nape of his neck. Double-barreled all right: Milano could trace the outline of each barrel just below his hairline.

"All right," Kirwan said, "hands behind you around the pipe. Slowly. Good. Now cross your wrists." One-handed himself, the gun barrels erratic against Milano's skull with each movement, Kirwan slipped the strap around the crossed wrists, worked it through its loop, wound it around and around, and finished by tucking the free end under the binding at the juncture of the wrists.

Tight and hard, Milano found, straining against the pressure,

[284]

pulling the strap against the riser. So much for the old man's failing strength. There was still plenty of it left. To what end? One prisoner taken and ready for questioning?

At least when Kirwan stepped back to look over his handiwork the gun no longer drilled painful welts into the neck. Evidently satisfied with what he saw, Kirwan propped the gun against the wall and went over to the desk. From the litter he extracted a long piece of cloth. A badly wrinkled, brightly colored necktie.

A necktie party?

A private lynching?

"For chrissake," Milano erupted, "you're making a mistake. I don't know what this is all about, I don't know any Passarini——"

"Please!" Kirwan looked pained. "That part of the game is over, Mr. Milano."

"What game?"

"Yours. That part of it." Kirwan made an impatient gesture. "Understand that you're beaten. But you can be helpful. Oh yes. But on my terms." He moved up to Milano, the necktie taut between his hands. "I'm sorry. But I think you might be heard outside."

"Listen to me, Kirwan——"

No use, not that Milano had expected it to be. He was gagged, the tie drawn between his teeth, knotted tight at the back of his neck right over the soreness left by the gun barrels. He tried to raise voice against the pressure, and it came out a growling in the throat. There was already a sour taste in the mouth from that necktie material and an outpouring of saliva saturating it.

A total wipeout. One prisoner, sir, ready for disposal.

Kirwan was doing some incoherent muttering in his throat too, as he went about his business. Impossible to make out the words, but from their rhythm he could have been reciting a set of rules to himself. Or instructions. Or the Ten Commandments.

No way of getting any clues from this, Milano saw, but that deliberate series of actions might provide something—anything—to get a handle on. Kirwan opened the familiar plastic shopping bag on the desk. Into it went the familiar Thermos bottle. That heavy-duty pair of shears. The flashlight. That tool like a pliers with a notary public's seal fixed on its nose. The last time out, that tool had been in two

[285]

parts. Now it was riveted together, the fresh rivet conspicuously shiny against the dull metallic finish of the tool.

And that was it. The same stuff that had been carted out of the basement next door on the introductory visit to Kirwan. Which had to mean that he was now packing to leave for that basement. But not to work on any boiler. You didn't kidnap somebody at gunpoint and then go make boiler repairs. Cracked as Kirwan was, there was a purposefulness about him. Marching to a different drummer, yes, but toward some well-defined objective.

All packed, Kirwan took stock of the prisoner.

"You see, Mr. Milano? All for that handful of Mr. Passarini's fireworks." There was no triumph in that croak, only querulous reproach. "And you still haven't come up with the answer, have you?"

Milano shook his head vigorously to indicate truthfully that no, he hadn't come up with anything.

"I'm sure," Kirwan said. He squinted up at the Naval Observatory clock over the doorway. "Almost four-thirty, Mr. Milano. So you'll get your answer very soon. At seven o'clock promptly. Worth waiting for. Oh yes."

Milano measured the distance to the desk. The phone on the desk was close to its edge. With a leg extended it might be possible to jar that massive piece of furniture and send the phone to the floor. And then —

For a chilling instant as Kirwan leaned over the desk it looked like the phone had drawn his interest too. Wrong, thank God. Part of the clutter was made up of tape recorder cassettes, a load of them. Kirwan drew them together into an untidy heap. He held one up to give Milano a proper view of it. "The rest of the explanation," he said, "is right here. In all of these. Oh yes. Marked in order." No more Captain Kirwan now but Professor Kirwan solemnly getting a seminar under way. "After the event — that should be not long after seven o'clock — you will make this clear to those in charge. Do you understand?"

Milano repeated that vigorous shake of the head, no, and Kirwan instantly turned wrathful. "You're not that obtuse, Mr. Milano. I said everything is here. The complete presentation. Complete. All

[286]

marked in order. For the proper authorities. Priceless." He was
gasping the words, hardly able to form them. "Priceless."

Jesus, Milano thought with foreboding, now all the old man has
to do to create a really wicked problem in getting out of this was to
drop dead of a paroxysm on the spot. So picking the lesser of the two
evils, he nodded enthusiastically in affirmation and was grateful that
Kirwan appeared to cool down as fast — and unpredictably — as he
had heated up.

"Good," he said. "That's all then. Until seven. You'll see."

There was a weatherbeaten raincoat slung over the back of the
swivel chair behind the desk. Kirwan laboriously got himself into the
coat, stuffed shotgun shells into its pockets from a box on the desk,
then made his way to the gun leaning against the wall and, as if
trying it on for size, tucked its butt under his armpit, the barrel
extending along his leg concealed by the coat. Evidently satisfied
with the fit, he hefted the gun in one hand, the shopping bag in the
other, and headed for the door.

He stopped in the doorway and turned to face Milano who, with a
foot already probing for the desk, had to withdraw the foot lightning
fast.

"In your original tongue, Mr. Milano," said Kirwan, *"nos
morituri."*

He moved off, and Milano could follow that hunched-over figure
along the hallway to the head of the stairs where it turned out of
sight. But the house was deathly quiet, and the painful progress
down the stairway was audible, step by tedious step. A brief silence.
Then the sound of the front door slamming shut.

That was at thirty-six minutes after four.

Ten minutes later, Milano realized that he was dead-ended.
Which, he knew, meant ten minutes shot to hell because he had
gone physical when he should have gone mental. He had displayed
exactly as much sense during that time as a mouse sealed in a shoe-
box. Strictly instinctive and physical. Had slid down to a sitting
position to ram his heel again and again into the leg of that
desk — like ramming it against a block of granite — and the result,
aside from a couple of the cassettes spilling onto the floor, was only

physical anguish. A bruised heel. Bound wrists, forced against the riser as he stretched out as far as possible to reach the desk, seemingly gnawed to the bone by their leather binding. Both shoulder joints on fire. Mouth, abraded by the necktie, like raw meat worked over with sandpaper.

Time to go mental.

Milano pushed himself upright and leaned back against the riser with eyes closed. Under physical constraint, he found, it wasn't easy to get a wild scramble of thoughts organized when the one constant among them was the raging need to get free of the constraint.

Never mind struggling to get free of the constraint right now. The immediate object was to make some sense of it. Think it out. Take it from there.

All right, the dim side. A wild-eyed certifiable case was roaming loose with a shotgun and a mess of backup shells in his pocket.

The bright side. The wild-eyed certifiable case wasn't really running loose. He and his shotgun were locked in that cellar next door where he would be busy at some project. Which would be completed at seven o'clock. After which —

A project.

Milano looked around the room taking stock. On the desk: telephone, penholder, lamp with a dent in its brass reflector, pile of cassettes, and what looked like a couple of old-fashioned blackpaper photo albums. Against the wall that antique safe. But now its door inscribed with the gilt *Witter & Son* was wide open, revealing just one lonely item, a cassette player.

The family treasure, that player? Hardly. So one might assume — one should goddam well assume — that these cassettes with their numbered-in-order explanation of Kirwan's coming event were the family treasure that had been stored in the safe. To be delivered — as well as someone bound and gagged could deliver them — to —

How had Kirwan put it?

Those in charge.

The authorities. Who would be showing up soon after seven o'clock.

But not Kirwan. Not the old man himself. Because he had other plans for himself after that mysterious event.

Take off somewhere. Disappear. The packed bags probably

already stowed in his car. Now all he had left to do in that cellar was what? With what?

In your original tongue, Mr. Milano. *Nos morituri*.

Hell, Milano thought, that wasn't just laying on the erudition, that gladiator's goodbye. We who are about to die —

*Nos morituri te salutamus*. We who are about to die salute you.

Not likely you'd get the message, Mr. Milano, you dumb wop, said Captain Kirwan in effect, but if by some miracle you do, you'll know I'm now signing off for good. I am going down with my event, baby. And why I did and how I did it is all on those tapes under your nose.

*Nos morituri*, Mr. Milano, and up yours. You really walked into this one, didn't you?

That hunched-over half-dead wreck ready to go on its mission. One shotgun, plenty of shells in reserve to stand off unwanted visitors to that cellar for quite a while.

One plastic shopping bag. Into it, one Thermos bottle. One heavy shears. One flashlight. One freaky-looking tool, freshly riveted.

That was what did it.

You fool around with the windowshade cord long enough, and suddenly the shade flies open and light floods in, dazzling you. All those years ago — it was even before he had teamed up with Willie — there was that gang of fake political heroes trying out extortion on those uptown hotels. A month of bomb threats, then an explosion. And more promised, until young Johnny Milano had tagged their Numero Uno and was allowed to be right there when the cops had invaded his little bomb factory. Dynamite evidence, said the cops happily, looking around. And one of them, pencil reversed in his hand, carefully nudged a curious tool into a plastic bag. A crimper, he said in answer to Johnny Milano's question. You fit your blasting cap and fuse to the head of the dynamite stick and you crimp them tight with this gimmick.

Dynamite stick. Blasting cap. Fuse.

Milano realized he had wildly bellowed "Kirwan!" under the gag when he felt the strain of it in his throat. Then panic grabbed him, the kind that starts an instant cold sweat over the whole body, sends pearls of it trickling down the face, wetting chest and belly, rolling off the fingertips.

Not arson. Dynamite. Somehow, Captain Kirwan, demolitions expert, had gotten himself a load of high explosive to play with.

A busy gardener now, planting the stuff around the dusty corners of that basement fortress.

And at seven o'clock tonight —

Superimposed on this was the image of Christine Bailey impatiently looking at that wall clock in the Rammaert Gallery just as Captain Kirwan's trussed-up, useless prisoner was now looking at this clock over the doorway. Ten minutes to five. In about ten minutes she'd be walking out of the gallery on her way over to the co-op's garage for the Toyota. Heavy traffic and all, she could easily make it here to Witter Street by six. Then upstairs to the apartment. And down below, Kirwan was getting things ready for the fireworks at seven.

Join the army. Learn a trade. Like Guy Fawkes.

That was the reason for that little private joke about Guy Fawkes.

And the laughter about Mr. Passarini's fireworks. But not the Coney Island kind.

So what was needed now, but fast, faster, fastest, was something sharp. Something with an edge to slice into this leather binding. That would be the advantage of leather over rope now. Once you just start slicing into leather it gave up easily, could be pulled apart.

Theoretically sound, but, as Milano saw, the only glass in sight were windowpanes well out of range. Metal. That brass lampshade. But if it could be jolted off the desk and drawn within reach, there didn't appear to be any edges to it. And bruising experiment had already demonstrated it couldn't be jolted off the desk.

Metal. The riser itself was iron, and maybe chafing the leather against it — given enough time — could serve the same purpose as cutting into it.

Maybe. Given enough time.

Milano leaned forward pulling the strap tight against the pipe behind his back and started drawing it up and down against the metal. With any luck, he thought, he could hit some imperfection on the pipe, some splinter of metal, which would start the cutting process. No luck at this level. He let himself down to his knees and again started that up and down motion of the bound wrists. No luck here either. Up there, down here, and probably wherever else you tested it, that pipe's surface was damn near frictionless. It wouldn't be a case of slicing into that leather or abrading it, it would be a case of eroding it.

But you desperately worked with whatever you had to work with.

Keeping your eyes on that clock naturally, so that you suddenly realized for the first time in your life that you could actually see the minute hand of a clock moving. It moved all right, while shoulder joints, drawn back unnaturally against the strain of those bound wrists against the pipe, felt more and more as if knifeblades had been shoved into them and were being slowly twisted into every nerve there. Stop to ease the agony, and the minute hand of the clock moved even faster. It was obvious now why tough old Guy Fawkes, after laughing off those fifty-six days of mustard and vinegar, gave up as soon as the rack got to work on his shoulder joints.

One half hour of this up and down against the pipe — thirty minutes which had the pains crawl together from each shoulder to join at the base of the skull, and then to crawl down the arms to the fingertips — and Milano knew that erosion wasn't going to work. He had suspected that well before the half hour was up but couldn't bring himself to know it for a fact.

At twenty after five he forced himself to accept the fact. And with the pains eased a little as he leaned back against the riser, forced himself to consider some bright possibilities.

All right, a lunatic was arranging to set off a blast next door. And — try to face this thought without coming apart — Christine Bailey was arranging to be there for the event. But what was to say that Kirwan, with his scrambled brains, could pull it off? As long as it hadn't happened yet, one might assume it wouldn't happen. A dozen things could go wrong with any such operation. A hundred things. Seven o'clock would come and go, no bang.

Oh yeah, thought Milano. Like those Friday morning arithmetic tests in good old P.S. 128. First you hoped Friday wouldn't come, but it always came. Then you hoped the test wouldn't come, but it always did.

And if a beautifully executed ambush was the gauge, there was a shrewd capability under the craziness of Captain-Professor Charles Witter Kirwan, that perambulating atomic plant with all valves leaking.

All. Valves. Leaking.

So at twenty minutes after five, Milano realized that he had a piece of sharp-edged metal within hand's reach. Incredible that he had missed it before. Proof, he saw, that he might have gone mental, but sure as hell not mental enough. And there was no point now banging his head against the riser as a payoff for such stupidity. That pleasure he would reserve for a more promising time.

A short length of pipe coupled riser to radiator. Extending from the near coil of the radiator was its valve. Smooth-surfaced, bright and shiny—every damn piece of visible metal in the building looked like it had been installed yesterday—but what had to attach it to the radiator would be a threaded stem, and those threads offered sharp edges. A spiral of them capable of chewing right through leather.

Given time.

Better not to think what it would be like if heat had been needed in these pipes. Just be grateful it wasn't.

When Milano went down to his knees again he had the feeling they had been skinned down to the nerve ends. Pushing his back hard against the riser he blindly fumbled behind him for the valve, loosened it with a shove of the fist, got a grip on it and started to carefully turn it. One turn too much, and it could land on the floor out of reach. And then talk about Tantalus and his troubles.

Slow turn by slow turn, the valve finally came off into his hand. He pushed himself upright and found with a probing thumb that he had about an inch of sharp, hard-edged thread to work with, and that the valve itself, serving as handle, offered the grip needed. He maneuvered it in his hand until the stem was forced between the top two layers of strap and started a thrust and pull motion, back and forth within the scant inch the stem provided. Almost lightheaded with the sense of being on the way at last, he felt the scrape of brass against leather.

The pain in hand and fingers now set in. It was an unnatural position to start with, the grip on the valve had to be unrelentingly, consciously tight because any slackening of it meant a chance he would drop it, and there was no changing hands without losing that one small spot being worked on and having to start all over again. So this was it. Back and forth, with an electric shock up to the elbow with every small thrust.

Patience. Concentration. A rhythmical sawing away at the exact mark. An uninhibited grunt—he sounded to himself like a happily rooting hog—whenever one of those jolts of electricity hit harder than expected. Plenty of punishment taken, plenty more to take. Because getting down to the bottom line, he told himself, he had no intention of settling for bloody goddam fragments of his woman now that he had finally met up with her. It was as simple as that.

Between grunts he became acutely aware of street noises. The kids. The traffic. The buses. Those buses especially. Everybody in town griped about its bus service, but it seemed that every couple of minutes another one of the damn things was squealing to a stop nearby, marking time briefly, and then racketing on its way. Only when he checked this on the clock it wasn't every couple of minutes, it was closer to every five minutes. Bad news. Even nightmarishly worse was the way those two hands of Naval Observatory up there moved to that vertical line marking six o'clock.

The kid noises faded away. Supper time. The traffic noises intensified. Coming-home time. And one of those cars could be the Toyota with Chris at the wheel. Or was there any chance that the car had been deliberately fouled up by Maxie Rovinsky in the garage? Gracie, that prime bitch—his worst case of mistaken judgment had to be Gracie MacFadden—had passed the word along about Milano's *melanzana*, and Maxie had sabotaged the car to save his old bachelor poker partner from a fate worse than death. Right now the car was busted down in the middle of the bridge. It would take hours before the trafic there was untangled.

And that, Milano warned himself, was the kind of thinking which meant that the Milano brain was now heading in the same direction as Kirwan's. Spinning off-center right into fantasyland.

Patience, concentration, and at twenty minutes after six Milano felt the threads of the valve stem meet resistance. Stick, scrape, stick, Stick again. Scrape deep. The feeling you got from a knife hitting the apple core.

Braced for disappointment, he pulled his wrists forward against the riser and there was a perceptible loosening of the binding around

[293]

them. He pulled harder and the severed strap, suddenly released from pressure, flipped around and around, but came up short at its initial loop. Still with a grip on the valve — you never knew — Milano worked the wrists against each other, twisting and pulling. The strap gave way completely. Only when it hit the floor did he let go of the valve.

He found then that he had no hands. No arms. Trying to raise them to get at the necktie between his jaws, he found they weren't attached to him any more. He had to will them into motion, raise them like lead weights, fumble at the knot in the gag with fingers that didn't belong to him. He finally got the knot open, pulled away the sodden tie.

He lurched at the desk, grabbed the phone from its stand and then, his hand failing him, dropped it. He scrabbled for it, holding it with the dead hand, the valve-wielding hand whose fingers couldn't seem to uncurl, and dialed with the other hand. For emergencies, you dialed 911. Like every other service in Magic City it had a bad name, it didn't work right, but, as ever, you used what was offered and did a lot of heavy praying while at it.

The praying didn't work this time. Milano listened incredulously to the busy signal, then slammed the phone down on the stand. Some screwed-up son of a bitch had a hangnail and wanted an ambulance. Or somebody's roast was burning in the oven, and fire engines were being called for. He counted one two three slowly, picked up the phone and dialed again. Now the praying worked.

The official voice was casually inquiring, female, Spanish-flavored. Milano cut through it furiously. "Listen. There is a bomb set to go off at seven o'clock in Four-oh-nine Witter Street, Brooklyn." The Spanish-flavored voice was still trying to do the official bit. "Shut up!" Milano shouted, and it shut up. "Listen to me, that's all. There is a bomb going off at seven o'clock in Four-oh-nine Witter Street, Brooklyn. An apartment house with a lot of people in it. At seven o'clock, do you hear? Now get moving, God damn it!"

He slammed down the phone again and on wobbly legs got moving himself, almost headlong down the staircase and out of there.

When he hit the street the sun was down, the street lights already

[294]

on, but there was still plenty of daylight without them. And no Toyota parked anywhere in sight.

He covered the distance to 409 in a stiff-legged painful sprint, some people in its doorway giving him plenty of room as he went by. He kept his thumb on the doorbell of the apartment, meanwhile savagely kicking the door, until the door was suddenly flung open and a stranger stood there glaring at him. It had to be the older brother. Odell. Not as tall as beanpole Vern but a lot wider. And looking mean. "Man, what the hell you — "

Chris was right behind her brother shoving him aside. "Johnny, where've you been? I was going to phone next door, but I wasn't sure you'd want — "

Milano waved a hand back and forth. "Never mind that. Kirwan's gone out of his skull. He's in the cellar here right now setting up a load of dynamite to go off at seven o'clock. A big blast right downstairs, do you understand?"

Odell looked like Kirwan wasn't the only one in the area out of his skull. Christine said to Milano in bewilderment, "What are you talking about?" But behind her in the kitchen somebody took serious notice, because Mrs. Bailey's voice rose in passionate appeal. "Oh, Lord Jesus!"

Bad manners maybe, but Milano pushed his way inside. They had all been at supper in the kitchen. Mrs. Bailey was now out of her chair looking terrified. Vern sat there gaping. No Lorena.

"Where's Lorena?" Milano demanded.

Chris motioned. "In bed. But Johnny — "

"No, just get her out of here fast. All of you get out. Don't take anything. Just hit the street."

Odell was frozen there. "Man, you sure you know what you're talking about? Kirwan? Him? And dynamite?"

"Kirwan," Milano said. "I got it straight from him." Too bad the truth had to be stretched like this, but, with luck, there'd be time for apologies at a later date. "He pulled a gun on me next door, tied me up, told me all about it before he headed here." He held up his crossed wrists to illustrate, and saw as they did that the wrists were grotesquely swollen, the swelling streaked with purple welts. "I couldn't get away until now. I already called the cops."

That was almost the convincer. The convincer itself came by way of a siren whooping louder and louder, the whoop descending to a groan and finally cutting out completely close by. Never knock 911, Milano thought, because sometimes it does work, doesn't it?

Vern moved from the kitchen table in haste. "I'll get Lorena."

"Hold it," Christine ordered. She said to Milano, "How much time is there?"

"Damn little. Kirwan said seven o'clock, and it's six-thirty now. Look, I have to go down and see those cops. All you do — "

She shook her head at him impatiently. "Odell, you get over to those back stairs. Start on top and get those folks moving. Vern, you take the front stairs. Don't waste time with talk. Just bang hard and yell them out."

"Yell what?" said Odell. "We yell dynamite, they'll know we have to be jiving 'em. We yell fire, they'll wait to make sure. You saw it happen."

"All right," said Chris, "then yell gas leak, hear? Gas leak. And loud. Bang and yell, that's all. And then get out fast yourselves. I'll take care of Lorena."

Going down the stairs, Milano could hear the banging and yelling start high above. The patrol car was parked at the front door. Two cops standing by it were looking up at the building. The street lights were needed now in gathering dusk. In the buildings across the way, tenantry leaned out of windows taking in the show.

Milano went over to the cops. "I'm the one who put in that 911 call," he informed them.

Both were cut to the same youthful rangy pattern, but the one with the Madman's style of luxuriant Viking mustache seemed to be senior. "About some kind of bomb threat?" he said doubtfully.

This is a bad dream, Milano knew. The kind where you're running from an unholy menace swinging an axe at you, and suddenly you're stuck knee-deep in ooze where you can't move.

He said between clenched teeth, "Look, the guy who owns this building went psycho. He's locked in that cellar right now setting up dynamite for a blow-up at seven o'clock. He told me that himself."

"He told you that himself?"

"He even showed me the stuff, for chrissake. But he got away before I could stop him. And it'll be seven o'clock goddam soon."

[296]

Upstairs, the convincer for the customers had been the appearance of the cops on the scene. Here, it seemed the convincer for the cops was the appearance of some customers. They came streaming out of the building, kids in the lead noisily making a ball of it, the older generation right behind—that elderly white couple among them, Milano saw, were the ones who had put the curse on Kirwan for their broken refrigerator—and never mind the dire need to get moving at once, a few had household goods in their arms, one had a fair-sized TV set, and there were also some dogs and cats being lugged along.

The sight of them spilling onto the sidewalk goosed Mustache into action. "That the way to the cellar there?" he asked Milano, pointing at the stone steps.

"That's it. But you won't get the cellar door open that easy. And he's got a shotgun ready if you do."

"We'll take a look," said Mustache. Hand on the butt of his pistol, he led his partner down the steps, Milano following close behind. Slipping the gun from its holster, Mustache banged the door with his other fist and shouted "Police! Open up there." A couple of tries in that direction with some added kicking at the door, and he turned to his partner. "Shit. Steel-jacketed. And probably a slide-bolt too."

"They'll have to burn through it," said the partner.

"He said seven o'clock," Milano pleaded. "That leaves only ten minutes. Just get the place cleared out, that's all."

"Yeah?" said Mustache with sarcasm, letting it be known who the expert was, but he moved with notable speed leading the way back to the street.

It presented a wild scene now. The one gratifying sight from Milano's angle was that of the Baileys en masse near the entrance of the building. Lorena, he saw, was in a bathrobe, and from the wrestling grip Chris had on her—one arm around her throat from behind, the other shoving up Lorena's arm in a half-nelson, it was evident that little sister had come along unwillingly and was still registering fierce protest.

For the rest, there were now more patrol cars parked near the original one, and down the street came yet another. Motor traffic was being bottled up, not only by drivers slowing down as they passed 409 to see what was going on, but by what looked to be the entire population of the block—those who weren't at their windows —crowding around to get a look at the action, whatever it was.

A sedan, unmarked but with a flasher on its roof, and with siren snarling, gave up trying to work its way through the thickening mass of foot and motor traffic, found an opening to the sidewalk beside a hydrant, and pulled right up on the sidewalk. Several men emerged from it—no uniforms there—and their leader was conspicuously the shortest and leanest of them, a pinch-faced, slit-eyed, thin-lipped character who moved up to Mustache by ruthlessly shoving aside anyone, man woman, or child, who stood in his way.

"Detective-Inspector Price," he said. "What is this?"

Mustache, a hand on Milano's shoulder to mark the informant told it fast, and Price looked over Milano. "I.D.?" he said. Milano fumbled for his wallet, extracted the driver's license, held it up for inspection. Price barely glanced at it. "Dynamite?" he said. "That your story?"

Jesus, though Milano, here we go again. The more desperately you want to be a trumpet sounding a clarion call, the surer it is you'll be read for a freaked-out harmonica player. "Man," he said to Price, "if it's a stiff, you can always hang me for it later, can't you?"

"And will," Price assured him. He turned to Mustache and pointed at Milano. "Keep him close until I say otherwise." Then he aimed the finger at an aide and said in a flat voice—no one, Milano thought, was ever going to say no to that voice—"You clear away this traffic. I don't care how, just get it clear of these premises in five minutes." The finger swiveled to the next case: "And you close up the block, outgoing only, no incoming except for official or press. Five minutes, that's it." Next case: "And you evacuate the building, hear? Clean. Get some of those uniforms on it. And bullhorn the place front and back." Final case: "And you—I want a street detail getting this stupid fucking crowd away from here." Price surveyed the face of the building. "If anything really comes off, it could turn those wall trimmings into shrapnel."

He never raised his voice over the deafening racket of car horns along the block, the mounting voices of the crowd, the incessant mechanical squawking of dispatchers' messages coming over the patrol car radios, but somehow there was no missing a word of his instructions, and the troop responded fast. Milano started on his way toward the Baileys, and was pulled up short by Mustache. "You heard the man," said Mustache. "Across the street and stay close to me." He started Milano off with a shove, and Milano, observing that the Bailey contingent was, along with all those in front of 409, being herded in the same general direction, yielded to this muscular persuasion.

Not that Mustache, despite a valiant effort, could win a place for them on the sidewalk across the street; the packed crowd there made an impregnable barrier. So he settled for a place between a couple of parked cars, a tight fit but offering a good view.

From there, Milano saw that Price's orders were, miraculously, having an effect. The motor traffic was thinning fast, the crowd before 409 was being driven into a wide semicircle clear of it, a few stragglers were hustled from the building, a bullhorn was bellowing warnings to anyone yet inside to clear out right now, and official-looking cars kept pulling up to the perimeter of the crowd disgorging official-looking characters who gathered around a gesticulating Price in conference.

Then the first TV mobile unit arrived, closely followed by another and another, all of them at least as much a feature of the crowd's boisterous interest as that abandoned building which, thought Milano, suggested an abandoned ocean liner, its bottom snatched out by an iceberg or whatever, waiting to go down.

And certifiable case Captain Charles Witter Kirwan down there in the engine room, match in hand close to the fuse.

He had to be. All logic said so.

It turned out that Detective-Inspector Price had his doubts about it. He broke free of the big brass, looking around until he spotted Milano and his escort, and walked across the street to join them. He said coldly to Milano, "You told me dynamite. Everybody else seems to be talking gas leak. What the hell is that about?"

"A way to get them out of the building fast. But it's still dynamite."

"Maybe," Price said. "Just remember, one way or the other you and me got a lot to clear up afterward." He looked at his watch. "Seven o'clock. You might as well know," he told Milano, "there was no way of getting anybody out of that cellar on deadline. Or what you claim is deadline. Are you sure the super is in there?"

"Not the super. The owner. He lives over there in that next house."

[299]

"The owner?" It was obvious that Price had more to say on this, but he wasn't given the chance. Christine Bailey, moving lightfooted past parked cars, fending off a cop, wedged herself into the narrow area occupied by the trio and confronted Milano. Price got as far as an outraged, "Hey, lady ——!" but she disregarded him.

She said breathlessly to Milano, "The boys are taking care of Lorena," giving him the pleasant feeling that in this case she was here to take care of him. "Johnny, you think it'll really happen?"

"Yeah," Price chimed in, choosing to overlook the almost indecently tight fit the four of them made. "That's a good question, Johnny." He held up his wristwatch on display. "It's after seven, Johnny. Or did you mean seven o'clock next year?"

It was after seven all right, Milano saw, time for a world-class false alarm. No dynamite. There never had been. Kirwan was acting out a role from his bad dreams, and somehow he had hooked John Milano into them. If the old man was in that cellar right now, all he was doing ——

The thunderbolt slammed deafeningly against Milano's ears. The impact of the bolt thrust him back against the radiator of the car he was leaning against. Chris screamed as she was driven up against him, face in his chest, arms going convulsively tight around his waist. Price and Mustache clutched each other in an off-balance embrace. High overhead, Milano saw with astonishment, a million diamond chips sparkled in a wide, descending arc before they abruptly blinked out. Glass, he suddenly realized, as a particle stung his cheek.

All in one thin fraction of an instant. The next fraction, a black tidal wave, a curling blackness along that sidewalk across the street from one end of 409 to the other, surged out over the roadway. A warm, stinking comber of dust rolling out and carpeting the world.

And in that final fraction of the same instant, Milano saw the building's outline seem to waver. Then it clearly wavered. TV aerials just behind the false front of the roof leaned toward each other. The fire-escapes on each side of the entrance shifted to a weird angle.

The crowd yelled. One wild yell and that was it as the brick walls tilted inward toward each other. There was a rending and grinding — monstrous jaws chewing chunks of brickwork, masonry, metal

[300]

pipe—as the roof caved in bringing down the floors beneath, one into the other. Then the walls themselves disintegrated in slow motion, the whole building dissolved in on itself, and with its collapse the air was again foul with that stink of warm dust. The street light was dimmed by it, but through the dimness Milano saw—trying to believe what he saw—that 409 Witter Street was now a vast pile of debris.

That's all there was of it. A great big pile of debris.

And incredibly, nothing—nothing at all of it except a few bricks and the twisted segment of a TV aerial—now littered the dust-covered roadway in front of it. Nothing. The building could have been mashed flat by a gigantic hand careful not to let anything slip between its fingers.

Chris, with that deathly grip on Milano, still wouldn't or couldn't, look. Price and his aide and Mustache could. They regarded the scene open-mouthed, and it was Price who found his voice first. "Son of a bitch," he said with awe. "Whoever he was, he sure as hell knew what he was doing."

And that, thought Milano, was as sweet a tribute as Captain Kirwan, demolitions expert, was ever likely to get. Especially, once the cost of his expertise was toted up.

Knew what he was doing.

And had left that pile of cassette tapes to tell about it.

The crowd had been stunned into silence until the last shifting and scraping of debris. Then someone on the sidewalk behind Milano cut loose with a loud "Whoo-ee," and that was the signal. Like an orchestra tuning up, voices rose here and there, mounted to a whole symphony fortissimo, ranging from the bassoon tragic to the piccolo comic. In the roadway, making its own internal combustion racket, a whole circus parade on wheels tried to jockey into position close to the debris: fire engines, an ambulance, a Brooklyn Union Gas Company van, an Emergency Squad truck. Everybody, it seemed, had to be in on the biggest show in town.

And, thought Milano, the way its scenario read, he could wind up with his face all over newspapers and TV screens. Where it would be spotted by such interested parties as Wim Rammaert and Willie Watrous who knew how to add one and one together. Rammaert especially, if he spotted the name Milano and the name Bailey in the same column of type.

Jesus.

Mister Hairpiece crooking a finger at his lady of all work. Miss Bailey, I must see you in the office at once.

Milano detached himself from Chris's deathlike grip. She looked across the street and shook her head wonderingly at the sight there. Milano said into here ear, "Where's the car?"

"The car?" She strained to remember. "Near Nostrand. It was the closest I could park."

Price prodded Milano's arm. "You. Romano."

"Milano."

"Yeah. Stay with me, you hear?"

"I'm with you," said Milano. He hastily thrust his keys into Chris's limp hand. "These are for the apartment. Get the family there fast. None of you say anything to anybody about me. Keep me out of it. I'm stuck here for awhile, so you all just hole up until I get clear. Do you understand about keeping me out of it?"

"Yes. But everything's gone," Chris said dazedly. "All their clothes — "

"Don't worry about that."

"And the woman from social services. She was supposed to — "

"Oh, Jesus," Milano said. "Wake up, baby, will you? Just get going. And remember what I told you."

He pushed her on her way as Price, that forefinger jabbing, was laying down the law to his aide: "Emergency can move in right now along with the fucking Fire Department. Get uniforms to back 'em up, but it's all handwork first. And ears. They're to climb around that shitpile slow and easy and keep ears open for anything that sounds alive under it. Move, move, move." Price looked at Mustache as if seeing him for the first time. "You too."

Mustache took off, shaking his head at the ways of the brass, and Price focused on Milano. "All right, let's have it. How come you were in a spot to get the score before the game even started? What's your line anyhow?"

"Private investigator. Watrous Associates. You know Willie Watrous?"

Price raised an eyebrow. "I think I heard some stories about him. If he's the one."

"If you heard some stories about him," said Milano, "he's the one. Now I want to talk deal with you. I got the score by way of a case I'm on. A very profitable case. But if there's any cameras or interviews aimed at me, that blows my cover and the case."

"Too bad," Price said coldly.

"It would be. So you keep me out of all this, and I'll hand you a little present from Willie and me."

"Will you now?" Price said with contempt. "You private outfit clowns are all the same, aren't you?"

"I don't mean that kind of present. I mean that the crackpot who pulled this off left an explanation of it in his house there for the first cop smart enough to find it. Could be somebody who'd like to get down on his record sheet just how smart he is."

"An explanation?"

"That's what he told me it was. I don't know what's in it, but I know where it is. And I left that front door open when I made my getaway. So if I told you now — strictly for public consumption — that he might still be in there with a loaded shotgun, you could walk in without worrying about a warrant, couldn't you?"

"I might," Price said. "With you along."

"That's the deal," said Milano. "I hand you that explanation or confession or whatever, and then I just bow out. You want me for a private talk afterward, you know where to find me. The name's Milano, by the way, not Romano. Just so you won't think I'm trying to pull anything on you."

"Milano. Mind telling me, Milano, if your case has something to do with that tall, dark lady who dropped in on us?"

Milano smiled. "Perish the thought, Inspector. How about the deal?"

It seemed that Price could almost smile too. He almost did. "For what it's worth, Milano," he said, "you got it."

So, thought Milano, as they moved across the carpet of dirt past the batteries of cameras toward the still unsullied Victorian grandeur beyond, his private business would continue to remain strictly private. For that matter, so would Lorena's — catering through an unshaded window to a crazy, murderous old voyeur plus a touch of blackmail to sweeten the kitty—and so would the family's private business be kept private. Johnny Milano and his woman and her family—John Anthony Milano, age forty, paterfamilias—were all well out of it.

Clear and free.

There was a strange new view through the window of the tower room. A gigantic heap of wreckage. Beyond the wreckage, the street light down the block shone on the newly exposed side wall of a brownstone.

Price wasn't interested in the view. He examined each cassette, studied its named and numbered and dated label, arranged the collection into two neat stacks. "Unlucky thirteen," he remarked. He looked around. "He had to have a machine for these things."

"Right in back of you," Milano said. "In that safe. And since you don't need me any more—"

"Take it easy," Price said. "First I want to know what I'm buying."

He locked the number one cassette into the machine, pressed the switch. The tape hissed. A violent coughing erupted from the machine, and Milano said, "That's him."

"There's got to be more than that," said Price.

There was.

"Sit back, light up, the text is yet to come," wheezed the voice oratorically.

"A comic act?" said Price.

The voice again. Price stood frowning as he took it in. Then he drew the swivel chair up to the desk and seated himself, an ear slanted toward the voice. It went on and on, punctuated by that cough. When it finally went dead Price switched off the machine and looked up at Milano whose mind was uneasily on the narrator's wheezing reference to a sexual adventure.

A perverse sexual adventure.

Lorena?

No, Milano decided. Kirwan came off scholarly precise in his language. Pedantically precise. Peeking through the kid's window would never fit his definition of a sexual adventure. No way.

"Well?" said Price.

[304]

"It's Kirwan all right," Milano said. "No question."

"Windy bastard too," Price said irritably. "And he still don't make all that much sense."

"It's only one down, twelve to go," Milano pointed out. He didn't know why he felt defensive about it.

"Maybe." Price nodded at the cassettes. "That could be the longest suicide note in the Guinness book. And no matter how long they are, the bottom line is always the same. Nobody loves me so I'll kill myself and then you'll be sorry."

"They don't all try to take along a building full of people though."

"No, they don't. But this could put that idea into a lot of fucked-up brains. A lot of them. Because what we've got here, friend, is a great big media event. Happy days for the newspapers and TV from here to Hong Kong. And these fucking tapes will be the cherry on top of the sundae." Price shook his head. "Crazy people. Crazy world."

"Fact," said Milano. He picked up the pieces of strap and the necktie from the floor and displayed them. "This is what he tied me up with. Mind if I mess up the evidence a little?"

"Don't be stupid. I can't mind what I don't know about, can I?"

Milano stuffed strap and tie into his pockets and finished off messing up the evidence by screwing the radiator valve back into place. "So —— " he said.

"Yeah," said Price, "you can take off now. One thing. There's that pair of cops near the gate outside. Tell them I want them up here fast."

Milano attended to the request, struggled through the solidly compacted mob beyond, and made it to Flatbush Avenue where there might be a cab heading Manhattan-way. He learned after awhile that if you wanted a cab to anywhere, the corner of Flatbush Avenue and Witter Street was not the place to find one. In the end he settled for the D train at the Church Avenue station — a lucky train that suffered no breakdown along the way — and so made it to Columbus Circle and to co-op in fair time.

No keys. He rang the apartment doorbell, picturing the disposition of the Baileys within. Lorena usurping the bed — what the hell, you had to make allowances for the kid right now — Mama probably holding her hand, the boys at the TV set getting a view through

[305]

news specials of what had been their home. Christine? Sitting on the edge of a chair waiting for his arrival.

No one answered the doorbell. No one answered the heavy pounding at the door. The picture of the Baileys abruptly changed. It was that goddam lightweight tin can of a car. His last closeup of Chris should have warned him she wasn't in shape to drive. Five of them packed into a peewee Toyota, including Lorena in a wild mood. They probably took the expressway too, to keep clear of the midtown evening traffic. There they were now, what was left of them in what was left of the car.

Still no answer.

Milano went down to the manager's office, borrowed the extra set of keys and let himself into the apartment. No one was playing possum there, no one had been there and left. He phoned the Village apartment, no answer there either. Naturally. Pearl and Lenardo had been notified of the car crash, had gone to identify the remains.

Which, Milano told himself as he put down the phone, was all a crock, of course. That morbid streak inherited from his mother who always had funerals on the brain.

The remainder of the pack of cigarettes was still in his pocket. He lit up, drew in deeply, never mind the lesson of that cancerous, wheezing voice on the tape. Crazy people, crazy world. The one sure thing in it was that anyone crazy enough to develop a meaningful relationship with Christine Bailey was going to wind up on four packs a day.

And an alcoholic in the bargain. He poured himself a large dose of Jack Daniels at the bar, but allowed himself only half of it in the first gulp. Standing there looking at the wall behind the couch, he removed the Seurat *Grande Jatte* from it and replaced it with a Max Beckmann triptych. Beckmann, the Expressionist, knew life. Those overwhelming figures, impassive in their agony.

And while Goya didn't buy impassive, he was another —

A key sounded in the door.

Milano doused the cigarette in his drink and reached the foyer as the door swung open. Chris stood framed there, a weighted shopping bag in one hand, the keys still poised in the other. She looked relieved at the sight of him. "Oh, yeah," she said.

"Where the hell have you been?" Milano demanded.

"What?"

He peered over her shoulder. "And where's the family? I told you to bring them along, didn't I?"

"They didn't want to come along. I left them at my grandmother's."

"What grandmother? You never told me you had a grandmother."

"You never asked me." Her voice became brittle. "And I have two grandmothers. One of them owns a house in Crown Heights section. Right off Eastern Parkway. It's not much, but it'll do for awhile. Now do you mind if I come in? Even if it's just to deliver a package?"

Milano stood aside, and she strode by, back rigid. She went straight to the kitchen, slapped the keys on the counter, hoisted the shopping bag to it and started removing from it some large, well-filled, screwtop jars.

Watching her from the kitchen entrance, Milano felt all his tensions evaporating. But it was easy to see from her motions, from the look of her, that she was under heavy pressure. Thick-headed of him not to take into account what she had just been through.

"I'm sorry, baby," he said. "I thought you'd be here when I got here. You scared me to death."

"No." She looked at him over her shoulder, still not altogether ready to forgive. "You scared yourself to death. That's something different."

"I guess it is." He moved back to give her room as she thrust jars into the refrigerator. "What is that stuff?"

"What do you think? Hog maw. Chitlins. Black-eyed peas."

"You mean that?"

"Oh, man," Chris said pityingly. "It's beef stew. Extra gravy. Piccalilli. My grandmother's. You never have anything to eat around here. I thought this would come in handy."

"It will. Did you tell the family about not mentioning me to anybody? Including your grandma?"

"Yes. None of us can figure why, but they said all right if that's what you want. Why is it what you want?"

"Because my line of work is strictly low profile. Good enough?"

"Not after what you did tonight. Johnny, do you know how much they owe you? How much I owe you?"

"Not a thing."

She tried to smile. "Is that how I rate?" she asked, and he saw that he was altogether forgiven.

"All right," he said, "this is what you owe me. The folks have no clothes now, no nothing. So you get on the phone and let them know that tomorrow — "

"Don't start that."

"I'm being practical."

"Don't be practical." Then it came out in a burst. "Johnny, why did he do it?"

"Kirwan? Try to forget him. It's all over."

"Not in my head. It's all jammed up there, so I can't really think of anything else. And the radio news was all mixed up."

"So was he. A real psycho. And half dead to start with. You didn't know he had terminal cancer, did you?"

"No. How do you know that?"

"He talked his head off into a set of tapes. That cop — Price — let me hear the first one. The cancer thing was on it."

"What else was on it?"

"Well," Milano said, "not too much you could get a handle on. But it's funny. From what there was — and from everything else I put together about him — I have a feeling he thought he could endow that house of his with money from the sale of those tapes after he was dead. Make kind of a museum out of it."

"He wanted to blow up a building full of people just for that?"

"Not just for that," Milano said. "There has to be more than that, what with so many tapes. And even that part of it doesn't make too much sense."

"Why not?"

"Because we have a state law which bars you from profiting from any such crime you commit. You can sell your story about it, but you can't keep the money. Which would have to mean your estate can't either. Matter of fact, I think the victims have first claim on any such money."

"Like Mama? For all that furniture and clothing?"

"Maybe," said Milano. "But don't count on it, baby. Remember, I am just theorizing. Anyhow, when it comes to getting up new furniture and clothing — "

"Hold it." Chris held up a hand. Red light. "Honey, you and I are going to have a very heavy talk on this subject right now."

"All right," said Milano, "you start."